New York Times Bestselling Author of *Simply Love*

MARY BALOGH

She entered a we
seduction, and a
that broke every

THE GILDED WEB

AND LOOK FOR THESE DAZZLING NOVELS FROM MARY BALOGH

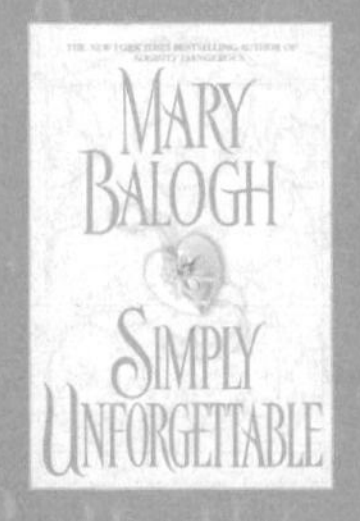

AVAILABLE IN PAPERBACK

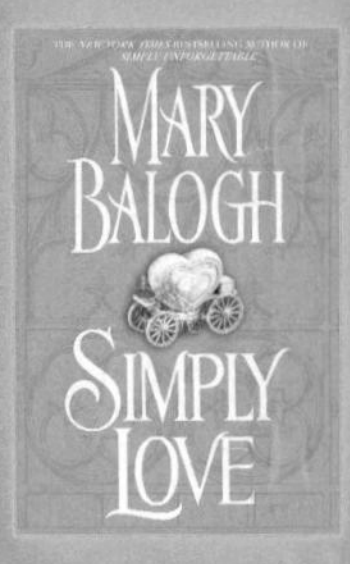

AVAILABLE IN HARDCOVER

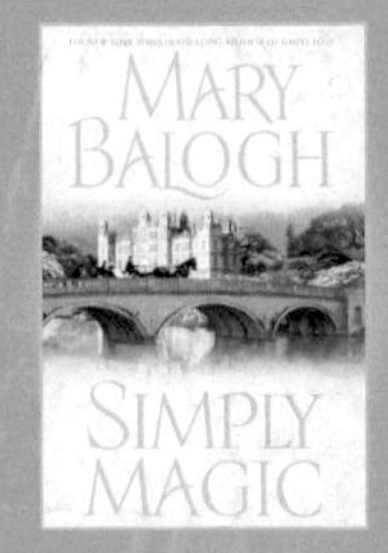

AVAILABLE IN HARDCOVER IN SPRING 2007

DON'T MISS MARY BALOGH'S SUMPTUOUS NOVELS FEATURING THE PASSIONATE BEDWYN FAMILY

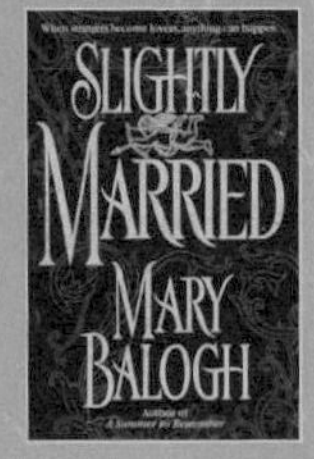

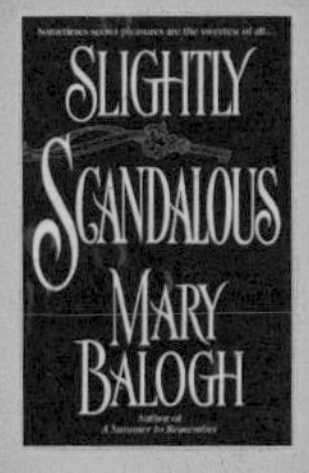

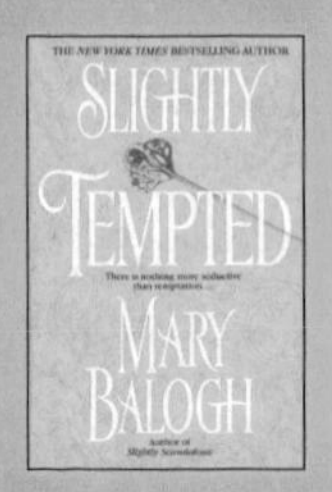

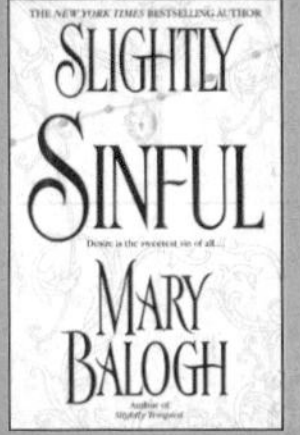

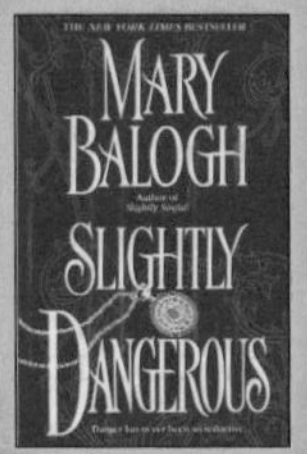

Available from Dell

PRAISE FOR THE NOVELS OF MARY BALOGH

SIMPLY UNFORGETTABLE

"When an author has created a series as beloved to readers as Balogh's Bedwyn saga, it is hard to believe that she can surpass the delights with the first installment in a new quartet. But Balogh has done just that."
—*Booklist*

"A memorable cast . . . refresh[es] a classic Regency plot with humor, wit, and the sizzling romantic chemistry that one expects from Balogh. Well-written and emotionally complex."—*Library Journal*

SLIGHTLY DANGEROUS

"*Slightly Dangerous* is the culmination of Balogh's wonderfully entertaining Bedwyn series. . . . Balogh, famous for her believable characters and finely crafted Regency-era settings, forges a relationship that leaps off the page and into the hearts of her readers."
—*Booklist*

"With this series, Balogh has created a wonderfully romantic world of Regency culture and society. Readers will miss the honorable Bedwyns and their mates; ending the series with Wulfric's story is icing on the cake. Highly recommended."—*Library Journal*

SLIGHTLY SINFUL

"Smart, playful and deliciously satisfying . . . Balogh once again delivers a clean, sprightly tale rich in both plot and character. . . . With its irrepressible characters and deft plotting, this polished romance is an ideal summer read."
—*Publishers Weekly* (starred review)

SLIGHTLY TEMPTED

"Once again, Balogh has penned an entrancing, unconventional yarn that should expand her following."
—*Publishers Weekly*

"Balogh is a gifted writer. . . . *Slightly Tempted* invites reflection, a fine quality in a romance, and Morgan and Gervase are memorable characters."
—*Contra Costa Times*

SLIGHTLY SCANDALOUS

"With its impeccable plotting and memorable characters, Balogh's book raises the bar for Regency romances."
—*Publishers Weekly* (starred review)

"The sexual tension fairly crackles between this pair of beautifully matched protagonists . . . this delightful and exceptionally well-done title nicely demonstrates [Balogh's] matchless style."
—*Library Journal*

SLIGHTLY WICKED

"Sympathetic characters and scalding sexual tension make the second installment in [the Slightly series] a truly engrossing read.... Balogh's surefooted story possesses an abundance of character and class."—*Publishers Weekly*

SLIGHTLY MARRIED

"Intriguing ... [A] whimsical Regency-era romance ... [filled] with homespun humor."—*Publishers Weekly*

"[A Perfect Ten] ... *Slightly Married* is a masterpiece! Mary Balogh has an unparalleled gift for creating complex, compelling characters who come alive on the pages."
—*Romance Reviews Today*

A SUMMER TO REMEMBER

"Balogh outdoes herself with this romantic romp, crafting a truly seamless plot and peopling it with well-rounded, winning characters."—*Publishers Weekly*

"The most sensuous romance of the year."—*Booklist*

"This one will rise to the top."—*Library Journal*

"Filled with vivid descriptions, sharp dialogue, and fantastic characters, this passionate, adventurous tale will remain memorable for readers who love an entertaining read."
—*Rendezvous*

Also by Mary Balogh

Simply Love
Simply Unforgettable
The Secret Pearl
Slightly Dangerous
Slightly Sinful
Slightly Tempted
Slightly Scandalous
Slightly Wicked
Slightly Married
A Summer to Remember
No Man's Mistress
More Than a Mistress
One Night for Love

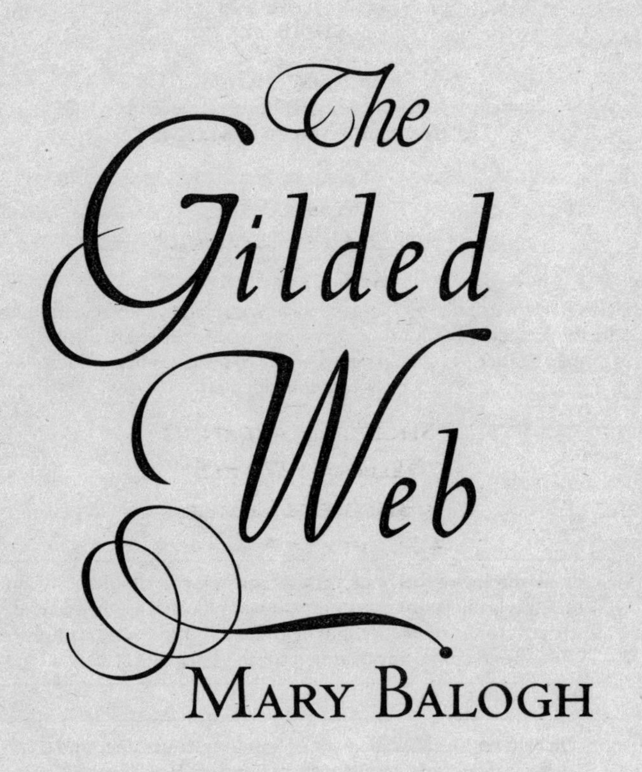

MARY BALOGH

A DELL BOOK

THE GILDED WEB
A Dell Book

PUBLISHING HISTORY
Signet mass market edition published December 1989
Dell mass market edition / December 2006

Published by
Bantam Dell
A Division of Random House, Inc.
New York, New York

This is a work of fiction. Names, characters, places, and incidents either are the product of the author's imagination or are used fictitiously. Any resemblance to actual persons, living or dead, events, or locales is entirely coincidental.

Cover art by Alan Ayers
Cover type by Ron Zinn

ISBN-10: 0-440-24306-8
ISBN-13: 978-0-440-24306-9

Printed in the United States of America
Published simultaneously in Canada

www.bantamdell.com

OPM 10 9 8 7 6 5 4 3 2 1

To Jacqueline,
my daughter, with love

ETERNITY

He who bends to himself a Joy
Does the winged life destroy;
But he who kisses the Joy as it flies
Lives in Eternity's sunrise.

—WILLIAM BLAKE

The
Gilded
Web

Dear Reader,

In its continued commitment to making my backlist available to readers again, Dell is republishing my Web trilogy, which has been out of print for a long time but is much in demand by readers, especially those who have discovered me only recently through the Bedwyn series and the Simply quartet. Here is the first book of the trilogy.

The Gilded Web was first published in 1989—a long time ago. I was surprised when I read it again recently to discover how much my writing has changed in the intervening years. Some would say the change is for the better; other readers have a particular fondness for my older books. It will be for you to decide what you think!

This is the love story of Alexandra Purnell and Edmond Raine, Earl of Amberley, forced by bizarre circumstances into an uneasy alliance not of their choosing. It is also, to a lesser degree, the story of James Purnell, Alex's brother, and of Dominic and Madeline Raine, Edmond's twin brother and sister.

Web of Love will tell Dominic's story. *Devil's Web* will tell Madeline and James's. I do hope you will enjoy this first book in the series and will come back for the other two when they are republished. I am more than happy to see some of my older books in print again.

Mary Balogh

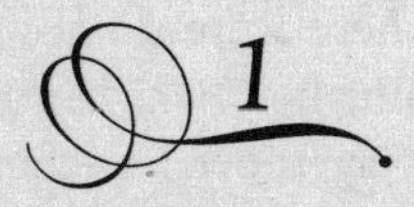

IT WAS A BITTERLY COLD NIGHT FOR EARLY May. It was not actually raining, but there was a heavy cloud cover, and the strong wind felt like a thousand knives to the scantily clad young lady who walked alone into its teeth. The thin dark cloak that she wore over an even thinner ball gown seemed like no protection at all, though she held it closed at the front with one hand and huddled inside it. The other hand held the loose sides of the hood tight beneath her chin.

Alexandra Purnell shivered and lowered her head. But she did not turn back to the ballroom behind her, despite the inviting glow of hundreds of candles through the long windows and the memory of scores of gay, brightly dressed guests. And despite the fact that the room she had just left was warm—perhaps even a little too warm, as the French doors into the garden had been firmly closed against the inclement weather.

No, foolish as it seemed, Alexandra preferred the discomfort of a solitary walk in the garden to the pleasures of the ballroom—for a short time anyway. In fact, she almost welcomed the weather just as it was. If it were warmer or less windy, doubtless there would be any number of guests strolling outside, and she would be unable to find any solitude at all.

She glanced back over her shoulder, but there was no one behind her. And there were no accusing faces at the French windows watching her make her temporary escape. Even so, she instinctively moved farther away from the lights of the house and closer to the dark back alley across from the stable block. It seemed that London dwellers were doomed either to live at some remove from their own stables or else to have them almost on top of the house.

Alexandra shivered again, and burrowed her chin behind the hand that held her hood firmly closed. She blew warm air down into her clasped hand. It was doubtless foolish to have run away like this. Her slippers were probably stained with grass. And her smooth chignon, which she had insisted upon despite Nanny Rey's plea that she try a hair fashion more suited to the festive occasion, would be flattened and disheveled by the close-held hood. And she certainly could not escape for an indefinite period. She would have to go back soon.

She was one-and-twenty years old already, she told herself in an interior monologue that had become very familiar to her mind over the past weeks. She was in her first and perhaps her only really active Season in London, which involved her in all the diversions of the *beau monde*. Papa had decided, quite without warning, that she must be given a proper introduction to society before her long-planned betrothal to the Duke of Peterleigh became official. They had taken a house on Curzon Street—Papa, Mama, her brother James, and herself. And they had met all the right people and attended all the proper functions in the month since.

She should be happy. Most young ladies would be ecstatic to be in her position. But she felt positively in her dotage beside all the other young girls who were making their come-out. And she could not feel comfortable with such a life. Nothing in her past had prepared her for the gaiety and frivolity of London. She was only now beginning to realize fully what a very strict and narrow upbringing she and James had had at Dunstable Hall. Almost any form of entertainment and personal pleasure had been frowned upon by Papa. Every thought and word and action had revolved around church and the Scriptures and Papa's firmly held notions of virtue and morality. And unlike James, she had not even been to school to discover that there was another world beyond home.

She had been intended for the Duke of Peterleigh for as far back as she could remember. She had met him only on a few occasions and then very briefly and formally. He did not live often on his estate, which adjoined theirs. He was twenty years her senior and spent most of his time in London on government business.

Alexandra had never questioned the fact that she would marry him when the time came. And she still did not do so. They had met a few times since her arrival in London, and she had found nothing to censure in him. He was in many ways like her father—stern and severe in manner, it was true, but surely an honest and an upright man. Unfortunately, he was also a busy man and did not appear at nearly as many entertainments as she was expected to attend.

And so there was an awkwardness about her come-out. She did not feel any affinity with the members of society around her. And she was not in search of a husband, or a flirt, as most of the other girls seemed to be. Papa did not like her to dress quite as fashionably as the others, and she could not bring herself even to dress her hair in a pretty fashion.

And there were the Harding-Smythes to contend with almost wherever she went. They kept her constantly aware of her inadequacies. Her aunt Deirdre, Papa's sister, always assumed that she lacked amusement and went out of her way to provide it. Her efforts were kindly meant, perhaps, but her ideas of amusement were not Alexandra's. Her cousin Caroline simpered and clung, more in an attempt to attract James than out of any real affection for her, Alexandra felt. And Cousin Albert appeared to have set himself the task of protecting an innocent young country cousin from all the evils and temptations of London. His manner toward her, toplofty and condescending, irritated her beyond bearing.

Alexandra blew again onto her cold hand. Had she been very rude to Caroline and Aunt Deirdre earlier? Did she owe them an apology? They had wanted her to return home with them that night so that she might accompany them to the shops on Bond Street the next morning. They had even secured her mother's permission before coming to ask her and had arranged to have a maid bring suitable clothes for her to wear the next day. But she had refused their invitation. She had not even softened her abruptness by offering some sort of excuse. She had been taught too well that telling the truth is always a virtue and that there is no such thing as a white lie.

They had left the ball soon after her refusal, as Aunt Deirdre had a headache. And at the same time she had been unable to resist the temptation to rescue her cloak and step outside for a moment's peace, especially as Albert had been smirking at her from across the room, and she knew he would come soon, remark on the singular misfortune of her having no dancing partner, and condescend to lead her out himself. Probably Mama still thought that she had gone with Aunt Deirdre. She really should be returning to the ballroom. Someone had signed her card for a set of country dances. She must not pay him the discourtesy of not being present when it began. Besides, Mama would scold if she were absent for a noticeable length of time and perhaps even report the fact to Papa the next morning. Then there would be trouble.

But Alexandra was fated not to return after all. As she was about to turn back to the house, she glanced almost absentmindedly at a closed carriage that was being drawn by four horses into the alley before the stable block just a short distance away.

And then the nightmare began.

Her back prickled to the knowledge that someone had stepped up behind her only a fraction of a second before a hand clamped over her mouth. Terror engulfed her instantly as she clawed at the hand and kicked back at her assailant with one slippered foot.

But her hands were soon dragged from her face and pulled firmly behind her back. Her cloak fell open so that the wind blew all its chill force against the delicate silk of her blue ball gown. She tried to shake her head, bend forward, kick herself free. But her efforts were all to no avail. Her hood had somehow been pulled down over her nose so that she could not even see.

"Got you!" a male voice said from behind her in tones of breathless amusement. "No use to struggle anymore now, young lady. You'll not be going such a long distance tonight after all. You should have stayed dancing. What in the deuce are you doing, Clem? Don't you have her wrists bound yet?"

"She is struggling like six cats," another voice said. "There. That should hold right and tight."

"Get the scarf for her mouth then," the first voice said. "We don't have all night, you know. A pretty pickle we would be in if she set up a screeching and we were caught. We could end up swinging."

"Swing yourself!" the second voice said indignantly. "I'm just doing this as a favor to a friend. I ain't in the habit of kidnapping females, y'know."

But Alexandra was not listening to the conversation. As he talked, the second man was stretching a scarf tightly over her mouth and tying it in a tight knot at the back of her head. And her hood was still down over her nose, so that she felt as if she were being bound in a sack. Renewed terror set her to kicking with fresh vigor and pulling uselessly against whatever it was that held her hands imprisoned.

"Grab her feet, Clem, will you," the first man said, "before my shins start getting bruises on top of bruises!"

And Alexandra was lifted unceremoniously from the ground and dumped none too gently inside what she realized must be the carriage she had seen pull out into the alley.

"There are limits to friendship," the first man grumbled before slamming the door and leaving Alexandra alone inside the dark interior of the coach. "Next time Eden has a wild scheme like this to execute, he can damned well do it himself."

The coach lurched into motion, and Alexandra realized that she was lying on a seat that must normally be exceedingly comfortable. But whose carriage was it? Who were her kidnappers, and where were they taking her? What did they plan to do with her? Ransom her? Did they imagine that Papa was a wealthy man? Murder her? She dragged again at her wrists, only to find that there was no way to loosen the bonds. She could feel the gag tight over her mouth, her hood halfway down her nose. And she began to draw fast and shallow breaths. She could not breathe. She was going to die. She was going to suffocate even before they had a chance to kill her.

Perhaps they were going to ravish her. Oh, dear God, she would rather die! Alexandra wrenched at her wrists again and found herself falling and quite unable to save herself from an awkward landing on the floor between the two seats.

The journey was not a long one. The carriage stopped, the door was thrown open, and the nightmare began again. If only she could see! She would not be so terrified if she could only see her captors and know that at least they were human.

"Oh, Lord, she fell off the seat," the first man's voice said. "Eden will have a thing or two to say if she has any bruises."

Alexandra had no chance to try once more to kick her way to freedom. Her head was toward the open door. One captor pulled her out by the arms, and she was immediately tipped forward and over the shoulder of the other, who proceeded to carry her up a flight of steps and into a lighted hallway. She could just make out a pattern of black and white tiles through the sides of her hood.

"Yes, I shall lead the way to her room," a third voice was saying. It was a stiff and disapproving voice. "But I don't like it, sirs. His lordship has never done anything quite like this before. She's all trussed up. It doesn't seem quite fitting somehow."

"Just lead the way, Palmer," the first man said breathlessly. "She ain't a featherweight."

Alexandra was bumped up a seemingly interminable

flight of stairs and finally set down on her feet for a brief moment before being pushed backward quite gently. She landed on what felt like a perfectly soft bed.

"Here," her captor said, fumbling beneath her until he found the bonds at her wrists. "I can't leave you like that, now, can I? But I'll have to tie you up somehow and leave on the gag. Can't have you screeching and disturbing the whole household. And can't leave you free or you'll only run away again and all my efforts will be in vain. I'll tie your hands to the bedpost here. No offense meant. Eden will be home soon. He'll deal with you."

Alexandra's struggles were not as frenzied as they might have been. She was feeling very close to despair. If she escaped from this man, she had a whole houseful of enemies to get past before she could regain her freedom. She made only muffled protests as her hands were tied quite firmly above her head. She shook her head furiously, but she could not uncover her eyes enough to see either her assailant or the room into which he had brought her.

And then she was alone, the room quiet and dark, all sound obliterated by the closing of the door. Alone to struggle for a freedom that she knew was next to impossible to achieve. Alone with her imagination. Alone and waiting for her real captor to come. Eden. He would be there soon. Soon she would know.

Alexandra struggled on.

DOMINIC RAINE, LORD EDEN, blew out his breath through puffed cheeks when he returned to the ballroom from the garden and saw Madeline, his twin sister, quite close by, flanked by her bosom friends Miss Wickhill and Lady

Pamela Paisley, the three of them laughing at something Lord Crane had just finished saying.

What a relief to see her there. He had made enough of a cake of himself as it was in the past hour. He had been justly served for jumping so hastily to conclusions. But it could have been worse—a lot worse. He would never have lived the matter down if his plan for Faber and Jones to bundle Madeline off to Edmund's house had been carried out. Her wrath would have been dreadful to behold. Not to mention Edmund's.

But all was well. Provided that couple of loose screws didn't still try to abduct her from the middle of the ballroom, of course. He would not put it past those two. The more difficult the scheme, the more likely they were to take the risk. And he was no better, he had to admit. He would not be able to resist the challenge if he were in their place. He must find them. Tell them the whole thing was off.

First, though, perhaps he had better warn Madeline. Tell her the whole story in such a way that she would think it all a great joke. He fingered his neckcloth to check that it was straight and sauntered over to the group of which his sister was a part. She flashed him a smile and finished the story she was telling to an attentive group. A burst of laughter greeted her final words.

She turned to her brother with a grin, her green eyes dancing up into his. "I thought you must have gone to the card room, Dom," she said. "I was prepared to call a physician for you tomorrow. It is unlike you to miss a single dance."

Lord Eden bowed to the group at large. "I have been taking a breath of air," he said. "It is like December out there. Will you waltz, Mad?"

He noticed that Miss Wickhill chortled as she always did

when he forgot himself and called his sister by the old pet name, something he did more often than not.

"I don't believe it," Madeline said, linking her arm through his. "Am I finally to dance with the handsomest gentleman in town? You are usually too busy leading out all the beauties."

"Of whom you are surely one, my dear," he said with a grin, drawing her away from the group. "Have I told you how I like your hair like that? I must confess I was horrified when Mama told me you had had it all shorn off, but it suits you, Mad. The short curls emphasize your large eyes and high cheekbones."

"I could wish it were darker or blonder or redder or some more definite color," Madeline said with a shrug, placing her hand on her twin's shoulder and waiting for the music to begin. "But to what do I owe the honor, Dom? You look rather as if you had seen a ghost."

"Not a ghost exactly," he said, looking at her rather sheepishly. "Just Sir Hedley Fairhaven."

She looked back at him expectantly. "Yes?" she said.

"At the bottom of the garden," he said. "Standing outside a traveling chaise."

Madeline frowned and fit her step to her brother's as the orchestra began to play a waltz. "Is this a riddle?" she asked. "I am supposed to guess what it is all about, yes? It was a new traveling chaise? It was missing one wheel? It was pulled by four grays you would cheerfully kill for? They had pink ribbons threaded through their manes? Sir Hedley had a ring in his nose?"

"He was waiting for a lady to elope with," Lord Eden said, twirling her as they reached a corner of the ballroom.

"Really?" Madeline's eyes sparkled up at him. "Are you sure, Dom? How deliciously scandalous! Who? Do tell me.

You did not challenge him to a duel in order to protect the lady's honor, did you? She wasn't one of your flirts, was she?"

She did not hear his mumbled reply.

"What?" she said, leaning toward him.

"I thought she was you," he said.

"What?" Madeline stopped in the middle of a spin. "You thought I was going to elope with Sir Hedley Fairhaven? Have your wits gone totally begging? If we were not exactly where we are at this moment, Dominic Raine, I would take you on for this. And black both your eyes too."

"Hush, Mad!" he said, flushing and glancing uneasily about him. "People will be looking. It was half your fault that I made such an embarrassing mistake, you know. You have been hanging around with Fairhaven all over London for the past month, and you distinctly told me just last week that you would marry him too if you chose to do so, and I was to keep my nose out of your affairs, thank you very much."

"And you know me so little," she said, dancing valiantly on, an empty smile on her face as she waltzed past friends and acquaintances, "that you think I would do anything so very tasteless and so very . . . stupid? How could you, Dom! To marry Sir Hedley, of all people. And to elope with him!"

"You must admit that you tried it once before, Mad," Lord Eden said. "How was I to know that you would not do it again?"

"Oh! I was eighteen," she said indignantly, "and fell in love with a uniform. And it is horrid of you to remind me of that youthful indiscretion, Dom. As if I have learned no wisdom and acquired no maturity in four years. Why did you think I was going to elope with Sir Hedley tonight, anyway?"

"I overheard him," he said. "I was sitting in one of the alcoves with Miss Pope and he was sitting just the other side of the curtain. I suppose he didn't know there was anyone there, because we . . . well, we weren't talking, anyway."

"I cannot imagine what you were doing with Miss Pope if you were not talking with her," Madeline said caustically. "But whom was he talking to and what did he say?"

"I don't know who the other man was," Lord Eden said. "But Fairhaven was planning to leave with some lady at midnight, and he was giving directions to the other about what to do tomorrow when the cat was out of the bag."

"And you assumed I was the one running away with him," Madeline said.

"I'm afraid so," he admitted, giving her a disarming smile.

"Why have you told me this, Dom?" she asked suspiciously. "It was surely not in order that I might have a good laugh at your stupidity."

"No." He grinned apologetically down at her. "It's just that at the time I wanted to be able to concentrate my attention and my fists on Fairhaven. I set Faber and Jones to spiriting you off to Edmund's so that I would know you were safe. I couldn't find them in the garden after my talk with Fairhaven. They doubtless took themselves off when they did not find you there. But I thought I had better warn you anyway."

"You set those two to . . . to kidnap me!" Madeline's voice had risen almost to a squeak. "I suppose they were to bind me hand and foot and gag and blindfold me?"

Her twin looked uncomfortable. "I don't think all that would have been necessary," he said. "But you know yourself that you would not have gone willingly, Mad. Especially if you had had your heart set on an elopement. I had to arrange it all hastily in the past hour. I did tell them to, ah, insist that you go with them."

"Oh, Dom," Madeline said, smiling dazzlingly at one of her favorite admirers, who was standing close by, watching her, "you have had a narrow escape, brother mine. I would have had your head on a platter for breakfast if your friends had laid one fingernail on my person. And I would wager that Edmund would have done the ax work for me."

"Yes, well," he said, "I thought I should warn you, Mad, to have an eye open for those two. I needn't have said anything to you, you know. I could have taken the chance of keeping quiet. This is all pretty embarrassing, as you might imagine."

"Pamela thought you were coming to ask her to waltz," she said. "I know she did, Dom. She blushed in that way she has whenever she sees you coming. And she always thinks that you are going to notice her. She really does have a painful *tendre* for you. You will dance the next set with her?"

"This is my punishment?" he asked, grinning ruefully down at her.

"Pamela is my friend," she said. "I do not consider it punishment for a gentleman to dance with her, Dom. She dotes on you, you know. And you really are very handsome. I see the way all the girls look at you. And so many of them this year are years younger than you and I."

"We will have to dust off a spinster cap for you soon," he said. "You are getting very close to your dotage, Mad. No, don't look at me like that. The next set it is for Lady Pamela. You see how contrite I am?"

Lord Eden duly danced with his sister's friend and unconsciously enslaved her even further with his charm and his sunny smile. There was nothing to keep him at the ball once the set was over. Miss Pope had proved a disappointment, perhaps because his attention had been taken by Fairhaven when he was kissing her. And Miss Carstairs had not appeared at all that evening, having contracted a cold in the head at Vauxhall Gardens a few evenings before. And since he was currently in love with Miss Carstairs, her absence made even the most glittering of social occasions dreary.

Besides, he was still feeling decidedly foolish over the Fairhaven affair. He had gone out to that carriage all fire and brimstone and brotherly outrage, ready to challenge the man to meet him at dawn on a foggy heath with pistols and seconds. He was fortunate to have got away without being challenged himself, but Fairhaven had appeared to have other matters on his mind, most notably, the little female who was lurking in the shadows obviously waiting for her lover's visitor to take himself off.

Lord Eden sallied forth from the ball to one of his clubs in the hope of finding some diversion to take his mind off the night's *faux pas*. If he were fortunate, too, perhaps he would run into Faber and Jones and persuade them that it would be as well to keep their mouths shut about the night's dealings or lack thereof.

He did not believe Miss Pope would start any awkward gossip. Even if she had heard, Madeline's name had not been mentioned. But it was doubtful that she had been aware of the scandalous conversation going on behind the curtain in the alcove anyway. He had kissed her with sufficient ardor to distract her as he had listened with all his attention. And she had looked suitably witless when he had finally lifted his mouth from hers. Perhaps that was why he had found her disappointing. It was far more intriguing to kiss a female whose manner left one in some doubt over whether one's hand would be welcomed or slapped if it chose to wander somewhere where it had no business to be.

It really was not all his fault that he had jumped to such a conclusion about Madeline and Fairhaven. Madeline really had tried to run off with a half-pay officer less than a week after her eighteenth birthday. Was he to blame if he had assumed that Fairhaven's traveling companion to Gretna was to be Madeline? She had said less than a week before that she would marry him if she chose. And it was just the sort of thing she would do, too, just to spite him. She never had got over the humiliation of being a full half-hour younger than he. Though to do her justice, she had never shown any indignation over the fact that she had been born female and had not therefore inherited one of their father's junior titles as he had.

What a very narrow and fortunate escape he had had that night! Lord Eden handed his hat and cane to the doorman at Boodle's and prepared to enjoy what remained of the night.

JAMES PURNELL WAS WATCHING the dancers. He had come from the card room just a few minutes before, where he had watched rather than participated. He had danced earlier, with his cousin Caroline and with two other young girls who had been smiling brightly as if they did not mind at all having no partner for the sets that had already begun.

He felt restless—as usual. He had been glad to leave the country, where he could never feel at home ever again, where his strained relations with his father were more in evidence than they were here, and where he was allowed no hand in the running of the estate. And yet he was not glad to be in London, where the endless social round seemed pointless and silly. It fell upon him to escort his mother and sister to almost all the events of the *ton*. A quiet soiree or a musical evening might coax his father abroad, but balls and routs and the theater were fitting only for females intent on making a showing with the people who mattered. Lord Beckworth stayed at home with his books and sermons.

Purnell watched broodingly the tall, slender young dancer in blue. She was somewhat older than most of the other unmarried girls, but she had all the freshness and glow of youth. He tended to notice her almost wherever he went, though he had never been presented to her or asked to be. Lady Madeline Raine. She was no prettier than a score of other girls in the ballroom. There was nothing particularly unusual about her short dark blond curls or her eyes, which might be blue or green—he had never been close enough to know which. Her figure was good but by no means unusually so.

He did not know quite what always drew his eyes. The sparkle, perhaps, that was absent from the women in his own family? Alex was perhaps younger than Lady Madeline Raine, but Alex had never been as young. She had never been given the chance.

Purnell shrugged his shoulders and turned to search the crowds for his mother and his sister. He saw the former sitting in an obscure corner of the room talking to a faded creature, who was doubtless a chaperone. He crossed the room toward them and bowed.

"Good evening, ma'am," he said to the faded creature, drawing some color to her cheeks and a surprised smile to her lips. "Have you seen Alex, Mama? I have ordered the carriage to be brought around."

"She has gone with Deirdre and Caroline, James," Lady Beckworth said. "They begged quite insistently that she be allowed to go. Your papa will not like it, will he? But there can be no real harm in her going, can there? Deirdre is his sister, after all."

Her son frowned. "I think Alex might be allowed to decide such matters for herself, Mama," he said. "She is of age, after all. Will you take my arm?"

He bowed again to the faded chaperone as his mother turned to say good night, and found his eyes straying once more to the dancers. Lady Madeline Raine was still waltzing with her twin, Lord Eden.

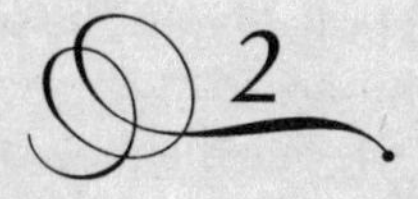

THERE WAS A SUGGESTION OF DAWN IN THE sky already before Edmund Raine, Earl of Amberley, returned home. He had spent most of the night with Mrs. Eunice Borden, his mistress. Indeed, it was becoming more and more his habit to stay with her. He found the relationship comfortable. As he was dressing and preparing to step out into the cold night, he found himself thinking, not for the first time, of suggesting to her that they marry.

It was difficult to put into words why he was finding the affair so satisfactory. And even more difficult to know why he was contemplating matrimony. Eunice was not a pretty woman. She was not even particularly attractive. She had a short, rather heavyset figure, strong features, and short, dark, very curly hair. Her manner was quite unflirtatious. She spoke in a forthright way that occasionally offended, but never left her listener in any doubt about her true feelings. She had acquired a well-deserved reputation as a literary hostess. Her salon was always worth attending during almost any evening of the week.

And she was older than he by three years. She was two-

and-thirty years old, a widow for the past six years. She had never made any attempt to conceal her age.

Lord Amberley looked behind him and smiled at Eunice as she lay in bed, the blankets neatly pulled up under her arms, her hands clasped loosely over her stomach. Her legs were stretched out side by side beneath the covers.

"Thank you, Eunice," he said, as he always did before leaving her. "You are very good to me, my dear."

"I am glad you came, Amberley," she said. She never called him by any other name. "I can always count on you for interesting and stimulating conversation. Do you think Mr. Denny a serious poet? I found his manner rather irritating tonight, as if he is somewhat in love with the idea of being a poet."

"That seems to be rather a failing of poets in general, do you not think?" he asked.

She thought for a moment. "Yes, you are right of course," she said. "And one can forgive a measure of eccentricity provided the creative genius is really present. In Mr. Denny's case, I rather doubt that there is any genius at all. I do not believe I will invite him again. I would not wish to have my salon gain a reputation for mediocrity."

"I think that is hardly likely to happen," Lord Amberley said, sitting down on a chair and pulling on one of his Hessian boots. "Would you consider marrying me, Eunice?"

She showed no outward sign of surprise or any other emotion. "I don't believe that would be wise for you, Amberley," she said. "I am too old to be thinking of giving you heirs. You will need to marry someone younger."

"And what if I am not too concerned about heirs?" he said, regarding her with a half-smile. "And what if I am satisfied with a more mature and sensible wife?"

"Then you are a fool," Mrs. Borden said. "It is your duty

to beget children of your own, Amberley. Personal inclination is of small consideration when you have an earldom to pass along."

"Are you saying no?" he asked. "Or are you open to persuasion?"

"I do not believe I am willing to give up my independence," she said. "I am quite satisfied to be your mistress for as long as you wish, Amberley. But your wife? No, I think not. We would not be nearly as comfortable together if we were married. We would begin to wrangle. Take my word for it."

Lord Amberley did not argue the point. He leaned over the bed to give his mistress the usual good-night kiss on her cheek—never on her lips—and took his leave of her.

He walked home, as he generally did, noting the signs of early dawn, the almost imperceptible lightening of the eastern sky. He was glad he had worn his greatcoat when he left the house the evening before, though it had seemed foolish to be doing so in May.

Eunice was probably right. It was better that they live their separate lives. The funny thing was that he could not remember quite how their affair had started. What exactly had happened to cause them to go to bed with each other that first time? He could not recall. He had never found her particularly attractive. He had enjoyed her salon and her conversation. He had grown into the habit of lingering until her last guest left, and then even beyond that. But when had conversation first given place to physical contact? He had never kissed her on the lips. He had started sleeping with her without any big romantic moment to herald the beginning of the affair. That had been more than a year before.

He had not had any other woman since. And that in itself was surprising. During the months of each year that he spent on his estate, he always lived a celibate life. But during his months in London he had often indulged himself with several women. He had remained faithful to Eunice, though, resuming their affair this spring after his winter at Amberley Court.

It was not a passionate affair. Indeed, he was quite sure that Eunice did not derive any pleasure at all from their couplings. She certainly did not participate in them beyond receiving him in a quite matter-of-fact manner, giving what she knew he wanted without either prudishness or coquetry. He often wondered what satisfaction she got out of their liaison. But perhaps it was in her attitude that he found his own satisfaction. In his busy life of responsibility for the happiness of others, it was refreshing to find someone who seemed more intent on giving than receiving.

He had expected that she would marry him. A desire to be the Countess of Amberley, to live a life of security as his wife, would have explained her willingness to submit to his embraces. And yet he was not surprised by her refusal. Eunice was not a woman to whom position and security would be overriding goals. She had been married very young to Mr. Borden and had been left with a comfortable independence eight years later. She did not appear to regret her widowed state.

Lord Amberley let himself into his town house with his own key. He always insisted that his staff go to bed at midnight whether he and Dominic were at home or not. Why keep a poor footman standing around asleep on his feet for most of the night merely because his master was too busy bedding his mistress to come home at a decent hour?

He climbed the stairs and walked the length of the upper corridor to his bedchamber. He yawned. Perhaps if the birds did not strike up too enthusiastic a dawn chorus outside his window, he would be able to snatch another few hours of sleep before beginning his day.

He stopped and listened. Was Madeline home? She did not come very often, as he had bought his mother her own town house four years before, having decided that she would be happier in her own establishment while in London, and naturally enough, her daughter had gone to live with her. But Madeline did come home on occasion, notably when Mama was otherwise engaged. His sister had been at the Easton ball last night, he believed. Dominic had been going to put in an appearance there too. Madeline must have returned with him.

She must be still awake. She certainly was tossing and turning in her room. He could hear her from where he was. Had something happened to upset her? It seemed unlikely. Madeline had a sunny nature and was not easily upset. Lord Amberley shrugged his shoulders and proceeded on his way.

And yet, standing fifteen minutes later in his dressing gown at the window of his bedchamber, looking out onto a street that was brightening into a new day, he sipped from a glass of water and wondered about his younger sister. What was she doing at home? Mama had not said anything about going away. They had not quarreled, had they? He frowned and looked toward the door of his room. Should he go and see if she really was still awake? Would she thank him for disturbing her even if she were?

He would do it anyway, he decided. He did not like to think of Madeline unhappy. Or perhaps ill. He must see if there was something he could do to help. He opened his door and walked back down the corridor. He stopped outside the door to his sister's room and listened. She was definitely still awake and apparently moaning and loudly fidgeting. Or was she indeed asleep and having nightmares? He tapped quietly on the door.

For a moment all fell silent within, and then the scuffling sounds increased in volume. Lord Amberley turned the handle of the door, found it unlocked, and opened it.

The curtains were not drawn either at the long windows or around the bed. He stared motionless for a moment at the figure on the bed, or rather twisted around and half off the bed. Madeline?

Her arms were above her head, apparently grasping the bedpost. Her head was completely swaddled in dark cloth. She was wearing a flimsy blue dress, but it was twisted awkwardly around her body and was pulled up so that her long slim legs were almost completely exposed.

"What on earth?" he said, striding toward her and putting his glass of water down on the side table so that he could help her. And she certainly needed help. Her wrists were bound to the bedpost, he saw with some horror. And it was a cloak that had wrapped itself completely around her shoulders and head.

She was a prisoner. Those mad twins! Would they never grow up? Lord Amberley felt a surge of anger.

"Hold still," he said firmly. "I shall have you free in a moment."

She lay still then, though it took him more than a few moments to loosen her bonds, which her struggles had doubtless tightened considerably.

"There," he said, expecting her at any moment to burst into an indignant tirade against Dominic. He reached down and tried to lower the skirt of her gown, but it was so tightly twisted beneath her that the task was impossible. He reached up to untangle her from the twisted cloak. Her hands were on his, plucking at them, but they were cold and nerveless. He pushed them away.

When he had pulled away the folds of the cloak, she was still not free. Her head and face were almost entirely covered by the hood, which was held very firmly in place by the green gag she wore. He pushed back the hood, feeling even greater fury. She looked up at him with wide and wary eyes.

Dark eyes.

Oh, God!

"Turn your head," he said tonelessly. "I will free you from that gag."

His fingers fumbled with the knot and finally loosened it. He slid one hand beneath her head and lifted it so that he could both remove the scarf and put back her hood. A cascade of thick dark hair fell over his arm with the hood and waved over her shoulders. He did not think to remove his arm for a moment.

She lay still, her head resting against his arm, staring up at him warily. Perhaps she did not realize that her legs were exposed to the thighs.

"Who are you?" he asked foolishly, and he slid his arm from beneath her head and stood up.

She opened her mouth as if to speak, and tried to lick parched lips with an equally dry tongue. She made an inarticulate sound.

"Here," he said, picking up the glass of water, "you must drink this. No, don't shrink from me. I will do you no harm."

He put one arm beneath her shoulders again and lifted her to a sitting position. He held the glass while she drank. Her hands, he could see, were temporarily paralyzed.

She turned her head away after she had taken a few sips,

and her long disheveled hair hid her face from his view. "You are Eden?" she asked, and coughed. "What do you want with me? I will not be intimidated. You may kill me if you wish, but I will not plead with my father to pay you a ransom. And I will not submit without a struggle to being ravished."

"Eden?" he said, straightening up and standing beside the bed. "My brother has brought you here?"

Her pale handsome face suddenly flushed quite painfully, and she pulled at the skirt of her gown. She had to lift her hips in order to loosen it. He kept his eyes on her face while she did so. She sat up abruptly on the side of the bed, and one hand collapsed clumsily beneath her as she used it to push herself upright.

"This is an outrage," she said, her voice shaking very slightly. "I demand to be released."

"I agree with you entirely, ma'am," he said quietly, and reached out to tug on the silk-tasseled bell-pull beside the bed. "May I know who you are so that I might communicate with your family? They must be frantic with worry."

"My father is Lord Beckworth," she said. "We live on Curzon Street."

"I know him," Lord Amberley said with a frown. "May I ask how you got here, Miss . . . ?"

"I was abducted," she said, "by two men. I was at Lady Easton's ball. They said that Eden would be here soon. But that must have been many hours ago."

"Lord Eden is my younger brother," he said. "Ah! Do come in, Mrs. Haviland. This lady has come to be here by some misadventure involving Lord Eden. Will you stay with her here, please, and see that she is made comfortable and has some refreshments, while I send for her father? She has been tied up and gagged for several hours. I believe she would appreciate having someone massage her hands."

"Oh, please," the dark-haired handsome girl said as he turned to leave her in some privacy, "not my father. Please, will you send for my brother instead? James Purnell. He will come."

Lord Amberley nodded and bowed to her, as the housekeeper, clucking her tongue, crossed to the bed and picked up one of the girl's hands. He left the room and closed the door quietly behind him. It was perhaps as well that the very first thing he must do was compose a swift note to the girl's brother. Perhaps by the time he had done so his present white fury would have cooled down just sufficiently that he would not quite throttle his brother when he went to his room to confront him.

Perhaps. Though he doubted it. The twins had always had a gift for getting into the most unbelievable scrapes. But this was not a scrape. Not by any means. A young girl had just been abused and terrified probably beyond his power to imagine, and her character and reputation destroyed, possibly beyond repair.

Oh, no, this was no scrape. Heads would surely roll over this.

THE AGONY OF FEELING the blood needling and knifing its way back through her hands was finally subsiding to a dull throbbing. Her fingers still looked and felt swollen, but she could begin to flex them. Her mouth still felt dry even after two cups of tea. Alexandra sat in the dressing room adjoining the bedchamber where she had been held prisoner. The Earl of Amberley's housekeeper sat with her, still clucking with concern after sending a maid scurrying for tea, and after chafing her hands and wrapping a soft shawl around her shoulders instead of the crumpled cloak. Alexandra had discovered the identity of her rescuer, though she had learned very little else. She still did not know any more about Lord Eden except that he was the Earl of Amberley's brother.

She had not asked, of course. Some explanation must be given for the happenings of the night, but she was not the one to do the asking. James would discover the truth. At least, she hoped it would be James. She prayed that her father's servants would have allowed the message to be taken to her brother. Her father would have to know eventually, she supposed. But she wanted some time to collect herself before he was told.

James would sort everything out for her. All she was thankful for was that it was over, that Lord Amberley had found her before Lord Eden came home. James would see to it that the truth came out. He would discover what motive a gentleman who did not even know her might have for having her kidnapped and held captive for the whole of a night.

Alexandra waited with an outer patience learned through long years as her father's daughter. Inwardly she was impatient to be gone, never to see this house again, never to see the Earl of Amberley again. She would burn with mortification, she knew, when she allowed her mind to dwell on the spectacle that must have met his eyes when he saw her on the bed. To have had a man in the same bedchamber as she was horrifying enough. But ten times worse, she had been stretched on a bed in a dreadful state of dishabille.

And then suddenly Nanny Rey was in the room and the earl's housekeeper on her feet. And her old nurse looked dearly familiar with her diminutive sparrow's figure, her sharp red nose, and the gold-rimmed spectacles that always looked for all the world as if they were ready to drop off the end of her nose. Alexandra would not run to her as she wished to do, or burst into tears as her body yearned to do. She merely clasped her hands very tightly in her lap and forced a bleak smile to her lips.

"I am afraid I have got you from your bed very early this morning, Nanny," she said.

"Thank the good Lord that Master James had the presence of mind to call me," Nanny Rey said, peering at Alexandra over the top of her spectacles. Indeed, she rarely looked through them. "Have you come to any harm, lovey?" She glared at the housekeeper as if that poor lady were solely responsible for all the woes of her mistress.

"Nothing that has not been put right already," Alexandra said. "Is James here, Nanny? May we leave now?"

"As fast as our feet will carry us," her nurse said. "We will wait in the carriage, though his lordship said you was welcome to stay in comfort here while he had his talk with Master James, and Master James himself said we was to wait here. But old Nanny wouldn't listen to the King of England himself if what he said wasn't in the best interests of my girl. Put your cloak on and your hood up, lovey. It is a chilly morning, May or no May. And thanks to you, ma'am." She nodded curtly in the direction of the silent Mrs. Haviland. "You will please tell Mr. Purnell that we will await him outside."

Alexandra looked about her in some wonder as Nanny Rey hurried her down a curved oak staircase to the tiled hallway she had glimpsed the night before. There were oak paneling and large paintings everywhere and a magnificent chandelier hanging from the domed ceiling. The experiences of the night before began to take on an aura of unreality.

She had never been so happy to see her father's carriage waiting at the bottom of a flight of steps. Her father's coachman handed her inside. Her attention was only momentarily distracted by a tall young man of pleasing appearance, who looked at her in some curiosity as he touched his hat and mounted the steps to enter the house. He was dressed in evening clothes.

Nanny Rey glared balefully at him and followed her mistress into the carriage. She pulled the velvet curtains firmly across the windows as the coachman shut the door.

INSIDE THE LIBRARY ON the ground floor of his town house, Lord Amberley found himself having an uncomfortable confrontation with James Purnell. He had expected an irate brother, bristling with fury, demanding satisfaction, perhaps even a duel. He had been apprehensive about the meeting, but he had been prepared for it. He would have thrown against such righteous indignation all the forces of reason and good breeding.

He had not expected a man of icy self-control, a man who said little, but whose dark eyes burned with something that seemed not quite anger. They were eyes that watched very directly and seemed to penetrate to one's very soul. No mannered speeches of carefully rehearsed platitudes would fool this man, Lord Amberley suspected.

"I am afraid Miss Purnell was the victim of some unknown prank last night," he said, "for which my brother appears to have been entirely responsible."

"Then I will speak with your brother," James Purnell said. He stood close to the library door, a cloak still around his shoulders, his hat in his hand. He had refused to have them taken from him or to take a seat. "Lord Eden, I believe?"

"I am afraid he is not at home," Lord Amberley said, "and in his absence it is impossible for me to say exactly what happened, since I did not feel it appropriate to question your sister too closely. But Miss Purnell was confined in my sister's room when I found her. I can only imagine that for some reason my brother thought her to be his twin. They are not unknown to such madcap activities."

"My sister does not resemble Lady Madeline Raine in any way," James Purnell said.

"I agree," Lord Amberley said. "Except perhaps in height and build. I can only suggest, sir, that you convey your sister home with all speed and return later to demand satisfaction from my brother."

"I certainly intend to do that," Purnell said quietly.

"We will hope that the events of the night will never be made public," Lord Amberley said. "I see no reason why there should ever be a blemish on your sister's name. Even so, I shall, if I may, call on Lord Beckworth after luncheon to beg permission to pay my addresses to Miss Purnell." His always firm jawline was more set than usual, his face pale.

James Purnell looked back at him with his burning eyes. One lock of straight dark hair had fallen across his forehead. "Frankly, Amberley," he said, "I believe my sister would be doing herself a disservice to ally herself to this family. But I can see that the offer must be made. I shall inform my father of your intention."

Lord Amberley bowed. "The time must be close to six o'clock," he said. "You will wish to take Miss Purnell home."

Purnell did not move for a moment, during which time he leveled a penetrating stare on his host. "Was she touched?" he asked quietly.

"No." Lord Amberley stilled his right hand, which he suddenly became aware had been clenching and unclenching itself at his side. "She was tied up and gagged when I found her, but I am almost certain that she had not been otherwise abused."

"You must understand that I will demand other satisfaction from Lord Eden if you prove to be wrong," Purnell said.

Lord Amberley bowed and felt a moment's relief as his guest turned abruptly to the door. But even as he reached for the handle, there came a jaunty tapping from the outside and the door opened.

Lord Eden's head appeared around it. "Edmund," he said, "who on earth was . . . ? Oh, pardon me. I didn't mean to intrude." He grinned cheerfully and made to withdraw.

"You had better come in here," Lord Amberley said. "This concerns you, Dom."

"Intriguing!" his brother said, the grin returning to his face. He came into the room, flung his hat down on a side table, and nodded genially to the visitor.

"Dom," Lord Amberley said, "can you explain what Miss Alexandra Purnell was doing in Madeline's room last night?"

Lord Eden looked blank. He glanced from his brother to James Purnell. "Have I missed something?" he asked.

"This is Mr. Purnell," Lord Amberley said. "I found his sister in Madeline's room an hour ago. She was tied to the bed and gagged. She seems to believe that you were responsible."

Lord Eden looked indignant. "Why, of all the . . ." he began. Then his face blanched. "Oh, Lord." He passed a hand over his eyes.

"What happened, Dom?" Lord Amberley's voice was quiet but it held an unmistakable note of authority.

"Those two loose screws must have mistaken her for Madeline," Lord Eden said, removing his hand from his face and looking first into the smoldering eyes of James Purnell and then at his brother. "I asked them to bring Madeline here. I thought she was just about to . . . Well, that is another story. It was all a mistake, anyway. When I found Mad was still in the ballroom, I thought no harm had been done. I might have known it was strange that Faber and Jones just disappeared without a word. Oh, Lord!"

"My sister has led a very sheltered existence," James Purnell said. "She has had a strict upbringing."

Lord Eden closed his eyes. "Oh, God," he said. "She must have been terrified. But I can't understand it. Both Jones and Faber know Madeline. Does Miss Purnell look so much like her? I say, Edmund, that wasn't her stepping into the carriage outside just now, was it?"

"Probably," Lord Amberley said. He held up a staying hand. "But this is not the time to rush out to make your apologies, Dom. Miss Purnell must be taken home without further delay. I suggest, sir"—he turned his attention to their visitor—"that you return later if you require satisfaction from Lord Eden, as I can well understand you may. I shall call at Curzon Street after luncheon."

James Purnell looked steadily at each brother in turn before bowing curtly and turning to the door without another word.

"Oh, Lord," Lord Eden said as soon as the door closed behind him, "what a coil!"

"I don't believe I have any sympathy to spare for you, Dom," his brother said, moving at last to sit heavily in the large mahogany-and-leather chair behind his desk. "Even if it had been Madeline I found, I would have been outraged. She was bound and gagged. Her hands were paralyzed when I released them, and she was quite unable to say a word until I had helped her to a drink of water. And you entrusted such treatment of our sister to two of your friends? Not at all the thing, Dom. And that is the understatement of the decade. I have a mind to level you with my own fists and leave nothing for Mr. Purnell to gain satisfaction from."

"I thought she was going to elope with that Fairhaven reptile," Lord Eden said. "I had to go after him, Edmund. I had to leave my friends to take Mad out of the way."

"You could not just have told her the game was up and set Mama to keeping watch over her?" Lord Amberley said wearily. "You never could take the easy and obvious course, could you, Dom? I don't see how I am to get you out of this. You will be fortunate indeed if you do not end up dead with a bullet between your eyes. And you will be honor bound to delope if it comes to a duel, you know."

"I deserve no less," Lord Eden said with bitter remorse. "The poor girl, Edmund. I have probably put her through a more frightening experience than I would feel looking down the barrel of Purnell's pistol. Do you know her? I cannot put a face to the name, I must confess. Is she very young?"

"She has backbone, I believe," Lord Amberley said. "She was not about to show me that she was afraid. And she told me I might kill her before she would beg anyone to pay a ransom for her."

"I am going to have to marry her, am I not?" Lord Eden said. "I have been trying to ignore the knowledge for the past few minutes. There is no other course open to me, is there? Unless Purnell lays me out cold, of course."

"That has already been taken care of," his brother said quietly.

"You mean you have made my offer for me?" Lord Eden asked, eyebrows raised. He looked at his brother more closely, and his eyes sharpened. "Oh, no, Edmund, not you. You have not offered for the girl, have you? You can't do it, old chap. This has nothing whatsoever to do with you."

"On the contrary," Lord Amberley said. "Miss Purnell has spent the night in my house, Dom. And I found her and was a few minutes alone with her in Madeline's bedchamber. I will be offering for her. You need have no worries on that head."

"Oh, I say," his brother said, flushing and confronting Lord Amberley across the desk. "I can't allow that, you know. You cannot always be taking my burdens on your shoulders, Edmund. I am the one responsible for this mess. I must be the one to marry her."

"I shall be calling on Lord Beckworth after luncheon," Lord Amberley said, a note of finality in his voice, "regardless of your plans, Dom. Now, if you will excuse me, I shall go and shave and tidy myself. My clothes were very hastily donned before I came down here."

"Lord Beckworth!" Lord Eden said. "She isn't Beckworth's daughter, is she? Good God, I wouldn't like to cross that character. But I seem to have done just that, don't I? I'm not sure I'll particularly enjoy crossing swords with the brother either, if it comes to that. And Miss Purnell, Edmund—is she pretty?"

"Quite remarkably lovely, I would guess, when she is properly groomed," Lord Amberley said from the doorway as he let himself out of the room.

IT IS THE MOST RIDICULOUS NOTION I EVER heard," Alexandra said. "I am all but betrothed to his grace, James. Why did you not simply tell the earl that? How can he possibly think of paying his addresses to me? You should have told him that the idea was quite out of the question."

"He is doing the honorable thing, Alex," James said. "You were compromised last night, and though I hope that somehow you can avoid this marriage, I must respect his willingness to do what is right."

"But Papa will not agree to let him speak with me. Will he? Mama? I will be mortified beyond all speech if I have to face him again. I had hoped never to have to do so."

"I do not see quite how your father can say no under the circumstances," Lady Beckworth said. She looked troubled. "If only you had not gone wandering outside on your own, Alexandra. You know that it was not at all the proper thing to do. Papa is going to be very angry with you, and with me too for not keeping a closer eye on you."

"It was not your fault, Mama." Alexandra got to her feet and paced restlessly to the window of her mother's sitting room. Her father had been called away by the arrival of the Earl of Amberley even before they had risen from the luncheon table. That was the first she had known of the earl's plan to offer her marriage. Nanny Rey had fussed her into bed as soon as they had arrived home that morning, and she had been there ever since.

"You said it was all a mistake, James," she said, turning back to her brother, who stood close to the door, his hands clasped behind his back. "Lord Eden had intended to kidnap his sister. I cannot imagine why he would have wished to do such a thing, but it is really a matter between them. The point is that he meant me no harm. And no real harm was done except that I spent an uncomfortable and rather anxious night. Surely a simple apology will do? But from Lord Eden, not the earl. What do you think, Mama?"

"I just wish you had come and told me that you were not going with Deirdre, Alexandra," Lady Beckworth said. "Then I could have sent James in search of you, and we would have been saved from all this inconvenience."

Alexandra's eyes widened as a knock at her mother's door heralded the arrival of a footman with the request that she attend her father in the salon.

"I do not wish to see Lord Amberley," she said, looking pleadingly at her brother.

He looked sympathetic. "I'm sorry, Alex," he said. "I don't think the meeting can be avoided. Just remember that you have done nothing wrong and have nothing to be ashamed of. Leave the talking to him."

"You must not keep Papa waiting," Lady Beckworth said nervously. "You know how very strict he is about promptness, Alexandra."

James Purnell crossed the room impulsively to his sister's side and held out his arm for hers. He looked unsmilingly down at her. "I'll take you downstairs," he said. "Damn the Earl of Amberley and his brother anyway. I beg your pardon, Mama. Effete aristocrats, both. And a sister who flaunts her beauty before the *ton* and flirts with all and sundry. Refuse him, Alex. To hell with him and his notions of honor." He did not apologize for the last blasphemy, as they had already passed beyond Lady Beckworth's hearing.

HE HAD BEEN MISTAKEN in his guess, Lord Amberley saw as soon as Miss Purnell entered the salon. She was not as lovely as he had thought. He had seen her on a bed, her long and shapely legs fully exposed to his view, her face flushed, her dark eyes huge with bewilderment and embarrassment and well-concealed fright. And her dark hair had been in luxuriantly disordered curls about her face and shoulders. It had been the setting and the circumstances that had given the impression of extraordinary beauty.

She stood inside the door now, looking at her father, a rather tall, slender woman who held herself very straight. Her hands were clasped quietly before her. She wore a day dress of brown stuff, well cut and clearly expensive, but dreary in color and unimaginative in design. Her hair was pulled back from her forehead and ears and dressed in a smooth chignon. Not a strand was out of place. She had strong features: dark long-lashed eyes topped by dark, slightly arched brows, a straight nose, and lips that were set now in a straight line. He was not sure how they would look when her face was in repose. She held her chin high. She had a firm, even stubborn jaw. Her face was rather pale.

"May I present the Earl of Amberley to you, Alexandra?" Lord Beckworth said in the heavy moralistic tones that characterized him.

He sounded always as if he were delivering a sermon, the earl thought as he bowed to Miss Purnell. And what a pretty farce this was, the two of them being formally presented for all the world as if they had not encountered each other under such scandalous circumstances just a matter of hours before. She turned her eyes directly on him. Her expression did not relax as she curtsied. She did not say a word.

"I have given his lordship permission to speak with you alone for ten minutes," Lord Beckworth continued. "It would be advisable, Alexandra, to consider well what it befits you to do for the honor of yourself and your family. I will wish you to remain in this room afterward, as I have a few words to say to you myself."

Miss Purnell dropped her eyes for the first time, Lord Amberley noted. But she raised them again almost immediately and looked at her father. "Yes, Papa," she said. They were her first words.

She did not move when Lord Beckworth left the room. Neither did Lord Amberley. He continued to stand with his back to the long windows, his hands behind him. Miss Purnell was looking at him quite steadily and calmly.

"Might I inquire after your health, ma'am?" he asked. "I will not insult you by saying that I hope you have recovered from your ordeal. I am sure you have not. But I hope that you have not taken any particular harm?"

"I am quite well, I thank you, my lord," she said. She had a steady, rather low-pitched voice, he noticed. It sounded quite different from the voice she had forced past dried lips earlier that morning.

"I will also not beg your forgiveness for the dreadful ordeal you have been put through by my family," he said. "Being a lady, you may feel obliged to grant that forgiveness, and really you ought not. What happened to you is unforgivable."

"There you are wrong, my lord," she said. "Nothing in this world is beyond forgiveness, and I understand that what happened to me was the result of an accident rather than malice. I am quite prepared to forgive Lord Eden. I wish you would not take it upon yourself to assume any of the burden of guilt."

"You were confined in my home, ma'am," he said. "I am guilty. I cannot make reparation for what you have suffered. I can only humbly offer the one thing in my power to give you: the protection of my name. I would be honored and indeed greatly relieved if you will accept my hand. I would gladly spend my life trying to repair some of the damage that has been done you."

"You make altogether too much of the matter, my lord," she said. "You owe me nothing. I thank you for the offer, but I must decline. I am to be betrothed to the Duke of Peterleigh by the autumn. Perhaps you had not heard. I am surprised that my father did not mention the fact to you."

Lord Amberley looked at the girl for a few moments before replying. She had not moved since she had first entered the room. She stood straight and proud, and appallingly innocent. He was the first to move. He took a few steps closer to her and removed his hands from behind his back.

"Yes, I knew," he said. "Your father did tell me. The Duke of Peterleigh is a prominent and highly respected gentleman. I can well imagine that you and your whole family are pleased with the match. And if you are rejecting my offer, Miss Purnell, I wish you a secure and happy future with all my heart. I only hope that no whisper of what has happened to you is allowed to escape this house and mine. If my hope is realized, then indeed my offer is unnecessary to your happiness."

"Why would anyone know or care about what happened?" she asked, her eyebrows arching higher and changing her expression suddenly, so that she looked for a moment like a vulnerable girl. "It was all a mistake, after all, and certainly I was not to blame for any of it. Nor were you, my lord."

He smiled grimly even as her chin came higher and her face resumed the set, disciplined look she had worn throughout their interview.

"I would guess that you are quite new to London, Miss Purnell," he said. "Am I right?"

She inclined her head but did not say anything.

"I believe my ten minutes must be almost over," he said. "Let me ask again quite bluntly, then—no, let me urge you—will you marry me?"

"No, my lord," she said quietly, without any hesitation at all, "I will not. But I do thank you. It was kind of you to come."

He inclined his head. "May I ask one thing of you before I take my leave, ma'am?" he said. "If word of your misadventure does escape and life becomes uncomfortable for you, will you receive me again? Will you give me a further chance to protect your honor with my name?"

"No," she said. "That will be quite unnecessary, my lord. I have a father and a brother to protect me, to make no mention of His Grace of Peterleigh."

He closed the remaining distance between them and held out a hand. "I will wish you good day, then, ma'am," he said, "and not distress you with my continued presence."

He thought for a moment that she would reject his offer of friendship. She looked at his hand before extending hers and placing it in his grasp. He looked up at her as he raised her hand to his lips. She looked quite steadily back, though her color heightened.

"Good day, my lord," she said. Her voice was low and quite calm.

ALEXANDRA STOOD WHERE SHE WAS for several moments after Lord Amberley had left. Then she drew a deep breath and crossed the room to the window.

What a dreadful ordeal! And how ridiculously unnecessary. What could have made the earl feel that he must come and offer her marriage just because his brother had made such a ghastly mistake? And why had Papa allowed him to speak to her when she had been unofficially betrothed to the Duke of Peterleigh all her life? Men had strange notions of honor.

She did not think she would have recognized the Earl of Amberley if she had passed him in the street. Indeed, she had scarce looked into his face earlier that morning, and anyway he had been wearing a dressing gown on that occasion. She had gained no impression of his looks or his coloring or his height—or even his age.

It had been a shock to find when she turned to him after Papa had presented him to her that he was a fashionable and distinguished-looking gentleman. And a young one too. He could not be nearly as old as his grace, and probably not much older than James. He had dark thick hair—though not as dark as hers—and blue eyes. They were kindly eyes that looked at one very directly and appeared to smile. He had a good-humored mouth. He was not particularly tall, though she had had to look up to him when he had stepped close to her. But he was powerfully built. She guessed that he was not quite the effete gentleman of James's accusation.

She had found his appearance quite disconcerting. Her memories of that morning would be humiliating enough even if the Earl of Amberley had turned out to be a plain, aging man. She had felt quite mortified to know that this young and elegant gentleman had seen her lying on a bed, her hair loose about her, her skirt twisted up under her and exposing almost all of her legs. She would dearly have liked to turn and run to her bedchamber so that she could hide her face in the covers of her bed. She had stood still instead and forced herself to both look at him and listen to him. She had even spoken. She had had to call on all the training of years for the discipline necessary to contain her discomfort.

She had found the whole interview quite thoroughly embarrassing. She had had little to do with gentlemen since her arrival in London the month before, and nothing whatsoever to do with them before that. She had lived an appallingly sheltered life at home. For years she had longed for her marriage and a home of her own and London, longed for freedom, though she had always known that in marrying the Duke of Peterleigh she would merely be changing hands from one severe taskmaster to another. But oh, being a wife would surely offer her more by way of independence and responsibility and self-respect than being a daughter. And a wife in London!

Yet she had found London bewildering and disappointing. She found that she was not at all equipped to mix socially with her social equals. While one part of her longed and longed to be gay, to abandon herself to the pleasures of the Season, the other part of her shied away from letting go of the discipline and the dignity of a lifetime. And this same part of herself led her frequently to long for escape, as it had the night before at the Easton ball.

And so she knew little about how to talk to and how to deal with a gentleman. She really had not taken at all well with the *ton*. She had not even known—ridiculous innocence—if it was proper to give her hand to the Earl of Amberley. She had not known if he was taking an unpardonable liberty by kissing that hand. Nothing like it had ever happened to her before. Yet she was one-and-twenty!

Certainly she had felt unusually flustered when his lips had touched her hand. The gesture had seemed alarmingly intimate. She had felt sensation sizzle along the full length of her arm. And she had despised herself for allowing such a little thing so to discompose her. If it *were* a little thing! She did not know.

The front door opened to the right of her window, and the subject of her thoughts emerged. Alexandra stepped back as a groom led forward a magnificent black stallion. She would not wish to be caught looking out if he should happen to glance up. But he did not do so. He mounted the horse, handed a coin to the groom, and turned the horse's head in the direction of the gates.

Alexandra could not remember seeing the Earl of Amberley before that morning, though she had been in London for a whole month. She hoped that she would never see him again. And she hoped that Lord Eden would not be sent to make his apologies. She really wanted the whole nightmare of the night before to be forgotten. She wanted life to be back to normal. His grace was to accompany them to the theater that evening and to attend Lady Sharp's soiree the following evening.

The door behind her opened and closed, and Alexandra straightened her shoulders and turned reluctantly to face her father. He was looking grim and tight-lipped, she saw with a sinking heart. His eyes were cold.

"So, Alexandra," he said, "you have seen fit to refuse the offer of respectability the Earl of Amberley was willing to make?"

"I refused his offer, yes, Papa," she said in some surprise. "It was quite unnecessary for him to make it. And besides, I am to be betrothed to his grace during the autumn."

"Perhaps his grace will not be eager to ally himself to a slut," Lord Beckworth said. "And am I to have you on my hands for the rest of my life?"

"A slut?" Alexandra's eyes were wide with disbelief.

"What do you call yourself?" her father asked, striding toward her. "You were brought to London at considerable expense and trouble to me in order to make your appearance in society. You were to be made a more accomplished bride for the duke. Last night you were sent to a ball with both your mother and your brother to ensure your respectability. Yet you hoodwinked your mother by sending your aunt and your cousin to tell her you were leaving with them just so that you would be free to slip outdoors unchaperoned. Who was he, Alexandra? I mean to have the truth."

"I did not send Aunt Deirdre, Papa," she said, bewildered. "And who is who? I do not understand."

"You have had all the benefits of a good and virtuous home," the baron said harshly, "but it has had little effect on your wicked heart, Alexandra. I want the name of the lover you were to have a secret tryst with."

Alexandra gaped at him. "I went outside to be alone for a few minutes," she said. "I find the crowds at social gatherings overwhelming, Papa, and sometimes long for the quietness of home. I did not intend to be gone for longer than a few minutes. And I did not plan to meet anyone. I did not know about the misapprehension Mama was under. I did wrong. I know that, and I beg your pardon, Papa, as I have already begged Mama's. You have taught me better than to wander about alone and unchaperoned. I have been justly punished."

"I left off thrashing you when you were sixteen," Lord Beckworth said. "God is my witness that I did my Christian duty in trying to instill the principles of virtue in you. Perhaps I should have continued with the thrashings even after you left the schoolroom. Perhaps I have failed in my duty after all. But you had beatings often enough, Alexandra, and they seem to have done little good. You are clearly of a stubborn and wayward disposition."

Alexandra had lowered her eyes to the floor from force of long habit. There was no point whatsoever in arguing with her father. She stood straight before him, her face impassive. "I am sorry, Papa," she said.

"We will be fortunate indeed if you have not brought permanent disgrace on your family," he said. "We will have to rely on the courtesy of the Earl of Amberley and Lord Eden to keep quiet about your scandalous indiscretion."

Alexandra raised her eyes to his for a moment, a look of incredulity on her face. But she resumed her former stance when she saw his reddened face and coldly angry eyes.

"You will spend the remainder of the day in your own room," he said. "You will occupy your time in reading your Bible. You will speak to no one until tomorrow. I shall have water and bread sent to your room at dinnertime. You will not communicate with the servant who brings it to you. Do you understand?"

"Yes, Papa," she said. Her voice was quite steady.

"Be thankful that your punishment is to last a day and

not a week," Lord Beckworth said. "I would suggest that you spend at least a part of the day in prayer, Alexandra. God may not be as lenient in his judgment as I have been."

"Yes, Papa," she said.

She lifted her chin and straightened her shoulders as she walked past him and out of the salon. A slut? A lover? Wayward? Oh, no, this was becoming insufferable. She met James on the first landing. He was clearly waiting for her. She looked meaningfully into his eyes and shook her head slightly as she turned to the staircase leading to the upper floor.

"I understand, Alex," he said quietly. "Is it to be for just the one day?"

She nodded briefly without turning back to him or slackening her pace.

"Did you refuse Amberley?" he asked.

She nodded again.

"Good girl," he said. "Good girl, Alex. It will not be too long until tomorrow. I have heard that the play is a bore anyway."

Alexandra, halfway up the staircase, looked back at him over her shoulder. She did not disobey her father's command—she had never dared disobey him—but a smile that would have been imperceptible to someone who did not know them passed between brother and sister.

"NO, REALLY, YOU FELLOWS," Lord Eden said indignantly, "it is no laughing matter, you know. We could all swing for kidnapping or something else if her family should decide to cut up rough. I could still end up peering down the wrong end of a dueling pistol. I didn't much like the look of that brother. A decidedly nasty fellow when aroused, I wouldn't be surprised. And all this is not to mention the fact that either Amberley or I will probably end up in parson's mousetrap over your atrocious bungling."

"She should make an active armful anyway," Mr. Clement Jones said with a grin. "She fought like the very devil. You had better tie her in the sheets before boarding her on your wedding night, Eden. She might do you some irreparable damage."

"I say, you fellows," Lord Eden protested as his two unsympathetic friends roared with laughter. The three of them were taking an early-afternoon ride in Hyde Park. Lord Eden had other pressing matters to attend to, but this meeting was of great importance too. "Between us we have done the girl enough harm as it is. There is no need to be vulgar or disrespectful. The point is, I need your word that not a breath about last night's doings will escape you. Not even when you are drunk. Faber? Jones? Your word of honor?"

"I call it a mortal shame," Mr. Faber said, having controlled his laughter finally. "It would make a priceless story, Eden. May we use it if we change the names?"

"Just try it, my friend," Lord Eden said, his customary good humor deserting him for the moment, "and you will be the one eating the barrel of a pistol. With my finger on the trigger! Your word, now."

"You have mine, Eden," Mr. Jones said. "Not that I think it necessary, mind. You should know us well enough to know that neither one of us would say anything to dishonor a lady. What is she like, anyway? Pretty?"

"Amberley says so," Lord Eden said gloomily. "Lord, what a coil! Forced to offer for a girl I haven't even met."

"Poor Miss Carstairs," Jones said, and winked at Faber.

Lord Eden groaned. "Don't even mention her," he said. "I

have to blank my mind. But I say, fellows, we might show a bit more sensibility. What about Miss Purnell? The poor girl must have suffered agonies. You know what females are like. And perhaps it doesn't suit her inclination to be thinking of taking on Amberley or me, any more than it suits ours to be taking on her. She is supposed to be half-betrothed to Peterleigh."

"Oh, Lord," Faber said, "she would be a fool not to fly into your arms, Eden. Or Amberley's. Peterleigh! He would probably whip the poor girl twice a week whether she deserved it or not."

"I have to go and call on my mother," Lord Eden said, "and half-throttle Madeline. All this is her fault. I just wanted to hear you give your word first. The lady's reputation has to be our main concern here."

Miss Carstairs, Lord Eden thought from the depths of his gloom as he turned away from his companions and headed his horse toward the Grosvenor Gate and his mother's house beyond. Trust one of those loose screws to mention her. He had been in love with her for all of three weeks, and it was real love this time. All those other times in the past several years when he had fancied himself in love, he had been merely infatuated.

But Miss Carstairs! She personified all that he found most desirable in a woman. She was small and fragile, with blond ringlets and blue, trusting eyes. She had a pouting rosebud of a mouth that his own lips ached to taste, and a tiny waist that he longed to span with his two hands. She spoke with the most adorable lisp.

And she was beginning to notice him. Three evenings before, he had had the unspeakable joy of seeing her carry the nosegay that he had sent her that morning, and she had smiled shyly at him over it as she lifted it to her nose. Her mother had even nodded graciously to him during the same evening.

And now he must renounce all thoughts of her. He must pay his addresses to a lady he had caught only the merest glimpse of that morning, a lady who had looked tall and thin and dark—not at all his type. That was if Edmund had not engaged himself to her already, of course. But surely, he would have had second thoughts on that matter. No, he would not. No one was more the soul of honor than Edmund or more eager to shoulder the burdens of his family. But surely the girl and her father would realize that his brother had no responsibility whatsoever for what had happened. Surely Edmund had been turned away.

He was going to have to make his own call on Lord Beckworth after his visit to Mama and Madeline. He certainly did not relish the prospect. He would not be wild with enthusiasm about confronting any father under the particular circumstances. But Beckworth! The man had not been in town long, but already he had gained a reputation as a harsh, moralistic killjoy.

Lord Eden had overheard him in White's one afternoon expounding his social theories. Every unemployed man and boy should be transported to a land where plenty of work could be found for them, and every prostitute should be stripped and whipped in the open streets before suffering a like fate. England should be preserved for God-fearing men and women who were ready to do their Christian duty at honest employment. Except for the rich, presumably. Lord Eden had felt taut with anger. Lord Beckworth, he had suspected, perhaps quite unfairly, was just the type who would relish watching corporal punishments, especially the stripping of the prostitutes.

And this was the man he must face after having had his

daughter abducted the night before and tied to a bedpost in the bedchamber of a bachelor establishment for the remainder of the night!

Lord Eden was thankful to arrive at his mother's house and have his thoughts distracted.

"Dom!" Madeline jumped to her feet when her brother was announced. "I was quite determined not to speak to you at all today and perhaps even for the rest of my life. But, you poor dear. We have just heard! I could have devised quite devilish punishment for you last night, but I would not have wished this particular one on you." She had crossed the room and taken his arm.

"Good afternoon, Mama," Lord Eden said, crossing the room to Lady Amberley's chair and bending to kiss her cheek. He patted his sister's hand amiably as he did so. "Edmund has been here before me, has he? Yes, it is something of an embarrassment, is it not? But it is the poor girl we must feel most sorry for. Do you know her, Mad?"

"I don't believe so," she said, "though I have been searching my mind. She is tall and dark, Hatty Temple said. But that description fits any number of girls, does it not? You have not been challenged to a duel, have you, Dom? Mama and I have been living in mortal fear that you might. Miss Purnell's brother was looking like thunder when he came for her, we heard."

Lord Eden disengaged his sister's hand from his arm. He had turned rather pale. "Edmund *has* been here, Mama, has he not?" he said. "It *is* from him you have heard all this?"

"No," she said. "Madeline went walking in the park with Miss Wickhill and her maid before luncheon. They met Miss Temple and she told them. It is a shocking thing, Dominic. I had hoped that there was no truth in it, but I see that there is after all. How can you possibly have done such a thing? The poor girl. I feel for her from the bottom of my heart."

Lord Eden sat down. He swallowed convulsively. "How did Miss Temple know?" he asked.

"She had heard it from her mother's dresser, who had heard it from the cook, who had heard it from the milkman, who had heard it...Do I need to say more, Dom?" Madeline asked. "Poor dear. Did you imagine that you could hush it all up? I suppose you have been busy silencing everyone abovestairs that could possibly have known, forgetting that scandal spreads faster than fire belowstairs. I am afraid the whole affair is probably the talk of the town by now."

Lord Eden rested his elbows on his knees and covered his face with his hands. "Oh, God," he said. "It couldn't possibly be worse, could it? Poor Miss Purnell. The innocent Christian in the lion's den. I shall have to get over to Curzon Street even faster than I had planned."

"You are going to offer for her, Dominic?" his mother asked. "I knew my son would do the right thing. I do feel for you, dear, though I must confess one is inclined to think you have brought it all on yourself. I suppose Miss Purnell was the innocent victim of what you had planned for Madeline? She told me about that. I really cannot approve of such high-handed treatment of your sister, even if your motive was a noble one. Sometimes, Dominic, I wonder if you will ever grow up."

"He is grown up," Madeline said, rushing to the defense of her twin as soon as someone else became critical of him. She came and sat on the arm of the chair beside him and took one of his hands in hers.

"He is willing to marry Miss Purnell. And you are willing to renounce Miss Carstairs, Dom. And you have such a *tendre* for her. I am sorry. What is Miss Purnell like? Will I like her as a sister-in-law?"

"I don't know," Lord Eden said. "I have had only the merest glimpse of her. Edmund says she is lovely. He is the one who found her, you know. And he has already rushed over there to make his offer. I don't think Lord Beckworth will pay much attention to his visit, though. Edmund is in no way responsible."

"But it is just like him to bear the burden," Lady Amberley said. "I do hope the father says no to him. Edmund will not like a forced marriage. I have hoped he will marry someone quite special."

"But she is all right for me, Mama?" Lord Eden asked.

"I consider the question quite irrelevant, Dominic," she said, fixing him with a steady eye. "You have very badly compromised the girl. You must marry her. Anyone with an ounce of sense in his head must see that. We will just have to hope that Miss Purnell is someone special too."

"Dom." Madeline raised his hand to her cheek and looked into his pale face. "I am so very sorry, dear. I feel dreadfully guilty, you know, because I am largely responsible for what has happened. If I had not teased you with Sir Hedley Fairhaven, you would not have made the mistake you made, and Miss Purnell would not have been abducted. I wish there were something I could do."

"You could go and marry Miss Purnell," he said sourly and ungraciously.

She bit her lip. "I wish I could, Dom," she said.

He squeezed her hand and jumped to his feet. "I know you do, Mad," he said. "But this is not your fault. You are not to think that. Cheer up now and smile at me. I don't want to leave here with the added burden of knowing I have made you miserable. Come on, you goose. It is not the end of the world. I am going to arrange for a marriage if I can, not an execution."

Madeline smiled bleakly at him. "I wish it had been me," she said, "tied to that bed, I mean. I could have had a good fight with you, Dom, with both feet and both fists and perhaps even my teeth. I would have left you with bruises and cuts to wince over for a month. And I would have thoroughly enjoyed myself. I cannot enjoy seeing you in such disgrace."

"Hm," Lord Eden said, turning to leave. "Good day to you, Mama. I am sorry to be such a constant source of disappointment to you. Perhaps one day I will be able to do something you can be proud of. Take it easy, Mad, and take off that tragic expression this minute. This is not the end of the world. It only seems to be."

"What a self-pitying little speech," Lady Amberley said as he reached the door. "You are my son, Dominic, and as such a source of enormous pride to me. You do not have to earn my love, you know. There is nothing you could possibly do to forfeit it. That is not to say that you do not do the most unbelievably stupid things on occasion. Go now and see what you can do to put this one right."

She smiled at his retreating back as Madeline withdrew a handkerchief from a pocket and blew her nose loudly.

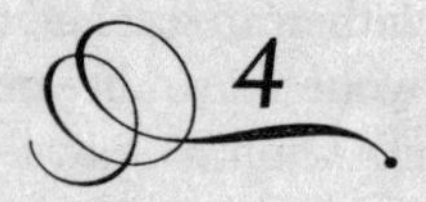

ALEXANDRA SAT VERY STILL, HER HANDS HELD in her lap, as Nanny Rey finished pinning her hair into its smooth chignon. She had thought her punishment would be over this morning. But it seemed not. Papa had summoned her to the salon again. He must have more to say to her. Perhaps he had decided that, after all, one afternoon and evening of solitary confinement with her Bible were just not enough. Indeed, she had rarely before known fewer than three days of such punishment. She had assumed that his awareness of her social commitments had influenced his leniency.

"There," Nanny Rey said, patting her on both shoulders from behind, "you had better not keep his lordship waiting, lovey. Not after yesterday. And why did you not drink the chocolate I had smuggled up to you last night?"

Alexandra met her old nurse's eyes in the mirror and smiled. "You knew I would not, Nanny," she said. "Indeed, you would have been shocked had I done so. You sent it only as a token of love, and for that I thank you. But you know that I will not knowingly disobey Papa."

"On your way, then," the nurse said, clapping her hands. "You don't want another day on bread and water, lovey."

Alexandra had a confused feeling of going back in time as a footman opened the doors into the salon and she stepped inside. Her father stood before the fireplace as he had the day before, the visitor before the windows, his hands behind his back. Only it was not the same visitor. This man was younger, taller, more slender in build, fairer of hair. But he was quite as fashionable as his brother. And his face looked as good-humored. He must be the Earl of Amberley's brother. There was a very definite family resemblance.

Alexandra folded her hands in front of her and lifted her chin. She looked at her father.

"May I present Lord Eden to you, Alexandra?" Lord Beckworth said.

She turned her eyes on the baron and inclined her head. He bowed.

"Miss Purnell," he said.

"Lord Eden has requested a private word with you, Alexandra," her father continued. "I have granted him ten minutes. I trust you will listen carefully and do what is right. You will retire to your mother's sitting room at the end of the ten minutes."

"Yes, Papa," she said.

But this was not to be an exact repetition of the day before, Alexandra found after her father had closed the doors behind him. Lord Eden did not stay by the windows, his hands behind his back, as his brother had done. He came hurrying across the room to her, his handsome face alive with concern.

"Miss Purnell," he said, "how you must hate me. How you must wish you could put a bullet between my eyes. I am most dreadfully sorry, you know. But I do not know even how to begin to beg your pardon. To say I am sorry is quite insufficient, but I can think of no words that are adequate."

She looked at him, at his eager, boyish face. He could not be any older than she, this ogre of sin and vice she had pictured to herself through one night of terror and another of tedious punishment. "You need not trouble yourself any further, my lord," she said. "I have already forgiven you. Did Lord Amberley not tell you that?"

"He did say that you were remarkably decent about the whole matter," he said. "But I find it hard to believe that you can have forgiven me, Miss Purnell. I can scarce think of anything more unpardonable that I might have done."

"We are all in need of forgiveness," she said. "How can we expect to receive it if we are not also prepared to give it?"

He looked somewhat taken aback. "You are more kind than I deserve," he said. "I have come to make things right if I can. I know that you cannot possibly wish to marry me. You must wish me at the bottom of the deepest ocean. I have heard that you have had an understanding with the Duke of Peterleigh. I cannot begin to compete with him in consequence. And you must have rather a poor opinion of the stability of my character. But you may be assured that as your husband I would spend the rest of my life trying to make up to you what I have taken from you."

Alexandra's eyes had widened. "Oh," she said, "you have come to offer for me too? It is quite unnecessary, my lord, as I told Lord Amberley yesterday. I am grateful that you have come to apologize, even though I had already forgiven you. But really you need do no more."

He looked with boyish earnestness into her eyes. "But you must marry me, Miss Purnell," he said. "I have severely compromised you. I am sorry from my heart that you have no choice, but really I do not think you have."

"No one need even know what happened," she said. "It was all rather silly nonsense anyway. I believe you refine altogether too much on it, my lord."

He reached for her hand and held it in a firm grip. Alexandra looked down at their clasped hands, embarrassed and not knowing if she should snatch her own away. He seemed not to be conscious of what he had done.

"The whole thing is already common knowledge," he said. "Did you not know? I did not think you could have escaped doing so. Servants, it seems, are not quite as discreet as we might hope. Amberley has already dismissed the footman responsible, but it is too late to repair the damage. I am afraid your reputation has been badly compromised."

"Oh, nonsense!" Alexandra turned away from him, using the movement as an excuse to withdraw her hand from his. "I was not in any way to blame for what happened. Everyone will realize that. And you made a mistake. Everyone will know that too. The whole matter will doubtless become a joke over which everyone will laugh heartily. I shall be horribly embarrassed to be seen in public for the next two or three days. But a little laughter never hurt anyone. I will be none the worse for it."

Lord Eden passed his fingers through his hair, leaving it considerably more disheveled than even the current fashion would allow. "Far be it from me to contradict a lady," he said, "but do you know much about the ways of society, ma'am?"

"I have lived my whole life on my father's estate," she said, "but I do assure you, Lord Eden, that I was brought up to know the difference between right and wrong. And I expect everyone who can lay claim to the name of lady or gentleman to know the same. I expect the same people to have a good deal of sense."

"Oh, Lord!" he said.

"So you see," she continued, folding her hands before her again and injecting a note of finality into her voice, "your concern is not really necessary, my lord. But I thank you for your visit and your offer. I will wish you good day. My father said ten minutes, and he does not take kindly to disobedience."

"Miss Purnell!" He strode impulsively toward her again and reached out both hands for hers. He did not wait for her to respond. He took her clasped hands and separated them with his own. "I beg you to reconsider. You do not know what is facing you when you leave this house. I cannot bear the thought that I have brought that on you. Marry me. I will not be a hard master, I promise you. I will treat you with the utmost respect and affection. I owe you that, though I do believe that I would offer the same to any wife. Please marry me. Allow me to protect you."

Alexandra was touched despite her embarrassment over his proximity and his hands clasping hers. She only just stopped herself from returning the pressure of his hands.

"Thank you," she said. "I truly thank you. But I am to marry His Grace of Peterleigh. There has been an understanding between us since I was in my infancy. I must leave now, my lord. My father will be very angry if I do not."

Then she did return the pressure of his hands before she realized what she was doing, pulled her own away, and made her way from the room before he had a chance to detain her further. She ran up the stairs to her mother's sitting room, thankful that at last the whole ridiculous and humiliating episode was at an end.

• • •

LORD AMBERLEY SAT IN Mrs. Eunice Borden's drawing room listening to her talk. Or rather not listening. She was telling him about a book of poems her latest protégé had presented her with the previous evening. He was smiling and watching her, not deliberately inattentive, but not listening even so.

"It is unusual for you to visit during the afternoon, Amberley," she said finally, breaking off quite abruptly what she was saying.

"What?" he said. "Oh, yes, I suppose it is. Do you mind, Eunice? Am I keeping you from something more important?"

"Not at all," she said. "I had planned to spend the afternoon reading, but I would just as soon spend it conversing with you. Something is the matter?"

He shook his head and smiled at her. "No, no," he said. "I merely felt the need of your good sense."

She looked at him closely for a few moments. "If you wish," she said, "we may remove to my bedchamber. Daylight does not seem quite appropriate to such activity, but that is no matter if it will content you."

He continued to smile at her. "Would it embarrass you, Eunice," he asked, "to be made love to during the daytime?"

"I believe it would," she said frankly. "Though it is quite absurd to feel so when the same thing happens, after all, whether the room is light or dark. Come along, Amberley, I can see it is what you wish."

He rose to his feet and looked down at her apologetically. "You are good to me, Eunice," he said. "You can read me like a book, can you not?"

"I can see that something is troubling you," she said, "and that somehow you are in need of me. Perhaps afterwards you will feel like talking about it. But only if you wish. I shall not pry into your affairs."

And she was as good as her word, Lord Amberley found. If she was embarrassed, she did not show it, but allowed him to take his pleasure beneath the bedsheets rather more lingeringly than was his habit with her and to sink into blissful unconsciousness beside her afterward. When he awoke, she was lying as usual on her back, her legs neatly side by side, her hands clasped loosely over the blanket, her eyes open. He felt a momentary regret that he had never been able to give her pleasure in their couplings. She seemed not to want it and had told him quite matter-of-factly on the only occasion when his hands had strayed that it was quite unnecessary for him to caress her.

He lifted his hand and stroked her cheek with one knuckle. "Thank you, Eunice," he said.

"I am always happy to give you pleasure," she said.

"Have you heard of the scandal?" he asked.

"I very much doubt it," she said. "I do not meet a great number of people outside my salon, Amberley, and quite frankly, I do not derive any pleasure from listening to gossip. Most of it is untrue anyway."

"This is all too real, I am afraid," he said. "Dominic took it into his head two evenings ago to kidnap Madeline in order to save her from an elopement that she had teased him into believing possible. He had some corkbrained friends of his take her to my house, tie her to the bedpost so that she would not run away, and gag her so that she would not disturb the servants' sleep. The scheme worked beautifully well except that the girl was not Madeline."

"And I can guess the rest of the story," she said. "The girl has been compromised and must be married. Lord Eden is too young to be faced with such a responsibility, so you are to wed her. It is quite what I would expect of you, Amberley. You have some misgivings about the girl?"

"She will not have me," he said, "or Dominic."

"She must be very new to London and society, then," Mrs. Borden said, "or of very firm character. Has she not yet found out what will happen to her?"

"I am afraid she must soon," he said. "The scandal broke yesterday when a new footman of mine gossiped."

"Then you must go back to her and renew your offer," she said.

Lord Amberley turned onto his side and raised himself on his elbow. "Yes, I am afraid I must, Eunice," he said.

She turned her head and looked at him. "It is making a decision that is hard, Amberley," she said. "Once the decision is made, then there is nothing more to worry about. You have decided to do what is right. Did you wish me to reassure you? Is that why you came? You are right. Of course you are."

"Oh, yes, I know that, Eunice," he said, the same smile on his face as he had worn downstairs earlier. "But I wanted to marry you, dear."

"You only think you do, Amberley," she said, "because you are comfortable with me and we share a friendship. But friendship is not sufficient for a good marriage. At least, for you it is not. You need more. You need passion, and you cannot get passion from me. Only comfort and companionship. We are only an episode, you know. We would have ended sooner or later. It is as well to end our association now when we still like each other a great deal."

"I will miss you," he said. "I notice that you are assuming that our affair must end if I marry Miss Purnell."

"Well, of course it must," she said. "I know you well enough, Amberley, to realize that you could not be unfaithful to a wife. And I believe you know me well enough to understand that I would not receive another woman's husband. We need feel no guilt over this afternoon. You are not yet betrothed, and I did not know of your obligation. But this is the end now. You must not return."

"No," he said. His smile was a little twisted. "I must not."

"Just tell me one thing," she said. "Will you be able to make a marriage of it, Amberley? Is there the chance that you will find with this Miss Purnell the passion you will need?"

"I think not," he said. "But I will make a marriage of it, Eunice. I will owe her that. She is quite blameless in all this, you know. A total innocent. I must spend my life making her a good husband. She was to marry Peterleigh."

"Then she is a very fortunate lady," Mrs. Borden said. "Peterleigh is humorless and egotistical. No woman could be happy with him. I would say that her misadventure was most fortunate."

He grinned unexpectedly. "Thank you, Eunice," he said. "I must get dressed and leave you now. I must try to find Miss Purnell tonight. If she has the courage or the rashness to go out, she will probably be at either Lady Sharp's soiree or the Higgins' rout. If she is wise, she will stay at home and I shall pay my call tomorrow morning."

It was impossible to know, Lord Amberley thought a few minutes later as he bent to kiss her cheek, whether Eunice was sorry to see him go or somewhat relieved that she no longer needed to render him a service that she did not enjoy.

LADY MADELINE RAINE WAS ENJOYING herself at Lady Sharp's soiree. There were advantages to being two-and-twenty and still neither betrothed nor married, she was discovering with pleased surprise. She had been rather fearful that this year she would be just too old to attract the female friendships and male admiration that had always come her way so easily. She had half-expected to find herself relegated to spinster status.

But it was not so. The younger girls seemed eager to be seen with her and to copy her fashions. And the gentlemen appeared to find her no less attractive for all her declining years. Indeed, they seemed to vie for her attention more than ever. There were three of them now conversing with her and Lady Pamela Paisley.

And one of them was Sir Derek Peignton, the adorable blond giant whom she had not encountered during all her previous Seasons, although he must be close to Edmund in age. She was quite in love with him. She had danced with him twice at the Easton ball and had allowed him to drive her in the park the afternoon before. He had touched his hat and bowed to her on Bond Street that morning when she had deigned to nod and smile at him.

She hoped it was real love. There was something to be said for having had five Seasons in a row and having been free to enjoy them to the full while she saw around her the girls with whom she had made her come-out seasoned matrons already, some of them with more than one child. But there was still that eternal female longing to belong to one man, to have the security of his name. She wanted to be married.

The only trouble was that she also wanted to be in love. And she had an annoying habit of falling in love with the wrong gentlemen or of falling out of love again just when she was thoroughly convinced that she was in forever. She had been in love with Sir Hedley Fairhaven at the start of the Season, though she could not now imagine why. The man was clearly nothing but a fortune hunter. She had probably imagined herself in love merely to assert her independence over Dominic, who had frowned his disapproval the very first time he had seen her dance with Sir Hedley.

Thank goodness at least Edmund did not interfere quite so openly. He had told her during her very first Season that she might choose her own husband, within reason. Those last two words, of course, had more meaning than had at first appeared. She had accused him of going back on his word when he had discovered a note from Lieutenant Harris giving details of their elopement plans and had told her quite plainly that it would not do and that he would not consent to the marriage even if he had to confine her to her room for a year.

But she had admitted long ago that on that occasion he had been quite right. She would not have been happy following the drum and she certainly would not have remained long in love with a man who was well known for his recklessness at cards and for his capacity to outdrink all companions. He had seemed dashing only because he wore a uniform and had a devil-may-care approach to life.

But no one could say that Sir Derek was ineligible—not Edmund, and not even Dominic, who was much harder to please where her suitors were concerned. Sir Derek was elegant and wealthy and charming and very, very handsome. She wanted to be in love with him. She wanted to be married and settled in life, and it would undoubtedly be very glamorous to be married to someone like him.

Madeline gazed around the crowded drawing room, well pleased with the evening. She chattered to the whole group and smiled on them all and exchanged special glances with Sir Derek—she was sure that he felt the same attraction she was feeling.

And she wondered if Miss Purnell was present or about to be. It was rather difficult to look around one for someone one has never seen before, or at least someone one does not remember to have seen before. And how could she possibly ask anyone? Everyone would know perfectly well the reason for her curiosity. It was very probable, of course, that Miss Purnell would not be there. Even if she had planned to come, the scandal would doubtless keep her away.

But Madeline hoped against hope that she would come and that somehow she would be recognizable. And it was very possible that she would be. She would surely have special treatment if she dared to put in an appearance. Madeline desperately wanted to see her. She wanted to see with her own eyes just what a very narrow escape Dominic and Edmund had had.

She still found it hard to believe that Miss Purnell had refused both of them. Under the circumstances the girl appeared to have had little choice but to choose one of them. And anyway, to refuse her two brothers! They were surely two of the handsomest and most eligible gentlemen in town. She had felt very grateful to Miss Purnell when she had first heard of the rejections, and inclined to like the girl. It was only after her first relief that perversely she had started to resent the woman who had refused both her brothers, when they had nobly been prepared to sacrifice their own happiness in order to protect her name.

Madeline was still part of the same group, though standing beside Sir Derek Peignton and in semiprivate conversation with him, when Maisie Baines joined them.

"Good evening, Lady Madeline, Lady Pamela," she said.

She fluttered her fan at the three gentlemen. "You really would not think she would have the nerve, would you?"

Mr. Sheldon looked across the room, over Madeline's shoulder, and raised his quizzing glass to his eye. "One would not expect her to have the *courage,*" he said in tones that set the color rising in Miss Baines's cheeks.

"Grandmama is in the card room," she said. "But I know she will wish me to remove to the music room now. One cannot be too careful of the company one keeps, Grandmama says."

Madeline turned her head to see the new arrivals.

"I cannot help feeling sorry for Miss Purnell," Lady Pamela said. "It is most unfortunate that she went walking alone."

"Grandmama says that she has come by her just deserts," Miss Baines said.

Miss Purnell was tall, Madeline saw, and almost exaggeratedly upright in bearing. Her chin was held high. Her face and manner were quite calm and self-possessed. She had very dark hair. She was not pretty. "Handsome" was perhaps a word that would describe her if everything about her did not look quite so severe. Her green gown was simple and unadorned. She wore no jewelry. And her hair, absent of all plumes or ribbons, was dressed in a plain chignon.

She had a hand resting on the arm of a man who resembled her to no small degree. He was taller than she, though not of immense height. He looked strong and agile. Indeed, he did not look as if he belonged in a London drawing room at all. His complexion was sun-darkened. His hair, dark, straight, and thick, was cut unfashionably long. One lock was fallen across his forehead. His face was as severe as his sister's—he must surely be the brother who had gone to fetch her from Edmund's—his jaw set in a hard line, his eyes watching the occupants of the room intently. Madeline did not remember to have seen either one before.

She disliked Miss Purnell on sight. She was proud and haughty. Madeline was very glad she had refused Edmund and Dominic. Madeline would not have enjoyed having such a woman as a sister-in-law.

"Would you like me to conduct you to the music room, Lady Madeline?" Sir Derek asked solicitously.

"No, thank you." She smiled up at him and felt a certain breathlessness. His gray eyes seemed very close to hers. His shoulders were very broad.

"May I take you to Lady Amberley, then?" he asked.

Madeline looked at him in surprise. "Mama is playing cards with Sir Cedric Harvey," she said. "I do not think she would enjoy being disturbed by me quite this early, sir."

He bowed and said no more.

Mr. and Miss Purnell had crossed the room to join that toad Albert Harding-Smythe, Madeline observed. The man had an air of enormous consequence, even though he apparently had very little else to recommend him. She had waltzed with him once the previous year and three times had had to endure his obsequious apologies and his secret leers as his coat front came into contact with her breasts. Since then, the sight of him had been enough to make her shudder.

"Poor Mr. Harding-Smythe is her cousin," Miss Baines was saying. "How dreadfully embarrassing for him. How can he cut his own kin? She ought not to put him in such a dilemma."

But if Mr. Harding-Smythe felt the dilemma, he showed no sign of doing so. Madeline watched incredulously as the man waited for brother and sister to come close, and quite deliberately turned his back on them and laughed heartily at something a near neighbor had said or not said. Miss Purnell's chin rose an inch. Mr. Purnell looked dangerous. His dark eyes burned from beneath the shock of fallen hair. He took two glasses of something from the tray of a passing waiter and handed one to his sister.

"She ought not to have come," Mr. Sheldon said, lowering his quizzing glass. "Poor lady. We live in a cruel society."

Madeline looked across the room to where Lady Sharp stood with the Marquess of Blaise. Why had she not come to greet the new arrivals? She was looking furiously angry and was glaring in the direction of the Purnells. She said something to the marquess, who raised his eyebrows, pursed his lips, and let his eyes roam insolently over Miss Purnell from head to toe. In the crowded room, a certain space had formed around the pair, who were sipping from their glasses and talking to each other. Miss Purnell's hand was steady, Madeline noticed.

"Forgive me, ma'am," Sir Derek said in her ear, "but I really believe your mama would wish you to join her in the card room."

"I am sure Grandmama will be shocked to know that I have been subjected to this embarrassment," Miss Baines said.

Madeline turned to look at her. "Why do you not remove yourself then," she said, "and go to the safety and respectability of your grandmother's side? Why just talk about it? Sir Derek, I am sure, will be only too happy to accompany you there."

Her voice was shaking, she heard with some surprise. She took hold of the side of her gown and held it against her so that she would not brush against Miss Baines as she passed her and walked deliberately away from her group, across the room, and across the empty space. She smiled.

"It is sometimes a disadvantage to arrive late, is it not?" she said gaily. "One finds that everyone's group is formed and everyone chattering so busily that often they do not notice one's arrival."

Mr. Purnell inclined his head but said nothing. His eyes looked quite decidedly dangerous, Madeline thought when she was unwise enough to look into them. She felt breathless again, as she had a few minutes before when looking into Sir Derek's eyes, but for a quite different reason. She turned her attention to the sister.

"Is it very improper of me to approach you when we have not been formally presented?" she asked with a bright smile. "But Dominic has told me about his atrocious misbehavior of two nights ago, and I feel partly responsible since you were mistaken for me. I am Madeline Raine, you know. Lord Eden is my brother. My twin, in fact. I think there is a special bond between twins. I do not fight nearly so much with Edmund—Lord Amberley, that is—as I do with Dominic. But we are not quite so close, either. Though I love Edmund dearly, of course."

She paused for breath and turned the full force of her not inconsiderable charm on brother and sister. She was horribly aware of the space that still circled them and of the stares and muted voices of the other occupants of the room. She opened her fan and fluttered it energetically.

"How do you do, Lady Madeline?" Miss Purnell said. Her voice was rather low-pitched and quite musical. She seemed perfectly calm and unaware of the zone of discomfort that encircled her. "I am pleased to make your acquaintance. I wish you would not feel badly about what happened two evenings ago. It was all nonsense and best forgotten about." She did not smile at all.

Madeline's smile was becoming painful. She fluttered her fan and looked up at the silent brother. And she felt again what a dreadful mistake she was making. He did not at all appreciate her coming to talk to them. Hostility burned from his eyes. His mouth was set into a straight line. She felt a twinge of fright until she remembered where she was—in the middle of Lady Sharp's drawing room, surrounded by a significant number of members of the *ton*.

"Are you enjoying the Season?" she asked. "I do not remember to have seen you here during the past several years. It is pleasant, is it not, to give oneself up to pleasure and to have nothing else to worry about for weeks on end? I suppose one would not wish to have a lifelong diet of such entertainment, but a moderate portion can be quite refreshing."

"Perhaps if one has nothing else to make life meaningful," Mr. Purnell said, "this is as good a way to pass one's life away as any."

His voice was quiet and far more refined than Madeline had expected. Her interest in hearing his voice for the moment obscured the words he had spoken. When she did comprehend his meaning, she flushed.

"Any new experience of life is worth having," Miss Purnell said, looking with reproachful eyes at her brother, "whether it be serious or frivolous, enjoyable or painful. We grow only by the variety of our experiences."

The anger disappeared from her brother's face, Madeline noticed. It was replaced by a brooding look. He watched his sister.

And then Madeline saw Edmund in the doorway, his hands behind his back, surveying the occupants of the room. She felt a surge of relief, though she did not know quite why. He represented no escape from the awkwardness of her situation. Mr. and Miss Purnell seemed quite ungrateful for the notice she had taken of them. And how was she to extricate herself?

She met her brother's eyes across the room and he smiled.

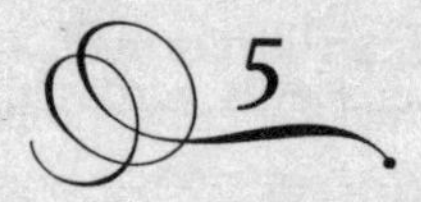

5

THE EARL OF AMBERLEY STOOD IN THE DOORway of Lady Sharp's drawing room, looking about him. He had been very reluctant to come even though his mind had been made up all day and even though he had not really expected to see Miss Purnell. With the gossip still fresh on everyone's lips, it was more than likely that she would remain at home for at least a few days.

But there was the chance that he would see her either here or at the Higgins rout. And so he had braced himself for the encounter. He would not, of course, be able to speak privately with her in such a public setting, but he must speak with her, prepare the ground somehow for the visit he must make to Lord Beckworth the following day.

He was definitely reluctant, however. He had always planned to marry by the time he was thirty, or soon after. But he had not expected ever to be pressured into a marriage not of his own free choosing. He had his title and his lands, and he was a wealthy man. He believed that he was reasonably attractive. He had planned for years the type of woman he would choose to marry when the time came. He would not be overly concerned with beauty or youth, and certainly money would not have anything to do with the matter. He would look for companionship more than anything else. He frequently felt lonely despite the presence of an affectionate family. And his wife must be intelligent, sensible, and reasonably well-informed.

But he had also planned to marry someone for whom he could feel affection. Someone with whom he could share the innermost depths of his life. Love! He wanted to love his wife deeply, with every fiber of his being. It was not necessarily a passionate physical love that he craved—he thought that Eunice had probably been wrong about that. He had no longing to be *in* love, to go about with his head in the clouds and stars in his eyes. But he wanted a wife who would be as dear to him as the very air he breathed. He had been a dreamer.

He had been contented with Eunice. She did not ignite him with passion, though he always found their beddings quite satisfactory, but she was the sort of person with whom he felt thoroughly at home. Being with Eunice was almost like being with any of his male friends at his clubs, except that there was the added attraction that she was a woman and willing to satisfy his physical need for a woman's body.

And now he must marry a stranger, a young lady whom he did not find physically appealing, and whose character and intelligence were quite unknown to him. And he must offer her the whole of himself, not just his name. He would do so with any wife, of course. He would never be able to contemplate a marriage of pure convenience. But under these particular circumstances he must work even harder at the marriage than he would normally do. Marrying him would go quite against the grain for Miss Purnell—she had already refused him once. He must find a way of making bearable for her a fate that she had done nothing to deserve.

Lord Amberley sized up the situation in Lady Sharp's drawing room almost immediately. Miss Purnell and her brother were easily distinguishable, stranded as they appeared to be almost in the middle of the room. People stood in groups all around them; there was the noise of talking and even laughter. Very few people were looking directly at them. But despite all these details, it was clear that everyone was self-consciously aware of the presence there of brother and sister, and wished they were somewhere else.

Miss Purnell was looking quite as proud and self-possessed as she had the day before when he had made his offer, though she must be perfectly well aware of the tense and hostile atmosphere around her. He felt a twinge of admiration.

And he felt more than admiration for Madeline. His sister did her fair share of irresponsible deeds, despite her two-and-twenty years. Her exploits frequently irritated him, as did her bewildering tendency to be passionately in love with a gentleman one week and oblivious of his very existence the next. He sometimes despaired of her ever growing up or of ever marrying. Occasionally he even felt he had made a mistake in allowing her almost a free hand in choosing her own future.

But there was a sense of rightness and justice in Madeline, and a courage that he had always been proud of. And never more so than on this occasion. She was standing with the Purnells, talking, glowing, and smiling as if she were in the most ordinary of social situations. He must go to her rescue. He met her glance across the room and smiled.

But before he could move forward, someone passed him in the doorway, and Lord Amberley stood where he was. The newcomer was the Duke of Peterleigh.

Peterleigh was a thin, balding man in his forties, with an air of haughty consequence. He had a reputation for strong and vehement opposition in the House to any bill that smacked of reform. To him wealth and position were virtues, poverty and social obscurity vices. The poor suffered deservedly, he was always loud to proclaim. His intolerance extended particularly to women. He was a firm advocate of the theory that good sense and docility entered the female frame through the back and posterior by way of a heavy male hand or whip. Lord Amberley disliked him intensely. And he could clearly understand why Lord Beckworth had chosen him for his daughter.

The duke looked about him now, quizzing glass to eye, and set out across the room. Miss Purnell looked noticeably relieved, Lord Amberley saw. Her shoulders relaxed. She half-smiled at the approach of her suitor, and looked at him with bright dark eyes. When he walked right on past her without pausing, and joined a group on the far side of the room, Lord Amberley's eyes were fixed on Miss Purnell. There was a moment of visible bewilderment, but a moment only. Her shoulders straightened and her chin lifted almost immediately. Her face was expressionless.

He strode across the room toward her, his smile firmly in place. He held out a hand to her as he approached.

"Ah, Miss Purnell, I was hoping to see you here this evening," he said. "How lovely you look tonight." He smiled warmly into her eyes, took her hand, and raised it to his lips. He did not release her hand, but laid it on his sleeve.

"Good evening, my lord," she said, her voice quite calm.

He smiled at her again and turned to her brother. James

Purnell was looking thunderous, Edmund was not surprised to find. "Purnell?" he said, nodding amiably. "Pleased to meet you again. Madeline? Are you enjoying yourself? I suppose Mama is playing cards?"

"Yes, Edmund," she said, smiling brightly at him. "With Sir Cedric. I have been making the acquaintance of Miss Purnell and her brother. There is really a quite excessive squeeze here tonight, is there not?"

Lord Amberley turned back to Miss Purnell, who had not withdrawn her hand from his sleeve, though he thought that perhaps she did not even know it was there. She was almost visibly holding on to her control.

"I must pay my respects to our hostess," he said. "Have you already done so, Miss Purnell? Perhaps you would be so good as to accompany me."

He really gave her no time to make a decision. He laid his free hand lightly over hers, smiled into her eyes, and led her to the far side of the drawing room, where Lady Sharp was conversing with the Marquess of Blaise and a small group of lesser personages.

"Ah, good evening, ma'am," he said to his hostess, making her his most elegant bow, and then returning his hand to cover Miss Purnell's, which still rested on his arm. "Mrs. Pringle? Blaise? Merridew? How do you do? I do apologize for my lateness, ma'am. But I see that your drawing room has not suffered from my absence at all. You must have gathered around you quite the most distinguished company of the Season so far."

As he smiled his most charming smile at his hostess, Lord Amberley wondered for one moment if people really did burst with indignation. If so, Lady Sharp looked as though she might be in imminent danger of doing so. Her smile, he was sure, bore some resemblance to the grimace of a jungle cat just deprived of its prey. He did not wait to find out what her reply would have been.

"You must have greeted Miss Purnell already," he said, "since she arrived earlier than I. But I cannot resist taking her about the room with me, you see. I am living in daily hope that she will consent to being my countess, but so far she has proved hard-hearted and kept me in suspense. I am afraid that I am very dishonorably trying to force her hand by making such a public statement." He smiled down at his companion. He had been gripping her hand quite bruisingly for the past minute.

She flushed and lifted her chin an inch in a gesture he was beginning to recognize as characteristic of her. She raised her eyes to his. They were quite empty of any readable message.

Lady Sharp gushed. Mrs. Pringle clasped her hands to her bosom and declared that she had never been so gratified by any news. The Marquess of Blaise exerted himself to bend a whole inch from the waist and give it as his opinion that Lord Amberley was a fortunate man. Mr. Merridew bowed to Miss Purnell and removed a jeweled snuffbox from his pocket. The Earl of Amberley smiled and waited. He felt the hand within his own stiffen just a little.

"Do come and meet Lady Fender," Lady Sharp said, her smile encompassing both Lord Amberley and his companion. "She will be quite delighted by the news. And, of course, you must not feel a moment's anxiety, my dear Lord Amberley. Any young lady worth her salt will play hard to get, you know, but no one in her right mind would think seriously of rejecting you." She tittered. "Is that not right, Miss Purnell? How delightful you look in green, my dear. I was saying so but five minutes ago to the marquess."

• • •

"WHATEVER AM I GOING to do, James? I am so mortally tired of this whole ridiculous situation, and so very, very angry." Alexandra sat on a straight-backed chair in her brother's dressing room the following morning, one arm hooked over the back, her chin on her fist. She watched as he pulled on his top boots.

"I still hate the thought of your marrying Amberley or any other member of his family," James Purnell said. "You will not be happy, Alex. How could you be, with a man whose brother can so carelessly involve you in scandal and so glibly offer to get you out of it again? What does marriage mean to such men? Or honor either? It is all a game. Compromise a girl through some foolish and careless trick and then marry her if something goes wrong. It is all as simple as that. I hate this age in which we live. I hate this society and its morals."

"Perhaps you are overreacting a little," his sister suggested, as if she were not the one most in need of comfort. "After all, we cannot blame Lord Amberley for what his brother did. His offer was generous under the circumstances. But I do consider his behavior of last evening unforgivable. I had refused him and released him from any obligation he might have felt. Now he has put me in a worse situation than I was in already. He has made my position impossible."

"He behaved in a quite disgusting manner," Purnell agreed vehemently. The front lock of dark hair, so carefully combed back from his brow fifteen minutes before, fell forward almost into his eyes again. "It was kidnapping just as much as what Eden did. How dare he take your hand like that for all to see, and kiss it! As if you are some sort of trollop, Alex. And then take you away on his arm and tell Lady

Sharp and whoever cared to listen that you are to be his betrothed. I cannot like it. I cannot like the man."

"And yet to be fair," Alexandra said, her eyes straying to the floor and staring right through it, "at the time, I felt some gratitude. Is not that shameful to admit, James? When he came across the room to me and kissed my hand, I wanted to look around on everyone there and sneer. How dreadful! I do not remember ever feeling that way before. And I felt like laughing in the face of Lady Sharp and Lady Fender and a half-dozen others when they thought that I might be made respectable after all. I hate to admit these feelings even to myself, but I did have them."

"Marry him, then," Purnell said, his expression softening for a moment as he looked up at his sister, his second boot in place over his pantaloons. "If you feel good about it, Alex, enter into this marriage."

"But I was coping last evening," she said, looking up at him with flashing eyes. "I would have carried it off alone, James, with some help from you. I would have stayed and finished my drink and left without giving anyone the satisfaction of knowing that I had even noticed anything amiss. I did not need help. If the earl had just not come along at that precise moment! I was bewildered at what his grace had done. And what can he have meant by walking past me as if he did not see me, James? No, don't answer that question. I am not so stupid or so naive that I do not know what he meant. He meant to snub me. He meant to show me publicly that I am now a soiled creature and quite beneath his notice. He meant me to know that there will be no betrothal and no marriage."

"And how do you feel about that, Alex?" Purnell asked, coming to stand in front of her chair. "Is your world shattered?"

"Yes, I think it is," she said, continuing to stare at the floor. "I am not sure I was excited by the idea of marrying his grace. In fact, I had no feelings either for or against the match, except that I looked forward to a greater measure of freedom. It is just that I have been brought up to the knowledge that I would be his wife someday. There is suddenly a void in my future. The thought is a little frightening."

"I know," he said. He reached out a hand and squeezed her shoulder. "I have lived with the void for a long time, and I still do not know how I will fill it. Or if I ever will. But you need a secure and happy life, Alex. You must have it. You have had little enough of happiness in your life so far, God knows."

She looked up at him. "You refer to Papa?" she said. "He lives his life as he thinks it should be lived, James. He means well. It is all anyone can do. I wish you did not hate him so."

"He thinks he is God," he said vehemently, squeezing her shoulder once more. "And I will be eternally thankful that he is not."

"He will be sending for me soon," Alexandra said. "Lord Amberley said he would call this morning. And I still do not know what I am to do. Oh, James, I have never known a nightmare like last night. First, that snubbing. It was dreadful, even though both Lord Eden and you had warned me what to expect. And then the duke. And finally Lord Amberley. I felt like a thing. A thing with leprosy. I have never felt much in control of my life, but last night I was totally at the mercy of others. I hated the feeling. I wanted to yell and scream and hit out at people. Is not that dreadful?"

Purnell stooped down on his haunches and looked into his sister's face. "I wish I could protect you from life, Alex," he said, his intense dark eyes glowing. "God, how I wish it! I have known some of the cruelty it can inflict. But I wish it would leave you alone. You are the only person in this world I have left to care about."

"James!" she said. She leaned forward in her chair and framed his face with her hands. "I wish you were not so bitter, dear, and so full of hatred. I do wish that. Can you not forget about what is in the past and cannot be helped? Can you not look to the future and make something bright of it? Besides, we are forgetting that there was one ray of light last night. There was the earl's sister. I have seen her before, you know, and always admired her beauty and gaiety, her ability to simply enjoy herself. Was it not kind of her to come and talk to us last night?"

"Kind!" he said, drawing back his head and getting to his feet again. "The girl likes to make grand gestures, Alex. She saw a chance for heroism. It was a chance not to be missed. For the space of a few minutes she was the focus of everyone's attention in that drawing room."

"I think you do her some injustice," Alexandra said gently. "She risked a great deal to put us at our ease. Perhaps other people will not like what she did and will shun her too."

Purnell laughed. "Her?" he said. "Taking a risk? Nothing is uncalculated with shallow, artificial little creatures of society such as she, Alex. She knew her brother was about to maneuver you into marriage. She ended up being the heroine of the hour."

"I liked her," Alexandra said.

"Then you must continue to do so," he said. "It seems likely that she will be your sister-in-law. Just don't expect too much in the way of love or loyalty, Alex."

The expected knock sounded at the door. Alexandra smiled briefly at her brother as he strode across the small room to open the door. She did not wait to hear the words of the footman who stood outside. She rose to her feet and smoothed out the cotton of her morning dress.

She was surprised when she reached her father's office to find him alone. She had expected the earl to be there. Her father was standing by the window, looking out into the street.

"Come in, Alexandra," he said, not turning at her entry, "and stand in front of my desk." One was very rarely invited to sit in Papa's presence, Alexandra reflected.

"Good morning, Papa," she said, clasping her hands loosely in front of her.

"I do not know what is particularly good about it," he said. He turned from the window to look at her. "Though I suppose we must make the best of the situation. I have had two visits concerning you this morning."

She looked inquiringly at him, but found her eyes dropping before the severity in his, as they had been doing for as far back into her infancy as she could remember.

"It seems we are no longer good enough for the Duke of Peterleigh," he said. "He sent a message to that effect with his secretary."

Alexandra said nothing.

"He did not even come himself!" Lord Beckworth's fist slammed down onto the desk before him with such force that Alexandra visibly jumped. "Lord Beckworth is to be communicated with now only through a secretary. Do you realize fully what disgrace you have brought on your family, girl?"

Alexandra raised eyes that long training had taught her to keep expressionless. "I think perhaps the Duke of Peterleigh is not worthy of us, Papa," she said. "I think little of a suitor who is not willing to stand by me even when I am the innocent victim of a silly prank."

"Silence, girl!" the baron roared, so that Alexandra squared her shoulders and lowered her eyes to the floor again. "Innocent, do you call yourself? When you tricked your mama and your brother in order to wander alone outside a ballroom? That is where bawds and strumpets display their wares. Have you not seen them outside the theaters and opera houses? You were issuing an open invitation. And you try to put all the blame for what ensued on Lord Eden? You are little better than a whore."

"Papa!" Alexandra's eyes blazed incautiously into his. "How can you say that to me? You know it is untrue. I was foolish, perhaps. But nothing worse. I have not been guilty of any great sin."

Lord Beckworth stabbed a finger in her direction. "You are committing the greatest sin of all," he said. "You are denying guilt, convincing yourself that sin is not sin. You are in grave danger of hellfire, my girl. My prayers will be devoted entirely to you today, that your heart will be softened and that you will beg for mercy. You will spend the coming hours on your knees. And when the Earl of Amberley calls on you this afternoon, you will receive him with humility and gratitude, and you will accept his offer of marriage. Do you understand me?"

"Papa," she said, "may I not just return home? Please?"

"Home?" he said. "Your home henceforth is with the man who is willing to lift you above your disgrace, Alexandra. It seems I have failed you. A fatherly softness and love have come between me and my Christian duty to train you properly for a life of virtue. I have failed with my son, and now I have failed with my daughter. I hope for the sake of your immortal soul that your husband will not likewise fail you. I advised him when he called on me this morning to be strict with you from the start. I advised him not to hesitate to beat you until you have learned obedience."

Alexandra clasped her hands more tightly in front of her. "I have tried to be obedient to you, Papa," she said. "I have tried all my life to make you and Mama proud of me. If I have failed, it has not been intentional, and my failure has not been your fault."

Lord Beckworth looked weary suddenly. He sank into the chair behind his desk and passed one hand over his bald head. "One tries and tries," he said. "One has a family and wants what is best for them. One wants them to grow in a knowledge of Holy Scripture and the principles of Christian virtue. And one does one's best to do one's duty, not sparing the rod, not allowing weak sentiment to stand in the way of what is right. And how does it all end? First James, and now you. You must marry Amberley, Alexandra. I can do no more for you."

Alexandra stood mute across the desk from him. She scarcely dared breathe. These moods of weariness and self-recrimination were more terrible than his moods of righteous anger. Her father's frequent sense of failure almost invariably led to a redoubling of his harsh attempts to pound virtue and morality into his family. She had always thought that once she grew up—reached the age of eighteen, twenty, one-and-twenty—she would finally be free of the tyranny of his terrible sense of obligation for her spiritual welfare. But it was not so easy to shake off the pattern of a lifetime when one was a woman, she had discovered as she reached each of those milestones of age. Always one must be dependent upon a man for the very means of survival. And wholly subject to his will.

"Go your room now," Lord Beckworth said, "and remain

on your knees until Mrs. Rey is sent to prepare you for the earl's visit. You will ignore the bell for luncheon."

"Yes, Papa," she said, and turned to leave.

"And, Alexandra." His voice held her still again, though she did not turn to face him. "If you refuse the earl's offer, I will consider it a sign from God that I must take on direct responsibility for your soul again. It will grieve me and hurt me probably more than it will you, but I will have to resume punishing your lapses in the only way your stubborn spirit seems to understand."

Alexandra drew a deep and silent breath, lifted her head, and proceeded on her way to her room, where she knelt obediently and unsupervised for almost three hours until Nanny Rey came bustling and clucking to her rescue. She prayed that feeling would never become so deadened in her that she would become bitter and cynical and hate-filled as James was. She prayed for James, that her deep affection for him would prove sufficient to keep alive in him the spark of love that had been all but quenched five years before.

LORD EDEN SPENT THE MORNING at Tattersall's. He did not go there with any intention of buying horses. He was quite satisfied with the ones he had. But his friend Faber was on the lookout for a new team of chestnuts and had asked him to go along to give a second opinion. And he had nothing else to do.

Indeed, he was feeling decidedly restless. The pleasures of the Season were beginning to pall, as they always did after a month or so. But this one had just become even more dreary than all the previous ones. Other years he had kept the same flirt throughout, convinced on each occasion that what he felt was true love. And yet he had found each time a few weeks after the Season was over and he was away from London that he had forgotten the girl.

It was really too bad that the one year when he was really in love, the flirtation was over even before the end of the Season. Miss Carstairs had refused to drive with him the previous afternoon, and had turned her back on him when he had called at her box at the opera the evening before. Her mother too had stared stonily down into the pit while he had been forced to make stilted conversation with the three remaining members of their party. He understood that he was in disgrace and was no longer considered a desirable suitor.

The prospect of balls and other entertainments for the weeks to come without the chance of coaxing a smile or a blush from Miss Carstairs was a dreary one indeed. It would be even more painful when she began to turn her attentions elsewhere, as she was bound to do soon. Everyone knew that old Carstairs had brought her to London with the express purpose of finding a wealthy husband for her before the end of the Season.

Lord Eden wished he had something to do beyond the usual daily round of amusements. He spent part of each summer on his own estate in Wiltshire, but it was a part of the country he had never allowed himself to become familiar with, and the estate was run by an aging but amazingly efficient bailiff who had been in charge of it since before his birth. His presence there always seemed redundant. He preferred to spend his time on Edmund's estate in Hampshire, where he had been brought up and where people and surroundings were familiar. But there was nothing very constructive for him to do there.

He wanted to be in the army and had done so since he was sixteen and had been befriended by the captain of the local regiment. He ached to be in Spain fighting old Boney, his days filled with physical activity, mental challenge, and danger. But Mama always became upset when he broached the subject. She had lost two brothers in the wars years before and understandably dreaded that her son might share their fate. Madeline too became genuinely distressed whenever he tried to confide in her. It was the only topic on which he could not talk quite freely with her. Edmund had never given his opinion either way. He would give his support if asked for it, Lord Eden was convinced. But he shied away from putting his brother in the dilemma of having to choose between his mother and sister on the one hand and his only brother on the other. And so he ached with empty strength and unchanneled energy.

The yard at Tattersall's was crowded with gentlemen eager for the auction to begin or contented to be in a place where they might converse and gossip freely, away from the inhibiting presence of ladies. Lord Eden frowned when he realized that he was standing directly behind a group that included Albert Harding-Smythe. He could not stand the man, and his companions were hardly more tolerable. But he could not move away. Faber, on his other side, was deep in animated horse-talk with an acquaintance.

"We have had to tolerate them until now because they are Mother's relatives," Harding-Smythe was saying. "Country bumpkins, of course. They have no idea how to go on in the genteel world."

One of his companions sniggered. "You gave the chit a masterly setdown last night," he said. "Perfect timing. She was left with her jaw hanging. The brother turned quite purple in the face."

"Yes, well," Harding-Smythe said on a sigh, "even cousins have to realize that there are limits to one's charity. The chit has a *tendre* for me. I have been beating her off with my cane ever since she arrived in town."

"Not your gold-topped one, I hope?" another companion said, recoiling in mock horror. "You would not want to damage that, now, would you?" The whole group guffawed loudly.

"It was all very amusing last night," a third fellow said, "but somewhat deflating to find out that Amberley is going to marry her. It was a dirty trick for her to arrive before him like that so that no one was aware of the betrothal and none of us knew how to behave toward her. I must say, I felt deuced foolish. One likes to be quite clear on the matter of whom one is obliged to be civil to and whom one must cut."

Lord Eden, standing behind the group, had gone very still.

"One does wonder if Amberley is not just too good-natured for his own good," Harding-Smythe said. "My cousin Purnell had probably frightened him into making the offer. He is the very devil, you know. Those of us who know the type would not be so easily intimidated, but Amberley is almost too civilized. I know that I would not be so easily drawn into offering a slut respectability. Do we know, after all, why she left the ballroom that night? In my experience, only one type of female wanders outdoors alone, and she is in search of only one thing: you-know-what."

His companions sniggered.

"I almost wish I had been wandering outside too," one of them said. "I might have been able to think of more amusing things to do with her after tying her to the bed than merely leaving her there."

"I wonder if Amberley untied her immediately upon

finding her, or if there was some, ah, delay," another said at the same moment that a third turned his head and met Lord Eden's eyes.

He turned back abruptly, coughed warningly, and said something in a low voice. The group lapsed into an uneasy silence. Lord Eden strolled forward.

"I have not seen you at Jackson's Boxing Saloon this age, Harding-Smythe," he said amiably, smiling at the uncomfortable gentleman in question. "It must be sheer coincidence that you go on the mornings that I don't. I seem to recall from last year that Jackson said you might become quite handy with your fives if you drank less and exercised more and were a little less wary of your opponents' fists. By this year I imagine you must be quite a bruiser if you feel no fear of a strong-looking gentleman like Mr. James Purnell. Perhaps you would favor me by taking me on tomorrow morning in a friendly bout?"

"I am not much in practice," Harding-Smythe said, darting sidelong glances at his listening and watching friends. "Besides, Eden, I have other appointments for tomorrow. I am a busy man."

"Ah," Lord Eden said. "I would not wish you to go out of your way to oblige me, my good fellow. Shall I just say that I will be there tomorrow and that if you are not, I shall consider you a damned coward as well as a scoundrel?" He smiled amiably at the group. "I wish you good day, gentlemen."

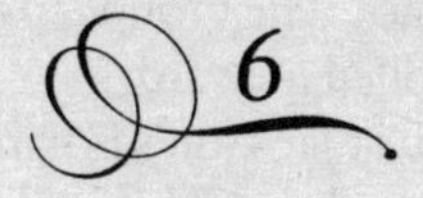

THE EARL OF AMBERLEY HAD A STRONG FEELing of *déjà vu*. He had been through it all before: the interview with Lord Beckworth; the salon at the front of the house; his standing position before the window—he had not been invited to sit down; the entry of Miss Purnell; her severe appearance—he was not sure if she wore the same clothes as on the previous occasion, but she looked very much the same; her proud, controlled bearing; her steady calm eyes.

And again they were left alone, she standing inside the door, he at the window.

He drew a deep breath. "Well, Miss Purnell," he said, "here we are again."

"Yes, my lord," she said. She was unsmiling, not hostile exactly, but perfectly impassive, it seemed to Lord Amberley.

"I am afraid I put you in a very awkward position last evening," he said. "I had not meant so to force your hand. Under the circumstances, I could think of no other way to act."

"At the time I believe I was grateful to you," she said.

"At the time?" He raised his eyebrows.

"It is not a pleasant feeling," she said, looking steadily at him, "to be stranded in the middle of a crowded drawing room surrounded by people who stare and whisper and are hostile. It is even less pleasant to be snubbed very deliberately and very publicly by the gentleman one has been brought up to consider one's betrothed."

"Peterleigh is not worth upsetting yourself over," Lord Amberley said, taking a few steps toward her. "A true gentleman would stand by his lady even if she were indeed guilty of some active indiscretion. Forgive me if my words pain you, but I believe you are well rid of such a man."

She raised her chin. "I was sickened by everyone's behavior last evening," she said in a low, rather hurried voice. "It was bad enough that they chose to judge me so harshly for something that was none of my own fault. For that alone I would wish to have nothing more to do with society for the rest of my life. What was worse was the way almost everyone changed as soon as you hinted that we might become betrothed. If last evening is an example of what 'gentility' means, then I am ashamed of the name 'lady.'"

"You are quite right in your judgment," he said gently. "Unfortunately, Miss Purnell, there is no perfect person on this planet and certainly no perfect institution. Our society protects itself through its strict moral and social standards. And such high standards inevitably lead to corruption on the one hand and to the type of hypocrisy of which you have been a victim on the other. But perhaps it is possible to overreact. There are good, if not perfect, people in this world. And an institution can have its value even if it is flawed."

"Then I am to accept that I must be a pariah unmarried,

but perfectly respectable as your wife?" she asked, looking very directly at him again.

He smiled. "You have a way of putting things, Miss Purnell," he said, "a very direct way that makes a person feel uncomfortable. The answer to your question seems so obviously to be no. But the world is not such a black-and-white place as you imply. Life is what it is. Society is what it is. There is very little we can do to change either. We must accept what we must and change what we can. And somehow preserve our own integrity."

"I cannot be such a creature of compromise," she said. "I have been in town for a month, my lord, and I do not like what I have seen. I would like to go home and forget I have ever been here."

"And is that possible?" he asked. "Have you put the idea to your father? Is he willing that you return home and remain there for the rest of your life?"

She looked back at him silently.

"I hate to say this, Miss Purnell," he said. "I really do. But I do not think you have any choice at all about your future, do you? You must marry me."

He expected her to argue. Her chin was at a decidedly stubborn angle. Her jaw was set in a hard line. She said nothing. He walked even closer until he stood just a few feet in front of her and the tilt of her chin became necessary so that she might see up into his face.

"I give you my word, Miss Purnell," he said, "that it will not be such a bad bargain. I do not believe I am either an evil or a hard-hearted man. I do not know of any particular vice in my character. I have managed to live close to a younger brother and sister whose behavior is occasionally wild without ever resorting to violence or undue irritability. And I have position and wealth to offer you as well as a home of which I am inordinately proud. Will you marry me of your own free will?"

Her eyes did not waver before his. They were dark, luminous eyes. "I will marry you," she said.

He smiled half-ruefully. "But not of your own free will?" he said.

She was silent.

"Will you tell me what it is in particular that makes you reluctant?" he asked.

She said nothing. He took one step forward and reached for her hands, which were clasped in front of her. They were very cold.

"You resent the chain of events that has made this necessary?" he asked. "It has all been quite overwhelming, has it not? The unfortunate mistake of identity; the fact that my brother did not return home in time to discover you and perhaps return you to the ball before you were missed; the fact that I had a new and prattling footman in my employ. You must feel that fate has been unduly unkind to you. But I am here now to protect you and care for you. Is that not enough?"

"I have accepted your offer," she said tonelessly.

"But you do not want to be married to me?" he asked.

"No."

He let go of her hands and walked away from her toward the window. He sighed. "I wish I did not have to persuade you into this, Miss Purnell," he said. "It has never been my wish to coerce any lady into marriage. The very idea of doing so is abhorrent to me."

"As you say, my lord," she said, her voice tight and controlled, "there seems to be little alternative now to what you have offered and I have accepted. Circumspection this morning seems somewhat pointless."

He turned and looked at her with a troubled frown. "I hate to see you unhappy with the situation," he said. Then he sighed. "But I suppose I can hardly expect you to be ecstatic about finding yourself betrothed quite unexpectedly to a stranger. I can only hope that in time I can teach you to be less reluctant. I shall spend my life as your servant, ma'am."

She dropped her eyes for the first time.

"Your father advised me," Lord Amberley said quietly, looking at her lowered head, "to keep you on a tight rein and not to hesitate to beat you when occasion arises. Why would he give me such advice?"

"I frequently disappoint him," she said, not looking up. "I am weak and thoughtless and often disobedient, even when I do not mean to be."

"Does he mistreat you?"

Her jaw tightened. "He is my father," she said. "He has the right to correct me in the way he thinks best."

"Does he beat you?"

"He has not since I was sixteen," she said.

"I see," he said. "And what punishments has he substituted for the corporal ones?"

"They are not called punishments," she said, raising her eyes and looking steadily and almost defiantly at him. "They are called corrections. I am required to pray and read Scripture when I have forgotten the peril in which I often place my soul."

"I see." But Lord Amberley was not at all sure that he did see. And he could not tell what her attitude was to what she described—whether bitter and cynical or accepting. He had an almost panicked feeling that he was betrothing himself to some alien creature, a woman with whom he might never find a point of likeness. "I assume that you would spend the rest of your life on your knees with an open Bible before you if you were to dare to refuse me?"

He supposed he had meant the words as something of a joke. But she did not smile or reply. She clasped her hands before her and raised her chin once more.

He strode over to her again and repossessed himself of her hands. "Listen to me, Miss Purnell," he said. "We both know that this betrothal must happen. I wish it did not, not so much for my sake as for yours. But the announcement must be made. Your father and society must be satisfied. Society will not be allowed to gloat, however. I shall see that you are taken away from here. I shall invite you and your family to Amberley Court. There you may spend the summer away from the public eye, getting to know me and the home that will be yours.

"And I hope—I will make every effort to ensure it—that you will find after all that this marriage is not so repugnant to you. I will care for you, Miss Purnell. I will lift this burden that accident and my family's carelessness have placed on your shoulders and give you contentment in its place. And I will not press for an early marriage. You may decide the date for yourself if you will. Will you agree to this?" He squeezed her hands.

"Yes," she said, looking him steadily in the eye.

"Splendid!" he said. "You have made me happy, Miss Purnell." He raised her right hand to his lips and kissed the palm. She flushed deeply, he noticed.

"I have accepted your father's invitation to dinner this evening," he said, "conditional on your acceptance of my offer, of course. Will you object to my inviting you to join me at the theater tonight with your family? I will not make the invitation public if you would rather not."

"It is necessary, is it not," she said, her tone bitter, "to show the respectable members of the *ton* that I am indeed now to be taken back into their favor."

"Yes," he said gently, "it is necessary."

"Very well," she said. "I am sure Mama and James will be delighted."

He smiled faintly to himself at her failure to assure him that she too would be delighted. "I will go one step further," he said. "I will arrange some sort of betrothal celebration at my town house here. You will be presented to the *ton*, Miss Purnell, as my honored bride-to-be. I will leave you now." He raised her left hand to his lips and kissed the back of her fingers.

He turned to leave. But he stopped as he reached the door and turned back to her. "I want you to know one thing," he said. "When you do marry me, Miss Purnell, you must rest assured that I will never under any circumstances lay a violent hand on you or on any children of our marriage. Neither will I ever impose prayer or Bible reading on you or them. God's word was never intended as an instrument of torture. It is the word of inspiration and of love in its purest and most unconditional form. I will never impose any form of punishment on you. And although in the marriage service you will promise me obedience, I will not hold you to that promise. Obedience is for servants, who are paid for their services, not for a wife, who is a man's companion and lover."

She did not turn before he left the room.

"GOOD LORD, MAMA, IT ISN'T true, is it?" Lord Eden looked very tall and restless, standing in the middle of his mother's sitting room.

"I am afraid it is, Dominic," she said, looking up from

her needlepoint at her younger son. "Do sit down, dear. You give me the headache, pacing about like that. Madeline will be home at any minute, and she is bound to be in the highest of spirits after driving with Sir Derek Peignton. He is her latest true love, you see. It will be too, too much for my nerves to have both of you prancing about before me. Not at your ages and with your sizes."

Lord Eden sat. "Edmund is to marry Miss Purnell," he said, stunned. "But she refused him the day before she refused me."

"It seems that Edmund did not consider his responsibility at an end there," Lady Amberley said, resuming her needlework. "The whole thing turned into something ridiculously nasty, as you must know, Dominic. And that poor girl was in the thick of it. Of course Edmund offered for her again—at least, I assume he is making the offer official sometime today. He certainly made it clear to several people last evening that he intended to do so. And it is only what we might have expected. Edmund can always be depended upon to look to the well-being of people he feels responsible for. Sit down, dear."

Lord Eden had leapt to his feet, but he sat again at his mother's quiet bidding. "And I can't, I suppose?" he said. "It should have been me, should it not? I should have been the one to see that I must go back and persuade her to reconsider. I should not have felt the relief I did when she refused. I had no right to feel relief. It is not right that it is Edmund doing this, Mama. It should be me. It must be me."

"I think not, Dominic," his mother said placidly, stitching on. "It is true that you were the one who unwittingly caused the girl's character to be destroyed. And I am proud that you acknowledged the fact and went to make your apologies and your offer to Miss Purnell. But it is true too, dear, that you are very young. Two-and-twenty is too young for a man to marry. Men, alas, do not grow up as quickly as women. That is not to say that they do not grow up at all. You have only to consider your brother to know that extraordinary steadiness of character can develop before a man's thirtieth birthday. But you are too young for marriage, Dominic. You would not do either yourself or Miss Purnell any good if you married her. Edmund would have realized that."

Lord Eden leapt to his feet again. "What nonsense, Mama!" he said, before flushing as she raised her head and her eyebrows. "Pardon me. I did not mean to sound so ill-mannered. But I *am* a man. It is just that I am your younger son and you see me as a boy still. And you have insisted on protecting me from any experience that will make me more of a man."

"The army," she said wearily.

"I was made to be a soldier, Mama," he said. "Can you not see that? I can find nothing else in my life to make it a joy to live. I need action and responsibility. I would find the latter at least if I were to acquire a wife. Miss Purnell is my responsibility, and I shall tell Edmund so."

"She is not a commodity to be wrangled over," his mother said with gentle firmness, folding her needlepoint and putting it to one side. "She is a person, dear, and undoubtedly a bewildered and unhappy person too. All her plans for her life have been totally overset in the past few days."

"And so have Edmund's," Lord Eden said. "I had not heard that he was even considering marriage yet, Mama, and he seemed quite happy with Mrs. B—. Well, anyway, he seemed quite happy. It is not right that he should be forced into this marriage. Miss Purnell is not remarkably pretty and she seems an overly serious female."

"Mrs. Borden is not right for Edmund either," Lady Amberley said. "I am quite relieved that he will be forced to give her up. And Edmund will—he is not the type to keep a wife and a mistress. I was very much afraid that he would drift into a permanent relationship with her, even marriage perhaps. I am not sure that Miss Purnell is the right wife for him either. Unfortunately, I have not even met the girl. But you can be sure that Edmund will make the best of the marriage. If the girl is at all likable or lovable, Edmund will both like and love her and bring her to like and love him."

Lord Eden sat silent, his hands dangling between his knees.

"We all owe it to Edmund to accept Miss Purnell as if she had become betrothed to him in the most regular manner," Lady Amberley continued. "I was extremely proud of Madeline last evening. Everyone else in that Sharp woman's drawing room was behaving with perfect snobbishness, avoiding the girl as if she had the plague. Madeline went and talked to her and risked being looked upon askance herself. I wish I had not been playing cards. I would have taken the girl on my arm and strolled from group to group with her. I would have dared anyone to snub her. Ridiculous people!"

Lord Eden had no chance to reply. The door to the sitting room swung open and his sister burst in, still wearing a lavender pelisse and chip straw bonnet. Her cheeks were flushed, her eyes sparkling.

"I heard you were here, Dom," she said, "and came right up. Mama, I thought I would be late for tea. What a love you are to have waited for me. Sir Derek's phaeton was the most splendid in the whole park, I do declare."

Lord Eden stood up and grinned at his twin. "Would it have looked so splendid with another gentleman in it?" he asked.

She put her head to one side and a finger to her chin, considering. "Well, perhaps with you, Dom," she said. "And now you have got the compliment you were looking for. Are you satisfied?"

"Do I hear wedding bells—again?" her brother asked.

"With Sir Derek?" she asked, removing her bonnet and twirling it by the ribbons before tossing it toward an empty chair. "How would I know, Dom? He has not asked me yet. But he is most excessively handsome. Even Mama admits that."

"So were Prescott and Mitchell and Roberts and What's-his-name from Dorset, and one or two others," Lord Eden said.

"You are not to tease me," Madeline said, tossing her pelisse in the same general direction as her bonnet. "You know you fall in love quite as often as I do, Dom, and I am always interested and sympathetic when it turns out that the girl is not quite the right one after all. Have you heard about Edmund?"

"Of course I have heard about Edmund," he said, scowling. "I have never heard such depressing news. Will she have him, do you suppose?"

"I don't believe she will have much choice," Madeline said. "You cannot imagine what it was like for her last evening, Dom. I felt dreadfully distressed to think that you and I were the cause of it all. But Edmund was perfectly splendid. You should have seen the way he turned on his famous charm for Miss Purnell. Even I was impressed. And the way he pokered up for Lady Sharp and all the tabbies!

He had everyone in the room fawning over him and practically eating out of his hand."

"Edmund ought not to do it," Lord Eden said, sitting down again as his sister seated herself on an ottoman beside her mother. "She isn't the wife for him, Mad."

"I'm not so sure," she said. "You would have admired her last evening, Dom. She was really quite magnificent. When everyone was loudly ignoring her, she looked just like a queen. I would have been howling with misery and mortification if it had been me. She did not break even when that horrid man, the Duke of Peterleigh, cut her very deliberately. And when Edmund took her about, she looked along her nose at the lot of them as if she were a dowager duchess. I think I am going to like her."

"We must all try to, dear," Lady Amberley said, turning to receive the tea tray that a footman had carried into the room. "She is to be part of our family. Edmund's wife. I shall try to love her."

"I just hope we do not have to see too much of her brother," Madeline said. "He gives me the shudders. He has such a dark and hostile look. And those eyes of his gaze quite through one as though one were a moth caught on a pin and spread out for his inspection. I have not once seen him smile."

"Some people do not," her mother said. "That does not mean that they are not perfectly civil people."

"He does not like me," Madeline said decisively. "He thinks me silly and frivolous and empty-headed. And the horrid thing is that I become all three when I am close to him. I don't like him. He rode past the phaeton this afternoon, and I smiled my best smile and waved to him. I thought his neck must be broken, such an effort it cost him to incline his head ever so slightly. And not a smile or a word."

"He will probably avoid the lot of us," Lord Eden said. "I don't imagine I am his favorite person at the moment either, Mad. And he probably resents even Edmund for forcing his sister into this marriage. He probably had his heart set on being brother-in-law to a duke. A mere earl must seem quite a come-down."

"You are being spiteful, Dominic," the countess said, handing a cup of tea to Madeline to take to her brother. "It is unfair to judge another on a very slight acquaintance or no acquaintance at all. I expect better of my children."

"I beg your pardon, Mama," Lord Eden said, pulling a face at Madeline as she bent to set the cup and saucer down on the small table at his elbow.

ALEXANDRA WAS NOT TO ESCAPE lightly after the Earl of Amberley had left her. She had promised that she would call on her mama to tell how the interview had gone. But she had hoped to escape to her room soon afterward to ponder the new direction her life had taken. However, when she left the salon, she found the butler bowing before her and informing her that she was to wait on Lady Beckworth in the drawing room. Her heart sank. Mama must have visitors.

She could not have been less pleased to see who the visitors were. Aunt Deirdre, Caroline, and Albert were all in attendance. They had not been near since the scandal of the ball. She had seen Albert, of course, the evening before, when he had snubbed her. Alexandra's eyes met her brother's across the room.

"Alexandra, my dear girl," her aunt said, rising from her

seat on a sofa and coming toward her with outstretched hands. "What very splendid news, to be sure. I was dreadfully distressed to hear of your ill fortune, as Caroline will tell you. I was so miserable with the migraines that I could not even come out to comfort you. I was never more pleased than when I heard this morning from Albert that you were to be betrothed to the Earl of Amberley. Such a very eligible gentleman, to be sure. I had to hurry over here to satisfy myself that it was indeed true. Imagine my feelings, my dear, to find that you were even then closeted with the earl. Is it true? Have you accepted his offer?"

"Yes, I have, Aunt," Alexandra said calmly. "I thank you for your good wishes."

Caroline shrieked and jumped to her feet. "I knew you would be respectable again, Cousin," she said. "Did I not say so, Mama? I was never more happy in my life."

"Thank you," Alexandra said, removing her hands from her aunt's and taking a seat close to her mother's.

"Of course," Mrs. Harding-Smythe said, "being a countess when you had expected to be a duchess is a little lowering, but you must not look at the matter that way, Alexandra. You must remember that under the circumstances you are fortunate to have found a husband at all."

Alexandra favored her aunt with a steady look that soon had the older lady busy smoothing the silk of her dress over her knees.

"It is a great relief to know that you have accepted the earl," Lady Beckworth said, leaning forward and patting her daughter on the arm. "You have done what is right, Alexandra, and doing what is right is its own reward. Papa will be pleased."

Alexandra looked across the room to where her brother was standing, one elbow propped on the high marble mantelpiece, one booted leg crossed over the other. He was looking broodingly back at her. She half-smiled, feeling her customary urge to push back the lock of dark hair that had fallen across his forehead.

"You are indeed fortunate, Cousin," Albert said. "It pained me to see you go into company last evening when you did not realize that it was not quite proper to do so. I am afraid I was absolutely powerless to help you. Had you waited for Amberley to bring you in, of course, everything would have been different. Everyone would have divined the truth and welcomed you. However, one can hardly blame you. You have not been in town long enough to understand such niceties of polite behavior."

"You are quite right, Albert," Purnell said quietly, causing his cousin, whom he usually ignored, to turn toward him in some surprise. "We are bumpkins indeed. We should apply to you more often for advice. In our backward part of the country, 'polite' means treating other people with courtesy and consideration for their feelings. I for one had no idea that Londoners speak a different language."

"I am sure everyone present in Lady Sharp's drawing room appreciated your predicament, James," Albert said, "and honored you for the way you stood by Alexandra. You will find, I believe, that no one will hold your loyalty against you."

Purnell inclined his head. "I will be forever grateful to the members of polite society," he said.

Albert seemed to suspect that he was being mocked. He turned back to the ladies. "You will be happy to know that you will be received by the *ton* again, Alexandra," he said. "That will perhaps make up somewhat for the unfortunate marriage you are forced to contract."

"Unfortunate?" said Lady Beckworth as her daughter's chin came up.

"They have the rank and the wealth, of course," Albert said, "if that is all that concerns you, Aunt. But I know that Uncle puts great emphasis on moral and religious virtue, and I must say I honor him for doing so. He could not have been pleased at having to accept the offer of such a man as Amberley."

"I do not know that any of the Raines are very bad, Albert, dear," his mother said, frowning, "except that Lady Madeline likes to flirt quite outrageously at a time when she should be thinking of donning a spinster's cap. She has not been able to trap a husband in four years for all her wealth and loose ways."

"I heard that she was going to elope with Fairhaven," Albert said. "It was to stop her from doing so that Eden tried to have her confined and taken home. Unfortunately, he took Alexandra instead. But Eden is even more wild than his sister. He is always fighting and provoking quarrels, I have heard. And no lady is safe with him, apparently. He thinks himself irresistible to the fair sex."

"It comes of the unfortunate fact that the old earl died ten years ago," Mrs. Harding-Smythe said. "The present earl was very young to take over all the responsibilities of his new position and the upbringing of two such ebullient children. The countess, poor lady, is placid and overindulgent. She has not been able to control them at all. The earl, unfortunately, takes after her. His is not a firm character. Not at all like Beckworth's."

"I will be marrying Lord Amberley, not his brother and sister or his mother," Alexandra said quietly. "I am sure that Papa would not have approved his suit if he felt him to be an unsuitable match for me."

"Oh, of course not, dear," her aunt hastened to assure her. "It is just unfortunate that having had such a father, you will find it quite impossible to find a husband worthy of him. My brother is quite without equal."

"My uncle probably does not know about Amberley's mistress," Albert said. "He has had her for a year or more, though I have never been able to see the attraction. Mrs. Borden looks and behaves altogether too much like a man for my tastes. However, perhaps it is that very fact that attracts Amberley. My uncle, of course, is too unworldly to have heard of such sordid matters. And under the circumstances, I suppose it does not signify a great deal. The important thing is that you are respectably betrothed, Alexandra. I am happy for you."

"Now, there is another word," James Purnell said, pushing himself to a standing position before the fireplace. "'Happy.' In the country it means joyous, contented, pleased. What does it mean in town, pray, Albert? No, don't answer now. I would like to hear a full explanation. Shall we leave the ladies to their tea while you show me your team? You are always assuring me that you have an eye for good cattle. I would like to learn from you."

Albert found himself looking up into his cousin's direct dark gaze and not particularly liking what he saw. He rose to his feet so that he was not at quite such a disadvantage, although he was still more than four inches the shorter of the two. He bowed when Purnell gestured toward the door, bowed again to the ladies, and accepted the invitation with as good a grace as he could muster.

"I am so gratified to see that dear James is willing to learn from Albert," Mrs. Harding-Smythe said. "He will be able to benefit such a great deal, you know, and Albert will be only too pleased to share his experience. Now, Alexandra, my love, do tell us all about your interview with Lord Amberley."

Caroline giggled. "Did he go down on his knees, Alexandra?" she asked, clasping her hands to her bosom. "Oh, I shall positively die if my future husband does not do so. I shall feel absolutely cheated."

Alexandra folded her hands in her lap and looked up at her aunt. "His lordship said all that was proper," she said. "And I accepted him."

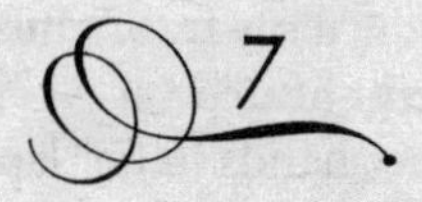

HOLD STILL, LOVEY. I HAVE ALMOST FINISHED." Nanny Rey was coaxing strands of Alexandra's dark hair into ringlets at the sides of her face.

"But I cannot wear it like that, Nanny," Alexandra said, "pretty as you have made it look. It just does not seem right."

"Such pretty wavy hair you have," Nanny Rey said with a cluck of the tongue. "Much prettier than that of any of the other misses I have seen since we have been here. And they all have curls and ringlets and the Lord knows what. None of them have their hair all confined as you do."

"I don't know," Alexandra said doubtfully, examining the results of Nanny's artistry in the mirror. "Papa has always said that a girl's hair should be down until she is sixteen and then up. He says that only vanity makes a lady want to show off her hair. I have never seen Mama's brushed out more than two or three times in my life."

Nanny Rey compressed her lips and viewed her charge's mirrored image over the tops of her gold-rimmed spectacles. "Your Papa also brought you to town so that you might learn how to live as the upper classes live," she said.

"Ladies here try to look pretty, lovey. They don't go out of their way to hide their beauty."

"Oh, dear," Alexandra said. "Is that what I am trying to do, Nanny? But I don't have any great beauty to hide, do I?"

Nanny Rey sniffed. "Not much," she said. "You could only be the most-sought-after young lady of the Season if you wanted to be, that's all."

"Oh, come now." Alexandra laughed. "You must own that you are somewhat biased. Though I do love you for saying so. Have I done the right thing, Nanny? But what does it matter whether it is right or not when it is the only thing I can do? Oh, but it feels so strange to be betrothed to a stranger. My life feels as if it has been turned quite topsy-turvy."

"I can't say either way," Mrs. Rey said, rummaging in a box in a drawer of the dressing table and coming out with a string of pearls. "I don't know his lordship. Perhaps you have been saved from the frying pan only to be cast into the fire, but I can't see that it makes any difference if that is so. You know how I felt about the duke."

"Yes," Alexandra said, bending her head forward so that the pearls could be clasped at the back of her neck. "And it seems that you were right all along. I was enraged by his snubbing me last evening. I suppose everyone else thinks he acted with perfect propriety, but I just cannot accept it. I don't like town ways, Nanny."

"There," the older woman said, patting Alexandra on the shoulder. "Perhaps this earl will marry you and take you away from this house, lovey. And perhaps he will teach you something about real life. Perhaps my girl will be happy after all."

Alexandra smiled and turned on the stool. "You are always telling me how unhappy I am, Nanny," she said. "You are absurd. I have never felt particularly so. Only a little restless perhaps, and eager to begin my own adult life."

She stood before the pier glass and surveyed herself from head to toe. She was wearing a new gown, a royal-blue silk, high-waisted, simple in design, perhaps a little lower at shoulders and bosom than she was accustomed to. The feathery ringlets at either side of her face touched her shoulders.

"Papa will not like it," she said. "He will say I look like a coquette."

"You look like a very pretty young lady about to meet her betrothed for dinner and the theater," Nanny Rey said firmly from behind her.

"I think I do like this gown," Alexandra said, "though I have been afraid to wear it until tonight. My hair feels strange. Well, Nanny, perhaps it is as well to begin a new life with a new look. I don't know."

"Are you ready to go down yet, lovey?" Mrs. Rey asked. "If not, I must leave you. I have a hundred and one things to do. I cannot stand around here all night long gossiping and admiring pretty young ladies."

Alexandra smiled and turned around. "I am going to stay here for a while," she said. "I do not need to go downstairs just yet. You go on, Nanny. Far be it from me to keep anyone from work."

She was afraid to go down. She acknowledged the fact quite freely to herself when she was alone. She was afraid to step out into the unknown as she would be doing when she left her room and went downstairs to join her parents and the Earl of Amberley in the drawing room. Her life would be forever changed, and she was bewildered by the speed with which it had all happened.

She had been contented with her life. Oh, not happy.

Nanny Rey was quite right about that. For years she had fretted against the restrictions of her home life. She had longed for the freedom she should have had when she left the schoolroom—the freedom to think and speak and do what she wished and what she thought right. The lifetime necessity of thinking twice about every impulse lest it offend some notion of propriety had become more and more irksome. The corrections—Lord Amberley had been quite correct to call them punishments—to which she was constantly subjected and which she could in no way fight had become an increasing humiliation.

Yet she had been content. With a life so restricted in its freedom and with her only real friend—her brother—from home so frequently, it was almost inevitable that she had developed a rich and intense inner life. Very little of her living was done outside herself, she often thought. Almost all was done inside.

She played the pianoforte, often for hours at a time, if she was not engaged in some other, imposed task and if she was not confined to her room as she so frequently was. If Mama came to the music room, she played music from the sheets kept in the stool. And indeed she loved all music. But if she were alone, she often closed her eyes, forgot her surroundings, and played from her heart. She should write down some of her compositions, James had told her more than once. But how can one write down the fleeting impulses of the moment? A butterfly is ruined if killed and spread out to be admired. A butterfly must be free. The music in her must be free.

She sketched and painted, sometimes outdoors, though she was rarely allowed to go far from the house, but more often indoors. She liked painting portraits, though there was a limit of subjects at home. And most of the people who sat for her—some of the servants, James, once Mama—were not happy with the finished paintings. She was not content to paint only what she saw with her eyes. She wanted to paint what she felt. She wanted to reveal the person as she knew him or her. And so colors and lines and textures were sometimes changed from the strictly realistic.

The last painting she had done of James—a year before—had shown him with his head thrown back, his hair windblown, his face lit by a warm smile. It was ridiculous, Mama had said. James never looked like that, and he was older than the very young man of the portrait. James himself had made no comment. He had merely squeezed her shoulder until it hurt and taken the portrait away. She did not know if he had kept it or destroyed it.

And she wrote endlessly—stories, reflections, poems. All the thoughts and feelings that might have been confided to a sympathetic mother or to a sister or friend were poured out on paper. It was mainly poetry that she wrote. The discipline of having to express herself through meter and rhyme helped her to formulate and organize her thoughts and sometimes to calm her feelings. She had never shown her writings to anyone. Only Nanny Rey and James even knew they existed.

And so she was not an actively unhappy person, she reflected, despite what Nanny and her brother believed. It was true that the older she got, the more irksome became the restraints on her freedom. And yet the certain knowledge she had always had that one day she would marry the Duke of Peterleigh had buoyed up her spirits. She had never known more of him than a brief and formal meeting every year or two could reveal, and had occasionally been chilled by his advanced age and distant hauteur. But she had always reminded herself that she would be a duchess and that she would spend most of her days in London.

During her month in London she had met the duke a little more frequently than ever before. But she had ignored any unease she had felt. The duke was not a warm or a charming man. He was not well-liked. Her flesh had secretly crept when she had thought that she must become this man's property to be used as he would. But there were compensations to outweigh these misgivings. When she married, she would finally pass beyond her childhood. Surely the duke would not dictate her every action as Papa had done.

And now all was changed. Alexandra sat down at one end of her high bed and clasped the fluted bedpost. She was to marry the Earl of Amberley. She was to be the Countess of Amberley. She still could not quite grasp the reality of all that had happened to her in the past few days. She had been so totally out of control of her own destiny. She always had been, of course, but she had never realized it as she did now.

She had been rather proud of herself at first. Apart from the terror she had felt during that night at the earl's town house and the dreadful embarrassment she had felt at being found by him in quite the state she had been in, she felt she had handled herself well. She had not given in to either hysteria or the vapors. And she was very satisfied with the firm, though polite, refusals she had made to both Lord Amberley's and Lord Eden's offers. For once she had had important decisions to make, and she had made them herself, according to her own wishes. She had felt her age for the first time in her life.

Even last night, at Lady Sharp's, during that terrible ordeal of knowing herself outcast, she had held on to her pride. She might have crept away or rushed away with

James as soon as she had realized what was happening. But she had not done so. She had held her ground and would have continued to do so for another five or ten minutes before making as dignified a withdrawal as she could. It was true, of course, that she had not expected the duke's snub. She was really not sure how she would eventually have reacted to that. She had not been given a chance to find out.

She had been touched and a little embarrassed by the approach of Lady Madeline Raine. She had recognized the girl's motive and had honored her courage and kind heart. She could not agree with James that her motives had been calculated and self-serving.

But what of Lord Amberley? He had come gallantly to her rescue—again she could not doubt his motive—and completely destroyed all her newfound pride. At the time she had been grateful. The moment of triumph had been irresistibly sweet as she had watched all the cold, condemning faces turn to warmth and deference. She had held to his arm as if it were the only solid anchor in a sea of troubles.

It was only when it was too late that she had realized the implications of what had happened. For one thing, she was bound to marry him. There was no further choice. Even if Papa had not been quite so insistent, there was her own common sense. For a whole hour she had allowed the cream of the *ton* to believe that she was about to engage herself to the Earl of Amberley. And this when she was already in the thick of scandal. There was no possible way she could have refused his offer earlier that afternoon.

And for another thing, she had just lost again an independence, a control over her own affairs that she had had for only one brief moment. Her father had always controlled her. The Earl of Amberley had taken over that control the evening before. He had seen her in a difficult spot, and with that dreadful male arrogance that all men seemed to share, he had assumed that she could not possibly extricate herself without his assistance. She was once again the helpless female, in the hands of a new and totally unknown owner.

She tried not to hate him. Indeed, she did not do so. He had made a great sacrifice in order to come to her rescue. He had sacrificed his own freedom, his own future. And all without any real obligation to do so. He was not the one who had compromised her. And there was kindness in him. If his behavior of the night before had not proved that, his words of that afternoon certainly had. He had tried his best to assure her that life with him would not be intolerable.

And those parting words of his had been kindly meant too. He would never strike her or punish her, he had said. Indeed, he would never even demand her obedience. She was not sure how far she trusted his words. How could a man never demand obedience from his wife? What if she defied him every day of his life? But the words had been soothing, and had opened to her mind a seductive glimpse of heaven.

A wife is to be a man's companion and lover, he had said. Strange, alien words! She knew very little about love apart from the deep bond of affection she shared with her brother. But the word "lover" seemed far more intimate than love. It brought to mind the strange feeling she had had the evening before with her hand on the earl's arm and his hand covering hers. And it brought back the distinct physical shock she had felt that afternoon when he had touched her palm with his lips.

She found the Earl of Amberley rather frightening. Despite all his kindness and his meddling male ways, there was a raw masculinity about him that she had never encountered before and had no idea how to cope with. The thought of being this man's property frankly terrified her. The thought that soon she must allow him marital intimacies threatened to rob her completely of breath. There was only panic to be gained from such a thought.

She resented such thoughts, such fears. Such dreadful helplessness! She deeply resented it. Though her rational mind, the more kindhearted and the fairer part of her mind, knew that Lord Amberley must be suffering from an equal feeling of frustration, she still resented him. She was betrothed to him, and there was nothing now she could do about that. When she married him, she would become his property to do with as he wished. She shivered. But he would not own her, for all that. She would see to it that he never owned anything more than her body.

He had a mistress. Albert had said he had a mistress. So she would be unimportant to him anyway. His life would not be utterly changed by this marriage as hers would be. He would still have his mistress. And he would still be a man—still essentially free.

A tap on the door of her bedchamber brought Alexandra out of her unwelcome reverie. James put his head around the door.

"He is here, Alex," he said. "Did you know? I thought you might like to have an arm to lean on when you go downstairs."

"Have I done the right thing?" she asked. "Did I have any choice? Oh, James, I am so frightened."

"Then it will be our secret, as always," he said. "Put your shoulders back and your chin up, Alex. That's my girl. I don't know if you are doing the right thing or not. I wish I did. I have always felt helpless where you are concerned. I want you to be happy more than I want anything else in the world. I don't like Amberley or Eden or Lady Madeline, but who am I to judge? Perhaps they are what you need. And I really cannot see any alternative. If you go back home, Papa will completely destroy your spirit. It is a miracle that he has not already done so."

"Oh, James." she said, reaching out for his hands. "It is not as bad as that. Papa has only done what he thinks best for me."

"He wants to make a slave of you!" her brother said viciously. The wayward lock of hair slid down across his brow.

"James!" Her tone was tender as she reached up to push back the hair. Her expression changed suddenly. "Is it true that Lord Amberley has a mistress?" she asked, flushing.

Her brother frowned. "Damn Albert!" he said. "Who knows if it is true? It means nothing anyway, Alex. Nine out of ten gentlemen you see around you have some female set up somewhere. Even Peterleigh, believe it or not. That paragon of virtue even has two children by his mistress. It is all something you need not know about. It is better that you do not know."

She closed her eyes. "But I do know," she said quietly. "I do know, James. And how am I now to respect Lord Amberley?"

"We must not keep him waiting," he said, reaching out an arm for her hand, "or Papa will have you on bread and water and down on your knees all day tomorrow.... Yes, that is good, Alex. You look as proud as a queen. Keep looking so. Keep all the hurt and the bewilderment and the fear inside you. It is better if no one ever knows. People will not try to hurt you if they think it cannot be done."

"James," she said. "Oh, dear James, I wish I could soothe

away the hurt that is in you. Sometimes one feels so helpless."

He laid a hand over hers as they left the room together, and smiled the smile that only she saw with any regularity. "If only you can escape from this web of our life," he said, "you will make me very happy. It is too late for me, Alex. But not for you. You must take the chance to live if it is offered you. I hope I am mistaken in Amberley."

His customary brooding mask descended on his face as they approached the drawing room. Alexandra, already straight-backed, lifted her chin an inch higher as a footman opened the double doors for them.

THEIR ARRIVAL AT the theater had proceeded without incident, Lord Amberley was relieved to find. They had not come face-to-face with anyone of consequence on the way in, but the theater had been more than half-full when he entered his box, and he had felt rather than seen eyes and lorgnettes and quizzing glasses turn their way. He had been too busy seating his betrothed, making sure that she was sitting in a position from which she might have a good view of the stage.

By the time he sat down beside her and looked around him, there was no visible sign that their entrance had caused any stir at all. He had been quite prepared to assume a haughty manner and to put his own quizzing glass to use if necessary. But it was not necessary.

He glanced with some admiration at the woman beside him. Her face was perfectly calm, her chin high, her shoulders back. She would not have crumbled, he felt, even if the audience had risen *en masse* and hissed her. She had a great deal of backbone, a great deal of presence.

Unfortunately, although disaster seemed to have been averted, it was not proving to be a comfortable evening. Lady Beckworth was gracious, though very grave. She rarely initiated conversation, though she would sustain it if someone else did so. James Purnell was taciturn, even morose. He spoke scarce a word. Miss Purnell was perfectly composed, quite distant, and almost silent. Lord Beckworth had declined to accompany the party to the theater, explaining that he disapproved of acting on the grounds that it was a form of lying, as was the writing of novels. He permitted his family to attend only because it was an acceptable pastime with the *ton*.

Altogether, then, the Earl of Amberley was feeling quite uncomfortable by the time the curtains came down to signal the end of the first half of the performance. He had tried repeatedly both before the performance and at appropriate moments during it to draw his betrothed into conversation. She looked encouragingly lovely in a gown more fashionable than any he had seen her wear and with her hair worn in a more becoming style than usual. But he distrusted her straight back and her lifted chin. They protected her against any snub she might receive from members of the audience around her. They also made her quite unapproachable.

"My mother and sister are in the box opposite," he said. "May I have the honor of escorting you across there, Miss Purnell, and presenting you? My mother, I know, is eager to make your acquaintance."

She turned her dark gaze on him, a look that always somewhat disconcerted him. Her eyes did not flutter over his face and neckcloth as the eyes of most females did. She always looked either deliberately away from him or so directly into his eyes that he had to restrain himself from pulling back so that she would not see into his very soul.

"Thank you," she said, "I would like that."

She was tall. He had noticed that before, of course. She had a good figure. One tended almost not to notice that fact, since the pride of her bearing took away something of her femininity. But the lower-than-usual neckline of her gown revealed the tops of well-formed breasts and the beginnings of the cleavage between. He knew that she had long, shapely legs. Her dark hair, in its severe chignon with the few ringlets as the only concession to the festive occasion, shone in the candlelight. He wondered if his memory of that hair all down about her face and shoulders exaggerated its almost voluptuous waviness.

She was a strange woman. She was obviously capable of exuding a breathtaking sexuality, and yet she walked beside him, her hand resting very lightly on his arm, her body not close enough to touch any part of his, controlled, withdrawn, sexless almost.

He touched her fingertips with his own and smiled down at her. "I have not had the opportunity to tell you how very lovely you look, my dear," he said. "I like your hair that way."

"Thank you," she said, and then she blushed hotly as he drew her more closely against his side so that another couple might pass them in the corridor. She stiffened very noticeably, and put more distance between them than before as soon as she was able.

"I am sorry," the Earl of Amberley murmured as he tapped on the door to the box where his mother was and handed his betrothed inside. He frowned slightly at her back. Was she frigid? Was he going to have to cope with that problem? He was not at all confident that he knew how.

Madeline jumped to her feet when they entered, abandoning two young men mid-sentence, it seemed. One of them was Sir Derek Peignton. She held out both hands to Alexandra and smiled brightly. "How delighted I am you have come," she said. "I was about to persuade Sir Derek to accompany me to your box, but I saw that you had left already. Hello, Edmund. I am very pleased, Miss Purnell, very pleased that you are to be my sister." She squeezed Alexandra's hands.

Alexandra smiled back. Lord Amberley watched with interest. She had lovely even white teeth. It was the first time he had seen her smile.

Lady Amberley was more restrained than her daughter in her greeting. She turned away from Sir Cedric Harvey, with whom she had been in conversation, and indicated an empty chair next to her own.

"How do you do, Miss Purnell?" she said. "Do have a seat. Yes, yes, Edmund, I realize this must be Miss Purnell, so I think we can dispense with the formalities. Let me look at you, my dear, and do you take a good look at me. Let us frankly size up each other."

Alexandra took the chair. Her composure seemed not to be affected by the countess's forthright manner. Lord Amberley took up his position behind his betrothed's chair and looked around him, one hand playing with the ribbon of his quizzing glass. He intercepted several interested and curious glances from the occupants of the other boxes.

"My younger son has treated you quite abominably, albeit quite unintentionally so," his mother was saying. "I am deeply shamed, my dear. I was more relieved than I can say when Edmund called on me this afternoon to tell me that you had honored him by accepting his hand. You must be quite apprehensive, Miss Purnell, and quite unsure that you have done the right thing. You may take my word for it that there is no more honorable gentleman in England than Edmund. I am partial, of course." She smiled and reached across to squeeze Alexandra's arm above the wrist.

"Thank you, ma'am," Alexandra said. "The honor is all mine, I assure you. I shall do my best to make Lord Amberley a dutiful and obedient wife."

"Gracious, child!" Lady Amberley leaned back in her chair. "You must do no such thing. It will only go to his head if you do so, and he will go around expecting it as his due from every female under his influence."

Lord Amberley watched the shoulders of his betrothed straighten. She made no reply.

"Let me present you to Sir Cedric Harvey," the countess said. "He is a dear friend of our family, and you will have to become acquainted with him if you are to be Edmund's wife."

Alexandra inclined her head as the older man stood and bowed to her in an old-fashioned courtly manner.

"Sir Cedric is an important person in my life, Miss Purnell," Lord Amberley said with a smile. "When I assumed my present title quite suddenly at the age of nineteen, he was there to save me from collapsing under the shock and strain."

Sir Cedric laughed heartily. "Even at that age you had a deal of sense, Edmund," he said. "Can't see that you would have fared much worse than you have even if I had not been available to help."

Lord Amberley touched the shoulders of his betrothed lightly and felt her stiffen again. He felt annoyance flare in him for a moment.

"Perhaps we should return to my box," he said. "It must be almost time for the play to resume."

"Edmund must bring you to call one afternoon, Miss Purnell," Lady Amberley said as Alexandra got to her feet. "And he told me this afternoon that he is going to organize a garden party in order to present you to the fashionable world as his future countess. I am delighted. We must get to know each other better, my dear, before we all retire to the country and are thrown into one another's company for almost every moment of the day."

As Lord Amberley and Alexandra left Sir Cedric's box, they almost collided with Lord Eden, who was on his way in.

"I say," he said, "are you leaving already? I saw you up here from the pit and came to pay my respects. How do you do, Miss Purnell?" He flushed quite noticeably as he bowed to her.

She curtsied. "I am quite well, I thank you, my lord," she said.

"Are you . . . ?" he asked. "Is it true . . . ?" He looked up at his brother. "Do I understand that congratulations are in order?"

Lord Amberley smiled. "I hope so," he said. "Miss Purnell has consented to be my wife, Dom."

Lord Eden looked back down at her, his flush deepening. "May I wish you happy, ma'am?" he said. "I mean . . ."

Lord Amberley was surprised to see his betrothed reach out a hand and touch his brother's sleeve for a brief moment. "Thank you," she said. And she smiled again, a smile that reached all the way to her eyes for a moment as brief as that during which her hand had lain on his arm.

"Edmund is a lucky dog," Lord Eden surprised his older brother by saying. "You will be wishing to return to your box. The play is about to resume, I believe. I shall see you later, Edmund?"

Lord Amberley raised his eyebrows. He was usually long abed by the time his brother came home, except on those now-ended occasions when he had spent many hours of certain nights in Eunice's bed.

"Later," he agreed.

LORD AMBERLEY WAS SITTING in his library several hours later, slouched down in a worn leather chair, a glass of brandy dangling from the hand that lay draped over the arm. He wondered if he should wait up for Dominic much longer. He yawned.

He was missing Eunice. He would give almost anything at the moment to be sitting with her in her parlor, just talking and talking. Why was it, he thought, that some of the profoundest truths one's mind was capable of grasping came to one during late-night conversations? His mind was always stimulated by Eunice. She was perhaps the most intelligent woman he had ever known. He needed a little of her sanity now.

He wanted to blank his mind to his own unenviable position. There was nothing he could do to change matters. Especially now, when his second offer had been made and accepted. The thought of marrying Miss Purnell was singularly unappealing, far more so tonight than it had appeared during the afternoon. He and she were universes apart. He could see no point of likeness at all.

She was not ugly. Quite the contrary, in fact. When he looked at her objectively, he could admit that she was rather lovely. She had a body that could be voluptuous and a face that could be beautiful. Indeed, she had appeared both to him during that first encounter in Madeline's bedchamber. But she was not voluptuous and she was not beautiful. He did not find her in any way attractive.

He could not quite explain to himself why not. Was it the character within that was unlovely? Yet she was perfectly well-bred. And she certainly had self-possession and dignity and courage that he could admire. But she was so totally untouchable. He had looked at her once at the theater when she was watching the action onstage. He had looked at her well-formed mouth and tried to picture himself tasting her lips with his mouth and his tongue. He just could not imagine it. His eyes had swept her body. He had tried to imagine it spread beneath his own in bed as it would be when they were wed. It could not be done. He could not picture himself making love to the girl, or even simply having intercourse with her.

Yet she was to be his wife!

Beckworth must be largely to blame for her strange character, of course. From a few facts she had let slip, he understood that she must have had an incredibly narrow and strict upbringing. And was that upbringing ingrained in her very character? Or was there some hope of softening her, making her more human with the patience of his regard?

And he must cultivate a regard for her. He must learn to esteem her, to respect her, to love her even. He could not tolerate in himself a willingness to do the right thing by marrying her if he ended his obligation there. Making her respectable was not simply a matter of speaking a few words at the altar so that she might acquire the protection of his name. It meant making her his wife, making her half of his life for the rest of his days. It would be a formidable task.

Lord Amberley sighed and lifted the forgotten glass to his lips. He was relieved when the door was suddenly opened and his brother's head appeared around it.

"Ah, you are still up, Edmund," Lord Eden said, coming into the room and setting his hat and cloak on a chair by the door. "I thought you would be in bed. I did not mean to be late. But it is Bates's birthday, you know—today, that is, and I had agreed to help him and a few other fellows celebrate it. I understood it was to be at the other end of the day—tomorrow, so to speak—but nothing would do but for us to toast him as soon as midnight struck."

"I have been having a brandy," Lord Amberley said, elevating his glass. "Have one, Dom?"

"No," his brother said. "I have had enough for one night. Listen, Edmund, I wished to talk to you tonight. About Miss Purnell. It won't do at all, you know. I am the one who should be marrying her."

"Too late, Dom," Lord Amberley said with a grin. "She prefers me."

"Poppycock!" Lord Eden said, jumping up from the chair he had just taken and beginning to stride about the room. "The poor girl just discovered what spite the *ton* is capable of, that is all. I heard what happened at Lady Sharp's. I should have been there. And I should have been the one to go back to Curzon Street this afternoon. I will marry her. I will go there tomorrow and explain."

"You will do no such thing," his brother said, yawning so that his jaws cracked. "The matter is all settled, Dom. Let's go to bed."

"It is not at all settled," Lord Eden said. His face was flushed. "Miss Purnell seems to be a sensible female. She will see immediately when I explain why things must change. She will be just as happy to marry me, I daresay. I can offer as much respectability as you, Edmund."

Lord Amberley placed his almost empty glass on a small table at his elbow and rose to his feet. "Enough, Dom," he said, a note of finality in his voice. "Miss Purnell is my betrothed. I owe her as much protection as if she were my wife already. Protection even against you. I will not have her harassed. You will have me to answer to if you try." He looked his brother steadily in the eye.

Lord Eden looked rebellious. His face was still flushed. "But you cannot possibly wish to marry her, Edmund," he said. "She is like a marble statue."

Lord Amberley's lips thinned. "Miss Purnell is to be my wife," he said softly. "You will do well to be careful of what you say about her, Dominic. I will not countenance any remark that even hints at disrespect."

Lord Eden ran a hand through his hair, leaving it considerably disheveled. "You know very well what I meant," he said. "You are taking her into the country—Mama said tonight. I am coming too, Edmund, unless you expressly forbid me the house. And I am going to take her from you. I am going to persuade her that she prefers me. I won't have you doing this for my sake. And I know that that is why you are doing it rather than urging me to do what is right. You do not want to see my life ruined. You would rather ruin your own."

Lord Amberley grinned unexpectedly into the tension that had developed between them. "Should we send for the dueling pistols now?" he asked. "Somehow I think not. We might damage the walls and books in here, not to mention each other's person. And we would undoubtedly alarm the servants. Leave matters as they are, Dom. If you had lived hundreds of years ago, you could have ridden off in a cloud of romance to the Crusades. Unfortunately, you are living in the very prosaic nineteenth century. Let us go to bed." He set a brotherly arm around the other's shoulders.

"I shall do it all the same," Lord Eden grumbled as his brother lifted the branch of candles and they left the room together. "I am not a boy any longer, Edmund. I wish you would realize that. This is entirely my problem, and I do not need your protection. I am going to take her from you."

8

LORD EDEN WAS FEELING MORE CHEERFUL than he had a right to be feeling, he thought, considering the fact that he was about to try to take on a life sentence. But the sun was shining outside, Lord Beckworth had not been home on Curzon Street, nor the rather disconcerting Mr. Purnell, and Lady Beckworth had been quite gracious, giving it as her opinion when he had waited upon her during the afternoon that it would be quite unexceptionable for her daughter to drive in the park with him. Miss Purnell herself had raised no objection.

And Miss Purnell was really not a bad looker after all, he was relieved to find. She was wearing a primrose dress that made her look far more youthful than anything else he had seen her in. The matching pelisse and straw bonnet she donned in order to ride out with him made her look rather like a ray of sunshine. He did not know quite what had given him the impression during his first interview with her that she was a thin, plain, and uninteresting lady. Indeed, when he thought about the matter, he believed that she had looked rather handsome the night before when he had seen her at the theater with Edmund.

Lord Eden handed Alexandra into his curricle and took his seat beside her. She was looking rather tense, but that was not unflattering. He was forever conscious of his age, which was not very advanced at all for a man. He was accustomed to not being taken very seriously by his elders. With very young ladies, of course, those below the age of twenty, he had had considerable success. But Miss Purnell was no girl. He was not even sure that she was not older than he. It was encouraging to know that she took him seriously enough to feel nervous with him.

"Are you comfortable?" he asked, smiling reassuringly at her. "Some ladies are a little apprehensive about the high seat, but you may rest easy. I handle the ribbons with great care, especially when I have a lady's safety in my hands. Even Edmund will admit as much."

"I feel perfectly safe, thank you," she said. "I trust your driving implicitly, sir."

Her voice was quite grave. Most young females of his acquaintance would have sounded breathless and even adoring saying the same words.

Lord Eden winced as he grasped the ribbons and gave the horses the signal to start. His arms were feeling deucedly stiff. He would have thought himself in better physical condition. Of course, the morning's boxing bout had been no ordinary one. He smiled to himself. Yes, there was another reason for his present cheerful mood.

"Did you enjoy the play last evening?" he asked conversationally, and settled into a pleasant verbal exchange of trivialities as he maneuvered his curricle along the streets leading to Hyde Park.

Harding-Smythe had put in an appearance at Jackson's that morning. Five of Lord Eden's acquaintances had had a bet on the question of whether he would do so or not.

Three of them had felt that the prospect of facing Eden's well-known fists would keep the man away. Two had believed that the challenge had been made so publicly that Harding-Smythe could not stay away without losing face.

It was difficult to make serious business of a boxing match at Jackson's. It was not easy to give one's opponent a thorough drubbing. Gentleman Jackson had not acquired his nickname without reason. Rigidly applied rules and gentlemanly etiquette determined that no one lost his temper and no one got seriously hurt at the famous saloon. The punishment of Harding-Smythe had had to be carefully planned.

Faber and two of his other cronies had volunteered for the task of distracting Jackson's attention. Not one of the three was up to the task of challenging the pugilist to a bout, but they had gathered around the man who had, making a great deal of noise and peppering Jackson with questions on strategy when the bout came to an early end. One true and rash friend had even offered his body for demonstration purposes.

They had created a long enough diversion. By the time Jackson had noticed the crowd of interested spectators gathered around the ring in which Lord Eden had taken on Harding-Smythe, that reptile was reeling and seemed not quite to know where he was or what he was doing there or from what direction the next punishing fist was likely to come. He had been down on the canvas, twice, but Lord Eden had stood over him, not laying a hand on him, finding just the right taunting words to bring him staggering to his feet again.

He would know for days to come that he had been used as a punching ball. He would be more careful in future of what he said about his own cousin and about Edmund.

Implying that Edmund had enjoyed Miss Purnell while she was still tied to Madeline's bed, indeed! Clearly the man and his friends knew nothing whatsoever about the Earl of Amberley!

The sore arms were worth enduring, Lord Eden thought, turning his horses carefully through the gates of the park and noting that the sun had brought out conveyances and horses and pedestrians by the score. The public and scathing setdown he had received from the lips of Jackson, no respecter of persons, was cheap at the price too, and the week's banishment from the boxing saloon for ungentlemanly conduct. He would cheerfully do it all again if he could.

Miss Purnell's chin lifted when they entered the park, he noticed with interest. She looked more like the proud and severe lady he had confronted a few mornings before with his marriage proposal. But the straw bonnet, trimmed with yellow and blue flowers, spoiled the effect. It was decidedly pretty.

"I wish I had been at Lady Sharp's two evenings ago," he said impulsively. "I would have had a thing or two to say to a few people. I would have made very sure that no one harassed you, Miss Purnell."

"Really, no one did," she said. "I was merely made to feel that I had been set down in the middle of an ice house. I had no idea that people could behave so, and for such a trivial cause."

"How you must hate me!" he said. "I marvel that you can sit there, ma'am, and be so civil to me. I cannot imagine what possessed me. Looking back now, I can think of a hundred courses of action that I might have taken under the circumstances. The easiest would have been to have stalked over to Fairhaven the moment I heard him talking of an elopement and drawn his cork right there. It would have been embarrassing in the middle of a ballroom, I suppose, but at least only I would have suffered. And he, of course. Though as for that, he deserves to suffer too. He has run off with Miss Turner and caused a pretty scandal."

"It is easy to think of the right thing to do or say after the event," Alexandra said.

"I wish I had been at Lady Sharp's all the same," he said. "If I had, I would have known sooner that you were in need of my protection. I would have been the one to take you about and present you as my future bride. And I would have been the one to call on you yesterday morning. And I would now be a happy man. Good day, ma'am."

He raised his hat to Lady Fender, who had given the signal for her barouche to come to a halt alongside his curricle.

"Ah, Miss Purnell," she called, nodding graciously at Lord Eden, "my felicitations, my dear. It seems that Amberley did prevail upon you, then, to accept his offer. I wish you joy. You cannot do better than to ally yourself to the Raine family, you know." The plumes of her bonnet waved again in Lord Eden's direction.

"Thank you, ma'am," Alexandra said unsmilingly. "I am very sensible of the honor that is being done me."

"She was present in Lady Sharp's drawing room?" Lord Eden asked as they drove on.

"Yes," she said.

"The old tabby!" he commented. "How do you do, my lord? My lady?" He bowed to a couple who passed them in a landau, nodding and smiling in Alexandra's direction.

Alexandra inclined her head. She did not smile, Lord Eden noted with some satisfaction, at any of the people they passed and greeted in the next few minutes.

"I want you to reconsider, Miss Purnell," he said abruptly, as soon as it seemed his conversation would not be overheard by a dozen people.

"My lord?" she asked, looking at him blankly.

"I want you to marry me," he said. "It is far more fitting. I am the one who compromised you. And besides, I am more of an age with you, better able to take you about and entertain you. Edmund is something of a dry stick, you know." He flushed at the disloyalty of his words.

"But the matter is no longer open for discussion," she said. "I have accepted Lord Amberley, my lord. And our betrothal is common knowledge already, as you can see for yourself this afternoon."

"It can be changed," he said. "A betrothal is not like a marriage. It is not binding. Besides, the summer is coming. We can leave town. We can marry immediately if you wish, and retire to my estate in Wiltshire. People will soon forget. I will be able to bring you back here next year or take you traveling. You will not have a dull life, Miss Purnell. I promise you that. And I promise to be a faithful and considerate husband."

"Why are you doing this?" she asked quietly. "There is no need, you know. I have been restored to respectability, as you can see. These people seem to be satisfied by the fact that I am now engaged to your brother. Why are you willing to face another scandal?"

"I want to marry you," he said. "I feel a deep regard for you, Miss Purnell. I love you." He looked at her, embarrassed by his own words. They were so patently overdone, so obviously untrue. And yet they did not feel entirely untrue at that moment. He had turned his curricle out of the main path and taken a quieter, more shaded one through the trees. The patterns of light and shade that passed over her, the sunny yellow of her clothes, the pretty straw bonnet, all made her look unexpectedly appealing. Her dark eyes fixed steadily on him enhanced her beauty.

"It is your brother, is it not?" she said. "You love him a great deal. I have noticed already that there is a closeness of regard in your family. I can sympathize with that. My brother is very dear to me. I think I would sacrifice a great deal to see him happy. You are prepared to sacrifice the whole of your future, my lord?"

"Oh, I say," he said, feeling himself flush and wishing that he could make his reaction more manly.

"I have really bungled, have I not? I really meant what I said just now, Miss Purnell. I do feel a regard for you. I do not know you, of course, but I have seen enough to find that I admire you greatly. Not many ladies would have lived through the last few days with as much dignity as you have shown. You are a woman of strong character, I believe. I would be truly honored to be entrusted with the protection of your name."

"I think I will like you too," she said, "when I know you better. You have done something rash and impetuous and you are willing to take the consequences. Unfortunately for me, I am the consequences. I do not enjoy my role, my lord, but I have been persuaded that my best course of action is to engage myself to marry your brother. I must live by that decision. All sorts of people, including me, would be embarrassed, if I were to change my mind now, today. I thank you, but I must beg you to say no more."

"I cannot give up so easily," he said. "I will not."

"Is it such a bad thing for your brother, then," she asked, "to be marrying me?"

He looked at her unhappily. This plan had seemed so right to him before he had begun to put it into operation.

He had been all persuasive charm, she all timid and yielding femininity. Why was it that now it seemed so wrong?

"I have succeeded in sounding very insulting, have I not?" he said. "As if you are a burden that either Edmund or I have to take on. That is not true at all, I do assure you. I really want to marry you, Miss Purnell. I find the prospect more and more appealing."

"And your brother does not?" she asked.

He felt himself flushing anew. "I do not know," he said. "I have not discussed feelings with Edmund. But I think for your own sake, Miss Purnell, that you will be better off with me. Edmund is a very private person. He does not mix readily with other people. I think he prefers to be alone. Perhaps he would not... Maybe he is not the sort of man who..." He drew a hand along his jaw and sighed. "I cannot talk for Edmund. It would be unfair. I can only talk for myself. I am not doing a very good job of this, am I?"

She laughed unexpectedly, a light, amused laugh. "Yes, I think you are," she said. "Not a very good job of persuading me to marry you, it is true. But you are doing a wonderful job of making me like you. You are an honorable man and a loyal brother, my lord. I am glad you asked me to drive with you this afternoon. I confess I have been feeling dreadfully depressed about this whole matter and unwilling to come out again to face people. I have not liked what I have seen in the past week. You have restored my faith in humanity."

"Well," he said, fingering the folds of his neckcloth, "that is something at least, I suppose. But I had hoped to be taken more seriously as a suitor. I will not give up this easily, you know."

"You will have to." She reached across and patted him briefly on the arm. "But I do appreciate the manner in which you have tried to make me feel wanted, as well as the concern you have shown for your brother. Perhaps I can ease your conscience. It is not on account of your inadvertent kidnapping of me that I have accepted Lord Amberley. Not at all. It is rather on account of the unfortunate way in which he chose to rescue me from embarrassment at Lady Sharp's. You are not to blame for this forced marriage, you see."

He smiled ruefully. "I do not know why you are so kind to me, Miss Purnell," he said. "In your place, I think I would hate me. But I cannot so easily put my conscience to rest. I will not deny that Edmund's happiness is important to me. But so is yours, you see. And I have certainly destroyed that. I have heard what Peterleigh did at Lady Sharp's, and I would dearly love to call him out, except that I have the feeling he would look down his nose at me as if I were a worm beneath his boot or—worse—a child fresh from the nursery, and refuse to come. But I will slap a glove in his face if you wish."

"I think the Duke of Peterleigh is best ignored," she said firmly. "But thank you. Are we to go down this path again, my lord? I believe it is the fifth time."

"Good Lord, is it?" he said. "I was just congratulating myself on having found a new thoroughfare that I had not seen before."

They both laughed.

"Edmund is giving a garden party next week," he said. "Mama is afraid that many people will not come on such short notice, but I will wager that there will be an admirable squeeze."

"Oh, dear," she said. "It was to escape a squeeze that I went outdoors alone at the Easton ball."

• • •

LORD EDEN PROVED CORRECT ABOUT the garden party. It was true that the invited guests had been given but little notice of the event—less than a week at a time of the year when every day presented them with a dozen entertainments among which to choose. But the prospect of attending such a betrothal party proved irresistible. Lord Amberley was one of the most eligible bachelors in town and had been the object of many a matchmaking mama's matrimonial hopes for several years past.

And Alexandra, of course, was the object of much curiosity. Despite the story that had been circulated, many wondered if it was likely that she had been abducted unwillingly by Lord Eden. The story of his having tried to kidnap his sister seemed somewhat difficult to believe when one thought about it. But why was it that it was the elder brother rather than Lord Eden who was to marry her? The whole scandalous episode was quite deliciously intriguing.

And so the vast majority of those invited and a few besides arrived at the Earl of Amberley's town house on a gloriously sunny and warm afternoon, which succeeded three days of clouds and chill and intermittent rain. Those who had not yet seen the newly betrothed pair together came in order to do so and judge for themselves whether it was a match of convenience or inconvenience. Others hoped to see Lord Eden present too and to observe for themselves whether he and Miss Purnell would exchange guilty looks or indeed any looks at all.

Alexandra had not wanted the betrothal party. She had never enjoyed the squeezes of fashionable society—indeed, as she had told Lord Eden, it was her attempt to escape from one that had led to all her troubles. To be the center of attention at such a gathering was terrible indeed to her.

Besides, she had not wanted her betrothal to be made so very public. Why pander to the expectations of a society she had come to despise?

However, Lord Amberley had felt that it was necessary to make such a public gesture—to present to the *beau monde* his prospective bride and to announce thereby her respectability. He was careful to choose his mother, the Countess of Amberley, as his hostess for the afternoon. And, as he had explained to Alexandra when he called at Curzon Street two days after their visit to the theater in order to take her to visit his mother, he wanted to show her off.

"I want everyone to see you, Miss Purnell," he had said, "and know what a very fortunate man I am."

Alexandra had made no protest. What was the point? She had agreed to this marriage. She must live by the consequences. But she felt the hypocrisy of it all.

Lord Beckworth too had considered some form of engagement party necessary. "We have all been brought considerable shame by your careless and scandalous behavior, Alexandra," he had said. "Everyone has been apprised of the fact that we are no longer good enough for the Duke of Peterleigh. And if you now marry the Earl of Amberley quietly and creep away to his estate in the country, how is everyone to know that there was not real substance to your disgrace? How is everyone to know that you are not with child?"

Alexandra had gaped and flushed painfully, swallowed the words that had leapt to her lips, and lowered her eyes. Her mother had shifted uncomfortably in her chair and coughed behind her hand. James had not been present at the time.

"We will all attend this garden party, Alexandra, and

you will behave with pride and decorum," her father had continued. "You will spend the whole of the day before it and the morning of it alone in your room preparing your mind."

And so she had had no real choice, she reflected as she stood in the receiving line with Lord Amberley on one side of her and his mother on the other. She was one-and-twenty years old, she was engaged to be married, and she was caught utterly in the unenviable position of owing obedience to two men. Lord Amberley had said he would never insist that she obey him. And yet when he had decided upon something as he had now, she had had no power to resist. Perhaps she was being a little unfair. Had she said to him in so many words that she did not want this garden party, perhaps he would not have insisted. Perhaps he did not realize just how abhorrent to her such a public display was.

"I think we have stood here long enough," he said at last, looking down at her with those smiling blue eyes that she always found so disconcerting. "Will you take my arm, my dear, and we will mingle with our guests?"

He also had a habit that she was still not used to of covering her hand with his as it rested on his arm and caressing her fingers. Alexandra did not believe he meant any familiarity—the gesture seemed almost absentminded. But she did not like it nonetheless. She felt uncomfortable waves of sensation sizzling up her arm and into her breasts when he did so, and she became more than ever aware of his physical presence. She became breathless and quite unable to relax or to concentrate on what was happening outside her own body. She felt out of control again.

"Shall we talk to my aunt and uncle?" he asked. "They are

almost my closest neighbors at Amberley. We will be seeing a great deal of them during the summer, I daresay."

"I would like that, my lord," she said. Relatives of his, neighbors, people she would meet frequently when she went into the country with him. The whole situation was taking on an appalling reality. "I have not met them before this afternoon."

She was not sure for the following half-hour whether she was comforted or further dismayed by the friendliness of Lord Amberley's Aunt Viola and Uncle William Carrington.

"It is time Edmund settled down," her uncle said to Alexandra, his eyes twinkling. "Our Walter will be twenty next spring, and of course young Dominic is of age already. But how can we expect any young lady to take them seriously when the greater prize is still unattached? You are doing our family a great favor, Miss Purnell."

"Gracious, William!" his wife scolded. "One would think that Walter and Dominic were in danger of going through life in bachelor solitude. They are mere babes yet."

"I wonder if mothers ever admit that their sons are grown up," Mr. Carrington said, smiling at Alexandra. "So, my dear, Edmund is bringing you into the country for the summer, is he? You will like Amberley Court. One of the loveliest estates in all England, I daresay. My sister certainly had an eye to what was good for her when she married Amberley. Edmund's father, that is." He laughed heartily.

"William!" his wife said. "You know very well theirs was a love match pure and simple. Take no notice of him, Miss Purnell. He is such a tease. One never knows when to take him seriously. We brought Anna with us, Edmund. I hope you do not mind. She is only fifteen, and some would say that she should not be allowed at a function such as this at her age. But she begged and begged until William said she might come. He never could say no to Anna."

"I am delighted to see her again," Lord Amberley said. "I see that she has discovered Dominic."

"I told her that she was to curtsy to him as to you and leave him to his adult companions," his aunt said, staring across the garden to her daughter and Lord Eden. "I might as well have saved my breath to cool my tea with."

Lord Amberley grinned down at Alexandra. "Anna has had a grand passion for Dominic since she was ten years old," he said. "She swears that she is going to marry him one day."

"I have already warned him that I cannot spare him my little girl to carry off to Wiltshire," Mr. Carrington said with a chuckle. "Anna will have to marry one of the Courtney boys."

"William!" his wife said. "The very idea. One of the Courtney boys! Besides, Miss Purnell, there is no question of Anna's marrying Dominic. He is her first cousin. It is just a stubborn case of hero worship. You will be thinking this whole family quite mad."

"On the contrary," Alexandra said quietly. "I have been realizing how pleasant it must be to have several close relatives living nearby. I have had only Mama and Papa and my brother James all my life."

"After a year married to Edmund," Uncle William said, "you will probably be wishing that you still had just your mama and papa and your brother close by, Miss Purnell. You will have Anna and Walter and Madeline and Dominic to plague the life out of you. Not to mention all the Courtneys."

"And not to mention you, William!" his wife retorted.

"Take no notice of him, Miss Purnell. You will be very happy with Edmund, I am sure, my dear, and we will be very happy to have a new young countess at Amberley."

Alexandra would have smiled if she had not at that moment felt Lord Amberley's hand on hers and looked up to see his blue eyes smiling at her.

"I have scarcely had a chance to talk to Lord and Lady Beckworth this afternoon," he said. "Shall we go and find them, my dear?"

"Yes," she said. "They are with your mother and Sir Cedric Harvey." She turned to smile at Mr. and Mrs. Carrington, whom she liked a great deal despite the fact that they seemed to inhabit a different world from the one she had been brought up in.

"They have the biggest hearts of almost anyone I have known," Lord Amberley said as they moved away. "Are you comfortable, Miss Purnell? I know it took a great deal of courage for you to come this afternoon. But I am glad that you did. I am very proud to have all these people see me with you."

He curled his fingers beneath hers and squeezed her hand. This time that strange sizzling sensation began in her throat and spiraled downward into her stomach.

"YOU REALLY WILL COME TOMORROW to take me to the Tower, Dominic?" the thin young girl clinging to his arm was saying. "Promise?"

"I have said I will, haven't I?" he said, smiling affectionately at her. "You have grown, Anna. At this rate, you may even reach my shoulder before another year has passed."

"I really do not mind if I never do, Dominic," she said.

"You are so tall. But I wish I would not merely grow upward." She sighed. "I wish I looked more like Madeline. Or Miss Purnell."

"You will, Anna," he said kindly. "By the time you make your come-out, you will take the *ton* by storm."

"Do you really think so?" she asked. "Really, Dominic? And will you be there to see it? I would like you to lead me into the very first set at my very first ball."

"By that time I will look old and decrepit to you," he said with a grin. "You will want someone younger and altogether more dashing, Anna."

"No, I won't," she said. "You know I won't. Do you think Miss Purnell beautiful, Dominic? I do, though Walter says she is too serious."

"I agree with you," he said. "And she is not always so serious. She is doubtless nervous this afternoon. And who would not be at her own betrothal party? I think you will like her when you get to know her."

"Yes," she said. "I am glad she is to marry Edmund. I like Edmund, though he is not nearly so handsome as you, Dominic. Or so tall."

He grinned. "I am going to return you to your mama," he said. "I see some friends of mine that I should pay my respects to."

"And you would not want them to see you with a fifteen-year-old cousin," she said with a sigh of resignation. "All right, Dominic. But I will grow up, I promise you."

He laughed. The party was even more of a squeeze than he had anticipated. His thoughts had taken a decidedly gloomy turn, and he needed the company of his friends to cheer him. The betrothal of Edmund and Miss Purnell was now very formal and very public. He could not possibly break it up without sacrificing all his honor.

He shrugged as he turned away from Anna and his aunt and uncle and crossed the lawn to a group of his acquaintances. The summer in the country would present him with a wholly new opportunity to see what could be accomplished.

MADELINE WAS SITTING IN THE CONSERVAtory at Amberley Court, her fingers absently playing with the velvety leaf of a pink geranium plant. She was staring gloomily out through the large windows onto a rain-soaked lawn. Her twin looked equally dejected, one booted foot resting on the window seat that extended around three sides of the room. His elbow was propped on his knee, his chin in his hand.

"It is not so much the rain," Madeline said. "Indeed, it is sometimes quite enjoyable to tramp along the clifftop or down on the beach with rain and wind lashing against one's face and hair. It is being home again, I suppose, after living for more than a month without a moment to spare for thought. The change of pace is too drastic."

"Elsewhere always seems so much preferable to right here," Lord Eden said without looking around. "Do you know what I mean, Mad? When I am in Wiltshire, I think I am living in the middle of nowhere, and I long to be here. When I am here, I fret for more social activity and hanker for a journey to London. And when I am in London, I tire of the shallowness and the tedium of it all and want to be somewhere else again. Is there something wrong with me?"

"It is not that I do not want to be here," Madeline said. "It is in the country that I am happiest. Perhaps if I never left here, I would not feel dissatisfied at all. But there is always the lure of the Season. Is there something wrong with me, Dom, that I still have not found myself a husband?"

He looked around at her. "I don't think so," he said. "In fact, I think you occasionally show some good sense, Mad. All the gentlemen who have shown interest in you for the last four years are nothing but loose screws, the lot of them, if you ask me. It does you credit that you have not married any of them."

"Oh, Dom!" she cried, showing the first spark of spirit in an hour. "What a lowering thing to say. It implies dreadful things about my charms if I cannot attract a worthy suitor."

"I thought you were keen on Peignton," he said. "What happened? Or should I ask, what did not happen?"

"He kissed me," she said, "at Edmund's garden party. It was most improper, Dom. He took me behind the summerhouse into the trees. I knew what he was going to do, of course, and I must confess I did not do much to dissuade him. He is exceedingly handsome, you must admit. Then he murmured something about having to talk to Edmund to discuss a settlement."

"A settlement?" Lord Eden said. "Nothing about undying love, Mad? No proposal?"

"No, nothing," she said. "I think he took for granted that I would marry him. He had good reason to, I suppose. I thought I would too."

"Well?" Lord Eden looked with some impatience at his twin, who was frowning at the tiled floor.

"I said no, I did not think that would be a good idea,"

Madeline said, looking up. "And I really did not think so. I did not want to marry him at all. I do not know what will become of me, Dom. That was the best offer I have ever had. And I really thought I loved him. I am two-and-twenty already. That is positively old. I cannot possibly appear next year for yet another Season."

"Peignton is all looks and surface charm," her brother said. "He is no great loss, Mad. Someday the right gentleman will come along, and you will live happily ever after. Why did you lose interest in Peignton, anyway? Isn't he a good kisser?"

"Yes, he is altogether too good," Madeline said. "I am not sure he has any business kissing ladies that way. He quite put me to the blush. But all the time it was happening, instead of just blanking my mind and enjoying it, I was remembering how he was so solicitous of my reputation at Lady Sharp's, wanting to take me to Mama so that I would not be contaminated by being in the same room as Miss Purnell. And he was so careful to avoid me for the rest of that evening after I had gone to talk to her. By the next day, of course, it was unexceptionable to consort with me again; Miss Purnell had made herself respectable by engaging herself to Edmund."

Lord Eden sat down beside his sister and crossed one ankle over the other knee. "She should be here soon," he said, "if the rain has not completely halted them on the road. You will help me, Mad?"

Madeline released her hold on the leaf and turned to look up at him. "I really don't think I ought," she said. "It would be far better to leave matters as they are, Dom. Edmund is betrothed to her, and he does not seem unduly unhappy about the idea. He will make the best of the marriage. Edmund is always so excessively kind to other people. Miss Purnell cannot help but like him and respect him."

"But it is not fair." Lord Eden looked earnestly at his sister. "Don't you see that, Mad? Edmund is always cheerful, always kind, always correct. He was only nineteen when Papa died. Three years younger than we are now. And ever since then he has been shouldering the burdens of this family, getting you and me out of scrapes, making sure that our lives are comfortable and carefree. One tends to forget that Edmund is as human as the rest of us. He has feelings and dreams and hopes just as we do."

"It is different," Madeline protested. "Edmund is not restless as you and I are. He is happy, Dom, happy as he is. And he is almost thirty. It is time he married. Miss Purnell is a good bride for him. She is a little strange, I will admit, but I admire her. She has great pride and self-possession. I am determined to like her."

"Sometimes I could shake you." Lord Eden uncrossed his legs and got to his feet again. "Mad, Edmund is being forced into a marriage with a stranger. And a rather strange stranger too, as you have just commented. He doesn't deserve that. Edmund deserves a bride who will love him and appreciate his goodness. He deserves a little happiness in return for that which he is so careful to spread around him. He was happy with Mrs. Borden, you know. Did you know about Mrs. Borden?"

"She was his mistress, I gather," Madeline said with a blush. "I saw her once, Dom. She is a perfect fright. What could Edmund possibly see in her?"

"I don't know," Lord Eden admitted, "but he liked her, Mad. I would not doubt he has given her up now. It is not fair. You have to help me persuade Miss Purnell that she prefers me."

"You were in love with Miss Carstairs just a little while ago," Madeline said, "though I thought her altogether too silly and childish for you, Dom. Have you forgotten her so soon?"

He rounded on her. "What a foolish question, Mad," he said. "I credited you with more intelligence and more understanding. You know that my feelings for Miss Carstairs have nothing to do with the matter. The point is that someone has to marry Miss Purnell. And who else should it be but me? Certainly not Edmund. There is no more reason why Edmund should marry her than there is that the man in the moon should do so. Can you not see that?"

Madeline got to her feet and tapped her hand lightly against his waistcoat. "Yes, I can, Dom," she said. "Of course I can. I just do not want to see you trapped in a bad marriage for the rest of your life, that is all. It would break my heart. But you are right, of course. It would be no better to see Edmund unhappy. But you see, I would not know that Edmund was unhappy because he would never let anyone see it. Oh, yes, I suppose I would know. But I would think, as I have always thought, that it is just Edmund, and that he does not feel things as strongly as you or I. Have I really felt that way about him all my life, Dom? How perfectly horrid I must be."

Lord Eden grinned down at her. "You will help, then?" he asked.

"I don't know how," she said. "Edmund would have my hide if he caught me at it. He considers a betrothal quite as binding as marriage, you know. And there was the announcement in London, and the garden party."

"You do not have to do anything," her brother said. "Just be willing to back me up when I invite her walking or riding. Come with us. Bring Purnell along with you. And be sure to give me a chance to talk to her sometimes without being overheard."

"Oh, famous!" Madeline said, raising her eyes to the ceiling. "I am to be the grand prizewinner, I see. Mr. Purnell gives me the shudders. One never knows what he is thinking. And usually one is thankful one does not. And those eyes!"

"You can rise to the challenge, Mad," he said. "You have never had a problem making conversation. Usually quite the opposite. And talk to Miss Purnell when you can. Nothing much. Just a hint here, a word there. Anything you can think of, without being too obvious. I mean to have her, you know, and I am usually successful with the ladies once I have set my mind to one."

"What a truly modest brother I have," Madeline said. "Perhaps the next few weeks will be quite as exciting as London after all. If only you did not have to be married to Miss Purnell at the end of it, Dom. I think I might like her, but she is all wrong for you. And Mr. Purnell is to be my portion, is he? Yes, very exciting."

"Perhaps you should set out to ensnare him," Lord Eden said with a grin. "We could have a double wedding, Mad."

"Oh, spare me," she said with a shudder. "I think I shall rush into the village and order a dozen spinster's caps. Large size. I shall pull them down over my eyes and my ears so that I might resist the strong temptation to flirt with Mr. Purnell. I would rather flirt with an alligator! Oh, Dom, is that a carriage I hear?"

Both stood very still and listened. Then Lord Eden crossed to the windows and peered through.

"Can't see a thing, what with the rain and the trees," he said. "But those are definitely horses I hear. Come along,

Mad, we should be with Edmund when he welcomes the guests."

"Do you think you might contrive to call me Madeline in public?" she asked. "The other is so lowering, Dom."

ALEXANDRA WAS SITTING quietly gazing through the carriage window. She was feeling relieved that her mother had finally fallen quiet. Lady Beckworth had scarcely stopped fretting since they had left London the day before. She thought the turnpike charges excessive when only two of them were traveling in the carriage; she wished Alexandra would not open a window to breathe in the air or to talk to James, who rode alongside them; she thought the service at the inns where they stopped for their meals slovenly—the servants would not have dared behave so if Lord Beckworth had been with them; the sheets were not properly aired at the inn where they had stayed the night before; they should have stayed there another night rather than risk traveling today in the rain.

Lady Beckworth had been terrified all day that they would be overturned in the mud. And indeed, the carriage had swayed and skidded quite alarmingly on a few occasions. But James had considered conditions quite good enough for travel, and Alexandra trusted her brother's judgment. Now they had turned through the imposing iron gates of Amberley Court and past the stone lodge and the nodding porter, and finally all was quiet as they waited for their first glimpse of the house. Meanwhile they traveled along a densely tree-lined winding driveway. It felt almost as if they were in an enchanted world. James had ridden on ahead, the driveway being too narrow to accommodate both a horse and a carriage traveling side by side.

Alexandra felt her heartbeat quicken. She really did not wish to be where she was. Despite all the publicity that had surrounded the event, she still had not adjusted her mind to her new status as the betrothed of the Earl of Amberley. It was rather strange perhaps that she, who had never known freedom and never expected to know it except in a very relative way as a wife rather than a daughter, had glimpsed it very briefly, lost it almost immediately, and now longed passionately for it.

And yet even that one glimpse had been elusive. How could she be free? If Lord Amberley had not renewed his offer after his grace rejected her, would she have been free of the domination of a man? She would still have belonged to her father, and for the rest of his or her life—she could not have expected any further marriage offers. Her fate would have been an unenviable one, to put the matter lightly.

Why, then, did she not just reconcile her mind to marrying the Earl of Amberley? He was not an unpleasant man. Indeed, he would probably be a far kinder and more indulgent husband than the Duke of Peterleigh would have been. He was certainly younger and more personable. And he had treated her with marked courtesy during the few occasions she had seen him before his return to the country more than a week before. At their betrothal party, in particular, he had taken pains to make it appear that he was actually proud to be her affianced husband.

Why not marry him willingly, then? Pride perhaps? How could she marry a man, knowing that he had offered for her only because he had felt that he had an obligation to do so? He could not possibly wish to marry her. He was a handsome man and a fashionable man. She was a plain, unfashionable woman who had felt all at sea in London. She had had no idea how to go on. She had not known until her arrival there how very different her life had been from that of most of her peers. She did not know how to enjoy herself or how to laugh. She did not know how to show her feelings at all. All her life she had been taught that self-control was one of the most important virtues to cultivate.

The Earl of Amberley could not possibly like her, then. And she could never willingly marry him, knowing that. Life at home with Papa would be preferable. At least that life would be familiar to her.

And did she like Lord Amberley? she asked herself, staring off through the trees beside the carriage. How could she know? They had not really had a chance to get to know each other in London. He had behaved honorably to her and had treated her with marked kindness and courtesy. He had been the perfect gentleman. But the perfect gentleman is not a real person. The Earl of Amberley was. But she had not glimpsed that person at all. He was a total stranger. And a stranger whom, despite everything, she still resented.

He thoroughly disturbed her. That was an absurd admission to make of a gentleman who had such easy, charming manners and such smiling blue eyes. But it was true nonetheless. She was aware of him physically in a way she had never felt with anyone else. She had never been afraid of meeting anyone else's eyes. Yet she was afraid to look into Lord Amberley's, afraid of... What? Drowning? She could think of no other word to describe the sensation.

And she had never been afraid of anyone else's hands. Oh, Papa's perhaps—large, blunt-fingered hands that could inflict pain until one had bitten the inside of one's mouth raw. But hands that had never hinted violence to her? Lord Amberley's were long-fingered, well-manicured hands that nevertheless looked strong. But she dreaded the touch of those hands. They aroused uncomfortable aches in her that she could not quell and that she did not want to feel. They made her aware of her own unawakened femininity.

She feared the Earl of Amberley because she sensed that he could make her into the sort of woman she had only dreamed of being and was frightened of becoming in reality.

Then, of course, there was the fact that he had a mistress. A woman whom he must be very well used to touching. And a woman whose experience would humiliate her and make her feel like nothing at all. She had never felt of much worth, yet she had dreamed of being a duchess, a person of some consequence. Well, she was to be a countess, a person of consequence still. Yet one who had been trapped into marrying a husband who did not really want her, who would lavish all his attention on a mistress.

Fortunately for Alexandra's peace of mind, her attention was distracted from such thoughts by a shriek from her mother beside her. She turned her head sharply to see that the trees on the other side of the road had given place to empty space. Even through the rain she could see a magnificent panorama spread out below them. They were perched on the side of a hill above a deep and wide valley, through which a river wound its way. In the valley were trees, meadows, cultivated lawns, fountains, ornamental gardens, and an arched stone bridge. Low on the hill opposite, and dominating all, was a Palladian mansion of a magnificence to make her catch her breath even at this distance.

"Ooh!" Alexandra's mouth formed the word even if no sound escaped her.

"We will never get down there in all this mud!" Lady Beckworth wailed, fumbling in her reticule for a handkerchief. "We will be overturned and go tumbling into the valley. We will be killed. Knock on the front panel for the coachman to stop, Alexandra."

But Purnell rode up beside the window before Alexandra could comply. The carriage eased to a halt at the same moment. Alexandra pulled down the window.

"You will be quite safe," he said, leaning forward so that a stream of water flowed from the brim of his hat. "The roadway has been heavily inlaid with stone. And the incline is not nearly as steep as you might imagine from here. The road descends quite gradually. Are you all right, Mama?"

"Your papa would never allow this," she said faintly from behind the handkerchief. "He would take us back to the nearest inn, James."

"I would not take any needless risk with your life, Mama," he said, "or with Alex's. Close the curtains over the window, Alex. Mama will not be so frightened if she cannot look down."

Brother and sister exchanged warm smiles before he rode on again. He laid his wet-gloved hand over hers where it rested on the window for a brief moment and squeezed it as he looked down into the valley to the house. Alexandra felt comforted as he rode away. The gesture of sympathy had nothing to do with muddy roads and an incline into a valley, she knew.

She did not close the curtains. Her mother's attention had become too deliberately intent on the Bible she had drawn onto her lap from the opposite seat to stray even once to the window. Her lips were moving in silent prayer. Alexandra gazed down in growing wonder and trepidation at the house and gardens spread out in the valley.

• • •

LORD AMBERLEY SAW THE APPROACH of two carriages and a rider from some distance. He was sitting in the long gallery, whose tall front windows faced east to the hillside that formed the main approach to the house. He had half-expected that their arrival would be delayed until the following day. There were many people who chose not to travel English roads during heavy rain. But he sat there anyway, unable to settle to any other activity.

His betrothal seemed so much more real to him now than it had when he was in London or even in the week he had been at home. In London he had been so concerned to save Miss Purnell from undeserved ostracism and then so intent on seeing that she was fully accepted again by all who had been prepared to shun her, that he had scarcely had time to consider the full implications for himself of his engagement.

And during his week at home, Miss Purnell's arrival had been comfortably in the future. He had much to do to catch up on estate business that his bailiff had been attending to during his absence. Only yesterday and today had it fully dawned on him that his fiancée was coming to his home. Not just a visitor to be entertained and waved on her way after a suitable time. But his betrothed. His future wife. The woman who would occupy this house with him for the rest of their lives.

The strange thing, the ridiculous thing, was that he could not picture to himself Miss Purnell's face. He could see in his mind a rather tall woman of proud and disciplined bearing. He could see dark hair worn in severe fashion. But there was a blank where her face should be. It was controlled and frequently impassive, he knew. Her eyes were dark. But he could form no vivid mental picture. All he could remember of her were wide dark eyes, flushed cheeks and dry lips, wild and luxuriantly wavy hair, long, shapely limbs, and a bed that looked invitingly tumbled.

But that was not Miss Purnell, he knew. Memory had played him false that first time. When he had seen her for a second time, she had been a different woman altogether. The heat of the moment had painted her lovely in his imagination. Miss Purnell was not very lovely, and she was not particularly attractive. She rarely spoke, she held herself stiff and aloof so that it was hard to imagine that she was made of flesh and blood. She flinched from his every touch.

And this was the woman he was to marry. This was the woman with whom he must share his home and his bed and his very self. His hostess. His closest companion. His lover. The mother of his children.

It was a daunting prospect.

Lord Amberley rose to his feet when he spotted the carriages. He watched them make their slow descent to the valley. There was no danger. The stones on the road made it impossible for either hooves or wheels to skid even in the worst weather, but it was natural for strangers to be intimidated by the drop on one side of the road. James Purnell must be the rider, he guessed. Miss Purnell and her mother would be in the first carriage. The other, smaller and plainer, was undoubtedly a baggage coach. Possibly Purnell had brought a valet and Lady Beckworth and Miss Purnell a maid, though it was unnecessary. He had been prepared to assign servants to them.

Lord Amberley left the gallery and walked through to the great marble hall when he saw that the carriages had reached the valley floor and had turned to cross the stone bridge and skirt the formal gardens before driving up to the marble steps at the main entrance to the house. Rain or no rain, he intended to be on the steps to greet his guests. He would have done no less for any visitor. For his future bride, even a winter blizzard would not have kept him indoors.

He greeted James Purnell, who was dismounting from his horse. A footman let down the steps of the carriage and helped Lady Beckworth to descend.

"Good day, ma'am." Lord Amberley took her hand and bowed over it. "How pleased I am that you have arrived safely. Welcome to Amberley Court."

He turned back to the carriage as Purnell offered his mother his arm and hurried her up the steps and inside out of the rain. Lord Amberley waved aside the footman and stretched out his own hand for Miss Purnell's. She put hers in it after a moment's hesitation.

"Welcome, my dear," he said, smiling up into her eyes. "Welcome to your future home."

The steps were already slippery with rain. He released his hold of her hand, placed both hands on her waist, and lifted her to the ground.

"It does not always rain here, I promise," he said gently, noting her hasty withdrawal from his touch. "I have ordered sunshine and warmth especially for you. Come on inside. You will wish to warm yourself and have some tea."

He gave her his arm and hurried up the steps with her. Did she even know that she had not uttered one word? he wondered. He looked down at her again as they entered the hall. Yes, that was what her face was like, of course. Every feature in place where it should be. A marble face. A statue's face. A face that could be plain or quite extraordinarily lovely, depending on the spirit that shone behind it. So far in his acquaintance with her, no spirit seemed to have been present. Except perhaps on that very first occasion.

She had a very small waist. Surprisingly, she had felt as light as a feather when he had lifted her a few moments before.

Lord Amberley turned his attention to his other guests. And suddenly all seemed noise and confusion. His mother, Sir Cedric Harvey, Dominic, and Madeline had all materialized from somewhere to add their greetings to his.

THE RAIN STOPPED DURING the early evening, the clouds dispersed, and a weak sun appeared over the western hills. The grass was wet, but Lord Amberley suggested a stroll in the formal gardens with his betrothed after dinner.

"The walks there are gravel," he explained, "and will not soak the hem of your gown."

Lady Amberley, who had looked cheered at the suggestion of fresh air and a little exercise, was obliged to remain indoors when Lady Beckworth pleaded fatigue from the journey. Sir Cedric Harvey remained with them. Lord Eden too hung back when he realized that his presence would make an odd number. He won a drowning look from his sister, who had already committed herself to the walk and who would be expected to stroll with James Purnell.

Alexandra held to the corners of her shawl as they left the house, and took Lord Amberley's arm only when it would have appeared pointedly rude not to do so. He was not a great deal taller than she, certainly not as tall as either James or Papa. Perhaps that was another reason for her discomfort with him, she thought as he led her across the cobbled terrace to the gardens, which stretched east of the house. She could not hide behind his shoulder as she could have done with a taller man.

"I am disappointed that it was raining when you arrived," he said. "I would have liked you to see the house and gardens from the hills in all their splendor. I am very proud of both, you see."

"They looked quite lovely even in the rain, my lord," she said. "I had no idea that Amberley Court would look as it does."

"I have a distant ancestor to thank," he said, "or perhaps political conditions at that time. The original house was built in the valley here in Queen Elizabeth's time for defensive purposes. We are only two miles from the sea, you know. Any house built on the flatland above would have been visible from the sea. And far less attractively situated, I think."

"James said he thought we must be close to the sea," she said. "But this is not the original house, my lord?"

"No," he said. "It was burned to the ground eighty years ago. The fire was a great tragedy. Many old family treasures were lost. However, my grandparents had excellent taste. They had the present house built, and my grandmother directed the construction of these gardens. You can see them in all their geometric precision from up in the hills. I will take you up there when the sun is shining, and you will see for yourself."

"You are fortunate to live in this part of the country, my lord," she said. "I find Yorkshire somewhat bleak, though I have lived there all my life."

"But not for the rest of your life," he said. "You forget that this will be your home too, once we are married."

He smiled down very directly into her eyes as he spoke, and touched his fingertips to her hand. Alexandra stiffened and looked around hastily to see that James and Lady Madeline were still close by. They had walked down a different path, but were still clearly in sight.

"I would like to think that our betrothal really begins today," he said. "I think of you as more than an ordinary guest. Do you think you could bring yourself to call me by my name? It is Edmund. And may I call you Alexandra?"

"If you wish, my lord," she said doubtfully. She had been taught that it was disrespectful to call any but servants and brothers and sisters by their Christian names.

"But you would feel uncomfortable doing so?" he asked. He had stopped walking and had turned to look at her. He was suffocatingly close.

"Yes," she said. "In my family it is not done. Mama and Papa do not use each other's names. But it will be as you wish."

"Not necessarily," he said. "Do you say so just because I am the man? I refuse to win your compliance on such nonsensical grounds. Mama was quite right in what she said to you at the theater. You must never give in to me just because I am your betrothed or later because I am your husband. Give in to me because you agree with me. Or else disagree with me and argue and fight to win your point if necessary." He smiled down at her, his blue eyes twinkling.

But she would not relax and join in his merriment. "How can that be?" she said somewhat bitterly. "Our society and, more important, our religion are built entirely on the idea that women are subject to their fathers and husbands. Can it be otherwise?"

"I think so," he said, the smile fading. "I disagree with your reference to Scripture, if indeed it is from there that you have taken your ideas. It seems to me that woman was created to be man's equal. Adam was bored, was he not, before Eve was created? It was not because he needed someone to lord it over. He already had a world full of creatures on whom he could exercise his love of power. What he needed was a companion, someone against whose wits he could sharpen his own, someone to discuss with, argue with, fight with, laugh with. Someone to love, no less. And what set me off into this sermon?" He was grinning again.

"And yet," she said quietly, "when men decide that a woman must marry, she has little choice. When men decide that honor dictates a certain course of action, honor becomes more important than a woman's inclination."

His grin disappeared. "Do you refer to yourself?" he asked. "I suppose you were coerced into this betrothal. But by circumstances more than by the will of men, surely. Did your father exert undue pressure on you? You said 'men,' not 'a man.' Am I the other? Or Dominic? Perhaps there is some truth in that. Undoubtedly there is. We are weak creatures, I will admit. Sometimes the problem is that it is impossible to know which course of action is right and which wrong."

Alexandra merely lifted her chin.

"But why are we so serious?" he said. "I believe the question was whether we call each other 'my lord' and 'Miss Purnell' or whether it is now appropriate to become 'Edmund' and 'Alexandra.' We will keep to formality for now, since it seems to be what you wish. But not after our marriage. Not without a fight on my part, that is. I do not believe I could call my wife 'Lady Amberley' or 'my lady.' "

"You may call me Alex," she said hastily. "It is what James calls me. I prefer it to my full name."

He took her hand again and drew it through his arm. He smiled. " 'Alex' it is to be, then," he said. "Thank you. I am doubly honored if I am to share the shortened form with your brother. You are fond of him, are you not?"

"He is the dearest person in the world to me," she said. "Many people do not like him because he is serious and frequently silent and cynical. He has lost his faith in the world, you see, and that is a dreadful thing to happen to any human being. But I know him as he really is. And as he used to be."

He was silent for a moment. They were standing looking into the rainbow colors created by the spray of water from a marble fountain at one side of the garden. "From what I have seen," he said, "I think he returns your regard. I am glad of that. I think it must be a good feeling to inspire such loyalty and affection in you, Alex."

She shivered at the sound of her name on his lips. Almost as if he had caressed her. "I am afraid I have not known many people in my life," she said. "James has been everything to me. I have lavished all my love on him. Edmund." His name was blurted out at the end of her speech, embarrassing her and causing her to pull her hand from his arm and move forward to the edge of the basin into which the water spilled. She held out a hand to the spray.

"Tomorrow I will show you the house," he said from behind her. "I hope you will grow to love it as much as I do." His voice sounded almost wistful.

MADELINE FELT AS IF THE SMILE ON HER FACE must be petrified. She would not be able to remove it if she tried. She chattered determinedly on despite the fact that she had little more than monosyllables in reply from her companion. What could she talk about? She could not remember ever having had to think of a topic of conversation. Talk usually flowed from her and around her. But then, she had never met anyone quite like Mr. Purnell: taciturn, brooding, and disturbingly handsome.

"Do you like the sea?" she asked. She had led him down a different path from that taken by his sister and Edmund. She was afraid that they would overhear her conversation, or lack of it, and think her very foolish. "We are very close, you know. Only two miles."

"I like it," he said. "It represents escape from this island."

She looked up at him, startled, and felt the urge she had had since the start of their walk to reach up and put back the lock of dark hair that had fallen across his brow. She resisted the urge now as she had done then.

"But do you wish to escape?" she asked.

He inclined his head stiffly. "There is only one thing that keeps me on these shores," he said.

"Oh?" Madeline gave in to curiosity before she could check herself. "What is that?"

She did not think he was going to answer. He looked at her, his face a blank mask. "My sister," he said curtly.

"Miss Purnell?" she said, turning onto a path that led even farther away from the other two. "But she is well settled now, sir. She is betrothed to my brother."

He did not reply. When she stole a look into his face, she could not fathom his expression. Contempt? But no, she was reading what was simply not there.

"Any lady would be fortunate indeed to have Edmund as a husband," she said a little more hotly than she had intended. "He is kind and utterly trustworthy. You need have no worries for your sister."

He inclined his head again. "As you say," he said.

Madeline was feeling anger in addition to the irritation his earlier silence had provoked. "If Miss Purnell turns out to be just half as kind and responsible as he, they will be happy indeed," she said.

Again she thought he would not reply. He stopped abruptly beside a fountain that was the companion to the one at the opposite side of the garden, and trailed his hand in the water of the basin. "Alex is not an ordinary girl," he said quietly. "She has had no ordinary upbringing. She has goodness and sweetness and, yes, a great number of other qualities too. But they are deeply repressed. I do not know if any man or woman has the skill or the insight to draw them out."

It was the most Madeline had ever heard him say. She felt an almost overwhelming impulse to place a consoling hand on his sleeve. She clasped her hands very tightly behind her.

"She is to be my sister," she said. "I am determined to try to make a friend of her. So is Mama. And so is Dominic. Where would you go, Mr. Purnell?"

"Where?" he asked blankly, shaking his hand dry and walking on again beside her.

"If you left England," she said. "Where would you go?"

He shrugged. "It does not matter," he said. "Away from here. Away from England. That is the only important thing."

"Away from yourself?" she asked tentatively. "Is that what you wish to escape, sir? It cannot be done, you know. You have to take yourself wherever you go."

She was sorry as soon as she had spoken. It really was a presumptuous and insulting thing to have said, even if it seemed likely to be true. Those very piercing dark eyes looked through her so that she was convinced that he must see the flowers behind her through her head. The mask came down over his face again.

"You are a philosopher," he said curtly. "I thought you were merely a very pretty and silly product of fashionable society."

Madeline winced. She supposed they were now even, having exchanged lowering insults. Though she had not meant hers to be an insult. Mr. Purnell was so hard to like that it seemed probable that he did not like himself. If he could learn to do so, perhaps other people would treat him more warmly and he would be happier. Then he would not feel the need to escape.

"We ride down to the sea quite often," she said. "There are magnificent cliffs and a lovely wide, sandy beach. Perhaps you would enjoy a visit there tomorrow. I think

Dominic is planning to invite Miss Purnell. Do you both ride?"

He nodded curtly.

And that was that for that particular line of conversation, she thought with an inward sigh. What next? The weather? Reminiscences of London? The house and its splendors? His journey? His home? What?

"Dominic wants to join the army," she said, "though both Mama and I vigorously oppose the idea. Mama lost two brothers in the wars, you know, and cannot bear the thought of the same thing happening to Dom. And I cannot let him go. We are twins, you see, and there is a special bond between us. I would not know a moment's peace if he were in Spain. I have heard that the heat and the rains and the mud there are quite as dreadful as the attacks of the enemy, though I do not suppose that is quite true. Not many men would actually die of mud and rain, would they? Though I have heard that the heat has killed men because of all the marching they have to do with heavy equipment and the lack of water and other supplies."

Prattle, prattle, she thought, listening to the sound of her own voice. Very silly, he had just called her. Why was it that she felt very silly with him? Other gentlemen had always made her feel interesting and witty.

But James Purnell, strolling along beside her, his eyes passing over carefully cultivated box hedges and flower beds and gravel walks, was scarcely listening. What had made him say that about wanting to escape? He had never put his deepest desire into words for anyone before, though he thought Alex knew. And now he had bared part of his soul to a young lady he despised himself for finding attractive. He had sworn to himself years ago that he would never again allow another person a glimpse into his inner self. He would never give anyone else a chance to hurt him.

"Soldiers must take risks," he said. "But then, so must we all, to a lesser degree. Life is a risk."

But one can minimize the risk, he thought, by putting on armor and being careful never to take it off.

ALEXANDRA CAME DOWNSTAIRS after breakfast the following morning, feeling almost cheerful. The sun was shining, transforming the view from her bedroom window from lovely to breathtaking. And she was to go riding with Lord Eden, Lady Madeline, and James. Lord Amberley was to be busy at estate business during the morning, so that he could devote the afternoon to showing them the house.

Riding had always been her favorite outdoor activity. Indeed, it had been almost her only outdoor activity. She liked to ride out onto the moors and drink in the wildness of it all with her senses. She had never been allowed to go alone and she was strictly forbidden to gallop, a wild and unladylike activity, according to her father. But it was one command that she had frequently disobeyed. When she was with James, they had often challenged each other to races, and gone galloping over the moors in neck-or-nothing fashion so that it was amazing that neither of them had ever had an accident.

She went out onto the terrace knowing already that she was going to enjoy the morning. They were going down onto the beach, Lord Eden had said. That would be a new and surely glorious experience.

Her three riding companions were already there, all mounted. So were Anna and Walter Carrington and Lord

Amberley, the latter holding the head of a dark mare fitted with a sidesaddle. Alexandra loved it on sight.

"Miss Purnell." Anna, her face alight with eagerness, brought her horse forward as soon as Alexandra appeared at the top of the marble steps. "Walter and I rode over to see if you had arrived safely. Mama said we might, though she warned us that we were not to disturb you, as you were likely to be tired after your journey. But you are to ride to the beach. May we come with you? Dominic says we may if it is all right with you. Please?"

Alexandra smiled. "Hello, Anna," she said. "Of course I have no objection to your coming. But have you ridden a distance already this morning?"

"Only three miles," the girl said, pointing vaguely up the hill behind the house. "You will see our house soon. Mama is going to invite you, though you do not need an invitation. Dominic or Madeline will bring you anytime you wish. Do come soon. I want to show you my colt and my dog. The dog has just had puppies—four of them. They are the prettiest things."

"Anna." Lord Amberley, leading the mare up, was laughing. "Pause for breath, dear. And may not *I* bring Miss Purnell to see the colt and the puppies? Why have I not heard about them, by the way? No, don't answer. I think everyone else is ready to ride."

"May I ride with you, Dominic?" Anna asked, walking her horse across to him.

Lord Amberley turned to Alexandra. "I wish I could come with you," he said. "Unfortunately, I have an appointment with my account books. Somehow they do not seem nearly as inviting as a ride. I shall have to keep reminding myself that I will be spending all the afternoon with you. I look forward to showing you the house. I warn you that I am inordinately proud of it." His grin was almost boyish.

Alexandra felt decidedly guilty as she placed her booted foot in his clasped hands and allowed him to help her into the saddle. She could not wait to get away from him. She felt suffocated by his presence, and so aware of him—his broad shoulders, his thick dark hair, his intensely blue eyes—that she could concentrate on nothing else. She wanted to ride free, to be alone with her own feelings, as she usually was. She did not know how to cope with such intense physical sensations.

"I shall see you at luncheon, Alex," he said, standing back so that she could join Madeline.

"Yes," she said, his use of her name catching at her breath. She could not bring herself to use his. She tried to smile at him. Why was it that her face felt stiff when she was with him, so that every expression was formed with a conscious effort?

"The tide is out this morning, according to Walter," Madeline said. "I am glad. The beach is a great deal larger when it is out. You will be able to see how very splendid it is. Five miles of glorious golden sand, Miss Purnell, and almost a mile from the cliffs to the edge of the tide. When the tide is in, it comes right up to the cliffs so that there is almost no beach at all."

"I am not familiar with the sea," Alexandra said. "But I love wild nature. I love the moors near our home, though they are desolate and can be dreary in poor weather."

"The sea is never dreary," Madeline said. "It is always different. Mama always says that it is the big frustration of her life. She likes to paint it, you see, but she can never capture in paint what she sees before her, she says. For my part, I have never tried. I prefer to paint something that stays still and does not change. Do you paint?"

"It is one of my great loves," Alexandra said, "though I do not believe I have any great talent. But I can sympathize with Lady Amberley. I can never quite reproduce what I see and feel. Perhaps that is the fascination of the task, though. Where would be the satisfaction in doing something that one felt one could do perfectly? There would be no challenge."

Madeline laughed. "You and Mama will get along famously," she said. "Shall we use first names, by the way? I hate calling you Miss Purnell. It makes you sound like an aging spinster. And I noticed that you called me Lady Madeline at breakfast. It sounds horribly formal when we are to be sisters, does it not?"

Alexandra smiled. Informality seemed to be a characteristic of the Raine family. Unfamiliar as she was with such an attitude, she was not sure that she disliked it. "Very well," she said. "I think that is a good idea, Madeline."

She looked closely at her companion as they rode on, talking easily. She envied her. How wonderful it must be to glow so openly with love of life. Madeline was perhaps not beautiful in any obvious sense. She had regular features and hair of no extraordinary color. In height and build she was not very different from Alexandra herself. Her eyes, which were a dark green, were her only unusual feature. And yet she gave the impression of quite vivid beauty. The full force of a sunny personality was in her face and in the graceful, energetic movements of her body.

"We should be able to see the sea in a minute," Madeline said. She raised her voice in order to include the group of four riding a little ahead of them. "There is a strange illusion when you first see the water, is there not, Dom? You would swear that it is much higher than the land. It can be quite frightening. You can imagine it rushing in to swallow up the valley and you in it. You used to tease me about it, Dom. Do you remember?"

Lord Eden turned to look back at them. He wore a boyish grin. "I used to tell you horror stories," he said, "that had you shrieking in terror."

"And then I would chase after you and beat you wherever I could lay my fists," she said.

"When you could catch me," Lord Eden added with a laugh.

"Brothers are dreadful horrors, are they not, Alexandra?" Madeline said, turning to her companion for support.

Alexandra met her brother's eyes and exchanged a smile with him. She could not remember a time when she had had cross words with James or when they had teased each other. She had always assumed that they had a normal relationship for a brother and sister. Was it possible that even in that they were different from others? But she did not care. She would not have things any different.

"There is to be a dance tomorrow at the Courtneys'," Anna said. "Everyone is to be there. Except me, that is. I have begged and begged to be allowed to go. I am fifteen, after all, and this is only the country. But Mama says no, and Papa will do nothing but make jokes. I will wear my feet out before I even make my come-out if I attend dances too soon, he says. Is not that ridiculous, Dominic?"

"It is hard to be almost grown up," he said, smiling indulgently at her. "I tell you what, though, Anna. When you do start attending dances, you will be so pretty that the men will not let you sit down all night. You will be able to dance to your heart's content."

"Oh, do you think so?" she asked, brightening.

"Of course," he said, "that is not much consolation at the moment, is it? We must have Edmund play the pianoforte one day and I shall dance with you in the music room. Just the two of us, and a waltz too. Agreed?" He winked at her.

"Oh, will you, Dominic?" She gazed eagerly and worshipfully at him.

Alexandra caught sight of the sea at that moment. They had ridden to the point at which the valley widened and the river spread into an estuary. The grass had coarsened and was interspersed with sand. Madeline was right. The water did seem higher than the land, even though it was far away, across a wide expanse of golden sand.

"Oh, look, James," she said. "How perfectly magnificent!"

Lord Eden rode up beside her. "It is lovely, isn't it?" he said. "Unfortunately, when one grows up in such a place, one takes it very much for granted. It is only since I have realized that this is not really my home but Edmund's that I have come to know what a very uniquely beautiful place it is. We always like to think that this is one of the most magnificent beaches in Europe, though we have not seen many more to compare."

Alexandra breathed in deeply. There was a salt freshness to the air that was irresistibly exhilarating.

"The beach is a lovely surface to gallop along," Lord Eden said. "I can remember many races here."

Alexandra turned to him with shining eyes. "Is it?" she said. "Oh, yes, I can see that you must be right. May we gallop?"

"Now?" he asked doubtfully. "Are you sure you are up to it, Miss Purnell? Edmund has not given you the friskiest horse from the stables, I see, but he has not given you the most sluggish either."

"It is perfectly manageable," Alexandra said. "Oh, please, may we?"

He looked at her assessingly. "Well," he said, "if you insist. Let me see, now. Do you see that black rock? The one that looks as if it must have toppled down off the cliff?" He pointed off to their right to a large rock isolated on the beach about a mile or more distant.

"Yes," she said, shading her eyes with her hand.

"I'll race you to it," he called with a laugh, spurring his horse forward in a spray of sand before Alexandra could guess his intent.

But she was not to be outdone so easily. While the others turned to watch in some surprise, she urged her horse forward and was after Lord Eden. The sandy surface was unfamiliar to her, but she gave the horse more rein as she became aware of the firmness underfoot and bent low over the horse's neck. With every fiber of her being she was aware of the thundering of the horse's hooves, the salt air whipping against her face, and the horse of her adversary just too far ahead to be caught.

She was laughing when she finally came up to him at the black rock. He had already thrown himself from the saddle and was reaching up, grinning, to swing her down to the sand beside him.

"Unfair!" she said breathlessly. "I demand a rematch, sir. With nothing less than a starting pistol."

"It would make no difference," he said. "Come, Miss Purnell, you must admit that you have met with superior horsemanship. If I were to give you a head start, I should still be waiting here ready to lift you down by the time you finished."

"You will rue those words one of these days," she said, and glanced back along the beach. The others seemed a great distance away. She began to feel uneasy. She should not have ridden off with Lord Eden like this, unchaperoned. Mama would have a fit.

He saw her look and grinned. "The others are coming this way, I believe," he said. "We might as well sit and wait for them."

He suited action to words and seated himself on a flat part of the black rock. After a moment's hesitation, Alexandra joined him there. It did not seem so very wrong to be alone with him like this. She liked Lord Eden greatly. He was sunny-natured, like his sister, handsome, charming, boyish. Yet totally unthreatening. She was as comfortable with him as she was with James.

She supposed that she should dislike him, or at least resent him. He was at the back of all her woes. Without him, she would not at present be at Amberley Court, trapped in a betrothal that was none of her choosing. But she could not resent him. She could almost imagine how that whole mad episode had developed, Lord Eden on the spur of the moment dreaming up an unnecessarily complicated and risky plan to save his sister from a rash elopement. Madeline would have been furious if everything had proceeded according to plan, of course. The two of them would have probably ended in a noisy fistfight. Alexandra smiled to herself as her mind contemplated behavior that was so alien to her own nature and experience. Yet she liked them both.

For his part, Lord Eden was feeling somewhat dazzled. In the past few minutes Miss Purnell had been transformed before his eyes into a strikingly beautiful young lady. Her cheeks were flushed from the exercise, her eyes dancing with merriment, her hair somewhat disheveled beneath the green riding hat she wore, her mouth curved into a smile.

For the first time he had become aware that she could be a vibrant and astonishingly lovely woman.

He had brought her on the ride in the hope of having a private word with her. He had hoped to charm her, to entice her into falling in love with him. He had not expected the task to be easy. Miss Purnell was markedly different from all the young girls he could so easily attract. She appeared to have far more character and to be far more serious. But he had set himself the task anyway.

He must rescue Edmund. Not that he had disliked Miss Purnell in London. Indeed, he had found her surprisingly likable and approachable during that drive in Hyde Park. But he had thought her overserious, not at all the right bride for Edmund. Edmund was quiet and serious himself. He needed a bride who would bring gaiety and brightness to his life. Miss Purnell could never do that. Together they would live a life of unrelieved gloom.

Those *had* been his thoughts. Now he was not so sure. Perhaps there was a great deal more to Miss Purnell than was apparent on a short acquaintance. Certainly the idea of marrying her himself was becoming far more palatable. But then, by the same token, perhaps Edmund too was finding the prospect of marrying her more appealing. Perhaps he would not be thankful after all for being rescued. And it would be deucedly awkward to announce to the world at this late date that Miss Purnell was to marry Dominic, not his elder brother.

Lord Eden gazed out to the distant line of the incoming tide. He hated having to deal with ticklish problems. Give him a daredevil deed to do and he would face it eagerly, without a qualm of fear. Give him a mental problem, and his mind stagnated and his head began to ache. As it was doing now. He shook the problem from his mind and turned back to his companion.

"You have done lots of riding?" he asked. "I will concede, you see, that you are an accomplished horsewoman. Almost worthy of racing against me." He grinned.

She raised her eyebrows and gave him a mock-severe look. "On the moors," she said, "there are miles and miles of wide open space. And I wager I would beat you soundly there. Indeed, I should probably have to ride back to you in order to bind up a broken limb. You would doubtless stumble into a foxhole or a rabbit hole."

He laughed. "I like any kind of outdoor activity," he said. "Hunting, fishing, fowling, playing cricket. Anything. Sometimes I think there are not enough activities in this world to use up all my energy. Perhaps I should try your moors sometime."

"I have never been allowed to spend much time outdoors," she said rather wistfully.

"Wiltshire is lovely too," he said. "That is where my own home is, you know, though I never seem to be able to get out of the habit of thinking of this as home. My estate is quite close to Stonehenge. I hope you will see it one day. Do you like to travel?"

"I do not know," she said with a smile. "In my mind, yes. I would love to see Paris and Florence and Venice and a hundred other places. But perhaps the discomforts of travel would make the reality less appealing than the expectation."

"Ah," he said. "Perhaps we will both see those places one day, Miss Purnell, when the wars are over. Perhaps I will take you on a gondola in Venice. In the moonlight."

She laughed. "And you will sing me a serenade?" she asked. "Or will you hire someone to do it for you?"

He looked sidelong at her smiling face. "I will have to think about that one," he said.

They sat in companionable silence for a few minutes as the other four riders drew closer. Should he say anything? Lord Eden thought. Should he suggest to her yet again that she change her fiancé? Damnation, the idea sounded ridiculous when put in quite those words. Like changing a hat or gloves. He said nothing.

"Dancing tomorrow at the Courtneys'," he said finally. "I will wager it is all in your honor, Miss Purnell. I must have a dance with you. May I?"

"It will be my pleasure, sir," she said. "Shall I write your name in my card now before it fills up?"

"By all means," he said. "I see Walter and your brother thundering along to reserve their own sets."

They were both laughing when the others came up to them.

Alexandra was feeling more carefree than she could remember being as she rode back along the beach with Anna on one side of her and Madeline on the other. How lovely it was to have friendly acquaintances, she thought. How much she had missed during her life. And how she wished now that she had accepted Lord Eden's offer of marriage. She could feel relaxed with him. She could enjoy his company. She could have been feeling happy if she were here as his betrothed.

But perhaps not, she thought after some reflection. Perhaps her feelings would be different if she really were betrothed to him. It was rather different being a gentleman's acquaintance and friend and being his future bride. It would spoil her pleasure in his company, perhaps, to know that she must be his wife, that at some time in the near future she must share the intimacies of marriage with him.

Her carefree mood was not to last for the remainder of the morning, she discovered as they turned their horses into the grassy valley again. Lord Amberley was riding toward them.

"I must have been mad," he said, drawing his horse alongside hers after greeting everyone, "to think that I would be able to concentrate on account books this morning. I have wasted an hour staring at columns and figures that refused to penetrate any deeper into my consciousness than my eyes."

"We have been along the beach for a mile," she said. "I raced with Lord Eden, but he beat me. It was unfair, of course. He was off before I was ready."

"That's Dom," he said. "He was fortunate he was racing against you and not Madeline. I assume you behaved like the perfect lady when you finally came up to him. Madeline would have launched herself at him, fists first."

They lapsed into silence. But it was not the comfortable silence she had felt earlier with Lord Eden. Alexandra found herself searching her mind for something to say. She found herself stiffening and feeling dull and uninteresting. She found herself so thoroughly aware of him that she forgot the presence of the five other riders quite close by.

"You are an experienced rider, then?" Lord Amberley said. "I was not sure when I was selecting a horse for you. I suppose I should have asked you at breakfast. What are your other interests, Alex? I know so little about you."

"I like music," she said, "and painting." She did not want to answer. She did not want any of her inner life to be known by this man. She wanted to protect herself against him.

"Music?" he said. "Do you play an instrument? Or sing? Or do you prefer to listen?"

"I play the pianoforte," she said. "I have no particular talent. I play for my own amusement."

He smiled. "I play too," he said. "I will enjoy showing you the music room this afternoon, Alex. I look forward to hearing you play. But if you are like me, you prefer to play when there is no audience. You must feel free to use the room whenever you wish."

"Thank you," she said. She glanced across into his face. Did he understand? He liked to be alone too? She could not bear it if he was forever encouraging her to play for him. She would not be able to do it. She would come to hate music.

"What do you like painting?" he asked. "I am afraid I have no skill with a brush. Mama likes to paint, though why, I do not know. Her attempts seem to frustrate her more than bring her pleasure."

"I can understand that," she said. "She is an artist, not just a dabbler, I would guess. No one who takes an art seriously can gain unalloyed pleasure from it."

He looked at her keenly. "Ah," was all he said.

"I have a library I am proud of," he said. "Do you read?"

"My father's library is restricted," she said. "I am afraid my reading has been confined mainly to the Bible and some sermons and poetry."

"Wordsworth?" he asked. "Have you read any of his poems?"

"No," she said.

"I will lend you my copy of his *Lyrical Ballads,*" he said. "Perhaps you will not like his poems. They are very different from what has been written in the last century. But if you like nature—wild nature, I mean—then I think you will at least understand what he is trying to do. He is intent on showing us the natural world not as we see it with the eyes but as we feel it with the heart." He laughed. "Am I making sense to you?"

She looked back at him with wide eyes. For the moment she had forgotten her awkwardness with him. "Oh, yes," she said.

The house had come into view ahead of them, past the green valley. It was quite breathtakingly lovely. Alexandra felt almost an ache inside her as she gazed along the gray stone of the eastern front with its pillared and pedimented entranceway and at the south wing with its tall arched windows. It was such a magnificent tribute to the work of man, and yet blended so perfectly with the scenery.

"I never look at it," Lord Amberley said quietly from beside her, "without feeling something like a lump in my throat and an almost unbelieving gratitude that it is mine. Why me? To think of all the thousands and millions of other people to whom it might have belonged! I pray that I will never take it for granted. Whenever I return from London and see it from the top of the hill, as you did yesterday, I wonder how I could have borne to leave it. I am afraid I may well become a hermit in my old age."

He smiled at her in that way he had that made his eyes impossible to look into. Alexandra turned away from him.

"It is lovely," she said, hearing the echo of her words long after they were spoken and realizing all their inadequacy to express how she had felt looking at it moments before when it had first come into view.

His voice was brisker when he spoke next. "I left my mother and yours in the gardens," he said. "I hope we will be able to offer Lady Beckworth sufficient entertainment while you are here."

"Mama is quite content to sit indoors with her sewing,"

Alexandra said. "I don't think anyone need worry about entertaining her."

"Well," he said, "I believe my mother has a few visits planned. You will find yourself much in demand, you know, Alex. Everyone I have spoken to in the last week is eager to meet my future countess. You are a great local event. I hope you will not find your life too demanding. I shall try to see that you also have time to yourself. You like to be alone, do you not? In that way you and I are alike."

Alexandra looked at him, startled. She had not thought that there could be any likeness between them. And she felt true alarm. Coming to Amberley had been ordeal enough. The prospect of spending a few weeks with her betrothed and his family had been daunting. She had been warned in London that she would also be called upon to meet and socialize with his aunt and uncle. Must she also meet other neighbors? But of course, she might have guessed as much. She had realized during her month and a half in London that her own family was unusually unsociable. It was not normal almost never to visit others or be visited by them.

"I shall be pleased to meet your neighbors, my lord," she said.

He turned to smile at her.

"Edmund," she corrected herself, and blushed.

11

LORD AMBERLEY WAS PLEASED THAT HIS mother had decided to join him during the afternoon, when he took his guests on a tour of the house. She was able to listen to Lady Beckworth's comments and answer her questions while he concentrated on those of his betrothed and her brother. He found himself nervous. He normally loved showing the house and its treasures to visitors, and he had looked forward to that afternoon. But in the event he found that Alex's opinion of what she saw was too important to him for him to relax.

She was to be his wife. They would live much of their life together in this house. And it was so very precious to him. It would depress him if she did not love it almost as much as he did.

The trouble with Alex was that it was so difficult to know what she was thinking or feeling. He could understand after knowing her for a few weeks that she had learned more self-discipline in her one-and-twenty years than anyone else he had known. He recognized that her very upright bearing, her raised chin, her impassive expression were a mask behind which the real woman hid. And it was his task to penetrate that mask, to persuade her to put it off forever with him.

It would not be easy. He did not even know who the real Alexandra Purnell was. He did not know how much there was behind the mask. He had had only a few tantalizing glimpses, most notably that morning. He had been enchanted when he had given in to his restlessness and ridden down the valley to meet her and the others. Her face had been flushed and animated, her eyes alive. And she had raced along the beach with Dominic? It was hard to imagine her doing anything so spontaneous.

What had been her feeling about the house when she had slowed her horse almost to a standstill as it had come in sight? She had seemed unconscious of both him and the others, who had ridden past them. And yet when she had spoken, she had been so lukewarm in her praise that he had felt rather as if he had been slapped in the face.

Lord Amberley took his guests first through the state apartments, through the grand dining room and drawing room and ballroom, full of treasures of painting and sculpture that had been gathered during the last century, first by his grandfather, and then by his father during his grand tour. The rooms were used only rarely, he explained, but at least once a year during the annual summer ball that his grandparents had made a tradition of in the neighborhood.

"My grandmother was responsible for the wall of mirrors," he explained in the ballroom. "Apparently she was afraid that in the country there would be too few guests to make balls splendid enough occasions. So every year we have candles and guests doubled in number."

Alex, he saw, was looking immaculate again after her ride of the morning. And she was distant from him, not hostile, not unresponsive, but totally unknowable. It was impossible to tell whether she liked what she saw or not.

He took his guests through the state bedroom with its gilded and painted ceiling and its ornate canopied bed hung with gold hangings, and listened to Lady Beckworth's enthusiastic comments. His mother was explaining to her that the room had never been occupied by royalty, though the one in the old house had reputedly been slept in by Queen Elizabeth herself during one of her progresses through the country.

He should have kissed Alex that morning, Lord Amberley was thinking. There had been a chance, when they had returned to the stables. The others had already dismounted and moved away. And he had thought of kissing her as he lifted her down. She had looked lovely. And he had set himself the task of getting close to her, physically as well as emotionally. He did not want to marry her without ever having touched more than her hand. And he did not want a marriage in which his only physical contact with his wife was the nightly ritual for the begetting of his children.

He must begin touching Alex, kissing her occasionally. It did not seem to be too difficult a task he had set himself. But with Alex it was. She made herself appear so thoroughly untouchable that he wondered how she would react to being kissed. And she was certainly not the sort of woman one looked at and dreamed of touching. He had let the opportunity pass him by in the stables that morning.

He led his guests into the library, one of his favorite rooms. It was a large room, three walls lined with bookcases and filled with books, which his grandfather and his father had collected and which he had added to.

"I have made it into a sitting room as well, as you

can see," he said, indicating the elegant Adam furniture grouped around the marble fireplace. "I spend a great deal of time here."

"What is the painting on the overmantel?" Purnell asked, strolling forward to examine the Apollo with his lyre more closely.

Lord Amberley joined him there after glancing at Alexandra, who was examining the books in one of the bookcases. She turned to him when he came up behind her a few minutes later.

"I did not dream that so many books existed," she said. "One could spend an eternity in this room and not be bored."

He smiled down at her. Her eyes were dark and wide and for the moment defenseless. "Will a lifetime of access to the room suit you?" he asked.

"Do you have that book of poems you told me about?" she asked. "The one about nature?"

She followed him to another bookcase, from which he took a leather-bound volume that looked as if it had been used a great deal.

"There are poems by two poets in here," he said. "Perhaps you will like Coleridge's too. They are splendid works of the imagination. I prefer the others because I can relate to them more closely. You might like to try the poem about Tintern Abbey. The scene described reminds me somewhat of Amberley."

She took the book from his hands and held it against her. "May I take it with me?" she asked.

"Of course." He smiled. "Anything that is mine is yours too, Alex."

She flushed and looked sharply down at the book.

"The music room is next to this," he said. "Come, I want you to see the pianoforte."

It was all so very splendid, Alexandra thought. Overwhelming. It was very clear that Lord Amberley loved his home. Not just his voice and manner as he showed them each room and pointed out its treasures revealed the fact, but also the details of the rooms themselves. The library was clearly a central room in his home. It was no mere showpiece. It was used. And the music room made her ache with longing. It was a large room and almost bare. The only major piece of furniture in it was the pianoforte, a rich work of art in itself, and with a tone to match, as she had been able to tell from running her fingers over the keyboard.

Anyone who did not truly love music would have crammed the room with other furnishings. Music must matter to Lord Amberley. She wished she could hear him play. But she would not ask him to do so. She hated to be asked herself.

"Alexandra is quite accomplished on the pianoforte," her mother said.

"Oh, are you?" Lady Amberley was smiling at her. "So is Edmund, you know, and Madeline to a lesser degree. She will not practice. Will you play for us, Alexandra?"

"Oh, not now," she said. "I am out of practice."

"Perhaps some other time," Lord Amberley said. "You must come here whenever you wish, Alex, and get used to the instrument. Each one is different, you know."

She was grateful to him for the quiet way in which he had smoothed over the moment. And quite overwhelmed by it all. How could she be this man's countess, mistress of this splendid house? The reality of her situation was becoming more painfully obvious to her as the hours and days went by. She ran her hand over the smooth shining wood of the pianoforte as her mother and Lady Amberley walked out into the great hall. James was already out there, examining the marble busts that lined the walls.

"Alex," Lord Amberley said from behind her, "you are feeling the pressure of being here as my betrothed, are you not?"

"Yes." She turned to face him, his book clasped against her.

"You need not," he said. "I will try not to put unnecessary demands on you. I like to use this room as an escape or at least as a place in which to be alone for a while. And the library too. You must feel free to do likewise. I would like you to start thinking of this house as your home. I am sure it is difficult. I try to imagine what it must be like for a woman, who must leave the home she has been familiar with all her life and go to live in her husband's. It must be unsettling in the extreme."

"Thank you." She tried to smile. "The house is lovely."

He took them into the green salon at the south front of the house, and explained that it had been designed and furnished especially for his grandmother, who disliked the main reception salon next to it.

"She objected to the heavy crimson color of the walls and furnishings," he said, "and to the ornate gilded chairs. Grandpapa would not change that room because he felt it made an impressive contrast to the marble hall for visitors. So he had this room done for her."

"They were always quarreling, those two," Lady Amberley said with a laugh. "But no one ever doubted their deep love for each other either. They always managed a compromise when their differences were irreconcilable."

"I wonder the countess would dare to express disapproval of her husband's taste," Lady Beckworth said.

Alexandra was enchanted with the room, which was all white and gold except for the green carpet. It was like a garden. She crossed to one of the long windows, which looked out on the rose arbor.

"Grandfather had it placed just there deliberately," Lord Amberley said, coming up behind her. "It seems almost an extension of the room, does it not? Or perhaps the room seems to be an extension of it."

"I think she must have been happy here," Alexandra said. "This room was made for happiness." Her heart ached with a longing that she could not identify.

Lady Amberley had already taken Purnell's arm and led him and Lady Beckworth into the long gallery.

"She used to sit here during the mornings with her sewing," Lord Amberley said, "though the room was not intended for such a use. I used to come in here sometimes when I could escape from my nurse, or from my tutor when I was a little older. When I was a very small child, I used to stand on the chair behind her—she always sat straight, never touching the back of her chair. I liked to watch the design of her embroidery take shape. She used to make me take off my shoes, but she would never scold or shoo me off back to the nursery. And when my nurse would finally come, Grandmama would always lie and say that she had invited me to visit her."

Alexandra turned and looked up at him. That ache had become almost unbearable. "How wonderful it must have been," she said, "to have someone—just one person—who did not always point out just your faults. And someone who would defend you even though both you and she must have known that you were in the wrong. You must have been distraught when she died. How old were you?"

"Thirteen," he said. "I grieved very deeply, as did we all. She was quite a character. But she was not my only advocate. Love has always been the ruling force in this family."

Love, not discipline? "Love?" she said, looking into his smiling eyes and clasping her book firmly against her stomach. "Is it enough? What about discipline and training?"

"Oh, I had my fair share of both," he said. "I always knew, sometimes quite painfully so, when I had done something that was unacceptable. But yes, love is enough, Alex. Discipline, even punishment, flow from it. I was never in doubt that I was loved quite unconditionally."

There was a tickle in the back of her throat that she had to swallow to control. She was on the verge of tears, she realized in some surprise. Had she always been loved by her parents? She was not sure. She had always assumed so, though she had felt too that she must earn their love. And sometimes, try as she would, she had not been able to live up to their expectations. Unconditional love?

He reached out and touched her cheek with his fingertips. "You will be part of this family, Alex," he said. "You will see for yourself."

She did not shrink from his touch. It comforted her, soothed the ache in her throat.

And then she closed her eyes as his mouth came down to cover hers softly, warmly. His lips parted over hers. She could taste him. He was part of the comfort of the room, the love that his grandmother had brought and left there.

But suddenly she was pushing against him with the book and staring at him in shocked disbelief. She could feel the color flooding her face. "Oh!" she said. And feebly, "How dare you!"

"Forgive me," he said. He did not move back from her. His blue eyes looked gently down into hers. "I did not mean to insult or to frighten you, Alex. I want to show you affection. You are to be my wife."

Her back was to the window. She thought she would suffocate or drown in his eyes. "Affection?" she said. "We are not married yet, my lord. You take liberties that you have no right to."

He took a step back. "I have been too hasty," he said. "Forgive me, please, Alex. I did not mean to upset you."

But he had upset her. Her feelings were in turmoil. The intimacy of the moment had terrified her almost to the point of panic. But it was, when all was said and done, only a kiss. How appallingly naive and straitlaced he must think her. And not without reason. It would have been better far to have passed off the moment without comment. And she had not been guiltless. She had invited his kiss, even though she had not realized at the time that that was what she was doing.

"Come," Lord Amberley said, holding out an arm to her, "let us join the others in the long gallery, shall we? It is my favorite room in the house."

Alexandra focused all her efforts on bringing herself under control. She felt so dreadfully foolish. And very bewildered. She straightened her spine, drew back her shoulders, lifted her chin, and took his arm.

But a footman appeared in the doorway before they reached it.

"Mr. and Miss Courtney have been shown to the drawing room, my lord," he said with a bow.

"How opportune," Lord Amberley said to Alexandra after sending the footman to take the same message to Lady Amberley in the gallery. "I am sure everyone is ready for tea. I am afraid I sometimes get carried away when I am showing off the house. I will show you the gallery and the chapel some other time. If you wish to see them, that is."

"Yes, I do," she said.

"Mr. Courtney is one of my more prosperous tenants," he said. "I had hoped that you would not be subjected to visitors until you had had a day to recover from your journey. But you had Anna and Walter this morning, and now this. I hope you will not mind."

"No," she said.

He looked silently down at her as they climbed the marble stairs to the drawing room. She dared not look across at him and meet those blue eyes at such close quarters. She only barely had her feelings under control.

"Say you forgive me, Alex," he said quietly just before they reached the double doors leading into the drawing room. "I am more sorry than I can say to have discomposed you."

"You have not discomposed me," she said, looking straight ahead at the back of the liveried footman who was about to open the doors for them. "And there is nothing to forgive, my lord."

" 'My lord,' " he repeated softly.

"Edmund," she said.

MR. WILFRED COURTNEY WAS an extremely large man, who creaked inside his stays but still filled every chair he sat in almost to overflowing. His powerful neck bulged from his high starched collar. His face was florid and genial, his head bald and shining. He looked like a prosperous farmer who lived off the fat of the land. And in his particular case, looks did not deceive.

His daughter looked as if she could not possibly be his offspring. Tiny and dainty, she had masses of auburn ringlets, large hazel eyes that looked eagerly on the world, expressive eyebrows and thick lashes, both of which features she knew how to use to advantage. Susan Courtney, apple of a doting father's eye, sister of four elder brothers, eternal pride of a mother who had never been more than passably pretty herself, had been raised to believe that life had more to offer her than another farmhouse and another farmer like her father.

She rose and curtsied low when Lord Amberley led Alexandra into the room, and again when the two older ladies and James Purnell followed them. She peeped shyly into his lordship's face when he presented Alexandra, and more searchingly into his betrothed's. She looked up at Purnell from beneath her dark lashes and blushed becomingly.

Mr. Courtney pumped Lord Amberley's hand and boomed his hearty congratulations. "I have been saying to Mrs. Courtney," he declared, "and she agrees with me, your lordship, as do all my sons and little Susan here, that you could not have done better for us all in these parts than to present us with a new countess. No offense, ma'am." He bowed and creaked in Lady Amberley's direction. "But we will be particularly honored to have two Lady Amberleys."

"Do be seated, sir," Lady Amberley said, nodding graciously in acknowledgment of his compliment and seating herself after gesturing Lady Beckworth to another chair. "Yes, we are all delighted at the prospect of welcoming Miss Purnell into the family. She has done us a great honor. Do sit down, Miss Courtney. How pretty you are looking, my dear. Gracious, it seems but last year you were a child."

The girl laughed. "I am all of seventeen, your ladyship," she said. "I have been allowed to sit at table with guests and dance in company for the last year now. Papa had an offer for me just after Christmas, but it was not a very advantageous one. He asked me, but I begged him to decline. It was Mr. Watson."

Mr. Courtney beamed fondly at his daughter. "We don't have to sell our little girl to the first bidder," he said with a rumbling laugh. "We can do better for her than Watson. I am sure you will agree, my lady."

"And yet Watson is one of the more reliable and honest of my tenants," Lord Amberley said. "Even if you could not accept his offer, Miss Courtney, I am sure that you must be gratified to have received it."

"Oh, quite so, my lord," she said, looking up under her lashes at James Purnell and blushing again. "But he is exactly twice my age. I must admit a preference for someone younger and more handsome."

Lady Beckworth had been looking disapprovingly at Susan Courtney from the moment the girl had opened her mouth. "Age and looks have little to say in the choice of a husband," she said. "I am surprised that your papa has allowed you a voice in the matter. He would probably make a far wiser choice than you." She turned to Mr. Courtney. "A child of seventeen cannot know her own mind, sir."

He laughed, seeming quite unoffended. "I always look at it this way, my lady," he said. "It is little Susan here who will have to live with a husband for the next forty or fifty years, not me. She should at least be allowed to choose someone who will not make her feel ill every time she has to look at him." He laughed heartily.

"You have a point there," Lady Amberley said, exchanging an amused glance with her son. "Ah, here come Madeline and Dominic. And Sir Cedric."

Miss Courtney jumped to her feet again and her father hauled himself to his.

"Ah, my lord and my lady," he said. "It is always a treat to look on youth and fashion. And good day to you, sir."

Susan meanwhile was curtsying to Madeline and darting glances at her fashionable muslin gown and short fair curls, and to Lord Eden and blushing.

"Why, it is Susan," he said, coming forward and reaching for her hand. "It must be two years since I saw you last. You were a mere child."

"I was sent to stay with my Aunt Henshaw last summer, my lord," she said. "And I am seventeen now."

"And all quite grown up," he said, grasping her hand and keeping it within his. "And it used to be Dominic, Susan."

"Oh," she said breathlessly, "it would not be seemly now, my lord."

"Do sit down," he said. "May I sit here beside you? You must tell me if you still like to play with all the new kittens on your farm."

"Twenty-three of them we had at the last count, your lordship," Mr. Courtney said with a booming laugh. "My Howard drowns the new ones whenever he can, but if Miss here gets wind of it, she cries until we are all fit to cry with her."

"They are such pretty, helpless creatures, my lord," she said, looking earnestly up into Lord Eden's eyes. "I do not know how anyone could be so cruel as to even think of killing them." She peeped across at James Purnell, who was sitting close by, his eyes on her.

"Do you eat beef and pork and mutton and chicken, ma'am?" he asked unexpectedly.

"Why, yes," she said with a blush. "We frequently have two meat dishes at a meal. More even if we have guests, as we frequently do."

"Do you not pity the cows and pigs and sheep and chickens?" he said.

"One does not like the thought of killing them, naturally," she said. "But one must eat, sir. I would not be able to endure watching the butchering, of course. I am perfectly sure I would quite faint away. I always do at the sight of the merest drop of blood." She shifted her gaze back to Lord Eden.

"Perhaps it is a pity for their sakes that they are not pretty animals," Purnell said.

Mr. Courtney laughed. "Right you are, sir," he said. "We would be overrun with animals. And talking of guests, my lord." He turned to address himself to Lord Amberley. "Mrs. Courtney sent me with the express purpose of inviting all present company to dinner tomorrow evening. Nothing very formal, you understand. Just four or five courses. A few more of our friends are to join us in the parlor afterward. Miss here has persuaded us to allow some dancing. Those of us who do not indulge in such exertions will play cards in the dining room when the covers have been removed."

Lord Amberley smiled at Alexandra, seated beside him on a love seat, and took her hand in his. "We would be delighted to accept your invitation," he said. "I have been telling Miss Purnell how eager I am to begin showing her off to my neighbors."

"And I don't wonder at it neither," Mr. Courtney said. "Such a lovely lady. Mrs. Courtney and I are only anxious lest you decide to wed somewhere else. You would doubtless be able to invite dozens of fashionable guests if the nuptials were in London, but here you would be among friends, my lord. Friends and well-wishers."

Lord Amberley smiled at Alexandra again. "We have not discussed the matter," he said. "But we will have to consider your suggestion, will we not, my dear?"

"Yes," she said, looking at his hand, in which her own lay, rather than into his eyes. She looked up at the beaming face of Mr. Courtney. "I think this is a good part of England, sir. Friends are important."

"Right you are, miss," he said. "I was about to take my leave with my little girl here, but I see the tea tray has just been brought in, and I never say no to a cup of tea." He patted his ample stomach and laughed. "Perhaps it would be as well if I sometimes did."

"Two of the officers from the regiment will be coming tomorrow night," Susan was telling Lord Eden. "They were at the Misses Stanhope's tea on Monday last and were excessively amiable. They accepted invitations from Sir Peregrine Lampman and Mrs. Cartwright as well as ours."

"Indeed?" he said. "I do not know whether to be pleased or dismayed, Susan. Am I to have to compete against uniforms?"

"Oh, la," she said, gazing at him with large hazel eyes, "you do not need a uniform to look handsome, my lord."

He grinned at her. "I take that as a compliment, Susan," he said. "Tell me, are there to be any waltzes tomorrow?"

"Mama said no at first," she said. "But Captain Forbes particularly asked her at the Stanhope tea and he is so very fashionable that Mama could not bring herself to say no. Besides, Howard reminded her that all our guests from Amberley Court must be familiar with the waltz, having just come from London. Mama has said we may dance a few."

"Splendid!" he said. "Will you reserve the first for me, Susan?"

"I do not believe I would be able to acquit myself well with such a fashionable gentleman," she said with a blush.

"Nonsense," he said. "What you do not know, it will be my delight to teach you, Susan." He watched her dark eyelashes fan across her flushed cheeks, and glanced downward to her well-rounded breasts, which were moving with her quickened breathing beneath the thin muslin of her dress.

Lady Amberley began to pour the tea from a silver tea urn into Wedgwood china cups, and Madeline rose to her feet to hand them around.

MADELINE AND ALEXANDRA WENT strolling in the rose arbor after the guests had left. The day was still sunny and warm. The air was heavy with the perfumes of many flowers and made drowsy by the droning of insects and the humming of bees.

"We grew up in close association with several of our neighbors," Madeline explained. "We were never made to feel as if we belonged to a race apart merely because we were from Amberley and had titles to our names."

"Then you must have grown up with many friends," Alexandra said. "That would have been pleasant."

"And enemies," Madeline said with a grin. "I never was popular with the boys because I always wanted to do whatever Dom was doing. And it was usually something forbidden or something deemed unsuitable for girls. Dominic and I were forever squabbling about the matter at home, though he would never criticize me in public."

"But surely you were not allowed to play with the boys, anyway," Alexandra said.

Madeline looked at her with a smile. "But of course," she said. "There were no rules. Only what we children imposed upon ourselves or upon those weaker than ourselves. Children are inveterate bullies, you know."

"I was never allowed playmates," Alexandra said. "The rector's children would have been considered suitable, perhaps, but they were all boys."

"None?" Madeline said. "What a sad little girl you must have been. You were doubtless very happy when the time came to go away to school."

"I was kept at home," Alexandra said, "with a governess. Papa could never find a school of whose rules and moral principles he sufficiently approved."

Madeline gazed at her in some horror. "You have never had friends?" she said. "How perfectly dreadful!"

"What one does not have, one does not miss," Alexandra said. "And I had James."

"Your brother stayed at home too?" Madeline asked.

"No." Alexandra reached out to cup a dark red rosebud between her fingers and bent over it to smell its fragrance. "He went to school and to university for two years. He did not finish there. He would not go back after... Well, something happened to upset him and he did not go back. He has always been my closest friend."

Madeline could think of nothing to say. It seemed unimaginable to her that anyone would be able to make a friend of the silent and morose Mr. Purnell. But if one had no choice and if one had never had a true friend, she supposed that it might be possible.

"You are a very good rider," she said, changing the subject. "I thought for a minute this morning that you were going to catch up to Dominic. And he is the best rider in our family."

"Riding has always been one of my main pleasures," Alexandra said. "I enjoyed the gallop this morning, though I should not have done so. It was always strictly forbidden at home."

"I could see that Dominic was enjoying your company," Madeline said. "Perhaps I should not say this, but he was disappointed, you know, when you refused him in London, and even more disturbed when he heard that you had accepted Edmund. I think he is still not happy about your betrothal."

"It has been altogether an embarrassing situation," Alexandra said after some hesitation. "Both of your brothers were placed in a nasty predicament. I have done what seems best under the circumstances."

"I believe Dominic has a *tendre* for you," Madeline said. She flushed at her own lie. "It is strange, but we have never heard Edmund say that he planned to marry. I think he might have turned into one of those men who are devoted to their homes and duties and never take a wife." She wished she had not started this particular speech. "Perhaps we should be thankful that he is to marry after all."

Alexandra said nothing, but her pace had increased. She was walking in the direction of the house, no longer showing interest in the flowers around her. Madeline bit her lip and hurried to catch up. No one had ever said she was good at intrigue. She had meant to make subtle hints. Instead she had been quite bluntly insulting. She had almost told

Alexandra that Edmund did not want her. And it was Edmund to whom she was engaged.

Damnation take her twin, Madeline thought in most unladylike language. In future let him do his own wooing and his own lying. It was quite nonsensical to think of him married to Alexandra anyway.

12

"NOT AT QUITE SUCH AN ANGLE, NANNY." Alexandra frowned as she felt the feather of her riding hat brush against her neck. "It is intended to be worn straight on the top of my head."

"Not so, lovey," Nanny Rey said, surveying her charge's mirrored image over the top of her spectacles. "Hats are meant to be worn somewhere on the head, but no one ever said they were to be worn at the exact center. Ladies' hats are meant to look fetching. This one looks fetching worn at an angle. A jaunty angle."

Alexandra laughed despite herself. "But I do not wish to look fetching or jaunty," she said. "I want to look correct, Nanny."

"Correct!" Her nurse sniffed and moved the hat up an inch on Alexandra's head. "With such a handsome lord as yours? And a kind man too, lovey. It is time you started to think about more than being correct."

Lord Amberley had stopped Nanny the day before as she was about to disappear down the servants' stairs. He had asked her if she found all to her comfort at Amberley Court and if there was anything he could do for her that might make her feel more at home. Nanny had answered in the affirmative to the first question and in the negative to the second, bobbed a curtsy, and made her escape. But she had been wholly enslaved by his blue eyes and his kindly smile.

Alexandra wandered to the window of her bedchamber after Nanny Rey had left. She buttoned her velvet riding jacket to the chin, glancing at the clear blue sky as she did so. She sighed. If only Nanny knew how much more she had thought about in the past two days than just doing what was correct!

She was to go riding northward through the valley with Lord Amberley. Just the two of them alone. She had been very reluctant to accept the invitation when she knew that James was going with Sir Cedric Harvey up onto the western hills to see the view from the top of the cliffs, that Lord Eden and Lady Madeline were going visiting, and that Lady Amberley and Mama were driving into the village of Abbotsford to call on the rector. She had not wanted to ride alone with his lordship, but James had not been his usual sympathetic self when she had appealed to him. He had told her that she must begin to accustom herself to the company of the man she had chosen to marry. And even Mama had considered it quite unexceptionable for her to ride alone with her betrothed on his own land.

So go she must. But she did not look forward to doing so. And there was the social gathering at the Courtneys' to look forward to that evening. She would meet an unknown number of Lord Amberley's neighbors and acquaintances. Her betrothal and coming marriage were becoming quite horrifyingly real to her. She felt as if a net were closing around her. She should not have come, she had thought more than once. Not to his home. Even her awareness of the foolishness of the thought did not amuse her. She had to come to his home sooner or later.

Of course, until she had arrived at Amberley, she had not known what Edmund's home meant to him. Home to her had always meant a house where she lived in relative seclusion according to prescribed rules. It had been the anchor of her existence, the place where she knew she was being trained for the real life ahead of her—the life of the Duchess of Peterleigh.

Amberley was different. Very different. Even after more than a month spent in London, Alexandra had not realized just how very different her life had been from that of most other people around her. Now she was beginning to realize it. Amberley was a place of happiness, a place where everyone seemed free to say and do whatever he or she wanted. It was a place of unashamed beauty. A place where love was important. And it was not the sort of love that she had been given. It was a warm and free love in which censure seemed to play very little part.

Amberley was a place of friendship, a place where one could be invited to dine with a mere tenant farmer and accept that invitation without any sense of either outrage or great condescension. It was a place where a child from the schoolroom could ride with his elders and talk freely with them. A place where children were free to play with those of lesser social status and where boys were free to mingle with girls. Where girls were sent to school so that they might befriend other girls, not withheld for fear that they might become contaminated by those of looser morals.

It was a place where people did things together for enjoyment, not in order to judge one another. She had been persuaded the evening before—by Sir Cedric—to go down to the music room to play the pianoforte. Not to give a recital to a silent and critical audience, but to accompany his singing.

"Will you oblige me by coming, Miss Purnell?" he had asked when everyone else was still drinking tea in the drawing room after dinner. "You play the pianoforte, I have been told, and I love to sing. Perhaps this will be my only chance to have you as an accompanist. In future, you may wish to make all sorts of excuses in order to avoid the pleasure."

"How very unfair you are being to yourself, Cedric," Lady Amberley had said with a laugh. "You know very well that I always come to listen to you from choice. He has a lovely baritone voice, Alexandra, as you will hear for yourself. I shall come along too. Would you care to join us, Lady Beckworth?"

It had ended up with them all going downstairs except James and Lord Eden, who had gone walking up into the hills. And it had been a relaxed evening in which everyone had been willing to play or sing, talent notwithstanding.

And Lord Amberley had talent, she had discovered. He had played a short Bach fugue that had held her spellbound for a few minutes.

And Amberley was a place where people touched and showed open affection.

Alexandra fingered the feather of her hat as it curled around her ear. She was staring sightlessly from the window. She had forgotten entirely that Lord Amberley might already be awaiting her downstairs. Yes, she was very strange indeed. Quite out of tune with her world. And not at all sure whether she wanted to try to fit in or whether she would deliberately hold herself apart from it all.

What would it have been like to grow up in such a place, with parents and grandparents who loved her unconditionally, as Lord Amberley had put it? Parents who did not make her feel that their love and the love of God must be earned and could easily be forfeited by a selfish or thoughtless deed? What would it have been like to have had friends with whom to play, in whom to confide? She had been fortunate to have James. She loved him dearly and had convinced herself for years that he was the only friend she needed. But James was five years older than she. And James had been away so much during her own childhood and girlhood.

What would it be like to feel free to chatter when there were older people in her company, and free to offer her opinions in the presence of gentlemen? Free to smile and to dress her hair and her person in order to draw the admiring glances of the people around her? Free to touch and be touched? Free to show affection, and free even to kiss?

She did have some of those freedoms, she supposed. She was one-and-twenty years old and she was betrothed to a gentleman who wished her to behave as his sister behaved and as Miss Courtney had behaved the afternoon before. She could be free of her father's world and become a part of her husband's.

And yet freedom was a relative term, she thought rather bitterly, turning sharply from the window as she realized that she had been daydreaming there altogether too long. Would she be able to call herself free in a marriage that had not been of her own choosing? And would she ever be able to be free in the way Lady Madeline was free? Or Anna? She had no practice, no training, in such an attitude to life.

THEY TURNED THEIR HORSES' heads up into the valley away from the sea. They soon passed the lawns and the orchard and the one small sheep pasture that was not upon the plateau above. Then the trees that covered the hillsides closed in around them, reaching almost to the banks of the river, and brought with them that sense of peace and seclusion that Lord Amberley valued most about his home.

He had always loved this part of the valley more than the wider, more open reaches farther down, and the sea. Here he could ride or walk, think or read, or merely drink in the beauties of nature around him. He could be alone with himself. Alone with God perhaps.

He had deliberately brought Alexandra here on their first outing together. There were many places he could have taken her even if he did not wish to repeat the route she had taken the morning before. He could have taken her to call upon his aunt and uncle or any of his neighbors. He could have taken her to see the view from the cliffs, as Sir Cedric was doing with her brother. Or into the village. Or to half a dozen other places.

But he had decided to take her to the place that meant most to him after the house itself. The temptation was to keep her at arm's length, to keep her on the outer fringes of his life, to keep private to himself the important things of his world. It was a very strong temptation, especially when, try as he would, he could not feel any closeness to his betrothed. It was not that he did not like her. He could not get close enough even to know if he liked her. She was unknowable. And the temptation was to keep himself equally aloof from her.

But he would not do it. They must marry. And he could not keep his wife on the outer reaches of his life. He must keep persevering in trying to draw her into his heart. He had tried the day before. But he was not at all sure that she had had any powerful feelings about the house. Except perhaps for the library. And his grandmother's salon. She had appeared to be affected by that. He had ruined the occasion, of course, by rushing his fences and kissing her long before she was ready for any such intimacy. If she ever would be ready. He was beginning to have serious doubts on the matter.

But he must try again. He must try to begin some sort of friendship with her. He must begin to trust her enough to open his innermost life to her.

"This is my favorite part of all my land," he said. "I come here often."

"It is quiet," she said, "and quite lovely."

He smiled at her. "It is good to have a quiet place to escape to, is it not?" he said. "Did you have somewhere at home?"

"Only the moors," she said, "and only if James was at home. I was never allowed to ride or walk alone, and it was never the same to take a maid or a groom with me."

"Being female is sometimes hard, is it not?" he said. "Here you will have much greater freedom, Alex. There are many private places on my land where you may go and no one will be any the wiser. You need not always be followed around by a servant. Or even by me. There is one place especially where you may wish to come. I will show it to you later."

Lord Amberley grimaced inwardly. He had not intended to be quite so rash. He had meant to open his life to her. Did he have to reveal his very soul? No one but he knew of that particular place.

"What would you have done," she asked abruptly, turning to look at him with her dark eyes, which could look so intense on occasion, "if you had not been obliged to marry me?"

He smiled and shrugged. "I probably would have drifted on," he said.

"For how long?" she asked. "Forever? For a few years? Would you have married eventually? Would you have continued your friendship with Mrs. Borden? Or perhaps you still do. I am sorry. I am being unpardonably ill-mannered. Please disregard my questions, my lord."

"On the contrary," he said, "you have every right to ask them. And to demand answers. I am sorry you know of Eunice Borden. Does the knowledge give you pain?"

"I would be foolish to allow it to," she said, staring straight ahead. "Wives are supposed to ignore such matters, are they not? Pretend they do not even know?"

"I would expect my wife to be furious to the point of violence," he said. "Fortunately, she would never have cause. Never, Alex. Eunice is part of my past. Not part of my present or my future. She is a perfectly respectable lady who just happened to do me the honor of being my mistress for a year. In your morality it probably seems impossible for a lady to be both respectable and a man's mistress, but it is possible, believe me. I will not dismiss her by saying that she is a creature of no account. I respect her deeply. But she is in my past nevertheless, by her insistence as well as by my choice."

He watched Alexandra swallow and flush and continue to stare straight ahead. It was impossible to tell if she was satisfied with his explanation. Perhaps in her moral world it was shocking indeed to discover that one's betrothed had been bedding another woman for longer than a year.

"Would you like to get down and walk?" he asked. "The horses will be very happy to graze here, I am sure, and on foot we can climb a little way into the hills. There are some magnificent views from up there that I would like you to see."

"Yes," she said, "that would be lovely."

He found again when he lifted her down from her sidesaddle, as he had the morning before, that her body was far lighter and more shapely than it looked. Her upright bearing and disciplined movements distracted the eye from her very feminine form. He was careful to hold her away from his own body as she descended and to release his hold on her slim waist as soon as her feet touched the ground.

"The weather is very warm," he said. "Would you be more comfortable if you removed your jacket and your hat?" He smiled apologetically down at her when he saw her stiffen and flush. "I am hoping you will say yes so that I may remove my own."

He did not know for several moments how she would respond. She was clearly engaged in a mental battle between inclination—it really was a very hot afternoon—and the strictness of a narrow upbringing.

"Yes," she said. "It is very warm."

"And warmer in the valley here," he said, "sheltered from any breeze that may be blowing." He unbuttoned his own coat and removed it with a sigh of relief. The air felt almost cool against the loose linen sleeves of his shirt. He hooked the coat over the branch of a tree above his head.

She was wearing a pale green silk blouse beneath her darker green velvet jacket. Despite its loose fit, its high collar and long sleeves, it seemed to emphasize her shape more than the tighter, more revealing gowns that she wore indoors. She had firm, generous breasts. She was struggling with the pins that held her hat to her hair.

"May I help?" he asked.

"This one will not seem to move," she said, exasperated. Her head was bent forward, both arms raised above it.

"Here, let me," he said, and was instantly reminded of another occasion when his hands had fumbled at the back of her head to remove a gag.

The pin finally came away and she took the feathered hat away with one hand. But his clumsy efforts had also pulled loose some of her hairpins. One side of her hair came cascading down from its smooth chignon to curl about her shoulder and over her breast. She looked up at him, startled and blushing.

Lord Amberley took a hasty step backward. She looked quite vividly lovely. He felt a totally unexpected stab of desire for her.

"I do beg your pardon," he said. "I am afraid I am no lady's maid."

"When Nanny Rey pins on a hat," she said in some confusion, gathering the long hair in her hands and twisting it up behind her head again, "she puts it on to stay." She stooped down to pick up two offending hairpins from the grass at her feet.

In one minute her hair looked even more severe than before, though not quite as sleek. Her shoulders were back and her chin high. Lord Amberley, hanging her jacket over a branch next to his and wedging her hat into an angle from where it was unlikely to fall, was left to wonder if he imagined the voluptuous woman who had stood before him a minute before. Alexandra Purnell was untouchable again and quite in command of herself.

THEY WALKED BESIDE THE RIVER for a while. It flowed along in its narrow bed almost without sound. Unseen birds sang in the trees. The grass was thick and springy underfoot, the smell of it heavy with summer. Alexandra consciously kept her chin up and her shoulders back, imposing calm on her mind, drawing on the peace of her surroundings.

The gently moving air felt warm and pleasant against the thin silk of her blouse and against her hair. If only she were walking alone or with James or even with Lord Eden, she would be feeling thoroughly happy. There must not be a lovelier place on earth. But she was not alone. She was with her betrothed, who had shown her nothing but kindness and courtesy since she had known him. And who had trapped her into this situation. She was alone with a man with whom she did not know at all how to deal.

She had been so very embarrassed a few minutes before. Even the suggestion that she remove her jacket and hat had unsettled her. She did not know why. Indoors she wore clothes that were far thinner and that covered far less of her than her blouse did. Perhaps it was the whole idea of removing part of her clothing in his presence. She had been strongly reminded of how very inadequately clothed she had been when he first saw her. And as if that had not been enough, he had had to help her with the stubborn hat pin. She had felt almost as if she must swoon with his arms at either side of her face, his hands on her head, her forehead almost touching the folds of his neckcloth.

And then her hair had come down as the final mortification. Papa felt very strongly about a woman's hair being confined at the back or top of her head. She could remember only one occasion since she had started to wear it up at the age of sixteen when she had appeared in her father's presence with it down. She had arrived home in the rain after a ride with James and had tied her damp hair loosely at her neck in order to come downstairs for tea. She had received a thundering scold in front of everyone, including the butler and a footman who had brought in the tea tray, and sent back upstairs without her tea. She had spent the rest of the day and all of the following one there too. She had been seventeen at the time.

She had felt as humiliated to have Lord Amberley see her with her hair all down around her as if her blouse had come off with her jacket. She had felt naked and defenseless. And she had not failed to notice how he had stepped back in embarrassment, though he had been courteous enough to take the blame and to apologize for being so clumsy.

"Do you feel up to a climb?" Lord Amberley asked. "If we go up a little way here, I can show you a splendid view back from the valley to the house."

"Yes," she said, looking up the wooded incline to her right. It did not look impossibly steep. She would have liked to gather her velvet skirt in her hands and run up the hill.

"Let me help you," he said as they began to climb.

It was really not necessary. The trees were more widely spaced than they appeared to be from below, and the ground between them was quite firm. But he took her hand in his nevertheless, lacing his fingers intimately between hers. Those long, sensitive fingers that rather disturbed her.

"This is a good test of fitness, is it not?" he said a few minutes later with a grin. He was a little breathless. "Are you all right, Alex?"

"Yes," she said. She was considerably more out of breath than he and thankful finally for the support of his strong hand.

"Ah, here we are," he said. "You will be able to sit and rest in one moment."

The trees thinned out before them into a small grassy clearing. They resumed a little higher up.

"I should have brought my coat with me for you to sit on," he said. "I wish I had thought of it. But look first, Alex, before you sit down. What do you think?"

He had released his hold of her hand. He set his hands lightly on her shoulders now and turned her to look down the slope over the treetops, and along the valley.

Her breath almost caught in her throat. It had to be—yes, it had to be the loveliest scene on earth. She had not realized that they had climbed quite so high. The valley beneath them looked almost like a green rug, its greenness broken only by the blue hairline of the river and by the gray stone house and its outbuildings and gardens in the distance. The blue haze on the far horizon must be the sea.

"It is lovely," she said.

His hands tightened on her shoulders for one moment before he released her. "Will you ruin your skirt, do you think, if you sit down for a few minutes?" he asked.

She looked back to him. She had wanted to stand and gaze for considerably longer. "I think not, my lord," she said, and lowered herself to the grass. She clasped her knees as he sat beside her. She could still see down to the house in the distance but had lost the total perspective of the valley below them and the path of the river.

There was silence for a few minutes. "Alex," he said at last, "we should get to know each other. Do you not agree? We are to be married. I do not know you at all. I rode beside you yesterday morning and you commented that the house was lovely. I showed you the inside of the house in the afternoon and you said it was lovely. We rode in the valley earlier and you said it was lovely. I have brought you up here to show you the view. And you think it lovely. I feel rather as if

I am pounding away at a very strong shield. Who is Alexandra Purnell?"

She tightened her grasp of her knees and gazed rigidly down toward his house. "I am sorry," she said. "I did not know I had offended you. I have not meant to do so. I have felt that all this is lovely. I have felt it deeply. I did not realize that the word was inadequate."

"And now I have hurt you," he said quietly.

"I am so inadequate to all this," she said, her voice almost angry. "You and your family—you seem always able to express your feelings freely. I cannot do so. Not in speech. I have been taught to contain my feelings. I cannot change now just because suddenly the circumstances of my life have changed. I cannot suddenly become like Lady Madeline or Lady Amberley. Or Anna. If I say something is lovely, I feel that it is so. I cannot express rapture. I do not know the spoken words."

"Pardon me," he said gently. "I have committed the error of believing that only I feel any frustration at our relationship. But yours, I see, is equal to mine, and probably worse. As my wife, you will be expected to live in my world and adjust to it. And my world is so very different from what you know. It is unfair, is it not?"

"Yes," she said abruptly, and pushed herself to her feet. She continued to look down into the valley. She breathed in lungfuls of the warm, fragrant air to calm herself. "I have read that poem. The one about Tintern Abbey. And read it and read it. It says everything that can be said and felt, does it not? I can never do as well. Oh, never. But it is at least possible to express feelings in the written word. In speech the words will not come."

"You write?" he asked.

"Oh." She turned to him. "Only to relieve my feelings.

Only to express thoughts that I cannot share. I do not even pretend that what I produce is literature."

"I am sorry," he said, "for flaring up at you just now, Alex. I seem always to be apologizing to you, do I not? I find you so difficult to come to know. And yet the more I am with you, the more I see there is to know. Forgive me."

She shrugged and turned away from him. "I know so little," she said. "I have had no experience in communicating with others."

"I know," he said. "Would you rather go back now? Or will you come to see the place I told you about earlier? Forgive me, Alex, please. I have not meant to upset you. Just as I did not yesterday afternoon. I hoped that we could get to know each other better this afternoon, become friends perhaps."

She turned toward him reluctantly. "I would like to see the other place," she said. "Is it close by? Is it as lovely as this?" She shrugged and half-smiled at her choice of word.

"Yes, it is close," he said. "It is rather different from this."

It was a stone hut built into the side of the hill at some undetermined time in the past for some undetermined reason.

"I used to think it was once a gamekeeper's hut," he said. "But why would it have been built so high up? Was it a hermitage perhaps when the old house was first built or when the old monastery still stood at the other side of the valley? I like to think so, but no one now living seems to know for sure. Indeed, no one seemed even to know it existed when I first discovered it as a boy. And everyone else seems to have forgotten about its existence since. Perhaps it would seem absurd to everyone but me that it is almost the most important spot on this earth to me."

It was very different from the clearing they had just left.

The treetops around them were just too high to allow a view into the valley. All that was visible around were the tops of trees behind them and stretching below and climbing the hillside opposite, and the sky above them. But Alexandra knew immediately what he meant. There was total seclusion, total peace, here.

She stopped herself from saying that it was lovely.

"Come," he said, pulling open the heavy wooden door of the stone hut and stepping inside. He had lit a candle by the time she reached the doorway.

There was a roughly carved table and bench inside and a bed of straw with a folded blanket against one wall. Against the other was another bench piled with books and papers, quill pens and an inkwell.

"It is my hermitage," he said, looking at her with an expression that was not quite a smile. He looked uncertain. "Sometimes I escape here for an hour or two. Sometimes I even spend a night here. At such times I usually invent some story about business taking me from home."

"Does anyone know?" she asked. "Anyone else?"

"No," he said. "I have never told anyone but you."

Alexandra turned away and stepped back out into the sunlit clearing. Why had he told her? Why had he brought her here and shown her? Was it so important to him that he befriend her? And yet he did not wish to marry her. His sister had told her that the day before, but she would have known anyway. He had not answered her question about whether he would ever have married or not. And he had spoken with warm affection about the mistress he had been forced to give up because of her. He had just admitted to great frustration at her terrible reticence.

He was making such a great effort for her sake. Did she

not owe him something in return? She owed him something, some vulnerability.

"You must be ready for tea," he said from behind her. His voice sounded weary.

She spun around to face him. "Thank you," she said curtly. "Thank you, Edmund." But the words sounded angry, as if she resented the web of obligation he was weaving around her. And she did not want to sound angry.

Perhaps he understood. He smiled, his blue eyes kindly again. "You are to be my wife, Alex," he said. "I do not believe a husband and wife should have secrets from each other."

"I will not come back here," she said hurriedly. "This is your place. It will remain so. I will never intrude."

He continued to smile. "Don't make a promise," he said. "Promises are so very binding on honorable people. Everything I have will be yours, dear, including this if you ever need it."

She felt her breath quickening as she looked at him—at his thick dark hair, his smiling blue eyes, the broadness of his shoulders and chest so very obvious beneath the linen of his shirt. She thought she would faint. But she owed him something.

"Kiss me again!" she said impulsively. Her eyes widened as she heard the words come from her mouth, and her heart began to thump in her throat.

He set his hands on her shoulders and lowered his head. His blue eyes searched hers. She closed her eyes.

His mouth touched hers lightly, his lips slightly parted as they had been the day before. She held hers steady, waiting tensely for the moment when he would release her and she would be free again.

But when she found herself a few moments later gazing

into his eyes a mere few inches from her own, noting their questioning expression, she knew that it was not enough after all. She had allowed something, but had given nothing. And she wanted to give something. She could not resist the need to give.

She lifted her hands to his sides and grasped the warm linen of his shirt. She raised her mouth to his and moved toward him as he bent his head to her again. She touched the strong muscles of his chest with her breasts, those of his thighs with her own. And she deliberately abandoned the aloofness that always kept her apart from others, private and contained within herself.

At some time over the next minutes—how many?—she took fire. At some time she allowed his tongue to part her lips, and opened her mouth to its more intimate penetration. At some time she allowed his hands to pull loose her hairpins so that her hair cascaded all around them. At some time she allowed those same hands to pull her blouse free from the band of her skirt and move beneath it and up along the thin silk of her shift.

And at some time she felt the thickness of his hair and the firmness of his shoulders, and pulled loose his own shirt so that her hands could caress the rippling muscles of his back.

When he raised his head again, she knew from the body pressed to her own, with a knowledge that had never been taught her, that she was desired. And she saw it in his face, in the heavy-lidded dreamy blue eyes that looked into her, far beyond her eyes.

There was a moment of choice, a moment during which she knew she was on the brink of an experience that would forever change her, forever decide the course of her life. A moment during which she wanted and wanted to pass beyond that brink, to give herself, to lose herself, to end the newly conceived struggle to assert herself. A moment only.

And then she panicked.

When she came to herself, she was almost at the bottom of the hill, the trees thinning before her, the river already in sight. The sobbing sounds that had finally penetrated her hearing were coming from her own throat. Lord Amberley was coming down behind her, she knew, though he had called her name only once, when she had first broken away from him and begun to run blindly downhill.

She slowed her pace when she reached the bottom, and began to walk in the direction of the horses, which she could see quite a distance downstream. She pushed her blouse back inside her skirt with frenzied hands.

"Alex," Lord Amberley said, coming up beside her and looking searchingly at her. He did not say anything more.

Alexandra averted her face. "It was all my fault, not yours," she said. "This will not work at all. You do not wish to marry me, and I do not wish to marry you. We have both somehow been trapped into this, and I think we both resent it. If I marry you, I will be forever stranded in a world in which I can never be comfortable. And if you marry me, you will be forever miserable. I cannot give you the love and affection and spontaneity that you want of me. I am incapable of changing. And I don't want to change. I must go away from here. I cannot marry you."

"Alex," he said, touching her arm briefly, but not leaving his hand there, "you are quite overwrought. I don't know if I owe you an apology or not. We were both involved in that embrace, but I should not have allowed it to get out of hand as it did. I have more experience than you. I should have known that you would take fright. I did not intend to allow matters to progress quite so far."

She was trying to confine her hair on top of her head again without any hairpins with which to do it.

"Here," he said, holding out a few in the palm of his hand. "I retrieved these. Alex, please don't do anything hasty. Allow yourself to calm down. Completely. Give yourself a day or two. Breaking off our betrothal would have terrible repercussions for you, I believe. And you know, what has just happened is not so terrible really. You are upset because this has never happened to you before. But passion between a man and a woman is not an ugly thing. Between two who are to be husband and wife it is even desirable, is it not?"

"I suppose it has happened to you a thousand times," she said, jabbing at her head with the one remaining hairpin and reaching for her hat, "and I am just one more victim to be seduced."

"That is not fair," he said quietly. "You know there was no seduction, Alex. And no, I am not familiar with passion. It is not an element of all relationships, you know."

"No, I do not know," she said, rounding on him, her face flushed, her hair untidy. "And I do not wish to know. I want nothing to do with you, my lord. Nothing at all. I want to be myself. I cannot marry you."

"And you cannot be yourself and my wife at the same time, you think?" he asked.

"No," she said. "No, I can't. I must leave. I will talk to Mama and James."

"Alex," he said, standing in front of the horses so that she had no choice but to look at him, "please don't be rash. Please don't. I am sorry for what happened. I should have known better. But you need me. I know that at the moment you think that any life would be preferable to being with me. But give yourself time to be sure that that is right.

Weigh the alternatives. I know I am not the man you would have chosen for yourself. But you need my protection. And I will give it willingly, Alex. And I will try to give you room so that you may grow accustomed to this life, which is so strange to you. Please do not act on impulse today or even tomorrow. Promise me you will wait for a few days at least."

She looked at him, her eyes stormy. "Oh, yes," she said, "I will promise. We both know that I cannot break this engagement. And we both know that I am being thoroughly unfair to you right now. And we both know that I need you, that I cannot function as a member of our society without you. You have my promise, Edmund."

He closed his eyes briefly, and she could see him draw a deep breath. "I am sorry for your bitterness, Alex," he said, "and sorry that you are so upset. Let me help you into the saddle again. We will go home in search of tea."

She rode the distance back to the house, her chin high, and blanked her mind. She must be calm before they got back. And she must hope that no one would see her disheveled state. She tried to forget that Lord Amberley was riding silently just half a length behind her.

13

"DA-DUM-DUM, DA-DUM-DUM," MADELINE SANG, grabbing her twin around the waist and attempting to twirl him into a dance. "We are going to waltz again tonight, Dom, and skip and hop and reel. Is not life wonderful?"

"Are you trying to tip me down the stairs?" her brother asked, shaking off her hands and resuming the absorbing task of straightening out his lace cuffs over the backs of his hands. "This is not the time or place to trip the light fantastic, Mad. Wouldn't I make an elegant descent to the hall if I went tumbling head over ears down the whole marble flight?"

"Especially since I would rush shrieking behind you," she said, giggling. "Come then, Dom, since you and I have emerged from our dressing rooms at identical moments, let me take your arm and we shall descend with all sedate dignity."

But as they began to do so, she struck up with "Da-dum-dum, da-dum-dum" again, descending the stairs to the hall below in time to the waltz tune she hummed none too musically.

"What has put you in such high spirits?" Lord Eden asked, hauling back ungraciously on her arm. "The prospect of dancing in Courtney's crowded parlor? The anticipation of dancing with Howard Courtney?"

She laughed gaily. "Howard is so very earnest and so very faithful," she said. "It just is not kind to make fun. I shall dance with him once, you will see. But those officers, Dom! I know we saw them only from a distance this afternoon, but how very splendid they looked. Why is a gentleman in a uniform so totally irresistible?"

"Imagine them out of a uniform in twenty years' time when the wars are long over," her brother said unsympathetically. "You have to live with a man, not a uniform, if you marry him, Mad."

"You are so unromantic," she said with a mock sigh.

"Besides," he said, "if you love a military uniform so much, why do you almost collapse in a fit of the vapors every time I mention donning one myself?"

"Oh, don't start that now," she said. "I positively refuse to talk about anything even remotely serious for the next twelve hours at the very least. And I am not planning to marry any of these officers, silly. Just dance with them. And perhaps flirt with them ever so little." She giggled.

"And probably be head over ears in love with at least one of them by tomorrow morning," he said. "You see, we are not the first down after all, Mad."

Sir Cedric, James Purnell, and Lord Amberley were in conversation together. Alexandra was talking with Lady Amberley. Only Lady Beckworth was still not downstairs.

"The carriages are ready," Lord Amberley said. "Perhaps you would like to start on your way, Dominic, with Madeline and Alex and Mr. Purnell? The rest of us will follow immediately."

Madeline smiled and took Alexandra's arm. "You and I will exercise a lady's right and sit facing the horses, Alexandra," she said. "It is not quite fair, is it? But men have so many privileges that are not available to us, that we must take what we can." She felt embarrassed about her attempt of the day before to further her twin's schemes to save his older brother from the fate of having to marry Alexandra. She had told Dominic earlier that she would have no more part in his plans. She was going to do her best to make a friend of Alexandra, whichever brother she ended up marrying.

Madeline chattered determinedly throughout the journey. Dominic could be trusted to do his part, of course, and she found Alexandra surprisingly easy to talk with when they were alone together. But Mr. Purnell made her thoroughly uncomfortable. It seemed to be inevitable that she be thrown into his company quite frequently at the house. But she felt his disapproval. He seemed so often to be looking at her from those intense and hostile dark eyes. Her high spirits over the evening to come were partly relief at the prospect of having other young men to look at and talk to and dance with. Other young men who would perhaps admire her. Madeline was used to being made much of, though she would admit that at the age of twenty-two she must expect admiration to begin to wane. One of these days she was going to meet the man she could really love and then she was going to get contentedly married.

"Farmhouse" was rather a misnomer for the solid red brick house that Mr. Courtney had built twenty years before. It was no mansion. It would have been lost if set beside Amberley Court. Nevertheless, it was an imposing building, quite comfortably large for a family of seven. Mr. Courtney was a tenant farmer, but one who was very comfortably well-off, more so than many a landowner. The greatest delight of his heart and of his wife's was to have guests. If they could entertain anyone from the Hall, their cup of joy was full. On this occasion, when eight people from the Hall sat down with them for a dinner of five full courses, their cup almost literally ran over. Certainly the quantities of food would scarce fit on the sideboard or on the plates of the guests.

The parlor had never been dignified with the name of drawing room. It might have been, being large enough to serve as a quite respectably sized ballroom on this occasion, as it had on others. But Mr. Courtney had a strong sense of his own place on the social scale. His wealth he would enjoy, but he had no pretensions to gentility. In his own mind and vocabulary, he was still a farmer, his house a farmhouse, and his main room of entertainment a parlor. If he did have an ambition to reach beyond his status, it was to see his daughter well married. He had no wish to see such beauty and refinement wasted on another farmer such as he.

Miss Courtney was seated beside Mr. Purnell during dinner and blushed and chattered her way through the meal even though she drew only polite response from him. By the end of dinner she had somehow got him to reserve the opening dance with her. Since the second dance was to be a waltz and Lord Eden had solicited her hand for that the day before, she was entirely happy.

Madeline continued gay, despite the fact that she had Mr. Howard Courtney seated beside her at dinner. She really did not dislike Howard. She would be quite happy to sit beside him and talk to him, and dance with him too, if he did not persist in looking at her with worshipful eyes and making stilted, worshipful speeches. She had told him four years before and several times since that she could think of him only as a childhood playmate and not as anything else. But nothing seemed to have changed. She might have been able to feel anger against him if he were not such a thoroughly likable person. He looked a great deal like his father. Indeed he seemed to be getting more portly every time she saw him. He had his father's geniality too, without his blustering joviality.

But Madeline refused to have her spirits lowered. All the other near neighbors were to come for the dancing too, including Sir Peregrine Lampman, who had always paid her such lavish compliments until he had married a woman ten years older than he two years before. Since then his manner had been distant. She suspected that Lady Grace Lampman was a tyrant. And there was Mr. Watson, the handsome poet farmer, whom Susan considered too old for herself. And of course her uncle and aunt and Walter. And there were the officers from the regiment stationed outside Abbotsford. Surely one or both of them would be handsome. One could not be an officer and not be handsome. It was strictly forbidden.

The younger Miss Stanhope was to play the pianoforte for the dancing, and the third Courtney son the violin. Not very impressive when one was used to London balls during the Season, as Mrs. Courtney had pointed out to her guests at dinner with apologetic voice and flapping hands. But a dance is a dance, Madeline reflected, brightening considerably when two officers in full regimentals entered the parlor and Mr. Courtney proceeded to present them to all the company already assembled. The one in front, the tall one, was extremely handsome, and the other was quite passably good-looking. Captain Forbes immediately solicited her hand for the first waltz, Lieutenant Jennings for the second. Captain Forbes was the very handsome one.

JAMES PURNELL HAD HIS DANCE with Miss Courtney. She was a harmless, empty-headed little girl who had been made much of by doting parents and admiring older brothers and who had ambitions to marry into the gentry. She might succeed, too. She was pretty enough and vivacious enough. And who was he to say that she would not make some gentleman a good wife? The chances were that she had learned many household skills from her mother. There was a time when he might have been attracted to her himself. He had been drawn to pretty, vivacious females.

Such days were over. He had discovered through hard experience that almost all individuals and all ways of life had their hypocrisy, their evil. Everyone, it seemed, was self-serving. It had become impossible to trust anyone. There was no such thing as innocence and selflessness and honor.

Almost no such thing. There was Alex, of course. His twenty-one-year-old sister who had never been given the chance to live. And having had all faith in humanity and all chance for happiness cut from his own life, he had come almost to live for his sister. She must be happy. There was a gentleness and a goodness in Alex, and a beauty of character that had been totally repressed behind the mask of feminine virtue put there through long years of harsh discipline by their father. There was a passion for life in Alex that he suspected, though no one else did, he guessed, especially not Alex herself.

Purnell stood and watched the dancers after the opening set was over. Fortunately, this dance was different from most London balls in that there were more gentlemen than ladies. The necessity to lead out some poor little wallflower and save her from humiliation was not present tonight. If only he could be sure that Amberley was the one who could bring Alex to life! But of course, it was not enough that she be simply brought to life. She needed to live in a world worthy of her, and experience had taught him that there was no such world.

If only there were! If only he could see Alex happy, then he could finally break away himself and go in search of… he knew not what. Could he ever find meaning? Could he ever forget? And could he ever throw off the training of years that had made him a person who could not communicate easily with others or relax or laugh or talk about trivialities? And did he want to be such a person anyway? He had rejected with bitter hatred the world of his childhood, the values of his father. But had he ever found a world or values to replace them? Was he looking for the impossible? Was Lady Madeline right when she had asked if it was from himself he wished to escape?

He found himself watching Lady Madeline Raine, as he did so often without ever intending to do so. She personified so much that he yearned for and despised. She was wealthy, privileged, beautiful. She appeared always to be happy. Was it an intrinsic part of her nature to be so, or had life never tested her? Would she crumble if she were called upon to suffer or to live with oppression as Alex had done for twenty-one years?

She was waltzing now with one of the officers from the regiment stationed close by, and glancing up at him, her green eyes laughing into his, her short fair curls shining in the candlelight. She was flirting with him. They made a handsome couple.

Why did he dislike the girl? She was harmless. Indeed, she tried her best, it seemed, to be friendly to Alex, and even to converse with him. She was sunny-natured. Was it her fault that she had had all her life what he wanted more than anything for his sister? Did he dislike her perhaps because she revealed his own inadequacies to him? Would he like to be that officer, to be able to smile at her like that, and talk as easily and as flirtatiously? Would he like to evoke that response in her instead of the discomfort and dislike he sensed when she was forced into his company?

No, he wanted nothing to do with the likes of Lady Madeline Raine. It was a weak and shallow woman like her who had caused his soul to be torn from him. If he ever took a woman again, it would be an entirely different sort. A woman who would cater to his needs and never want anything for herself. A stupid notion, of course! He would want no such woman. Was he his father all over again?

He looked abruptly away from Madeline to find that the eldest Courtney son was also gazing at her, an almost comical look of unrequited love on his face. He had not looked like that a moment ago, surely? But no, there was nothing of love in his feelings for the woman. He would like to bed her, that was all. He would like to have her beneath him, to show her that a physical encounter between a man and a woman was a great deal more real and raw than the romantic, flirtatious encounter that her manner suggested she expected.

Good God, he thought, appalled at himself, he wanted to hurt her.

"Is one permitted to walk in the garden for fresh air?" he asked Howard Courtney.

Howard seemed quite happy to have his train of thought broken. He grinned broadly. "I'll join you if I may, sir," he said. "I don't suppose you would care to see our hogs? The boar won a prize at the fair last week."

"I think I would be quite delighted to see your hogs," Purnell said with a wry smile, "provided we can do so without having to bring the smell of the pens back inside with us again later."

LORD EDEN WAS WALTZING WITH Susan and thoroughly enjoying the sensation of holding her small, very shapely form. He held her at arm's length, of course, as propriety demanded, but the Courtney parlor was not excessively large and there were twelve couples twirling about it, not to mention a few other people sitting or standing around the edge of the floor, which had been cleared for the dancing. Under the circumstances there was more than one opportunity to draw his partner close enough that they almost touched.

"I would not have believed it, Susan," he said, smiling down at her bright, pretty face. "What has happened to the little girl I knew but two years ago?"

"She has grown up, my lord," she said, sweeping him a look from under her lashes. "Are you sorry?"

"Yes, indeed I am," he said, winning for himself what he had hoped for: a direct and questioning look from those large hazel eyes. "The little girl used to call me Dominic."

"It seems unseemly still to do so," she said, blushing prettily. "I am a woman now."

"Oh, and so I had noticed, Susan," he said. "But come, I want to hear you say my name."

"You are unkind to bully me," she said, and raised eyes shining with unshed tears to his interested gaze. "Gentlemen all seem to think that they can tease me because I am female and may not fight back."

"Susan!" he said, gentle concern in his voice. "I did not mean to tease. I certainly did not intend to bully. Come, I will make no more demands of you. You may call me what you will. Smile at me and tell me you forgive me."

"Of course I forgive you," she said. "It really is excessively hot in here." She raised appealing eyes to his.

"Then I will take you somewhere where it is cooler," he said. "Outside?"

"I really should not," she said. "But perhaps just outside the door."

"Just outside the door" proved to be a rather dark stretch of lawn on the opposite side of the house from all the farm buildings. And Lord Eden walked for all of ten minutes, the girl's slim arm drawn through his, her voice a whisper close to his ear. He spent the whole time in some discomfort, resisting the urge to steal a kiss. The trouble was that she was just the type of female that he found most irresistible. She made him feel large and protective and older than his years.

But she had almost wept at his familiarity in suggesting that she call him by his name. She would either have the vapors or deal him a stinging slap to the cheek if he tried to kiss her. And besides, he was not free to indulge in a flirtation with Susan Courtney or any other female, appealing or otherwise. He had pledged himself to marrying his brother's betrothed. And he must not put off the siege indefinitely, or those two would be married and Edmund would be doomed to a life sentence indeed.

"Shall we go back inside?" he suggested, hugging Susan's arm closer to his side for a moment. "I would hate for you to catch a chill."

"I suppose so," she said wistfully. "It is so pleasant out here. I could walk for an hour."

"I think perhaps your mama would be displeased with me if I kept you out here any longer," he said gently.

She raised large eyes to his in the darkness. "Other people do love to gossip," she admitted. "Yes, take me back inside, my lord. I know that you would not do anything unbecoming a gentleman, but they may not know that."

Lord Eden squeezed her hand and restrained himself with great difficulty from proving her judgment of him quite wrong.

ALEXANDRA FOUND HERSELF UNEXPECTEDLY the center of attraction, being newly betrothed to the Earl of Amberley. It was a novel experience for her to find her hand solicited for every dance. She even found herself relaxing far more than she ever had in company, warmed by the unpretentious friendliness of her fiancé's neighbors and relatives.

It was a great relief to have this dinner and dance to attend. She did not know how she would have endured an evening at home. How would she have talked with her betrothed? Looked at him? She had been able to avoid both under the circumstances. And it seemed that he too had avoided her, sitting close to Sir Cedric during tea and talking about sheep and crops while his mother had drawn her into conversation; sending her to the Courtneys' in a different coach from the one in which he traveled; leading Mrs. Courtney in to dinner; and choosing dancing partners other than herself. She did not look forward to the one waltz he had reserved with her later.

Alexandra had the uncomfortable feeling that she had behaved very badly that afternoon. As a gesture of some openness, she had asked Lord Amberley to kiss her. Yet when he had done so, she had blamed him and accused him of trying to seduce her. How very unfair she had been. He had been quite right about that.

And she had told him she would not marry him. She had been prepared in her embarrassment and shame to break off their engagement and go rushing away from Amberley. Where had she envisaged going? Back to Papa? Fortunately, Lord Amberley had kept a cooler head than she and had persuaded her to promise not to make a decision for two or three days. And she would have to back down, of course. It was just one further humiliation to know that he had been more sensible than she.

Even apart from that, though, there was all the embarrassment of remembering what had happened to cause her hysteria. She had expected a kiss like that of the day before. And indeed that was what she had got. It would have ended there had she not chosen to invite more.

What had happened then seemed very unreal to her mind. Her life had been almost totally without powerful physical sensations. The clandestine gallops on the moor with James were the greatest physical exhilaration she had ever known. There was nothing with which to compare her embrace with the Earl of Amberley. It had been an experience so very carnal that the mind had not been part of it at all. She had been all need, all aching, panting need to touch, to explore, and to be touched, to be . . . possessed. She had wanted him closer, much closer. She supposed she must have wanted that which she knew happened in the marriage bed. But she had never thought of that before in terms of need or desire.

And she could not now. She was repelled by the memory of her own mindless longing. She could not resist stealing surreptitious glances at the earl all evening, recalling that it was with him she had done such things. It was his naked flesh she had felt beneath her hands, his hands that had been beneath her blouse, even beneath her shift, his mouth and his tongue that had so ravished her own, his body that had pressed so intimately against hers.

It was almost beyond belief. In his formal evening wear he looked so remote from her, so refined, so handsome. Alexandra shivered and felt the heat of the parlor close around her.

"May I have the honor, ma'am?" The very dashing Captain Forbes was bowing before her, hand extended, his white teeth flashing in the candlelight. Miss Stanhope was pressing single notes on the pianoforte while Colin Courtney tuned his violin again. Two sets were forming for a country dance.

Alexandra smiled and placed her hand in the captain's.

LORD EDEN WAS BREATHLESS at the end of the same vigorous country dance. He had spent precious breath laughing at the elder Miss Stanhope, who had declared when he had asked her to be his partner that she had not danced in ten years but that she would accept anyway and proceed to prove to all who cared to watch that she could keep up to any of the young people. But she had a disconcerting and amusing way of shrieking when he twirled her down the set at the conclusion of each pattern. Consequently, Lord Eden had twirled her harder each time.

"I shall be able to boast to the rector tomorrow and for the next month that I danced tonight with the most handsome and dashing gentleman in the county," she said, patting him on the sleeve when he had returned her to her seat at the end of the set. "That is, if I ever recover enough breath to live through the night." The normally prim Miss Stanhope giggled like a girl. Her cap was slightly askew on her crimped curls.

Lord Eden made a suitably gallant reply and looked about him for Alexandra. She had also made one of his set with Captain Forbes and had looked quite handsome with her cheeks flushed and one lock of hair worked loose from her chignon and curling down onto her shoulder. He made his way across the room to her.

"Shall we go in search of a drink, Miss Purnell?" he asked. "There is a bowl of punch in the dining room, I believe, and some lemonade."

"Lemonade, please," she said gratefully.

He took her arm. "I thought that Miss Letitia Stanhope's fingers would fly off her hands at any moment," he said, "she was playing the pianoforte so fast. And poor Colin Courtney looked more as if he were trying to saw through the strings of his violin than to play it."

She laughed with genuine amusement. "Don't be unkind," she said. "I must admit to enjoying this dance far more than I liked any of the grand balls I attended in London."

"There speaks a true country miss," he said. "You have a good point, you know. The friendliness of a small gathering like this is worth a great deal, is it not?"

"It is all so new to me," she said.

"Would you care to walk outside for a few minutes?" he asked. "I believe it is quite proper to do so. The garden is small, and it seems to me there must be some other people outside already."

"The fresh air would be pleasant," she admitted, and put

her arm in his again after he had taken her empty glass and returned it to a tray.

There were indeed a few people strolling on the lawn where he had walked earlier with Susan. "Are you really enjoying this part of the world, Miss Purnell?" Lord Eden asked when they were strolling across a different lawn past small flower beds.

"I like it very well," she said. "Everyone has been kind."

"Did Edmund take you riding in the valley this afternoon?" he asked. "That is always his favorite direction for a ride. Edmund is something of a lone wolf, you know. He is throughly good-natured and generous and takes his responsibilities very seriously. But I believe he is never so happy as when he is alone with his books or with his trees or his thoughts."

Alexandra did not reply. They had reached a stile leading into the farmyard. The country smells of animals and manure were around them.

"I will take you up on the hill to see the view from the cliffs tomorrow if you wish," he said. "That direction is more to my taste. One feels caught up in the wildness of nature—it is always windy on the clifftops, you know. One realizes in such a place how vast the world is and how full of possibilities for excitement and adventure."

"That is what you dream of?" she asked, turning to look up into his eager face. "James is somewhat the same. He would like to travel to other lands, though I do not believe he knows quite what he would do when he got there."

"Oh, I do know," he said, "though I will probably never achieve my ambition. I want to be part of England's army. I want to fight against the French. I want to go to Spain."

"You wish to serve your country?" she said. "That is a

noble ambition, my lord, though a dangerous one. Why can you not do it?"

"I had two uncles who died years ago," he said, "both in the same campaign. Can you imagine such rotten bad luck? They were Mama's brothers. My mother is a very sensible and placid lady, but she closes up like a clam whenever I even hint at going myself. I have never had the courage to press the point."

"It is hard to go against one's parents," she said. "We are all brought up to respect their superior knowledge and wisdom. But it is harder for a man, I think. I know James has found it harder to be obedient to Papa."

"Has he?" he said. "Then I can sympathize. Though my mother would not stop me if I told her that it is what I want more than anything in life. She would even see to it that she did not shed a tear when I went away. But can I do it? That is the question. Can I do that to her, knowing that I may never come back? What do you think, Miss Purnell?"

"There are so many considerations to weigh," she said. "Love and duty to your mother. Loyalty to your country. Your own need to commit yourself to a cause. What does your brother say?"

He smiled down at her. "Edmund doesn't," he said. "Edmund believes firmly that everyone has the right and the duty to make his own decisions about his life, though I do know that he will support me in anything I decide. But I do not need his permission, you know, although he is the head of the family. I am of age, and I have my own fortune."

"Then you must do what is right," she said. "But the decision will be difficult because sometimes all the thought and reflection in the world will not reveal clearly what is right and what wrong. You must pray about it and have faith that your decision will be the right one."

He continued to smile, and reached out with his hand to cover hers as it rested on the stile. "I admire you, Miss Purnell," he said. "You can advise me to pray while looking me straight in the eye. And I would wager that you are not even blushing. Most of us go faithfully to church every Sunday and yet are far too shy to mention any part of our religion outside that hour. Are we not strange?"

"Yes," she said. "Religion has always been so much a part of my everyday life that I did not realize that I would embarrass you by what I said. I believe I am the strange one, though. I have realized during the past few weeks that I am strange."

"No," he said, "just different. I like you, Miss Purnell. You are not at all silly or frivolous or flirtatious as other females are."

"Oh, dear." She smiled fleetingly. "I am not sure that that is a compliment."

His hand closed over hers and lifted it to his lips. "It was meant as a compliment," he said. "Will you marry me, Miss Purnell? I shall buy a commission in the army and fight for England and for you. You will be my inspiration, for you are a strong person. I would be proud to fight and have you to come home to. Will you? Please say yes."

He looked down eagerly into her dark eyes, shaded by the night around them.

"I am betrothed to your brother," she said calmly.

"But you will not be happy with him," he said. "With him you will never be quite sure that your marriage is not one of convenience only. You do feel that doubt already, do you not? With me you need not feel that way. I would be proud to have you as my wife."

She turned away from the stile to face him. Her hand was still in his. "I cannot believe you would continue to feel so," she said, her voice more agitated than it had been, "although you may believe so at this moment. But if you only knew how you tempt me. If only you knew how very weary I feel and how unsure of myself today." She leaned tensely closer to him. "Will you—?"

But she was not to complete the request, whatever it was to have been. Both of them became aware of voices approaching from the other side of the stile. Both had been unaware of James Purnell and Howard Courtney coming toward them across the farmyard.

Lord Eden, releasing Alexandra's hand and turning toward the approaching pair, was surprised to hear Purnell laughing and talking amiably to his companion before he became aware of them standing at the stile.

"Let me guess," Lord Eden said, raising his voice. "You have been showing Mr. Purnell your prize boar, Courtney. And you are supposed to be inside dancing with the ladies."

Howard Courtney was grinning as he came up to the stile. "Your guess is right, your lordship," he said. "And as I saw it, there were not enough ladies for everyone to dance with inside anyway. That will be Mama's and Susan's idea of a successful dance."

"Mr. Courtney put fresh straw on the ground for me to stand on and would not let me touch a single animal, Alex," James Purnell said, unaccustomed amusement in his voice. "With luck, no one will know I have been in the barn and the pig pen." He exchanged a grin with his sister under the interested gaze of Lord Eden. "Is there a waltz soon? Will you dance with me?"

"I am engaged to dance the next waltz with Lord Amberley," she said. She turned back to Lord Eden. "Thank you for bringing me outside for some fresh air, my lord. Shall we go in again?"

He offered his arm and leaned close to her ear as the other two men moved on ahead of them. "I shall take you up onto the cliffs tomorrow," he said. "We will talk further."

LORD AMBERLEY WAS RELIEVED TO FIND THAT his betrothed was being so well received in the neighborhood. He had expected as much, of course, but it was gratifying to see it happen, and on this of all days. The ladies had all talked to Alexandra. Most of the gentlemen had danced with her, and those who had not already done so had reserved sets with her later in the evening, or at least made themselves pleasant to her.

He thought she was pleased. At least he thought she had recovered some of her composure. He would not have expected her still to look distraught, of course, but he would have known if she was still upset. Her back would have been very straight, her chin high, her manner quite aloof. As it was, she smiled and talked. She looked rather lovely, dressed in blue.

And the time had come for his waltz. He had hesitated about reserving it with her. She would undoubtedly be happier away from him for the rest of the day at least. But it was their first appearance in public among his neighbors. They must be seen together.

He bowed to Lady Lampman and smiled at Alexandra,

with whom she spoke. "This is my waltz, I believe, my dear," he said. "Are you enjoying the evening, Lady Lampman?"

"Oh, exceedingly," she replied, her eyes searching the room for her husband, who was talking to a group of men in the doorway. "It is pleasant to have more company once again, my lord, now that you have returned to Amberley."

He inclined his head in acknowledgment of the compliment and reached out a hand for Alexandra's. "Miss Stanhope and Colin are about to begin again," he said. "They are to be greatly commended for providing such spirited music. Shall we give them our compliments at the end of the dance, Alex?"

"Yes," she said. He noticed that she did not look up into his face.

They danced in silence for a while, the thumping of the pianoforte and the scraping of the violin, the high-spirited voices and giggles of the young, and the rumbling conversations of the not-so-young closing in about them.

Lord Amberley felt the smallness of his partner's waist beneath his hand and looked down at the shining smoothness of her hair. He watched her dark lashes fan her cheeks. And he marveled anew at the passion he had unleashed in her that afternoon. It had been so totally unexpected.

Had he been better prepared, perhaps he could have guarded against what had happened. As it was, he had kissed her even more tentatively than he had the day before, and noted that she neither flinched nor withdrew. He had wanted more. He had wanted to put his arms around her and kiss her somewhat more lingeringly. He had asked her with his eyes if he might. And she had signaled yes.

And then he had simply lost his head. He was ashamed to remember now how the unexpected touch of her very shapely body against his full length had inflamed him, and how he had used his expertise to open and invade her mouth, and to get his hands beneath her clothing. He had not touched her breasts only because she had had them pressed against him.

He had behaved like a boy with his first woman. Within a very few minutes he had allowed himself to become fully aroused, so that his only thought before she panicked had been to lay her down, lift her skirt, and find his ease in her.

He had been totally, shamefully selfish. It was true that she had been hot and aroused in his arms, as ready as he for full intimacy until she had taken fright. But he had known that she was a total innocent, that his kiss the day before had doubtless been her first. He had had no business rushing her into such a very hot and raw embrace even though she had led the way. She had not known where they were going. He had.

He was deeply ashamed of himself. And he could not blame her for the things she had said afterward. He only hoped, for her sake, that he could salvage their betrothal.

"I would have to say you are the belle of the ball, Alex," he said. "I am glad I had the forethought to reserve this dance at the start of the evening."

"I like your neighbors," she said. "They are kind people."

"Yes," he said, "I am fortunate. I would like to take you to meet some of the other people of the neighborhood, Alex. Some of my laborers. Most of them live in the village. I know they will be agog to meet you and talk to you. I have always maintained a close relationship with them. I refuse to see them as nonentities who do my work for me."

"That will be pleasant," she said.

"Tomorrow morning?" he asked.

"I have promised to ride out to the cliffs with Lord Eden," she said.

"Ah," he said, "you will enjoy that, Alex. All the power of God is there. You will know what I mean when you get there. I must visit my people alone tomorrow then. I have not had a chance to visit most of the families since I returned from London. Perhaps you can accompany me some other day."

"Yes, perhaps," she said.

He felt disappointed. He had never looked for company in any of his self-imposed estate tasks, though both his mother and Madeline frequently visited his laborers, especially if there were any sickness or a birth among them. He wanted to take Alex. He wanted her to be interested in his life.

He looked down at her, hesitating, not knowing if he should refer to the afternoon or not.

"Are you feeling better?" he asked at last very quietly. "Have you recovered, Alex?"

"It was all my fault," she said, looking hurriedly up at him and away again. "You did no more than I asked. I was foolish. You must think me very silly."

"No," he said, "definitely not that, Alex. Am I forgiven, then?"

"There is nothing to forgive," she said. There was a short pause, during which she darted another look up at him. "I would rather pretend none of it happened. Please let us forget."

"It is forgotten," he said, bending his head closer to hers. "Your happiness and comfort are my only concern, Alex. Now and always."

The music had stopped almost without their realizing the fact. Mr. Courtney suddenly clapped Lord Amberley on the shoulder at the same moment as his hearty voice boomed out at them.

"I was just saying to Mrs. Courtney," he said, "how wonderful it is to see young love, my lord, if you will pardon me the familiarity. All the exertions of an evening of dancing, and still too intent on exchanging sweet nothings to hear the call to supper." His hearty laughter was joined by that of those people still left in the room.

Lord Amberley smiled ruefully at Alexandra. "Shall we talk to Miss Stanhope and Colin while we may?" he asked.

"Yes," she said, her smile somewhat strained.

LORD AMBERLEY WAS SITTING in the breakfast room the following morning, conversing with Sir Cedric and waiting for Alexandra to come down. He hoped to have time to show her the gallery and perhaps even the chapel before she went riding with Dominic and Madeline. Madeline had decided the night before to join the expedition to the cliffs, as had James Purnell.

Sir Cedric Harvey spent a month of each summer at Amberley Court and had done so for many years. He had been a close friend of the former earl and had kept up the friendship with his widow. He spent the months of the Season in London, as did she.

Lord Amberley often wondered why the two of them had not married. His mother was not yet fifty years old, and she was still a strikingly good-looking woman. Sir Cedric was no more than a year or two older. He was a widower of long standing, his wife having died of consumption after only three years of marriage. He was a distinguished-looking man, though his silver hair made him appear somewhat older than his years.

But they had never married or shown any signs of a romantic attachment, though they undoubtedly shared a firm friendship and an affection for each other. His mother, of course, had been deeply in love with his father and almost inconsolable in her grief for the first year or more after his death. Sir Cedric took with him wherever he went a miniature of the wife he had lost when she was barely twenty years old. Perhaps one loved like that only once in a lifetime, Lord Amberley reflected.

"Don't let me keep you if you have business to attend to," Sir Cedric said at last, noticing that his companion had finished his breakfast. "I shall wait for your mama and Lady Beckworth, as I have promised to accompany them into Abbotsford this morning. Ah, the idle life, Edmund. There is a great deal to be said in its favor."

"No, you are not keeping me," Lord Amberley said. "I am going to stay until Alex comes down in the hope that there will be time to take her to the gallery before she goes riding."

"Oh, but Miss Purnell is in the music room," Sir Cedric said. "I heard someone playing when I returned from an early-morning walk, and looked in to see who it was. She looked most self-conscious, so I withdrew immediately. I always know when someone prefers to be alone. And she did not even invite me to remain and sing!"

Lord Amberley laughed and rose to his feet. "I shall leave you then," he said, "if you do not mind. Perhaps she will still be there."

She was. He could hear the muted tones of the pianoforte from the hall. He hesitated outside the door for a moment before turning and going into the library instead. He did not wish to disturb her if she really did need some time to herself. But for all his wish not to eavesdrop, he found that the sounds of the instrument in the next room drew him to the door that adjoined the two rooms. He stood and listened, trying to identify the tune she played.

It was intricate, haunting. Indescribably sweet and romantic. Whatever it was, it was something he had never heard before. He could not even guess at the composer.

He knocked at the door when the music came to an end and opened it. She had risen to her feet already and was standing beside the pianoforte, the color high in her cheeks.

"I do beg your pardon," she said. "Am I disturbing you?"

"What was it?" he asked. "I heard the end of what you were playing, Alex. It was beautiful. But I cannot identify it."

"Oh, it was nothing," she said, shrugging and looking embarrassed. "I was just letting out my feelings."

He stared at her. "You mean that it was your own composition?" he asked.

"Yes," she said. "It was nothing."

"I was carried away by the beauty of it," he said. "Have you composed other music too?"

"I play for myself when I am alone," she said. "I really do not know what I play."

"You mean you have never written any of it down?" he asked.

"No, I could not," she said. "Words are difficult enough. I struggle to express in written words what my feelings are. I could not possibly do it with music."

She was very uncomfortable. Her cheeks were still flushed. Her eyes were on his neckcloth. She was twisting her hands together.

"Forgive me," he said. "I have told you that you may escape here and be alone. I did not purposely eavesdrop. I merely waited until you had finished before coming in to ask if you would like to see the gallery before you ride."

"Is there time?" she asked.

He smiled. "Madeline is not the earliest of risers after a late night," he said. "I would guess that we have plenty of time."

"Then I would like to," she said. "You have said that the room is your favorite?"

"Yes, in a way," he said. "It contains all the family portraits. We were extremely fortunate that the old house did not have an impressive gallery. As a result, all the family portraits were kept in the town house and so escaped the fire."

She took his arm and Lord Amberley looked down at her curiously. What more was there to discover about his betrothed? There was the outward disciplined, serious, dispassionate woman, beyond whom the world was not meant to see. At the start, despite that first encounter with her, he had assumed that there was nothing else. But he had discovered since, her beauty, her exuberance, her deep love of beauty, her creative talent, her passion. And yet he felt that he still did not know her.

He was still not comfortable with her, or she with him. And yet he was becoming more and more convinced that she was worth the challenge, that he had quite by accident won himself a priceless prize for a bride.

MADELINE WAS SITTING IN LONE state in the breakfast room when her twin found her there a little while later.

"Well, Sleeping Beauty!" he said. "You were too busy dreaming of officers and scarlet uniforms, I suppose, to think about waking up in good time for a mere ride."

"Don't tease at this hour of the morning, Dom," she said. "You know I am not at my best until my brain has been awake for at least an hour. Do I have to go on that dreadful ride?"

"Dreadful ride?" he said. "You have always liked the cliffs, Mad."

"But I don't like the company," she said. "It really is not fair, Dom, that every time you decide to accompany Alexandra anywhere, I am expected to join you with Mr. Purnell."

"Well, you must admit," he said, "that I would never get anywhere with Miss Purnell if I were obliged to entertain the two of them together. And you have nothing better to do."

"How do you know that?" she asked. "Captain Forbes and Lieutenant Jennings said they might call sometime today."

Lord Eden grinned. "Ah, I might have guessed as much," he said. "Which one are you in love with, Mad? Or are you in love with both?"

"Don't be horrid!" she said. "And what about you, Dom? You seemed much taken with Susan last night. Is she replacing Miss Carstairs in your heart?"

His grin faded. "Be serious," he said. "I am going to marry Miss Purnell, Mad. I asked her last night, and I don't think she was going to say no. We were interrupted by Howard and her brother."

"Oh, Dom!" she said. Her coffee cup clattered back into its saucer. "Are you still planning that? It is all wrong, you know. It seemed all very well a few days ago before she arrived. But can you not see the impossibility of it now? She is formally betrothed to Edmund. Everyone knows. She was presented to everyone here last night as his future bride.

What would happen now if you were to take her away from him? Edmund would be the laughingstock, and you would be in disgrace. The scandal surrounding Alexandra would be redoubled. I doubt that Edmund would receive you ever again. And besides, Dom, you would be very unhappy married to Alexandra. She is not right for you."

"There I think you are wrong," Lord Eden said. "She is a very sensible and understanding female, Mad. And she is not near as sober as she seems to be on first acquaintance. I think it altogether possible that I will grow to love her."

"Oh, Dom!" she said.

He flashed her a grin. "I saw you waltzing with Purnell twice last night," he said. "Perhaps we can have that double wedding after all, Mad."

"What an appalling thought," she said. "I mean, both weddings. I danced with him a second time only because Mr. Courtney took hold of my hand before the last waltz, placed it in Mr. Purnell's, and declared that he simply must see us dance together once more. Sometimes his lack of conduct is quite mortifying. I could tell that Mr. Purnell was as delighted as I was. He spoke scarce a word the whole time."

"Well," he said, "you must keep him talking this morning. Will you, Mad? I need some time alone with Miss Purnell."

She sighed. "Keep him talking about what?" she asked. "Do you have any ideas, Dom? I used up all of mine long ago."

He got to his feet. "Will you be ready soon?" he asked. "It's not going to take you half an hour to have your hair done or something like that, is it?"

"Twenty minutes," she promised. "Go away, Dom. You are interfering with my digestion."

But it wasn't Dominic who was making her toast taste like wood, she thought with a sigh as he left the room. It was the prospect of riding with Mr. Purnell.

She had been surprised the evening before when he had asked her to waltz with him. She had expected that he would be as relieved as she to find himself free of the necessity of being in close company with her for an evening. She had accepted, but she had refused to have her evening spoiled. Or at least she had tried to refuse. She had smiled up at him as gaily as if he had been one of the officers.

It had been difficult to keep that smile in place after a few minutes. He had looked directly down at her from those dark, unfathomable eyes of his and not responded to her smile, though he had made some effort at polite conversation.

She had been suffocatingly aware of him, of his tall lean body, his dark intense eyes, that lock of dark hair that seemed always to find its way across his forehead no matter how many times he pushed it back. Madeline usually liked to feel aware of the gentlemen with whom she danced. It made her feel more feminine to be held by an attractive man and to sense the pull of that attraction. She also liked to be kissed and had several times allowed a favored gentleman a taste of her lips. But the excitement of such moments had always been light, flirtatious, exhilarating.

She felt none of those things with James Purnell. He was very attractive, probably more so than any other man she had ever known. But the attraction she felt was not a pleasant feeling. It was not the sort of feeling that caused her to bubble over with high spirits and excitement. She could not imagine being kissed by him in the harmless way of other gentlemen during brief stolen moments, in an alcove or a shaded place in a garden.

Indeed, the thought of being kissed by James Purnell made Madeline's stomach lurch and her knees weaken. But not in pleasurable anticipation. He would not be gentle with a woman, she sensed. He would not be content with mild flirtation. It would be a dangerous game indeed to allow him close to her. And the thought was not exciting in any way. At least not in any pleasurable way.

She was afraid of Mr. Purnell. He was from an alien world. She would not be able to control him as she had easily been able to control all the gentlemen who had had a part in her life for the past several years.

"Are you enjoying the dancing?" she had asked brightly. "I think it is quite splendid, even though we have only a small room in which to twirl and only a pianoforte and a violin to supply the music."

"And an abundance of men to admire you," he had said.

She had laughed. "Do they? How very flattering."

"You thrive on it, don't you?" he had said. "Hearts galore to capture and bruise."

"And to break and throw away," she had said with a gay laugh. "Tomorrow I will find more and begin all over again."

"Perhaps someone will return the compliment one of these days," he had said.

Something had been burning behind his eyes. And it was only as she had smiled into them that she had realized that he was serious. And it was at the same moment that she had realized just how very afraid of him she was.

"You are serious," she had said, her smile frozen in place. "You think me heartless. You think I break hearts?" She had felt anger rise in her. "Name one, sir. One heart I have broken."

"Howard Courtney's," he had said without hesitation.

"Howard?" she had said. "Howard was a childhood playmate. He knows that I do not return his regard. Am I to blame if he still sighs over me?"

"You behave toward him and speak to him as if he were a slightly amusing toy," he had said. "Is he worth no more merely because he is the son of a tenant farmer of your brother's and one of your rejected flirts?"

She had been speechless with anger and with the need to defend herself. But the music had come to an abrupt end and she had been given no opportunity to do so. By the time they were forced into company together for another waltz, the moment had passed. His contempt was hidden behind his usual taciturnity; her anger had turned her to ice. They had said almost nothing to each other. If he looked at her out of his dark eyes, she did not know it. She looked—and smiled—at everyone in the room except her partner.

And now she must ride with him. Talk with him. Keep him somewhat apart from Dominic and Alexandra. How could she? What could she say? How could she be civil?

Madeline sighed and pushed back her chair. There was no point in postponing the evil moment, she supposed.

ALEXANDRA WOULD HAVE KNOWN without having to be told that the gallery was Lord Amberley's favorite room in the house. There was, of course, the extraordinary beauty of the room. It extended the full width of the south wing, one wall almost entirely consisting of tall windows. The ceiling and frieze were painted with delicate gold-leaf filigreed patterns. Yet there was nothing to distract the mind long from the portraits that hung there.

And it was clearly these portraits that were the center of

his home. They represented Lord Amberley's family, and his family obviously was very central to his life. Alexandra felt almost like an intruder as she listened to the pride and affection in his voice and looked at the painted faces of strangers.

This was the family of which she was to become a part. It was strange, she thought, that when one became betrothed to someone, one imagined that only two people were concerned in the contract. And then one became aware that many other people were also involved: the immediate families, aunts and uncles, neighbors. And even the dead. She would become part of this family when she wed Lord Amberley. Part of this rich heritage.

Why was it that she had always been almost unaware of her own heritage? Her parents had never talked about their ancestors. She had never known any family members beyond them and James, except for Aunt Deirdre and Albert and Caroline. Family, tradition, the past, had seemed not to matter in her home. Only the Bible and the moral laws. Only doing what was right and avoiding what was evil.

"These are my grandparents," Lord Amberley said, pausing before two life-size portraits. "They are very like, though both were considerably older when I knew them."

The grandmother who had loved him as a child and aided and abetted him when he played truant from the nursery! Alexandra looked with curiosity at the stern, handsome lady in her tall powdered wig and ball gown with the wide padded hips.

If only she had had someone like that in her life. Would it have made a difference? Would Papa have allowed a grandmother to help her break the rules of the house? She had never known her own grandparents. Her mother's parents had lived for many years after her birth, but their home had been in Berkshire, and they had never traveled the distance to Dunstable Hall.

"Come to the windows," Lord Amberley said quietly from behind her. "Perhaps I have bored you with all my talk of people you have never known, Alex. But the view outside is splendid at least."

It was only then that Alexandra realized that she had said almost nothing since they had entered the gallery. Her thoughts had been intensely private and rather painful. She had still been caught up in that private world that her music had taken her into, despite the embarrassment she had felt at being questioned by Lord Amberley and at knowing that she had been overheard.

"Oh," she said, turning to him, "my silence does not indicate boredom. I like this room, Edmund. And I am fighting the urge to say it is lovely." She flashed him a smile. "I like to paint portraits. I am always fascinated by other people's attempts."

He smiled as they crossed to the windows. "You can see where you rode two days ago," he said. "Not quite to the sea but a long way down the valley. I always like the view of the hills from here. They seem to point to eternity. It always seems an appropriate setting for a family gallery."

"That is the chapel?" she asked, pointing to a small building close to the house but a little higher up the hill.

"Yes," he said. "I don't think there is time to go there now, Alex, but I would like you to see it. It is very small and utterly peaceful. Is it not strange that some buildings can be filled with the presence of God?"

"Is it used?" she asked.

"It was every morning during my grandfather's and my father's time," he said. "The servants were required to drop whatever they were doing when the bell rang and assemble there for devotions. I dropped the custom two years after I succeeded to the title."

"Why?" she asked. "Do you not feel a responsibility for the spiritual welfare of your servants?"

"No," he said. "One's spiritual welfare is a personal matter. I could force my servants to come to chapel and behave devoutly. Would I be bringing them closer to God? I think it unlikely. I have made it known that anyone may use the chapel at any time, from myself on down to the lowliest scullery maid. I have on occasion encountered a servant at prayer there."

"Papa would not agree with you," she said.

"And you?" he asked.

"I don't know," she said. "For all my religious devotions and all the importance of religion to my life, I do not believe I have ever felt close to God. Or really wished to be. I can never be worthy of God."

"But of course not," he said. "He does not expect us to be. You must go into the chapel, Alex. Go alone. If there is daylight outside, you will see that you are among the hills. If not, then you can remind yourself that you are. You will feel incredibly close to God. And you will realize that he is not a God of censure and vengeance. Those qualities are for men who habitually misunderstand God. God is love. Nothing else. Just simply that."

"It would not work," she said. "Love alone would not work. There would be chaos."

"Yes," he said. "There was the crucifixion. A chaotic end for a messiah. But there was also the resurrection. Love triumphant, you see."

It was a sweet, seductive theory. But far too simple to

represent an absolute truth. Alexandra smiled ruefully and turned away from the window.

"Madeline and Lord Eden and James will be waiting for me," she said.

"Yes," he said. "I must not keep you from your ride. The sea will look splendid from the cliffs this morning in the sunlight."

He led her back to the marble hall, where the three riders were indeed awaiting her. Talking to them were Howard Courtney and his sister.

Howard bowed and looked awkward when he saw the earl.

"Howard has business here with Spiller, Edmund," Lord Eden said. "Susan was sent by Mrs. Courtney to satisfy herself that the ladies have taken no harm from their exertions of last evening. We have prevailed upon her to come riding with us. I have already sent to the stables to have a horse saddled. Do you not envy Purnell and me? We are to have three ladies between the two of us. That is what I call fair odds." He grinned and looked thoroughly pleased with himself.

"I could not possibly allow you such a triumph, Dom," his brother said with a laugh. "Give me ten minutes and I shall make a sixth. The village will not run away if I postpone my visit for one day or even perhaps half a day." He smiled down at Alexandra.

"I never expected any such outing, my lord," Susan said, looking up at Lord Eden with her large hazel eyes and glancing up under her lashes at James Purnell. "I expected everyone to be still abed. I would have been quite happy to take tea with the housekeeper while Howard was busy with the bailiff."

"How glad I am that we had not already left," Lord Eden

said, smiling dazzlingly at her. "I would have been out of all charity with Mrs. Oats if she had had you all to herself for the next hour. Howard, you may return home when your business is done. I shall see that Susan is returned safely to her mama."

15

LORD EDEN QUICKLY FORGOT ANY ANNOYANCE he might have felt at having his plans for a private talk with Alexandra thwarted. It was, after all, a beautiful summer's day, and he had a pretty girl riding at his side, protesting blushingly that she should have declined joining the outing because she was not properly dressed for it. He was able to assure her in all truth that she made a charming picture on horseback in her light muslin dress and straw bonnet. There was plenty of time to spend with Miss Purnell.

He and Susan fell a little behind the others as they rode up the tree-shaded roadway on the western side of the valley.

"Well, Susan," he said, "you were much in demand last night. I was disappointed to find it impossible to have a second dance with you."

"All the gentlemen were most obliging," she said with a blush.

"And will you tell me now that I do not have to compete with a uniform?" he asked with a grin. "I thought that Captain Forbes and Lieutenant Jennings would come to blows over who should lead you into the final set."

"The lieutenant is Baron Renfrew's brother," she said. "I was never more surprised in my life. Do you know him, my lord?"

"Never heard of him," he said.

"He said that I dance more gracefully than all the ladies at Almack's," she said. "But I think he was flattering me. That cannot be true."

"I have not danced with all the ladies at Almack's," Lord Eden said. "But I tell you what, Susan. I have *seen* all the ladies at Almack's, and there is none prettier than you."

"Oh," she said, looking at him sidelong beneath her lashes, "you are funning me. I am not a grand lady. My gowns are not as fashionable as Lady Madeline's or my hair stylish. I am only the daughter of a farmer."

"Well," he said, "all the breeding and dressmakers and hairdressers in the world cannot make a girl lovely, Susan. Nature takes care of that. And I would have to say that nature took very good care of you."

She sighed. "How lovely it must be, though," she said, "to be able to be fashionable, to be able to go to Almack's and to other assemblies where the really important people go."

"They are vastly overrated entertainments, I assure you," he said. "I found last evening far more amusing than all the other balls I have attended this Season."

"Oh," she said, "I am sure you are just saying that, my lord, in order to be chivalrous."

"Not at all," he said. "You did not attend all those other balls, you see, Susan, but you were at last night's." He grinned at her.

They reached the top of the hill. An area of coarse grass and stones stretched ahead of them, buffeted frequently by the strong salt breezes from the sea. Grazing sheep dotted the landscape for as far as the eye could see. Lord Eden smiled at his companion and urged his horse forward in order to catch up to the others.

He was very tempted to flirt with Susan. She was all prettiness and big eyes and feminine frailty. It was so easy to flatter her and make her blush. He was intrigued by the changes two years had wrought in her. She had changed from a girl whom he had treated with indulgent condescension into a young woman whom he wanted to treat far differently. He would like to hold her in his arms and feel her soft curves against him. He would dearly like to kiss her.

But he really must not indulge in anything more than the mild, teasing flattery that he had used on his three encounters with her in the past few days. For one thing, being a nobleman and necessarily a gentleman of privilege also limited a man's freedom. His brother had taken him aside when he was eighteen and had begun to have a roving eye where females were concerned. One must choose with care the females with whom one intended to flirt, Edmund had said. It was cruel and ungentlemanly to set up hopes where one's intentions were not serious. And it was unthinkable to seduce any virtuous girl, no matter how low her birth. He must never assume that because he had rank and fortune, he had a right to any woman who took his fancy.

He had always heeded his brother's advice. And so girls like Susan were beyond his reach. When his need for a woman was strong, he always turned to those who were quite willing to oblige and who had no illusions about his intentions. He always paid handsomely for their services. But he had never set up a mistress. He had always been preoccupied with the latest love of his life and with dreams of marital bliss with her.

It was a shame about Susan. It would be easy to draw her into a pleasant flirtation, he knew. But there was the other reason why he must not do so. He glanced ahead to where Miss Purnell was riding beside his brother, looking elegant, if not dazzling, in a brown riding habit and hat with a yellow feather.

He found that he did not feel nearly so reluctant about marrying her as he had when he had first decided that he must relieve Edmund of the responsibility of making her respectable. He rather liked Miss Purnell. She was far different from his usual taste in women, it was true. He was habitually attracted to small, shy, pretty girls who made him feel protective. But Miss Purnell was not ugly. Far from it, in fact. When one really took a good look at her, one had to admit that she was decidedly handsome. She might even be beautiful if she would let herself be.

She did not have that soft, helpless femininity that he was always drawn to, of course. She was dignified and self-possessed. Yet he did not find her unattractive. He did not feel the need to protect her, but he did find his masculinity challenged by her. He had never thought of the army and marriage simultaneously as he had the evening before. If he had married any of the other girls he had loved, then of course he would have had to stay at home to take care of his wife. He could not have endangered her peace of mind by putting his own life in danger on a battlefield.

But the night before, it had suddenly seemed a splendid idea to marry Miss Purnell, buy a commission in the army, and sail off to Spain to win glory for his country and his wife. She was the sort of woman he would want to impress. She would spur him on to brave deeds. And she had seemed to understand the night before. She had wavered in her answer to his proposal. He would be able to win her, he was sure.

And so he must put his youth behind him. He must not allow himself to be too much impressed by Susan's prettiness or give in to the pleasant possibility of a summer's flirtation.

He smiled at her. "Do you like riding on the cliffs, Susan?" he asked.

"I do not like to be close to the edge," she said. "I become quite dizzy in high places. Whenever we walk close, I always cling to Papa's arm or Howard's, and then I feel safe."

"Don't worry," he said. "I see the others are all dismounting here. The horses will graze quite happily while we walk forward. Let me help you down. Then you shall take my arm and feel quite perfectly safe, I promise."

"I hope I will not spoil your pleasure, my lord," she said anxiously. "I really do not want to go too close."

She set her hands on his shoulders as he took her by the waist to lift her to the ground. But somehow she lost her grip, with the result that she swayed against him and slid along the length of him before her slippered feet finally touched the ground. She blushed hotly, and her long lashes fanned her cheeks, hiding her eyes completely from his view.

"I do beg your pardon," he said, releasing his hold of her as she brushed down the skirt of her dress. "How clumsy of me!"

"It was my fault, my lord," she said breathlessly, peeping up at him. "I was not quite ready."

Lord Eden offered her his arm and regretted anew that she was as untouchable to him as a vestal virgin. He was having to make a concerted effort to control his breathing.

• • •

ALEXANDRA DID NOT HOLD to anyone's arm as they approached the edge of the cliff. She was enjoying the almost bleak emptiness of their surroundings, the coarse grass underfoot, the fresh breeze, from which they had been sheltered just a couple of minutes before. She was reminded of the moors except that there was a salt tang to the air here. She felt exhilarated. She wanted to throw off her hat, spread out her arms to the wind, and run.

And then she came to the crest of a slight rise of land, and her heart somersaulted inside her. The world fell away almost at her feet, and the sea sparkled far below and stretched to the dark blue horizon. The wind whipped her skirt against her legs. She drew in deep lungfuls of air and closed her eyes for a moment. She looked around for James so that she might share the moment with him.

But it was Lord Amberley who stood at her shoulder.

"It takes your breath away when you are not used to it, does it not?" he said. "Indeed, it does so even when one knows what to expect."

"It is magnificent," she said, and turned back to gaze out over the sea and downward to the white line of the waves breaking against the beach far below. She could see the rock to which she and Lord Eden had raced two days before. She was grateful that Lord Amberley did not say anything. It was not the time for small talk. And to put into words what she felt was quite as impossible now as it had been the day before when she had seen an equally magnificent, though quite different, view from above the valley.

"I think there is nothing as awe-inspiring as wild nature," she said, breaking the silence at last. "Tamed nature, gardens, can be appreciated with the senses. But this"—she drew in a deep breath again—"this one feels here." She placed a hand against her ribs. "It is too deep for words. It is almost an ache. Do you know what I mean?"

"Yes," he said quietly. "Perfectly."

She turned her head toward him after a minute more of silence. She smiled fleetingly. "I might also say that it is lovely," she said.

He smiled back in some amusement. "You were quite right yesterday about the inadequacy of words," he said. "It was foolish and quite unreasonable of me to hope that you would respond to the places I love with the words I have never been able to find for myself. But then, I have never been called upon to do so. I am a very private person, as you may have realized, Alex. I have a close relationship with my family, but my deepest feelings I have never shared."

She had been looking into his eyes. But they were so very blue in the sunlight, so very kindly, that awareness of his physical presence returned and broke the rare ease of their conversation. She turned sharply away.

"Is the cliff quite sheer?" she asked. "Is it possible for it to be scaled?"

"Oh, yes," he said, "though it is very dangerous to do so, especially in this particular place. I did it for the first time when I was thirteen years old, with Peregrine Lampman. He is two years younger than I. It was strictly forbidden, of course. We would not have been caught except that Perry got stuck close to the top. He had made the mistake, I believe, of looking down, and then would not move up or down or sideways for all my cajoling. I had to run home for help. I felt like something of a hero until all the excitement was over and Perry had been borne home by his father. I did not feel quite so heroic after a sound thrashing. I believe poor Perry suffered a like fate."

He was grinning when she looked back at him. "Your parents must have been frantic with images of what might have happened," she said.

"Oh, yes," he agreed. "I realized that even at the time. I have always vowed that I will bring my sons here myself when they are of suitable age, and perhaps even my daughters too if they are anything like Madeline, and supervise them on a climb. Perhaps that will destroy the lure of it as a forbidden activity."

Papa would never handle a situation in that way, Alexandra thought. A forbidden activity was wrong, an offense against God as well as the moral laws. Supervising such an activity merely because one knew it would be attempted anyway was moral weakness. It merely taught children that wrongdoing is sometimes excusable. That was what Papa would say. He would approve of the thrashing. He would doubtless have added a week or more of confinement to the schoolroom or a bedchamber.

She was not at all sure that Papa was right. She could almost picture the intense pleasure and sense of adventure and achievement Lord Amberley's children would derive from climbing the cliff with him. And such a shared activity would bring him closer to his children. There would be the bond of love between them, not of fear.

They would be her children too! The thought caused a nasty lurching of her stomach and made her realize that she was still looking at her betrothed. She turned away to gaze down at the beach and the breakers again.

"There is another way down," he said. "A little farther along." He pointed to their left. "There is a fault in the rock that forms a quite effective and reasonably safe path. It makes for exciting exercise, though it is quite unappealing to children, of course."

"May we go down?" she asked, turning to look at him with bright eyes.

He looked surprised. "Now?" he said. "When I said the path is safe, I perhaps exaggerated somewhat. It is not wide and it is steep. It has to be descended with great care."

"I will be careful," she said. "May we go down?" She felt an almost urgent need to do so. She felt as she did on those occasions at home when she begged James to gallop across the moors with her. Almost as if she would burst if she could not somehow give vent to pent-up energy. James had never needed much persuasion.

Lord Amberley looked back searchingly into her eyes. "We would have to leave the horses up here," he said. "It is a walk of three miles at least back to the house from the bottom of the cliff."

"I will enjoy the walk," she said.

He still seemed undecided. Then he smiled suddenly. "I will take you down there on one condition," he said. "You must hold firmly to my hand every step of the way."

"Yes," she said, and she smiled openly at him in her eagerness.

"We had better see if Dominic and your brother will take our horses back for us," he said, turning to look for the others. Lord Eden was standing a short distance away, farther back from the edge of the cliff, with Susan Courtney clinging with both hands to his arm. James Purnell and Madeline were strolling back toward them along the clifftop, side by side, not touching.

MADELINE HAD BEEN HAVING a difficult morning. Inevitably she was paired with James Purnell. She was becoming almost resigned to the fact. She had been able to see, when Susan arrived and agreed to join them on the ride, that that young lady would have been just as pleased to ride with Mr. Purnell as with Dominic, but Madeline had not allowed her hopes to soar. It was unlikely that anyone would think it polite to leave her to her twin's company. Besides, it was clear that Dominic fancied Susan. He would probably be head over ears in love with her within a few days at the most.

And so she had ridden with Mr. Purnell and walked with him for a few minutes along the cliff top and exhausted every topic of conversation known to man. It was not that he was silent. He was not quite that ill-bred. But he never initiated a topic, and his comments and responses to those she introduced were terse and entirely to the point. He never left her any room to expand on a theme. He said only what needed to be said. Did he not know that in polite conversation one forced oneself to say a great deal more?

By the time they were strolling back toward her brothers, Madeline was fuming with suppressed rage. Her elder brother's idea of climbing down the cliff path, then, something she had not done for years, was entirely irresistible.

"Oh, I will come with you, Edmund," she said, her face glowing into life. "I can think of nothing more exhilarating. Dom, do come with us. Mr. Purnell can take Susan back to the house."

Lord Eden glanced down at his companion—clinging to his arm with both hands, Madeline noticed, and looking decidedly pale—then regretfully back at his sister. "No," he said, "you go, Mad. I will stay with Susan. She is afraid of heights, you know."

Perhaps it would not take him a few days to be in love, Madeline thought, noting the protective way his free hand came across to pat one of Susan's reassuringly. Dom looked as if he had fallen already. Perhaps it was not a bad thing, either, although Susan was just the helpless, clinging type of female that always attracted Dom and was quite wrong for him. At least she would keep him away from Alexandra. And the infatuation would not last long. Dom's infatuations never did. And neither did hers, for that matter, she thought philosophically.

"Is there a way down?" James Purnell was asking. "And are you really prepared to tackle it, Alex? I will come too, of course."

Madeline turned away from her twin with an inward sigh as he assured everyone that he would take Susan back to the house and send stable-hands for the horses.

Madeline and Purnell led the way down. She declined the assistance of his hand. She knew from experience that the path was quite safe, though it would seem dangerous if one did not know it. If one walked close against the cliff face, even spreading one's hands on the rock, one could stay decently far from the edge. Time had made the surface underfoot grassy and quite firm. It was only the height and the sheerness of the drop at the edge of the path that gave the illusion of danger.

A little more than halfway down, the path opened out onto a much broader ledge. From there on the path was narrower and steeper, but the danger seemed to be past because the beach was so much closer. Madeline enjoyed every step of the descent. Although Mr. Purnell turned back frequently to see if she needed assistance, the obligation of making conversation had been taken away from her temporarily. She felt great regret when he finally jumped down the few feet from the end of the path to the beach and turned to lift her down. And it was only then that she realized that now she would be with him for all of the three-mile walk home.

She set her hands on his shoulders and jumped. Edmund and Alexandra, she could see when they both looked up, were still no farther down than the broad ledge.

"Will Alexandra be all right, do you think?" she asked. "I must confess I was surprised that she allowed herself to be persuaded to make the descent."

"It was probably Alex who suggested it," he said. "She has a great deal of energy and courage when she forgets herself and breaks free."

He looked as if he were talking to himself, Madeline thought, his eyes narrowed and looking upward. That lock of dark hair was down over his forehead again. He was not wearing a hat.

"Edmund will see that she is safe anyway," she said. "I have been told that Papa was the first to bring me down here, but I can remember doing it only with Edmund. I always felt as safe as I could possibly be. It seemed impossible then that he could ever slip. We have gone up too on occasion. That seems very much safer, though it takes considerably more exertion."

"You seem to have been given a great deal of freedom as a child," he said, turning to begin the walk along the beach.

"Yes," she agreed. "I did not even realize that it was so until I began to meet other people and found that their upbringing was often a great deal more restricting. Do you disapprove?"

He walked with his hands clasped behind him, she noticed. She was glad that he did not offer her his arm. "No," he said. "If I had children..."

Madeline looked inquiringly at him when he did not immediately continue. He was grimacing. His eyes were on the sand at his feet.

"If I had children," he began again, "I would see to it that they had a happy childhood. If I planned to have any, that is."

"You do not wish to have children?" she asked. "Or to marry?"

"No to both questions," he said curtly. "Why bring children into this world knowing what is ahead of them? Better to leave them in unknowing oblivion."

"But you cannot know what is ahead for them," she said. "Life has a great deal of happiness and pleasure to offer. I have even known happy people among those who seem to have nothing at all to celebrate."

"Death is ahead for every child that is born," he said harshly.

"But one cannot dismiss the value of the whole of life just because death is its inevitable end," she said. "Sometimes when I think that I must die, that there is no avoiding the moment, I am consumed with terror. But Edmund once told me how to cope with such moments. Look back on your life, he said, and ask yourself quite honestly if you would have missed it, given the choice. I think I would hate not to have lived at all."

"You have lived a privileged life," he said. "Some people have nothing pleasant at all to look back upon."

"I cannot believe that," she said. "Oh, yes, I know I am privileged. I find nothing more horrifying than the journey into London, when one has to drive past all the dreadful signs of poverty. But there are very poor people who are happy. I have met some. I don't believe that any life need be filled with unrelieved despair."

"You are a romantic," he said. "Your attitude is typical of those who have never been called upon to suffer."

"That is unfair," she said. "I have been fortunate, yes. More fortunate than anyone has a right to expect to be, perhaps. But I have suffered too. My father died when I was twelve years old. I was still at an age when life seemed safe and secure and incredibly happy. And then Papa died quite suddenly. And Mama was gone for a long time too. She was here with us the whole time, but she suffered what must have been a living death. Suddenly the world was a wide and dark and frightening place. And yet life is still worth living. The experience has taught me that happiness is to be enjoyed to the fullest right now. It is a gift that should not be wasted. And it can give us the strength to live through the troubled times."

"And how does one get one's strength if one has never been allowed to be happy?" he asked. "And one's faith that life is worth living?"

"I don't know," she said. "Are you referring to your sister? She is a strong person, I believe. And I don't think she shares your cynicism with life. Happiness is possible for her. Edmund can make her happy."

He stopped walking and looked back along the beach. They had walked almost to the head of the valley. Madeline looked back too. Alexandra and her brother were on the beach, but they were standing still below the cliff path. They were a long way back.

"Perhaps," he said. "I hope you are right. Perhaps there is that much justice in this world. I would see some glimmering of meaning if only Alex could be happy."

Madeline shook her skirt as they stepped onto grass at last. But her hem had not picked up a great deal of sand. The beach was firm and damp.

"You are very self-pitying," she said. "You and Alexandra had a hard upbringing, I think. You have not known a great deal of happiness. But you are alive now. You are still young. There is still a great deal of happiness you can make for yourself if you will. I think you are so much in the habit of feeling sorry for yourself that you have doomed yourself to a life of misery and martyrdom. You cannot have suffered that much in fewer than thirty years of living."

It was a very unmannerly speech. She might have spoken to Dominic thus with no fear of offending beyond an angry moment. It was not at all the way to talk to a stranger. She would not have done so had she not still been feeling cross at having to spend a whole glorious morning with a difficult companion.

She looked across at him when he did not immediately reply. She was already framing an apology in her mind. But she swallowed the words when she saw the expression on his face. He was looking straight ahead, to her everlasting gratitude. His face was tense, his dark eyes burning with fury.

"What do you know of my life, of my past?" he said. She was positively frightened by the quiet control in his voice. "Only someone quite silly and totally lacking in imagination or sense will announce to another that he cannot possibly have suffered because he has not yet reached his thirtieth year and because he is still alive. You know nothing beyond your own life of frivolous pleasure. Nothing!"

Madeline had to increase her pace to keep up with his lengthened stride. The trouble was, she could not even feel anger at his outburst and his judgement of her character. She had the uncomfortable feeling that she had deserved both.

"You are right," she said. "It was a silly thing to say. But I did not mean quite what I said. I merely meant that life is what you make of it. There is no point in brooding on the past, however bad it might have been. Life is to be lived. And there is still possibly a great deal left for you as well as for me. Is it not wrong to reject the gift of the future?"

"Gift?" he said, turning to look at her. His voice was full of contempt. "And who, pray, is the giver? God? If there were such a being, I would hurl his gift back in his face. You are a romantic."

"And that is supposed to set me down and make me feel like a worm?" she said, anger finally coming to her rescue again. "I would prefer to be a romantic than a cynic, sir. Who is usually the happier of the two, may I ask? And you are an atheist, I perceive. Then I am truly sorry for you. And I can understand why you feel as you do about life. The man without God is a man without hope."

He laughed without amusement. "Another quotation from your brother?" he asked. "I wonder if you have ever had an original thought."

"Now you have gone too far," she said, stopping short and glaring up at him. "I believe that calls for an apology, sir."

He stopped too and looked down at her, his eyes cold. "Let me see," he said. "I make an elegant bow first. Thus? And then I say that if I have offended your feminine sensibilities, I will offer my tongue to be cut from my mouth. Or do you prefer to dispense with the theatrics? I am sorry. I believe I made an insulting remark about your intelligence."

Madeline frowned. She felt very close to tears, but she was not going to give him the satisfaction of knowing that she was deeply hurt. "Why do you hate me?" she asked.

He made an impatient gesture and began to walk on. "More theatrics," he said. "Do you want me on my knees before you?"

"You hate me," she said. "It is not just dislike. It is not just contempt for someone you think foolish. You hate me."

"Nonsense!" he said. "We can hate only those who are important to us in some way. In what way could you be important to me? You are the sister of Alex's betrothed. We have been forced into company together and are likely to be again. Neither of us is particularly happy about that. We do not like each other. I don't think it is a matter for soul-searching, do you? I suggest that we be civilized and keep our conversation to neutral and essentially meaningless topics."

"And yet," she accused indignantly, "when I have tried to do just that, I bear the burden almost entirely alone. You have almost nothing to say on any topic, and you will begin none of your own."

He stopped again and looked at her, his expression unfathomable. "Take my arm," he said, offering it to her. "How much farther do we have to walk? Upward of a mile, would you say? I shall tell you about my years at school, shall I? And if I run out of anecdotes on that topic, I will tell you about my two years at university. You may say 'Really?' and 'Is that so?' and 'How splendid!' in the right places, if you wish. Beyond that you may relax your mind. I shall entertain you."

Madeline glared back at him for a moment before thrusting her arm almost vengefully through his and striding on.

He began to talk.

THE PATH FELT VERY DANGEROUS. THE CLIFF face was warm and hard against Alexandra's shoulder, the path firm beneath her feet. But the sheer drop to the beach at the edge of the path, the steep slope of the path itself, the wind howling around their feet and whipping at her skirt and hat, the sunlight sparkling on the water far below, the gulls crying from above and swooping down around them: all thrilled her with an intense excitement.

Her heart beat fast. She could never remember such exhilaration. She knew she should not look down—she might get dizzy if she did so. Lord Amberley and her own good sense had told her that before they started. But how could she resist? The edge of the tide stretched for miles, its surface ridged with the ever-moving waves, the ones closest to the beach breaking in a spreading line of foam. And the golden beach swung in a great arc right beneath her feet. She stopped numerous times to drink it all in. There might never be this much happiness again.

She clung obediently to Lord Amberley's hand during every moment of the descent. But she did not feel threatened by his touch or his nearness. Both added an assurance of safety. Besides, he made no attempt to intrude into her thoughts. He said nothing, moving when she moved, stopping when she stopped, seeming to sense her need for silence. Perhaps he shared it.

He spoke for the first time when they reached the broad ledge more than halfway down. "Madeline and your brother are down on the beach already," he said. "Do you mind being so far behind?"

"No," she said. "I don't want to hurry. I don't want this ever to end." She closed her eyes and turned her face to the wind. Then she opened them again and looked at him guiltily. "But you will want to be home as soon as possible. You have work to do."

"Nothing that will not wait," he said. "I would far prefer to be here with you, Alex. I feel almost like a boy again, escaping my responsibilities."

"Escape is so rare," she said, turning her face to the wind again, "and so very precious. I do not want ever to think of anything beyond this moment. I will not think."

"An admirable resolution," he said. "Shall we continue on our thoughtless way? Be careful, Alex. The path is narrower for the rest of the way. Hold firmly to my hand."

It was unnecessary advice, since she had not relinquished her hold of it since they began the descent. But he grasped hers more tightly as he led the way down, letting it go finally only so that he could jump down onto the sand and reach up to lift her down after.

"What a pity," she said, setting her hands on his shoulders and allowing him to lift her from the ledge. "I don't want to set my feet on safety and sanity again."

"Then we shall not force you to do so, madam," he said, holding her to the full extent of his arms and swinging her in a circle. "You shall stay up there for the rest of the morning. I shall carry you home."

Alexandra shrieked and giggled. "Set me down," she said. "Oh, set me down before my arms break."

He set her feet down on the sand and she turned from him toward the distant line of the sea. "Oh, how beautiful it is," she said. "How beautiful. How wonderful it is to be alive and to be here." She snatched her hat free from her head and held her face up to the sun.

Lord Amberley stood behind her, transfixed. She was a different woman again, the one he had held in his arms and lost his head over the day before. Except that this was no sexual passion he watched. This vibrant, beautiful woman, whose face had just laughed down into his, whose dark eyes had glowed with wonder, was part of the very wildness of nature about her. She was alive! Could this be Alexandra Purnell? He unconsciously held his breath.

"It would be altogether too dull to stroll sedately back to the house, would it not?" he said. "And to do something as mundane as arrive in time for luncheon. Shall we play shameless truant and walk out to the edge of the sea?"

"May we?" She spun around to face him and he released his breath. She was still the same woman, the one whose existence he had not suspected until the day before. Her cheeks were glowing, her eyes sparkling. She was smiling.

"We may," he said. He swept her a bow. "I am lord of the manor, ma'am, and I say we may. Would you care to take my arm?"

"No," she said. "I want to run. All the way to the edge of the water. I have never run in my life." She held up her skirt with one hand and set her face for the water's edge.

Lord Amberley, laughing, watched her go for a moment before following her. She was not trying to run from him or to race him. She held her face up to the sunlight and set her body against the wind. But she had slowed to a walk by the time he caught up to her, and was holding her side.

"Oh," she said, gasping for breath, "I am not very fit. Oh!" She stood still, panting and laughing.

"Ma'am," he said, bowing and laughing back at her, "perhaps now you will conduct yourself like the lady you are and avail yourself of my support."

"Oh, gladly, sir," she said, slipping her arm through his and walking forward at a much more sedate pace. "I have always wanted to do that. To run on the moors, my arms spread to the wind. Absurd, is it not? I forget I am no child."

"There is an eternal child in all of us," he said, "thank goodness. A time to be silly and absurd and utterly irresponsible."

They did not talk for a while. But Lord Amberley watched her in wonder. She was gazing about her with a bright, animated face.

"One could imagine oneself all alone in the world here, could one not?" she said when they finally came to a stop no more than three feet from the incoming tide. "But one would not feel lonely. It is much easier to feel lonely in the middle of Almack's. Here there is a vast and powerful presence. God, I think."

"Some people find such surroundings frightening," he said.

"Ah, yes," she said. "People who have always been surrounded with activity and other people might feel that way. People who have never been alone with themselves. Sometimes I have longed for friends, for a more exciting life. But in many ways I have been blessed. I have learned not to be afraid of silence. Not that there is ever silence in nature. Listen!" They stood very still and listened to the roar of the sea, so immense and elemental that it could be mistaken for silence. "Oh, I have had so little of nature."

Her arm was still linked through his. He turned so that they could stroll along the sand beside the water. The sparkle and exuberance had gone from her, he saw with some regret, but there was still a barrier gone from her. Her more peaceful mood seemed still to be relaxed. She did not walk beside him with stiff spine and raised chin. Her face was not a disciplined and expressionless mask. One glance down at her showed him that she was still beautiful.

And he found as they strolled along together that the absence of conversation between them was not at all uncomfortable. After a few minutes he was able to relax almost as much as he could during solitary walks in the same place. In some ways even more so. It made for contentment to know that there was someone beside him in tune with his thoughts and feelings. For the first time he began to feel that perhaps a marriage between them would be possible. Perhaps she was even beginning to overcome her distrust of him. Certainly there had been no evidence of it since they had left the house.

He would like to make more of the moment. He would like to stop walking again and just stand and gaze out to sea with her beside him, his arm around her waist, holding her against his side. He would like to put his arms right around her, hold her against him, kiss her even. Not with passion. The passion had gone out of the morning several minutes before. But just from the contentment of the moment. He wanted affection to grow between them. He wanted to be close to her. He wanted a real marriage.

And he knew suddenly and with some amazement that he would not after all have been happy with Eunice. There had been affection between them, yes, and she had been incredibly kind to him. They had shared a stimulating friendship. But he could not have strolled like this with Eunice, silent and contented. And he could never have even dreamed of holding Eunice in his arms out of mere affection. She would have allowed it, as she had allowed him the deepest intimacy of all whenever he had wished for it. But she would have given like a mother to a child, because of his need. She had no emotional need for him. He did not want another mother. He wanted a wife.

Yes, he needed a wife. He had often thought that he could very easily develop into a hermit when Madeline and Dominic finally moved away permanently and when his mother was not in residence. The thought had sometimes seemed attractive. But a solitary life would not satisfy him after all. He wanted to share his life with a woman. And he wanted children. There was too much need in him to give love to make the life of a hermit a possibility.

And soon he was to have a wife. Alex. And he was beginning to think that he wanted her, despite all the strange prickliness of her character. It was not just that he must learn to love her. He thought it very possible that he would grow to love her. And now, today, hope had been born in him that she might after all allow herself to be loved.

He touched her fingers with his and smiled down at her. "All truants have to creep home eventually, alas," he said, "unless they become runaways. Shall we run away to sea, Alex, and never return? Or shall we go back and think of a plausible excuse for our lateness on the way? We must have missed luncheon by an hour."

"It would mean three days in our rooms at least with Papa," she said. "And prayer and fasting and Bible reading the whole time."

"Would it?" he said. "Will a cold luncheon instead be sufficient penance?"

"Yes," she said, turning with him to walk up the beach to the head of the valley, her arm no longer linked through his, but their hands clasped together again.

It was possible after all, she thought, and her spirits rose anew. It was possible to be free, to do something merely because one wanted to do it. And not have to face consequences. Freedom despite the chains. It was altogether possible to be happy.

And it was possible to be with Lord Amberley and not resent him. It was possible to walk with him, to have her hand in his, to look occasionally into his blue eyes, to talk with him, to laugh with him. Even to be silent with him, as she was now. It was possible.

She thought that she might even endure his kiss at that particular moment without losing herself and without panicking as she had the day before. Today everything seemed possible. It seemed possible that she could marry him and live comfortably with him. It seemed possible that marriage, even one not of her own choosing, need not be a prison. Marriage would bind her to this man, but within those bonds she could perhaps be free. After all, was not life itself very similar? One was bound to life and could not escape death. But there was freedom and happiness to be achieved within it.

"You must be very weary," he said when the house was well in sight. "We have walked several miles."

"Decidedly footsore," she admitted. "But I suggested the walk, remember? Thank you, Edmund."

Lord Amberley's bailiff was waiting for him at the foot of the steps leading to the main doors. Both Madeline and Lady Amberley were with him.

"Edmund," Madeline called, hurrying toward him and Alexandra, "whatever has kept you for so long? Mr. Spiller was going to ride for you, but I have been assuring him for almost the last hour that you were not far behind Mr. Purnell and me and could not be longer than a few minutes."

Lord Amberley looked inquiringly at his bailiff. "Miss Purnell and I have been playing truant and strolling by the water," he said. "What on earth can be so important that it cannot wait?"

"It is Joel Peterson, your lordship," the bailiff said. He was dressed for riding. He was twisting his hat in his hand.

"What about Joel?" the earl asked with a frown.

"Oh, Edmund," Lady Amberley said, "the poor man has upset a cart and could not get out of the way of it as it fell. He has been carried home, but it is feared that he is badly hurt."

"I was on my way there," Mr. Spiller said. "But I thought you would want to come with me, your lordship."

Alexandra withdrew her hand from Lord Amberley's as he stepped forward.

"Yes, indeed," he said. "He is badly hurt, you think? How on earth did he come to upset a cart? When did you hear of this, Spiller?"

"Close to two hours ago, my lord," the bailiff said. "Seth Harrison rode over as soon as it happened."

"And I had to be from home!" Lord Amberley said. "Well, Spiller, let us waste no more time. You have had my horse saddled?"

"He is all ready in the stable yard, my lord," the bailiff said.

Lord Amberley began to stride in the direction of the stables.

"Edmund?" Alexandra called, her hand outstretched to him.

He stopped and turned back. "Mama," he said, "Alex has had no luncheon. Will you see to it?"

"PAPA WILL BE MOST vexed if he ever finds out how you have been behaving, Alexandra," Lady Beckworth complained. "I wish he had not declined the invitation to accompany us here. I feel altogether unable to cope with you. You are so headstrong that only your father seems able to tame you. James is no good at all."

Alexandra sat on a stool in her mother's dressing room, where she had been summoned after her late luncheon. She had not wanted to eat, but Lady Amberley had taken her arm and insisted.

"I know just what an appetite good sea air can arouse," she had said. "And as for being late, my dear Alexandra, think nothing of it. I had three children who were invariably late for meals despite the existence of a nurse who had a ferocious bark but no bite at all. All three of them quickly had her wrapped around their little fingers, especially Dominic. I am only too glad to see Edmund take the time to show you around."

"But that poor man," Alexandra had said. "Who is he?"

Joel Peterson was one of Lord Amberley's field laborers, she discovered. He lived in the village with his wife and two half-grown boys.

"Edmund will be disturbed by this accident," Lady Amberley had said. "He always takes anything to do with his workers very personally, almost as if he is solely responsible for every sickness or accident that happens. He has an overdeveloped sense of responsibility. But you will love him for it, dear, as I do. It is always better to be that way than to be careless and insensitive, is it not?"

Lady Amberley had sat at the table drinking tea while Alexandra ate. Alexandra had forced herself to swallow the food that was set in front of her, though she did so with difficulty. "And I had to be from home!" Lord Amberley had said. They would have been at home if she had not suggested descending the cliff path. Lord Eden, it seemed, had arrived back and left again to take Susan Courtney home before news of the accident had arrived. And Lord Amberley would have been at the village if she had only agreed the day before to accompany him there.

"It was unfortunate that his lordship was from home when Mr. Spiller came looking for him," Alexandra said now to her mother without looking up.

"That is not the point," Lady Beckworth said. "I daresay the bailiff could have taken care of the matter himself. That is what he is employed for, I take it. But for you to be so long alone with his lordship is disgraceful, Alexandra."

Alexandra looked up in surprise. "Yesterday you said it was quite unexceptionable to go riding with him, Mama," she said.

"And so it was," her mother said, "for one occasion, Alexandra. But that was yesterday afternoon, and already this morning you have been alone with him again for upward of an hour. What will Lady Amberley think of your morals? I dread to think what your father would have to say to you and to me if he were here now."

Alexandra looked down at her hands, which were spread in her lap. "We walked down close to the ocean," she said.

"You scrambled down a steep path to the sand," Lady Beckworth said. "A most unladylike activity, Alexandra.

Your father has not raised you to behave in such a hoydenish manner. What is worse, James seems to think that you were the one to suggest such a mad scheme. Is this true?"

"Yes, Mama," she said.

"I cannot understand it," Lady Beckworth said. "And then to stay on the beach for a whole hour after James and Lady Madeline had come back home. How is anyone to know what you were doing there?"

"I have told you, Mama," Alexandra said, "that we walked down to the water."

"I am not sure I can trust you to tell the truth," her mother said. "Your father was never convinced that you did not leave the Easton ballroom to meet a lover, Alexandra. And now your behavior appears quite inexcusably wanton."

Alexandra's hands were clenched into fists in her lap. But she said nothing. What was the use? There had never been any point in arguing with Mama and Papa. Indeed, she had learned that doing so usually brought on its own punishment.

"Well, you are justly punished," Lady Beckworth said. "While you were engaged in your immoral behavior on the beach, whatever it was, perhaps that cart driver was dying. And apparently he was asking for his lordship. If he dies, Alexandra, before his lordship can reach him, I believe you will know who has judged you. A far higher authority than I or even your papa, I fear. I expect more decorous and more godly behavior from my daughter."

Alexandra was on her feet, panic in her eyes. "Mama," she said, "the man was not that badly hurt, was he? Oh, please say he was not that badly hurt."

"I have no idea how badly injured he was," her mother said. "Such matters are none of my concern, Alexandra.

But I believe you know what your father would direct you to do now."

Alexandra stared at her wildly for another few moments before turning and fleeing from the room.

LORD EDEN WAS WHISTLING to himself as he turned the gig from the laneway leading to Courtney's farm onto the main roadway from the village to Amberley. Susan. He grinned. It was almost worth having missed the scramble down to the beach with the others just in order to have spent an extra hour with her.

He did not think he had ever encountered anyone quite so timid. She had always been the same. He could remember her as a child insisting on climbing trees with her brothers, but invariably getting stuck in a lower branch, terrified to move until someone went to her rescue. He could remember her once crossing the river in the valley on stepping-stones and having to be almost carried from the loose one in the middle.

Even as a child she had always been as wide-eyed in her gratitude for rescue as she was now. She had been very apologetic about keeping him from the cliff path earlier and had valiantly offered to return to Amberley alone if he really wished to go. Yet all the while she had clung with both hands to his arm as if she thought the wind would blow her over the edge if she released her hold. As if he would have left her alone there! And as if he would have allowed any harm to come to her!

Lord Eden turned his thoughts to Alexandra. He had certainly missed his chance to follow up his advantage of the evening before. Perhaps he would have a chance to talk to her that afternoon. It seemed likely that Edmund would spend his time about estate business, having lost a few hours during the morning.

Poor Edmund. He had never particularly enjoyed having guests. He had always preferred a quiet life, sometimes even a solitary one. He spent time with his family, of course, because he was familiar with them and comfortable with them. And he always dutifully both issued and accepted social invitations. But he would hate the obligation he now had to be sociable, to take Miss Purnell about, to entertain her. He must long to get off on his own as he so often did when they were all at home.

But of course courtesy and duty always came first with Edmund. Having spent time after breakfast showing Miss Purnell the gallery, he must have been looking forward to a quiet hour or two in his office or riding around the estate or doing whatever he had planned to do. But then he had discovered that Susan had been invited for the ride too and had felt obliged to join the group in order to even the numbers. Poor Edmund!

The object of his thoughts hailed him at that moment and came riding up alongside him.

"You have been into the village?" Lord Eden asked. "You wasted no time, Edmund."

"Joel Peterson has just died," Lord Amberley said. And indeed his face was unusually serious and pale, his brother saw now that he looked at him more closely.

"Joel?" he said, pulling back on the ribbons so that the horses were scarcely moving. "Whatever happened?"

"He had a cart loaded with hay," the earl explained. "He pulled it over to let another vehicle past, it seems, and tipped it. It fell on him."

Lord Eden grimaced. "It killed him instantly?" he asked.

"No." Lord Amberley was very pale. "He was taken

home and was conscious too. He died just a short while before Spiller and I got there. Apparently there was no way of saving him. But I wish I had been there. He was worried, apparently, about what would happen to his wife and sons. But I always look after the widows and orphans of my workers. He knew that. He must have known that, must he not, Dom?"

"You have never failed," his brother said, "or Papa or Grandpapa before you. Yes, Edmund, he would have known that they would be cared for."

"I wish that I had been there to reassure him all the same," Lord Amberley said. "If I had arrived just fifteen minutes sooner, I could have done so. Fifteen minutes, Dom. Poor Joel. He was a conscientious worker."

"Is anyone with his wife now?" Lord Eden asked.

"Half the village," the earl assured him. "And Spiller, of course. He will make all the arrangements for the funeral. I stayed for a while. But my presence put a strain on them, you know. Mrs. Peterson seemed to feel obliged to treat me like an honored guest when obviously she was beside herself with grief. She needed to give way to it but could not do so as long as I was there." He smiled rather sadly. "We are a race apart, are we not, Dom?"

Thcy rode on side by side and turned through the gates onto the narrow tree-lined driveway leading to the valley road.

"You saw Susan safely home?" Lord Amberley asked. He did not wait for an answer. "Will you and Madeline entertain Alex this afternoon, Dom? And her brother and mother, of course. I need to be alone for a while."

"You know you don't need even to ask," Lord Eden said, and eased back on the ribbons as the road began to descend and his brother rode on ahead of him.

• • •

WHEN JAMES PURNELL WENT in search of his sister later in the afternoon, he found her in her bedchamber staring out through the east-facing window.

"You have been all alone here, Alex?" he said. "Why?"

"That man," she said tonelessly, "the one who was hurt. He is dead."

"Yes, I know," he said. "The whole family seems to have taken it rather hard."

"I went downstairs," she said. "When I saw him coming home, I went down to ask him. He scarcely spoke to me. He brushed past me and went upstairs. It was Lord Eden who told me. And when I came back up here, I saw him ride away again."

"Amberley?" he said. "Doubtless he had business to attend to, Alex."

"He went up the valley," she said.

Purnell frowned and came to stand beside her. "You are upset?" he asked. "You feel abandoned? I think you are becoming attached to him, aren't you?"

She looked at him bleakly. "It's my fault," she said. "All my fault, James. I am like a blight on everything I touch."

His frown deepened. "What is this?" he said. "What are you blaming yourself for, Alex? You were miles away from the accident. You did not even know the man."

"I insisted on going down that path," she said, "just like a child who must have its treat now. We would have been home a couple of hours before if I had not."

"Nonsense, Alex!" he said, taking her by the shoulders and turning her to him. "You are developing a conscience like Papa's. Don't do it. Of course you are not to blame. You are Amberley's betrothed, Alex, and a guest in his house—by his invitation."

"Last night," she said, "he asked if I would go to the village with him to meet some of his laborers. I said no. I was feeling spiteful and I said no, I had promised to go riding with Lord Eden."

He dropped his hands. "I had hoped that this was going to work for you," he said. "I thought perhaps you could be happy with Amberley. But there is something between you? Some problem?"

"I don't know," she said, turning from him wearily. "He has been kindness itself. I could not ask for someone more courteous or more willing to please. And now that has become the problem. I feel oppressed with kindness, hemmed in, totally inadequate. And the one time when I might have helped, offered a word of comfort perhaps, done something for the widow and her children, he is behaving as if I do not exist. As if I am of no importance. Do I make sense to you, James? I am afraid I don't to myself."

"Yes, I think so," he said. "You have never had a relationship with anyone but me, Alex. And we have always sympathized with each other to an amazing degree. Now you are discovering that it is not easy to be a part of someone else's life."

"I don't think I can make him happy, James," she said. "How can I? I do not know anything about giving happiness."

"Yes, you do," he said. "You are the one ray of happiness in my life, Alex. You do not have to try. You can just be. But listen to me. You must not blame yourself for what has happened today. Amberley does not, I am sure. He chose quite freely to go with you this morning, and he seemed not to be regretting the choice the last time I saw him. Tell me you will give up this feeling of guilt."

"I will try," she said. "But, James, he got there fifteen minutes after Mr. Peterson died. Fifteen minutes! And the man had wanted to talk to him."

Purnell was tight-lipped as he looked at his sister. "Come on downstairs now," he said. "Captain Forbes has called and wants Lady Madeline to go walking with him. She wants you and Eden to accompany them. You had better go, Alex. I don't like to see you brooding like this."

"All right," she said, her tone flat, "I will go walking, James. Are you coming too?"

"No," he said. "I had my fill this morning. I am going to play billiards with Sir Cedric."

"You do not like Madeline, do you?" she said, fetching a straw bonnet from her dressing room. "I do. She tries her best to be friendly, and I do admire her lighthearted way of facing life."

"Her frivolity, you mean," he said. "No, she and I do not quite see eye to eye, Alex. Are you ready?"

And yet, James Purnell found, watching the four of them leave on their walk several minutes later, it seemed strange not to be going with them. It was a subdued group that set out, both Lord Eden and his sister seeming genuinely upset by the morning's fatal accident.

It was a novel experience, Purnell thought, to see Lady Madeline without some of her customary sparkle. But she looked quite as pretty as usual in her sprigged-muslin dress and chip-straw bonnet. And the captain was certainly appreciative.

Well, he thought, turning away in the direction of the billiard room, let her flirt. She had a man with her this afternoon who was likely to be willing to accept her flirtation for what it was worth and return its like. She would not be forced into anger this afternoon or be subjected to insults.

She would be a great deal happier. And so, he thought as he let himself into the billiard room and found the older man already there and waiting for him, would he.

17

LORD AMBERLEY WAS LYING ON THE STRAW mattress in the stone hut, his hands clasped behind his head. The door was propped open. The afternoon sun slanted through it, its rays almost touching him.

His mind had calmed. It had been one of those freak accidents that are so upsetting because they seem so utterly meaningless. He himself was in no way to blame. The equipment had been quite sound. Spiller had assured him that it had been checked only the week before. It was regrettable that he had been unable to talk to Joel before he died, but the man must have known somewhere at the back of his pain and his knowledge that he was about to die that his wife and sons would be well-cared-for.

Perhaps the most upsetting aspect of any death to those left behind, he thought, was the feeling of terrible helplessness. One always wants to do something, but very rarely is there anything to do. His own sense of frustration had been distressing. He had known that he was not needed at that cottage. Appreciated, yes. But needed, no. His people could not be themselves in his presence. So rather than put a constraint on them when they were already overwrought, he had left.

He wanted company. For the first time in his memory he wanted someone with whom to share his emotional turmoil. He wanted Alex.

He turned the idea over in his mind with some surprise. But it was true. He wanted to be with her as he had been that morning—quiet, relaxed, knowing that she shared his mood. And he wanted her with him as she had been the previous afternoon for a brief while. He wanted to make love to her.

And for the first time he felt sorry that he had not gone to her when he had returned home earlier. He could have talked to her, brought her here with him. Perhaps he would not even have needed to come if he could have walked with her as he had that morning, or sat with her somewhere quiet—the conservatory perhaps. She had been in the hall, had she not, when he went into the house with Dominic? Had he even spoken to her? He could not recall.

He sighed and pushed himself into a sitting position. He had a great deal to learn about sharing his life with someone else. It was all very well to think of love, to dream of the perfect marriage. But nothing could be accomplished if he retreated to his private world whenever anything happened to ruffle his calm. Love was not just a word, a passive emotion. It was a full-time, lifelong commitment.

THE MORNING ON THE cliff path and the beach might never have been. There was a tension between Lord Amberley and Alexandra again that both had hoped on that morning to ease.

Alexandra did not turn entirely inward upon herself, but

she could not let go of the guilt that had nagged at her after the death of Joel Peterson. Had she gone with her betrothed to the village as he had asked, he would have been there when the injured man was brought in. He would still have died, of course, but Lord Amberley would not have been left with the feeling that he had neglected his duty—playing truant, as he had jokingly put it when they were on the beach.

She knew that he grieved for Mr. Peterson and felt for his family, but he had said nothing to her. He had shut her out of his innermost feelings with his usual calm, kindly manner. She felt more punished than she ever had by her father. She was being treated as a person who had not taken his life seriously and who would not be invited to take a glimpse into it again.

When Lord Amberley and his mother visited the cottage in the village the following morning, they seemed genuinely surprised when she asked to accompany them.

"You really do not need to do this, Alex," Lord Amberley said, taking her hand in both of his. "Such a visit is painful even when it is clearly one's duty to make it. It is not your duty."

She went anyway, but she felt chastised by his words. Was she to be an ornament in his life, not a participant? She might have used the moment to look into his eyes, to smile, and to explain that if she was to feel any freedom, any meaning in the marriage she must make, then she must become involved in his life. But she looked at his hands that held hers and drew back her shoulders.

"I would like to express my sympathies to the widow," she said in a voice she had not meant to sound cold.

"I think it a splendid idea, Alexandra," Lady Amberley

said. "The people of the village will not forget it, you know, and they will respect you for it as they do Edmund."

Nothing improved between them in the following two days. They went to church together on Sunday with the rest of their families, and sat next to each other in Lord Amberley's pew. They greeted acquaintances together afterward, and Alexandra was presented to other people she had not met before. They took tea at the Carringtons' in the afternoon. She attended the funeral with Lord Amberley and his family the following day, again insisting on going despite his gentle insistence that she was under no obligation to do so.

But there was no closeness. And it worried Lord Amberley as well as Alexandra. He wanted to atone for his *faux pas* of the day of Joel's death. He wanted to talk to Alexandra, to penetrate behind that barrier and draw her into his inner life. But she was unapproachable again. She was not hostile or sullen or silent. But she was far away from him. He was left to wonder if he had imagined the afternoon in the hills and the morning on the beach.

He must find the opportunity to talk to her once more. He must bring that bright, vibrant Alex to life again. He must. He thought he was growing to love her. And he did not want to discover that he loved a dream, a woman who did not really exist. But how was he to begin? He was a man who could do a great deal for others when occasion demanded it. But he had no practice in giving himself. He had tried with Alex, more than once, but he was not successful. They were no nearer now to having a close relationship than they had been the morning they had become betrothed.

• • •

THE CARRINGTONS HAD PLANNED a picnic for the day after the funeral. All the residents at Amberley had been invited, as well as the Courtneys and the officers of the regiment. Madeline was in high spirits, the gloom of the previous few days behind her. She arrived in Alexandra's dressing room just as Nanny Rey was dressing her mistress's hair.

"What a beautiful shade of pink your dress is," she said. "Most pinks are thoroughly insipid. I avoid the color altogether, of course. With my dull hair color I have to choose something more vivid."

"Your hair dull, Madeline?" Alexandra said, meeting her eyes in the mirror. "But it is so lovely—so shiny and healthy."

"I wish I had yours instead," Madeline said. "It is such a glorious color. Why do you not leave some of it unconfined?"

Alexandra met Nanny Rey's eyes in the mirror and laughed. "We were just having a dreadful row on that topic when you came in," she said. "Oh, go on then, Nanny. Enjoy your triumph. Yes, the curls beside my face and on my neck, if you please."

"I am glad I came," Madeline said.

"So am I, my lady," Nanny Rey said, regarding her over the top of her glasses and nodding her head.

Alexandra was rewarded later when Lord Amberley was handing her into the barouche with the other ladies. "How very pretty you look, Alex," he said. "Quite dazzling, in fact. And what has set you to giggling, Madeline? Have I said something funny?"

Madeline raised her parasol over her straw bonnet, gave it a twirl, and grinned at Alexandra.

The picnic was to be held about a mile from the Carringtons' house, close to the ruins of an old abbey that had been destroyed centuries before, at the time of the dissolution of the monasteries. It was a quiet, picturesque spot among the trees, close to the top of the valley that led down to Amberley Court.

Everyone except Lady Beckworth and Mrs. Carrington walked to the picnic site. Lady Amberley looked vastly relieved when her sister-in-law good-naturedly offered to ride in the barouche with Alexandra's mother.

"Viola is just thankful to have an excuse to ride," Mr. Carrington called out for all to hear.

"Oh, nonsense, William!" his wife replied. "I can outwalk you any day of the week, as you know only too well and Walter and Anna can attest to."

"I would ride myself," Mr. Courtney added, "except that I know there would be those to say I am incapable of moving so far of my own volition."

Two of his sons laughed.

Altogether, it was a merry group that walked across fields and climbed over stiles. Lady Amberley walked thankfully on the arm of Sir Cedric, breathing in the warm smell of vegetation and declaring to him privately that she would have been compelled to scream or steal away on a midnight walk if courtesy had forced her to spend one more day either indoors or seated in a carriage.

"You must call on me if you ever decide on the midnight outing," he said seriously. "I really would not wish to think of you outdoors alone at such an hour."

"I might just come knocking at your door one night," she said with equal seriousness. "Though what the servants would have to say belowstairs if we were seen would create a sensation to last for the next ten years."

Lord Amberley walked with Mrs. Courtney, shortening his stride for her convenience and listening amiably to a detailed account of every plant that was flourishing in her vegetable garden and every one that was not, and assuring her at regular intervals that, no, she was not boring him in the least. And surprisingly, he thought, glancing around him in some contentment, she was not.

Susan walked with Lieutenant Jennings, blushing and lowering her lashes as he talked, peeping upward at James Purnell, who was with her brothers, and at Lord Eden, who was with Alexandra.

Madeline was happy to be with Captain Forbes, with whom she felt thoroughly comfortable. She was familiar with his particular brand of flattery and flirtation and knew well how to react to it. It was a relief to be able to relax her mind and prattle cheerfully on about topics that mattered little to either him or her. It was such a treat not to have to wonder what he was thinking of her intelligence or what was hidden behind dark, unfathomable eyes. The captain's eyes were gray and twinkling.

Lord Eden had taken Alexandra determinedly on his arm. He must speak with her. He had lost too much time, and his purpose had cooled. Her response might also not be as favorable as it had been several nights before. But despite all, he was contented to have her with him. As unlike his usual flirt as she was—or perhaps because of that fact—he liked her and found himself able to relax with her and talk sensibly on topics that really mattered to him. One did not have to talk trivialities with Miss Purnell.

It was almost impossible to imagine what the abbey must have looked like, Lord Eden explained to Alexandra, though one could still see the floor plan quite clearly, and the bases of most of the columns that had lined the nave of the large chapel were still in place. He took her to show her what he meant.

"What a shame it is that it was so completely devastated," she said. "So much history obliterated in the name of religion."

He shrugged. "That is life, I'm afraid, Miss Purnell," he said. "War is as bad. We are fortunate that the sea is between us and Europe. We would see a lot more than the destruction of a few old monasteries if we lived there."

"I would hate it," she said, "even though I know it is necessary to fight oppression."

"Yes, it is," he said, looking at her eagerly. "You talk about history being obliterated, Miss Purnell. But have you thought about how history is being made now, at this very moment, in Spain? If the French are put to rout there and pushed back elsewhere, those who fought against the forces of Bonaparte will have made history. They will have made Europe safe for decent people again. The world safe. How wonderful it would be to be part of the making of that history. Instead of a mere distant witness."

Alexandra seated herself on one of the broken columns. He looked very eager and very boyish pacing back and forth before her as he was. And very handsome.

"It is the only thing you really want to do, is it not?" she said.

He stopped in front of her. "Yes, the only thing," he said. "I think I will have regrets for the rest of my life if the war ends without me."

She smiled. "I think you should go, then," she said.

"Do you?" He looked at her, arrested, for a moment. Then he stooped down on his haunches in front of her and looked up into her face. "Do you really, Miss Purnell? You are the only person who has ever said that to me. Mama and Madeline almost have the vapors at the merest mention of my purchasing a commission; Sir Cedric tells me that I must consider my mother's feelings very carefully before I do anything impulsive; Edmund says I must decide for myself. Only you have told me that I should go."

"But that is not sufficient reason for doing so," she said. "His lordship is right. The decision must be yours. But I think a person should do what he feels he really must do, even if other people's feelings are hurt. Maybe I am wrong. All my life I have been taught that one must do what is right by some outside standard, by some rules that other people have laid down. But I am beginning to think that that is not always so. Perhaps you will have to hurt your mother and your sister. In order to give your life meaning, perhaps that is what you have to do. I don't know. I really am not qualified to be giving you this advice."

He caught at her hands and held them tightly in his own. "I love your advice," he said. "It is what I feel. But to hear it from someone else's lips seems so much more important. Yes, I must decide for myself, Miss Purnell. I must decide yes or no and then live by that decision. It is very immature, is it not, to dream and to fret and never to do?"

"But very normal, I think," she said. "It is sometimes the most difficult thing in the world to do what we want to do or else to finally turn our back on it. It is so difficult to be positive. It is so much easier to dither, to allow ourselves to be carried along unhappily by life."

"You are so very wise," he said. "I don't believe I have ever known a lady I admired so much, Miss Purnell. You make me feel a courage and a determination that I have always lacked." He lifted one of her hands to his lips.

"Oh, no," she said. "I cannot possibly give you something that is alien to your nature, my lord. And I don't think I am really very wise. I was merely thinking aloud just now.

I am not a very positive person, you see. I have never been taught to consider it a virtue to think for myself."

"Then it must be that we bring out the best in each other," he said, squeezing the hand he had just kissed. "I think perhaps we were meant for each other, Miss Purnell. Do you think we were?"

She looked down into his boyish, handsome face and ached to say yes. Simply to say yes and let the consequences take care of themselves. The prospect was for the moment, and quite unreasonably, very attractive.

She returned the pressure of his hands and smiled fondly and a little sadly down at him.

"Dominic, here you are! I knew that you could not have wandered away already. Hello, Miss Purnell. I do so love your dress. I wish I were older and could wear something as pretty myself." Anna had come around the pile of stones that had hidden them from the rest of the picnickers.

"You look as pretty as a picture just as you are, youngster," Lord Eden said. "In two or three years' time you will quite outshine all the other girls and they will hate you for it."

"Will they?" she asked eagerly. "Will they really, Dominic? How splendid that will be."

Alexandra joined in Lord Eden's laughter.

"Walter and Colin Courtney want to go down into the valley," she said, "and now several of us want to go too. Mama says there will be time before tea. Do you want to come, Dominic?"

"If someone twists my arm, I suppose I might," he said. "But not if it means fishing anyone out of the water, mind. I am past such pranks. I might ruin my Hessians." He grinned at Anna and tugged affectionately at the ribbon that held her bonnet closed beneath her chin.

They strolled back to the others and found that indeed most of the young people were on their feet. Colin and Howard Courtney and Walter had already begun the descent. Madeline and Captain Forbes were looking down through the trees. Lieutenant Jennings was talking to Susan.

"I really do not know if I ought," she was saying, looking up at him through her lashes. "The hill is steep and I will delay you and spoil your afternoon, sir."

"It would be my pleasure, Miss Courtney," he said with a gallant bow.

"What, Susan?" Lord Eden said. "You are not afraid, are you? We will have to see that you regain your courage. You must take the lieutenant's arm and mine. One on a side. That way you cannot fall even if you try to do so."

"Oh, you are very kind," she said, looking up at him with large eyes and doing as she was bidden.

Purnell waited until Sir Cedric came to the end of a sentence and rose to his feet. He strolled over to a disconsolate-looking Anna.

"I do not believe for one moment," he said, "that you are so chickenhearted as to need my arm. But would you like to take it anyway, Miss Carrington, so that we may descend the slope like a sedate adult pair?"

"Oh." She looked up at him and blushed. Then she smiled, turned an eager face to her mother, and linked her arm through his—for the world as if she were being led into a quadrille at St. James's, her father said with a chuckle to Mrs. Courtney beside him.

"Mr. Purnell is a kind young man," Mr. Courtney said. He shook his head. "Young people! Running up and down hills for the simple pleasure of doing so. If I were to go down, it would take a team of oxen to haul me back up again." He laughed merrily at his own joke.

"It would be easier to float down the river to Amberley, would it not?" Mr. Carrington said, causing his neighbor to guffaw loudly again.

"William!" his wife scolded. "That was not at all a genteel thing to say. Take no notice of him, Mr. Courtney. William likes to tease."

"The river might overflow its bank, though," Mr. Courtney said, "and cause a flood."

The two men chuckled as Mrs. Carrington clucked her tongue, Lady Amberley exchanged an amused glance with Sir Cedric, and Lady Beckworth looked disapproving.

Lord Amberley got to his feet. "Shall we do something less energetic than climbing, Alex?" he said. "Shall we stroll along the top?"

THE DESCENT OF A STEEP wooded bank was not nearly enough exercise for the young men. They must cross the river too, an activity made all the more challenging by the fact that the water at this particular part of its slightly downhill course was fast-flowing, though not deep.

"Those two stones in the middle have disappeared since I was last here," Walter said, pointing. "They were always loose. I'm not at all surprised that they have gone. Though where did they go, do you suppose?"

"Washed away to sea?" Colin suggested, and won a withering look from his brother for his pains.

"Taken by the village boys, more like," Howard said.

"Wouldn't they be too heavy?" asked Walter.

But the problem of what had happened to the stones was forgotten in the intriguing question of what they were to do to get across the gap without wetting themselves to the knees.

"You could jump," Madeline suggested, coming up to them on the arm of Captain Forbes. "I think it would be possible. And the suspense of not being quite certain would definitely add a thrill."

"Father would not be amused if we missed, though, Lady Madeline," Howard said, giving her an adoring look despite the foolhardiness of her suggestion. "We are all in our best rig-outs."

"What is the problem?" Lord Eden wanted to know. "Oh, no stones. And I suppose it is imperative that everyone go across? Yes, of course it is. How foolish of me to ask the question. We will just have to carry out new stones."

The men and boys set about this exciting task with a will, while Madeline and Anna joined in the search for suitable stones. Susan hovered in the background. In no time at all Captain Forbes and Lord Eden were staggering to the bank and across the stones already in place with a huge flat-bottomed rock in their hands. When that was in place with no further casualty than a splashing of water on Lord Eden's Hessians, Lieutenant Jennings and James Purnell set out with an even larger rock and bridged the final gap.

"Now," Lord Eden announced, "we may all troop safely across and admire the grass and trees on that side of the river."

Walter was the first across, followed by the captain and the lieutenant. He was taking them to the top of the hill opposite, from which vantage point they might command a view down the valley to Amberley, a sight denied them from the picnic site because of a bend in the river. Everyone else politely declined such energetic exercise. Captain Forbes, it was true, hesitated when Madeline showed no eagerness to accompany him, but she waved him on.

"Oh, do not mind me," she said airily. "I see Amberley almost every day of my life. Why would I wish to climb a hill in this heat merely to see it from a distance?"

"Are you coming across, Dominic?" Anna asked. "Usually I am forbidden to go near the river, but I know Mama will not mind my crossing if you are with me."

"I shall stay here," Susan said timidly. "I would fall in, I know I would. But please do not let me spoil anyone else's pleasure."

"Come on, Miss Carrington," Howard said. "Come with Colin and me. There is a good fishing spot farther along the bank. Let's see if we can find it."

"Oh, yes," she said, brightening. "Walter has promised that he will take me fishing this year, but he never does."

She went running lightly across the stepping-stones, holding her dress above her ankles, Howard in front of her and Colin behind.

"Susan," Lord Eden said, amusement in his voice, "will you not cross over even if I hold your hand very tightly? The stones are quite steady, you know. You would have to try very hard to fall in, I swear."

"Oh, no," she said, favoring him with a wide-eyed look from her hazel eyes. "Please, my lord. I would positively die of fright. But do go with Lady Madeline and Mr. Purnell. I shall go back to Mama."

"I would not dream of deserting you," he said good-humoredly. "Come, we will stroll along on this side. I shall walk next to the bank so that you cannot possibly slip and fall. Will you take my arm?"

"Oh, how kind you are," she said, slipping an arm through his.

• • •

MADELINE WAS LEFT WISHING she had gone with the captain after all. How had it happened so suddenly that instead of a whole crowd of people surrounding her, she was left with a silent Mr. Purnell? How mortifyingly embarrassing!

She turned and smiled brightly at him. "I cannot resist crossing the stones," she said. "We used to do it frequently as children. But it was far more dangerous because the two middle stones used to be very unsteady. And of course, being children, we used to dream up all sorts of games to make the crossing even more dangerous. Like having to walk backward or having to hop on one foot. We even did it blindfold once, but we got into dreadful trouble then because Dom fell in, and I jumped in after so that he would not have to face the punishment alone."

"And what was the punishment?" he asked. "A thrashing?"

"No," she said. "That was why I jumped in. Dom would doubtless have been beaten, but Papa would never beat me because I was a girl. I thought he would not be able to thrash Dom and not me if we were guilty of the same offense. I was right. We were sent to the kitchen to wash our clothes and a whole pile of other clothes besides. What a horrid task it was. It took us hours of scrubbing and rubbing and stirring and pegging out. And then we had to iron everything afterward."

"And were you cured of crossing the river blindfold?" he asked.

"Oh, yes," she said. "The next time we did it, it was with our ankles tied together, I believe." She laughed.

"I shall come across with you," he said, and set out across the stones without further ado.

Madeline's heart sank. She had been hoping that he would decide to go back up the hill to join the others. She followed him across the stepping-stones, placing her hand in his when he stopped to assist her over the largest gap. And whose decision was it to turn when they reached the other side and begin to stroll along the bank in the opposite direction from that taken by Anna and the boys? she wondered a few minutes later. Neither had suggested it, but that was where they were strolling nonetheless.

"Do you feel the necessity for us to make noise again today?" he asked. "I do hope not. I believe I ran out of both school and university stories a few mornings ago."

"No," she said, "I would not wish you to exert yourself, sir. I am quite happy to commune with nature for a few minutes, if you are."

But how could one commune with nature, she thought, when one was feeling thoroughly irritated with one's companion? How could one appreciate the varying shades of green around one and the sound of the breeze in the branches of the trees and of the water rushing by? She might as well be blind and deaf.

"This is ridiculous!" she blurted after a few minutes.

He turned an inquiring look on her, his eyebrows raised, that one lock of hair down across his forehead again. "What is ridiculous?" he asked.

"You walking along in silence; me walking along in silence," she said. "Sometimes silence can be deafening. I cannot hear anything else around me."

"Your life has been filled with trivial noises," he said. "Prattle. Gossip. Talk of fashions and other trivialities. Anything to fill the silence. It is no wonder that silence is loud to you. It is something quite alien to your experience."

"Oh!" Madeline stopped walking and turned to face him. "How obnoxious you are. You must always cast me in the role of silly, giddy female. A few days ago you were very angry with me, demanding to know what I knew of your life, and said that only someone very silly would presume to know what had happened during thirty years of another's life. But you are doing exactly the same thing. You assume you know everything there is to know about me, and you have concluded that that really is not a great deal."

"Am I not right?" he asked, infuriating her further by his failure to show suitable contrition. "Is not life for you the pursuit of one amusement after another?"

"No, it is not," she said. "But of course you will not believe me. I am a woman beneath your contempt, obviously."

"What else is there?" he asked. "Who is Lady Madeline Raine? What is important to you in life?"

"My family is important to me," she said. "Dominic. Edmund. Mama. Amberley Court." She turned to walk on.

"You are more than twenty years of age, are you not?" he said. "Have you found nothing to replace this home in your affections? It is not yours really, you know. It is your brother's. Have you not been altogether too busy enjoying yourself and adding to the list of your male conquests to do anything as dull as getting married and having children?"

"You are older than I am," she said indignantly. "And you are unmarried. Is it different for women? Can women prove their worth only by marrying and giving birth? I want to marry, and I want to have children, but I do not want to do either merely for the sake of respectability. I want to marry for love. I want my children to be born out of love. You see? You are wrong. If I were as silly as you think, the only thing on my mind would be matrimony. Almost all the girls with whom I made my come-out were married long ago."

"Love!" he said, his voice a sneer. "You are always the romantic, are you not? People do not marry for love. They marry to suit their personal interests. And women do not bear children from love. They bear them because some man lusted after them."

"How horrid you are," she said. "How very horrid. I would pity the woman you l-lusted after, as you put it. How ugly it would seem to have your child."

It was only as the words were already beyond recall that she realized how very shockingly unladylike they were. How could she possibly have even thought such things? But she was not given a chance to burn with shame and embarrassment, as she undoubtedly would have done. James Purnell caught her arm in a painful viselike grip and jerked her closer to him.

"You know nothing!" he said. "You know nothing of what it would be like..." The pressure on her arm increased even further, and he shook his head in frustration.

Madeline was very frightened. His dark eyes burned into hers. His face was harsh with fury. She thought he was going to do her violence. She set her hands defensively against his coat.

She had always enjoyed being kissed. There was a deliciously naughty feeling about allowing a man's lips against hers, and an exhilarating challenge about knowing just when she must push him away and smile apologetically at him.

But there was nothing enjoyable about James Purnell's kiss. His mouth came down bruisingly on hers, cutting the soft flesh behind her lips against her teeth. His hands held her arms like vises, forcing her against him so that she was aware of every hard contour of his body from her shoulders to her knees. She felt as if she were being ravished. And the embrace—if it could be called that—was quite beyond her control, quite beyond her power to end.

When he finally lifted his head, he did not immediately release his hold on her or put her from him.

"You are playing with fire, my lady," he said very quietly. "It would be better far for you to keep to games that you can win. Flirt with the captain. He seems to be the perfect gentleman. I am not. Stay away from me if you know what is good for you."

He took his hands from her arms, and she pushed away from him. She said nothing. She was too bewildered, too frightened still. She turned and brushed at her skirt with unsteady hands.

"I am sorry," he said curtly from behind her. "You have done nothing to deserve such treatment. No woman should be subject to violence. I am sorry."

She turned without a word and began to walk back the way they had come. She had to make an effort not to stumble. Her legs felt decidedly unsteady. He walked beside her, a little distance away. They were silent.

I AM JUST A SILLY GOOSE, I KNOW," SUSAN SAID, peeping up at Lord Eden from beneath her lashes. "Everyone must become very impatient with me. I spoil everyone's enjoyment."

"Just because you would not cross the river?" he said. "Nonsense, Susan. From my experience, the grass is just as green and the trees just the same height on this side as they are on the other. It really is of no consequence at all that we are strolling on this bank instead of that."

"But not just crossing the river," she said. "There was my fear of the cliffs a few days ago. And yesterday Lieutenant Jennings was obliging enough to invite me to ride. Howard came too and we called on Nancy Morton to come with us. But I was afraid to move at a faster pace than a canter when everyone else wanted to enjoy a gallop. Everyone said that it did not signify, especially the lieutenant, but I know that I was a burden on them."

"I'll bet you weren't, though, Susan," he said gently. "Oh, to your brother, perhaps. Brothers are dreadfully impatient and unsympathetic creatures, are they not? But not to anyone else. I do not find your fears in any way burdensome."

"Do you not?" she asked wistfully. "You are excessively kind. You were always kind to me even when I was a nuisance of a little girl. Do you remember rescuing me from the tree?"

"Indeed I do," he said. "One of your brothers—Harold, was it?—was telling you that since you had got up there on your own, you could jolly well get down on your own too."

"But I would still be up there if you had not come and helped me down," she said.

"What were you doing on that branch, anyway?" he asked. "You had gone up after one of the kittens, had you?"

"Yes," she said. "You were my hero for a long time after that, my lord."

"What?" he said. "Past tense, Susan? You mean I am no longer your hero?" He grinned at her.

"Oh," she said, and blushed. "It would not be fitting now, my lord."

"Indeed?" he said. "What a shame. I think I rather fancy being a hero."

"Of course," she said, "I still admire you greatly. You are kind, my lord. You are not impatient with weakness."

"You refer to yourself again?" he said. "But you are not weak, Susan. You merely have an excess of imagination and sensibility. There is nothing wrong with that. On the contrary. Who wants a woman who is always brave and independent and never needs a man's help at all?"

"Oh," she said, "I am not at all like that, am I?"

He looked down at her, at her wide-eyed, rather anxious look, her mouth a little rosebud as it formed another "Oh." Yes, she was just exactly the sort of female that most appealed to him—small and sweet and helpless. Quite adorable, in fact. He would like to wrap her in his arms and protect her from all of life's ills for ever after.

He was unaware that they had stopped walking until he found himself gazing into her wide hazel eyes and glancing down at her mouth. It drew him like a magnet. One taste. Oh, just one taste.

He straightened up and smiled regretfully down at her. "Susan," he said. "Dear little Susan. We must not, you know. It would not be fair to you."

"Must not what?" she asked, her eyes wide with innocence.

"Was I the only one having wicked thoughts?" he asked with a shaky smile. "I would like nothing more in this world than to kiss you, Susan. But it really would not be fair to you if I did so."

Her eyes were swimming in tears suddenly. "I do not know what I have done to make you think I am of such easy virtue," she said. "I have given you no cause, my lord."

"Susan!" he said, taking her hand between both of his and patting it. "I thought no such thing. But you look so very fetching this afternoon, and these surroundings are so lovely and so peaceful. I confess I almost lost my head and kissed you. But only as a sign of my regard, you see. If it was wrong of me to feel that way, the fault is all mine, believe me. You have been the perfect lady, Susan."

Her tears spilled over. "I try," she said. "I know that Papa is only a farmer and a tenant of his lordship. I know I am no grand lady. I know I may not aspire to winning your admiration, my lord, or that of any other grand gentleman. But I try to be genteel. And I have never allowed a gentleman to kiss me. I am sure I would faint quite away if anyone tried."

He patted her hand once more and reached in his pocket for a handkerchief. "What a monster you must think me," he said. "Dry your eyes, Susan, and say you forgive me. Will you? I did not mean to frighten you or give you a disgust of me. Truly I didn't. Forgive me?"

She patted her eyes dry and returned the handkerchief into his outstretched hand. "Of course I forgive you, my lord," she said. "Though there is really nothing to forgive, I am sure. I am just being a silly goose."

"Come," he said, offering his arm again. "It is time I returned you to your mama, Susan. Besides, I think it must be close to teatime, and I for one am hungry. Are you feeling better now?"

"Yes, thank you," she said. "You are very kind, my lord."

Lord Eden, remorseful over his own clumsiness and insensitivity, was quite in love as he slowed his pace to help his companion up the steep slope of the hill.

ALEXANDRA STROLLED ALONG THE top of the hill beside Lord Amberley. He did not offer her his arm.

"Dominic was showing you the abbey ruins?" he asked. "Is it not a tragedy that so little remains?"

"Yes," she said. "It must have been beautiful. These are such peaceful surroundings for a religious house."

They strolled on, gazing down the tree-studded slope of the hill.

"He wants to join the army in Spain," she said. "Lord Eden, that is."

"Ah," he said, "he has told you that, has he? I believe he is really serious about the matter. Mama has been hoping it was a boyish whim. But Dominic has passed somewhat beyond boyhood."

"He should go," she said. "He told me earlier that he will be forever sorry if the war ends and he has not been a part of it. I think he would, too. He would always feel that his life was unfulfilled. A person's life is too precious to be controlled by others, is it not?"

"You think I try to control Dominic?" he asked. "It is not so, I assure you. I have always told him that he must decide for himself what he wants of life and then do it. He is quite free to join the army anytime he wants."

"There are more ways of controlling another than just giving commands, though," she said. "That is Papa's way. Then there is the way that puts constraints on another that are quite invisible and that neither party may be even aware of. Do you know what I mean?"

He looked at her, frowning. "I am afraid not," he said.

"Lord Eden says that your mother would allow him to go if she knew that he really wished it, and he has said what you have just said to me. That is, that you have given him the freedom to decide for himself. Indeed, he tells me that he does not even need your permission to buy a commission. But don't you see that you are binding him hand and foot with love?"

"Binding him?" he said. "With love? Is that not rather a contradiction in terms?"

"No," she said. "I do not know quite how to explain myself. If you and your mother—and Madeline—ranted and raved at Lord Eden and forbade him to go, he would have something to fight against. He would be able to decide either to obey or to rebel. But as it is, he has the obligation of knowing himself loved, of knowing that he has the power to hurt people he loves in return. And he knows that he will cause suffering if he decides a certain way. You are not setting him free simply by saying that he may decide for himself. He is not free at all."

He had stopped walking. He stood gazing out across the

valley. "Then there is no such thing as freedom," he said. "Or no such thing as love. If what you say is true, then the two things cannot exist side by side."

"I don't know," she said, standing beside him. "I have not thought this all out. I am thinking as I speak. You can set Lord Eden free. You can tell him that he must go, that your feelings and your mother's feelings are secondary to the great pride you will feel for him if he fights for his country. You can hide your terror that he will die. If you do this, you will do so because you love him. You see? Freedom and love side by side."

Lord Amberley turned to her and smiled. "It is a daunting thought," he said, "that love can sometimes be a destructive force. I am not sure I believe it. I will have to think over what you have said and see if I can find a flaw in it. Are you fond of Dominic?"

"Yes," she said. "He is eager and youthful."

"And yet," he said, "he did you a great wrong."

She smiled and turned to walk on.

"But you do not see it that way, do you?" he said, walking beside her again. "You see me as the author of your troubles, do you not? I am the one who trapped you into all this." He gestured around him with one arm. "It is the same thing that we have been talking about, is it not? I have put chains on you."

"You meant well," she said. "I know that. And you yourself had to make a great sacrifice in order to do what you thought must be done to help me."

"But you resent the fact that I did so," he said.

"I had refused your help," she said. "You had done what honor demanded, as Lord Eden did. I refused your offer, and I also told you, if you remember, that I would not need your return if the situation got nasty. Your obligation was quite at an end there."

"But, Alex . . ." He caught at her arm and brought her to a stop. He turned her to face him. "You were suffering. And you would have suffered much more. Both during that evening and in the days to come. And I believe your father would have made you suffer. You would have continued to do so for the rest of your life. How could I stand by and see that happen?"

"It was not your problem; it was mine," she said. "I have been made into a thing again, as I have been all my life, a commodity—and rather a nuisance of a commodity—to be passed from hand to hand. I don't want to be owned. I don't want to be a thing. I want to be me. To make a life for myself, I would hope. To suffer if necessary. But I want it to be my life and my suffering. My choice."

His face had turned rather pale, she noticed. The customary smile had totally disappeared from his eyes. "I have never wanted to own you, Alex," he said. "I have told you from the start that you are free to be yourself here."

"Yes," she said, "but I must marry you. You would never dream of setting me quite free, would you? You are too gallant to risk allowing me to suffer scandal and ostracism and punishment at my father's hands. How very free you leave me, Edmund."

He stared into her eyes for a long time before speaking. "You wish to be free?" he said at last. "You would prefer that to marriage with me?"

She stared mutely back.

"Let us not be hasty," he said, passing a hand over his eyes. "I must think, Alex. It cannot be done. I cannot see you exposed to all that." He was silent for a while before looking up into her eyes. "The Amberley ball is to take place in just over a week's time. Let us wait that long. After that, if I know you unhappy still, if we both feel as you do now that we cannot make a successful marriage out of our union, I will allow you to break our engagement. I will not argue. I will allow you to be free. Do you agree to this?"

She shook her head. "I want you to break the engagement," she said. "You insisted upon it. You break it."

"Alex!" he said, aghast.

"You constantly watch over me!" she said. "Like a spider over a fly. Except that yours is a benevolent tyranny. But I am caught in your web, Edmund. Your gilded web. I am to be protected at all costs. It will be easier for me if I am the one to break the engagement. I will not be seen as such an abandoned creature. I don't want your protection, Edmund. I have never asked for it. I am smothered by it. I cannot breathe."

"Very well," he said curtly, his eyes holding hers. He was still very pale. "Unless something happens between now and next week to change matters, I will break our engagement after the ball. Does this please you?"

"Yes," she said. "Yes, it does."

He laughed suddenly, rather bleakly. "I will be a pariah," he said. "Have you ever heard of a gentleman breaking off his engagement, Alex?"

"No," she said.

"Sometimes..." He took a deep breath and let it out slowly. "Sometimes—in the past few weeks—I have felt that we are both quite mad."

And unexpectedly they smiled at each other as if a great tension between them had been lifted.

"Alexandra Purnell," he said, "I have never known anyone quite like you, and I believe I must thank my good fortune for it. You look quite remarkably pretty this afternoon, by the way. Have I told you that before?"

"Yes, Edmund," she said, "but it bears repeating."

"Does it?" he said. "You have such very beautiful hair. Why do you usually confine it all so ruthlessly?"

"Papa's training," she said, "and force of habit. I feel very conscious of myself with any of it down, and imagine that everyone is looking at me."

"You are probably right there," he said. "I have not been able to keep my eyes from you this afternoon. And if you are to be mine—or almost mine—for only a week longer, I plan to let my eyes feast their fill."

She smiled rather ruefully as he reached up and undid the bow that tied the wide pink ribbons of her straw bonnet beneath one ear. She lifted her chin to make his task easier. He eased the bonnet from her hair and dropped it to the ground.

He framed her face with his hands and trailed his fingers through her ringlets. He smiled into her eyes.

"And how am I to let you go?" he asked, his mouth very close to hers. "Tell me that, Alex. The chains of love work both ways, you know."

But he did not give her a chance to reply or to show in any way the shock his words had created in her mind. His lips touched hers very lightly, closed, brushing teasingly across hers until she tipped back her head, parted her lips, and invited his kiss.

It was not like the last embrace they had shared. She found that her arms were up around his neck and her breasts against his coat, but his hands at her waist held the rest of her body away from his. His mouth opened and moved over hers, teasing, tasting, caressing, but he did not use his tongue. She felt all the masculine attractiveness of him without any of the threat of the physical unknown.

He still held to her waist when he had lifted his mouth from hers, and she forgot to remove her arms from his neck.

"I envy the man you will finally choose for your own, Alex," he said.

"No one will ever have me," she said with a rueful smile. "Will you return to Mrs. Borden?" She flushed, mortified, as she heard the words come from her lips.

"No." He smiled. "I have told you she is in my past, Alex. She will remain there, no matter what happens between you and me."

"I'm sorry," she said.

He grinned. "If I thought your question was motivated by jealousy," he said, "I would readily forgive you. Shall we go back for tea and hope that some kind soul has kept us something? I suddenly realize that I am hungry."

He stooped to pick up her bonnet and watched as she tied the ribbons beneath her chin.

"Is Mrs. Rey the one responsible for the interesting angles?" he asked. "Hats to one side, ribbons tied beneath one ear? If so, I shall have to tell her that she is a born seducer. One would never suspect it of such a birdlike little person. Now, you, on the other hand, have to have everything straight and no nonsense. Perhaps I should be grateful that you did not create your own hair." He pulled at one ringlet and watched it curl back into place again.

"Nanny is a holy tyrant," Alexandra said, taking his offered arm and beginning the walk back to the picnic site.

"If I decide to marry you after all," Lord Amberley said, "and if you decide to marry me, I shall have to raise Mrs. Rey's salary and tell her to continue the good work."

• • •

THE FOLLOWING MORNING, ALEXANDRA was riding with her brother along the cliff top, a safe distance from the edge. The day was cold and damp. Heavy clouds hung low over the water, looking as if they were about to disgorge their moisture at any moment.

"I am going to be leaving here soon, Alex," Purnell said. "I know that you have been invited for the whole summer and that I promised to accompany you here for moral support. But I don't think you really need me any longer. Do you?"

"But why must you leave?" she asked. "You just admitted yourself, James, that this must be one of the loveliest parts of the country. And everyone is excessively kind. What will you do? Where will you go?"

He shrugged. "I don't know," he said. "I am not going back home, Alex. Not now that you are safely away from there. I haven't yet decided where I actually will go."

"Can you not reconcile with Papa?" she asked, looking across at him with pleading eyes. "He is your father, James. I know that you feel he wronged you, and indeed he did, but he did what he thought was best at the time. Papa always does what he thinks is right."

"Yes," he said viciously. "The trouble with him, Alex, is that he believes no one else can possibly be right. He would probably find fault with God if they ever came face-to-face."

"James!" she said, distressed.

"I cannot forgive him," he said, "even if he acknowledged that what he did was wrong and begged my pardon. Oh, perhaps then I would. But of course he will never do any such thing. He interfered with my life in an unpardonable way. And in the process he destroyed all my hopes of future happiness and irrevocably altered the course of two other lives. Whether for better or worse, who is to say? No, I cannot go home, Alex. Home! I have no home."

"Yes, you do!" she cried passionately. "Home is where I am. You will always have a home with me."

He smiled tenderly at her. "Amberley Court?" he said. "You have done well for yourself after all, Alex. You will be happy here?"

"I don't know," she said, her expression guarded. She shivered as a gust of wind caught her in the face and tugged at her cloak. "I don't know, James. I think it very possible that I will not marry Lord Amberley after all."

"What?" he said. "You do not like him, Alex? He does not treat you well? I must confess that I have grown to respect him, suspicious as I was at first."

"It is not that," she said. "I like him very well. He is exceedingly kind. Compared with the Duke of Peterleigh, he is kindness itself. I don't think I could ask for a better husband."

"What, then?" he asked.

She shrugged. "I don't know," she said. "I think perhaps I woke up when this scandal happened. I mean, really woke up for the first time in my life. I suppose I was never happy—both you and Nanny Rey were always telling me that. But I did not know myself unhappy. I was quite content to be groomed as the bride of a stranger, though I knew all the time that as a husband he would be very similar to Papa. He would have been a strict and a demanding master, I believe. But I had always accepted that. It was only when suddenly his grace would have nothing to do with me and Lord Amberley and Lord Eden were vying for my hand that I realized what pawns women are in a man's game."

"I am afraid you are very right," he said. "But surely Amberley would be different, Alex? I would say you are fortunate to be engaged to a man who will not oppress you."

"I know you are right," she said. "I think if he had asked to marry me for any other reason, I would be happy, or contented at least. But he asked me because he felt he must, James. And even after I had refused, he came back and more or less forced himself upon me in order to save me from humiliation and ostracism. And I am grateful. Of course I am grateful. But can you not see, James, how very helpless it all makes me feel? How very useless?"

He looked across at her and said nothing for a while. "Yes," he said. "I think I can imagine, Alex. And sympathize. I always knew there was extraordinary strength in you, if only someday you recognized it yourself. So you will reject Amberley even though you know that you could be happy with him?"

"I keep telling myself that I am a fool," she said. "But, yes, I think I will have to."

"Does he know?" he asked.

"He is going to break off the engagement himself," she said, "after the ball next week, if I have not already done so."

"He cannot do that!" Purnell said, appalled. "That would be unbearable humiliation for you, Alex. I will call him out if he does any such thing."

She smiled at him unexpectedly. "No," she said. "It is what I want. I don't want to be treated as the helpless female who must be protected at all costs. I will honor him if he does it, James, more than I can say."

He shook his head. "You are a strange pair," he said. "Are you sure you do not love each other, Alex?"

Her smile faded. "No," she said. "But I respect him."

"This rather changes my plans," he said. "I was hoping to leave tomorrow. But you are going to need me, by the look of it."

She smiled at him. "I want you to stay, James," she said, "but only if it is what you wish. I am not going to lean on you anymore. You are free to go and do what you wish. Or to stay here. I have kept you from your own life for long enough."

"Alex!" he said, drawing his horse to a halt and staring at her. "You really have changed. I love what I am seeing and hearing, though I must admit I think you are doing a cork-brained thing where Amberley is concerned. But what are you going to do? Life with Papa will be hell after all this."

"I will not be living with Papa," she said. "I have been thinking about it all night. I will apply for a position as a governess or companion. You must admit I am eminently suited, James. I am used to a dull and disciplined life. But at least this will be a life of my own choosing."

He shook his head. "Where are we, by the way?" he asked. "We must be miles from the house. We had better start on the way back."

"Why must you go?" she asked. "And why so soon?"

He shrugged. "I am restless, I suppose," he said. "I have to get away, Alex, somewhere where I can unleash all the energy and anger inside me without hurting any innocent person."

"But you are not hurting anyone here," she said.

He smiled grimly. "I think I am going to leave this country altogether," he said. "Go somewhere where I am not expected to live an idle life as a gentleman. Somewhere where I can use my muscles and my brain."

"I will miss you," she said. "Write to me?"

"Of course," he said. "Oh, of course, Alex. You must know that you are the only important person in my life. Without you, it would lose all meaning."

"You are going tomorrow?" she asked bleakly.

He hesitated. "I will wait until this ball is over," he said. "Not to protect you, Alex. But I want to know what your fate is to be."

"Good," she said, and smiled across at him. "That I will have you for another week, that is."

They rode onward in silence, both alone with their thoughts. Purnell's plans had been complicated somewhat. He had planned to leave the next day. He was shaken by what had happened the day before. He had looked on the world and its people with some contempt for the past five years, but his hatred had never before focused upon one person, if one discounted his father. Never on an innocent person.

And really, the rational part of his mind had to admit, there was no reason at all why he should hate Lady Madeline Raine. Hate was a powerful emotion. She had done nothing to offend him. And yet he could not look at her or even think of her without wanting to hurt her. He had recognized his feelings during the Courtneys' dance, but he had thought himself sufficient master of his own impulses that he would never actually do her violence.

Even the tongue-lashings he had given her had disturbed him. He was not normally openly ill-mannered, especially to a lady. Yet the day before, he had used physical violence on her. It was true that all he had done was embrace her, but despite all appearances it had not been an embrace. He had wanted to hurt her with his hands and his mouth. He had wanted to lay her down. He had wanted to take her right there on the hard ground.

And it was only afterward, when he was no longer touching her, when she had turned away from him, that he had felt the full horror of his own actions. Only then, when it was far too late, had he wanted to take hold of her with gentle hands, to gather her against him, to soothe her with his mouth and his voice and his body.

And that impulse of sudden tenderness had alarmed him almost equally with the violence. No, not that again. Never that again.

And so he had decided he must leave. For Lady Madeline's sake and for his own, he must go. Alex did not need him any longer, he had concluded. Amberley would look after her. And yet now that situation had complicated. He was delighted at Alex's newfound spirit. It was what he had always hoped for, and had always thought possible, though he could have wished it to show itself in a way other than the rejection of a man who would undoubtedly make her a good husband. But he knew he would not be able to leave until he knew more certainly what was to happen to his sister.

And Alexandra for her part was feeling an unreasonable mixture of exhilaration and depression. Exhilaration at the fact that she had finally been able to sort out all her confusing feelings of the past weeks and know that she had her own life in her hands and that she could, within certain limits, do what she wished with it. The outlook was bleak—a breaking-off of her engagement, a dreadful scene with Papa, a future as a servant. But it was her future, and she felt excited at the prospect of being able to shape her own destiny for the first time in her life.

But there was depression too. James was going away, probably for a long, long time—perhaps forever. And she must not even try to hold him back. Indeed, she must encourage him to go, to find his own destiny. James must go in search of whatever it was that would release him from the terrible bitterness he felt against life.

And there was depression to know that she must go away from Lord Amberley just at the time when she realized she was beginning to care for him. He was a truly kind man. She doubted she would ever meet his like again. And a very, very attractive man. She had feared his touch at first because she had not understood the physical responses it evoked. Now she did understand. His touch appealed to the sexuality that had long been suppressed in her, that she had always been taught was the sin in her.

That sexuality could blossom at Lord Amberley's touch. She knew that. When he touched her, when he kissed her—even when he looked at her with those smiling blue eyes—she came alive in a way she had never known and never dreamed of. She had known of the physical duty marriage would bring her, but she had always expected it to be just that: a duty, the most unpleasant one of her married life. Something she would do because she belonged to a man and existed to bear his children and give him pleasure.

But she wanted to be intimate with the Earl of Amberley. She wanted to go beyond kisses, beyond the touch of hands and bodies. She wanted everything, everything there was to experience, even that always dreaded penetration of her body that she knew was at the heart of the marriage act. She wanted him inside her body. Edmund!

And yet she had decided that she must leave him, for no other reason than that he had offered her marriage in order to protect her. She must have windmills in her head! And he would end their betrothal because he respected the freedom of others too deeply to hold her to an engagement that was against her wishes.

Mad! She must be mad, Alexandra thought, the wind buffeting her from behind as she rode beside her brother, back along the cliffs toward Amberley. She was excited and depressed, jubilant and unhappy, all at the same time.

19

"WELL, DOM." LORD AMBERLEY, HIS COAT collar pulled up, his hat drawn forward, felt reasonably comfortable despite the chill of the morning. He and his brother were riding side by side on the road from the village, having just called on Mrs. Peterson to see how she and the boys did. "It seems an age since we had the chance of a talk together."

"That sounds ominous," Lord Eden said. "Do you have something particular on your mind, Edmund?"

His brother laughed. "No," he said. "Merely a certain elder-brotherly envy. You do attract the females, don't you?"

"Do you mean Molly Sugden just now in the Peterson cottage?" his brother asked with a grin. "I have never given her any encouragement at all, I swear. She is altogether too buxom for my taste."

Lord Amberley laughed. "You must admit that she showed unusual devotion," he said. "I wish I had counted the number of curtsies she bobbed in your direction. If I can count that high. I had two, one when I entered and one when I left."

"I can't help it if I am the handsomest Raine in the family," Lord Eden said.

"And the least modest," his brother said. "And there is Anna, Dom. She has a sad case of hero worship. I don't believe any other person exists in this world for her but you."

"She will grow out of it," Lord Eden said. "Wait until she is taken to London to be presented. She will have all the bucks swarming around her. A very fetching little thing, Anna. Give her time to acquire some curves and some allure, Edmund, and she will be slaying male hearts by the score."

"What about Susan?" Lord Amberley asked.

"What about Susan?" His brother frowned.

"She is smitten, Dom," the earl said. "And you have been doing nothing to discourage her, as far as I can see."

"Oh," Lord Eden said, "so there was a serious point to this conversation after all. You are wrong, though, Edmund. She is not smitten, and I have not been encouraging her. She actually started to cry yesterday when I told her I should not kiss her. She was hurt that I would think she wanted such a thing. You need have no worries on that score."

His brother looked incredulously at him. "You told her that you should not kiss her," he said. "Meaning, I suppose, that you had worked yourself and her into a happily romantic mood in which a kiss seemed the obvious next step?"

"Yes, well, you know," Lord Eden said, "we were down in the valley, Edmund, and nothing would do but everyone else had to cross the stepping-stones to the other side. Susan would not go across. I had to stay with her. What else could I have done? It was deuced quiet and shady down there, and Susan is such a pretty little thing. I would have had to be made of stone not to want to kiss her. But she did not want to be kissed, so no harm was done."

"Dom," Lord Amberley said, "are you two-and-twenty or twelve years of age? What did you expect her to say? 'Please'? Any self-respecting female would have reacted just as she did if a man said that he should not kiss her. Any woman with any pride, that is. Of course she wanted to be kissed, numbskull. And now she probably wants it more than ever. You are both playing hard to get, but I don't believe you even realize the fact."

"That's utter nonsense!" Lord Eden said uneasily. "I wouldn't trifle with Susan's feelings. And I can't marry her."

"Because she is the daughter of a tenant farmer?" his brother asked. "It would not be the most advantageous match imaginable, it is true. And many people would look askance. But you have a comfortable fortune, Dom. If she is what you want, marriage is not impossible."

"Yes, it is," Lord Eden said, staring fixedly ahead. "I have other plans."

"The army?" Lord Amberley asked.

"That too," his brother said. "But I was referring to other plans. I am still determined to free you, Edmund, as I said I would when we were still in London. I still plan to marry Miss Purnell myself."

"Indeed?" Lord Amberley broke a short silence. "And what does Alex have to say to this, Dom?"

"She has not said no," Lord Eden said. "I have every hope that she will say yes if she can just get over the feeling that she will be acting dishonorably to break off her engagement to you. You could talk to her, Edmund. And you need not feel as you did in London that you must do the noble thing for my sake since you are the elder brother. I want to marry Miss Purnell. I love her. I think."

"I see," Lord Amberley said quietly. "I seem to be standing in the way of a mutually happy match, then."

"Yes," Lord Eden said, glancing at him uneasily again, "you are, Edmund."

They turned into Amberley park and rode side by side in silence.

"You are not offended?" Lord Eden blurted at last. "This will be the best outcome for all three of us, will it not? You will be free again, and Miss Purnell and I will marry according to our inclination."

"If you say so," Lord Amberley said. "Don't forget, though, that I am betrothed to the lady. Until there is some announcement to the contrary, I am committed to that relationship. And to protecting her honor. Be careful, Dom. Don't do anything to compromise that honor. Not again."

Lord Eden winced. "Admit you will be happy to be released," he said.

Lord Amberley smiled rather grimly. "My feelings at least are my own private property, Dom," he said. "We will leave this topic of conversation for now, if you please."

Lord Eden glanced at him, not feeling quite the hero he had expected to feel at this moment.

"There is another thing," Lord Amberley said as they began to ride down the slope into the valley.

His brother groaned.

"About the army," the earl said. "When are you planning to buy your commission, Dom?"

"Eh?" Lord Eden looked with some surprise at the other. "You know Mama would have an apoplexy if I did, Edmund. Though Miss Purnell has been helping me build my courage. I shall have to prepare Mama very carefully over the winter. Perhaps next spring."

"Perhaps Bonaparte will be defeated by next spring," Lord Amberley said. "Why not sooner, Dom? If you really are determined to go, Mama and Madeline must face your leaving sooner or later anyway."

"Yes." Lord Eden glanced uneasily at his brother. "I have to make the decision, don't I? I am no longer a boy. But I don't want you to be caught in the middle, Edmund. I don't want you speaking up for me and incurring Mama's wrath. Worse, if I should be killed"—he drew a deep breath and kept his eyes fixed on the road ahead—"if I should be killed, I don't want you blamed at all."

"I would not dream of treating you as a child and arguing for you to either Mama or Madeline," Lord Amberley said. "But once your decision is made, Dom, and once you have spoken to them, I shall support you. If they come to me asking me to plead with you, I shall tell them I am more proud of my brother than I ever thought to be."

"Really?" Lord Eden's face had brightened to boyish eagerness. "You would not think me irresponsible, Edmund?"

"Irresponsible?" Lord Amberley said. "To give up your comfort and your safety to fight for your country against tyranny and oppression, Dom? To be willing to give up your very life? I am consumed with admiration."

Lord Eden grinned at him and turned his horse out of the roadway as they reached the valley. "I am going for a gallop down to the beach," he said. "I shall see you later, Edmund."

Lord Amberley watched him go, feeling as if he had a lead weight in his stomach. Dominic and Alex! She had not said no, Dom had said. He thought she would say yes if she were free to do so.

She was officially his betrothed, and he was not even free to flatten his brother and relieve him of his front teeth for such words. He had already promised to let her go after the ball the following week. Not just to allow her to break off their engagement, but to do it himself if he was not convinced by that time that she would be happy with him or that there was a reasonable chance that he could make her happy.

It would be terrible enough to let her go and see her disappear from his life. It would be dreadful beyond words to see her the bride of his own brother. And the happy bride. Dom seemed to think that it would be a mutually happy union.

Well, then. So be it.

Lord Amberley turned his horse in the direction of the house. He would not even be able to be assured that she was safe and secure. She would be the wife of a soldier. Perhaps even in Spain following the drum. Somehow he could not imagine Alex married to a soldier and sitting comfortably at home while he risked his life every day. She was just the sort of woman who would go, too.

And he loved her. He had known it surely for several days. He had known at least that he had a physical passion for her, that he desired her. Perhaps it was only as a result of the previous day's conversation that he had also learned to appreciate her character, the strength of purpose that made her want to stand alone rather than be protected from the nastier side of life.

Perhaps it was only now, today, that he could fully love her. And he did. She was today as necessary to him as the air he breathed, even more necessary to him than the beloved home he was approaching.

Damn Dominic! And damn his stupid sense of honor

that would not let him remove those teeth and break his brother's nose and a few ribs for good measure! Lord Amberley felt a vicious and quite uncharacteristic need to punish someone.

LORD EDEN FOUND MADELINE in the conservatory an hour later. He almost did not see her. She was hidden behind a large fern. Only the movement of her hand as she pulled the needle through the cloth she was embroidering betrayed her presence.

"Here you are, Mad," he said. "I have been searching for you everywhere. What on earth are you doing sitting so quietly here on your own?"

"Sewing," she said, without looking up.

"I can see that, you goose," he said. "But why alone like this and hidden from view?"

She shrugged. "It's a horrid day," she said. "I don't feel like going out."

He seated himself on the window seat beside her and looked at her searchingly. "What is it?" he asked. "And don't say, 'Nothing,' as you are about to do. We can see through each other's lies in a glance; you know that."

She jabbed her needle into the cloth and set down her work in a heap beside her. "I am so unhappy, Dom," she said.

He reached out and took her hand in his. "I thought you were rather enjoying yourself," he said. "Forbes seems very taken with you, and you were busy flirting with him during the picnic yesterday. I expected to hear that you are head over ears in love—again." He grinned.

But she did not look up to see his expression. "He kissed me," she said.

"And that is cause for such misery?" Lord Eden said. "You didn't like it, I gather. That is no matter for grand tragedy, Mad. There are plenty of other fish in the sea. What about Jennings?"

"It was Mr. Purnell who kissed me," she said.

"Oh." He sat beside her silently for a while and then squeezed her hand. "Do you want to tell me about it, Mad?"

"He hates me," she said. "I don't know why, Dom. I have never done anything to offend him. Well, I have said a few nasty things, I suppose, but they have been a result of the hatred I feel in him, not the cause of it."

"'Hate' is a pretty strong word," Lord Eden said with a frown.

"I know," she said. "But I chose the word with care, Dom. He hates me. I can tell every time he looks at me or talks to me. I don't know how I was trapped into being alone with him yesterday. I have been trying to avoid him. But somehow it happened."

"And he kissed you," Lord Eden said. "You are not making much sense, Mad. That does not sound like the action of a man who hates you."

"It wasn't really a kiss," she said. "It was an insult. It's hard to explain, Dom. It was horrible."

"He didn't try anything more than that, did he?" he asked, his voice turned hard. "If he did, Mad, tell me. I'll draw his cork for him, guest or no guest. He is not my guest, anyway. This is Edmund's house."

"No," she said. "He just kissed me. And then told me to stay away from him. And then apologized."

"I should give him a good drubbing anyway," Lord Eden said angrily. "Who does he think you are?"

"No," she said wearily. "Leave it, Dom. Please leave it."

"Stay away from him, then," he said. "There are other

people to entertain him, Mad. Concentrate on falling in love with Forbes or Jennings or even Watson. Enjoy yourself."

He did not hear her mumbled reply.

"What?" he asked.

"I love him," she said.

There was an appalled silence. "Purnell?" he said. "You love Purnell?"

"I hate him," she said. "I am afraid of him. And I am obsessed with him. I can't understand it, Dom, or myself. Or him. He is horrid to me and thoroughly cynical about everything. I know he hates himself. I think he is very unhappy."

"That is no reason for making everyone else around him miserable," Lord Eden said indignantly. "Especially my sister. Can't you just forget him, Mad? Let him look after his own problems?"

"No," she said, looking at her free hand, which she spread in her lap. "I can't, Dom. I have tried. I tried to fall in love with Captain Forbes yesterday. Usually it would be easy to do. Normally by now I would be swinging from clouds and hearing wedding bells. But not this time."

"Well, then," he said, "someone else. Soon you will meet someone else and it will happen again."

"Maybe," she said bleakly. "But I don't think so. I love him."

Lord Eden swallowed and squeezed his twin's hand again. He could think of nothing to say. Least of all the news he had come to give her. That could wait for a while. He had decided to stay until after the ball anyway. He had some unfinished business here at Amberley before he could rush off to war.

"What about you?" Madeline asked, looking up at her

brother eventually. "I think you are in love with Susan, aren't you?"

He looked at her and smiled nervously. "She is a sweet little thing, isn't she?" he said. "She has certainly grown up since I saw her last."

"Susan is a sweet conniving little thing," she said. "She is out to get herself a husband above her station, Dom."

"Oh, come now," he said. "That is unfair, you know, Mad. She can't help being pretty and charming. And there is nothing wrong with wanting to better oneself. But she certainly isn't flirtatious or conniving. What a ridiculous idea. She won't even call me by my given name or let me kiss her. Are those the actions of a conniver?"

"Yes," she said, and smiled unexpectedly. "But it is cruel of me to say so, Dom, when you have such stars in your eyes. Enjoy your flirtation. You will not marry her anyway, I know. At least, I hope I know. You will tire of her soon enough. You always do, and all your flirts are almost identical to Susan in every way."

"There is no one else like Susan," he said indignantly. "And I am not flirting with her, Mad. I can't. I am going to marry Miss Purnell."

She grimaced. "Oh, no, Dom," she said, "you cannot possibly be still entertaining that idea. It's ridiculous. Far too much time has passed. And I think that she and Edmund are admirably suited. I really do. And I think they are developing a regard for each other. You will only make a cake of yourself if you try to play the hero and rescue her from an unhappy match. Just like Don Quixote."

"I like her," he said. "I think we will make a good match. And she has not said no, you know. I have told Edmund too."

"Told Edmund?" she said. "That you are going to try to take Miss Purnell from him? Didn't he throttle you?"

"No," he said. "He was remarkably civil about it. I would say he was relieved, Mad."

"And Alexandra has not said no?" she asked. "You have asked her, then, Dom?"

"Yesterday," he said, "at the picnic. I think she is relieved too."

"Oh, Dom," she said, grabbing for his other hand and holding tightly to both of them, "there will be a terrible family rift over this. You cannot expect Edmund to take this lightly, you know, for all his seeming relieved. He will be the laughingstock. You can't do it. It would be better far to let him marry her, even if they do not love each other. They are both very honorable people. They will respect each other and probably even develop an affection for each other. Perhaps more. Who are we to say? Don't do it, Dom. Please don't. Oh, I know you have conceived the notion out of a sense of honor, but really it would be a dreadfully dishonorable thing to do. It really would, Dom."

He squeezed her hands in return. "Don't take on so, Mad," he said. "Sometimes I don't know what to think or what to do. I am a man already—in years anyway. But I feel so much like a boy still. I can make up my mind to something, and then I talk to someone else and have my mind changed again. And I never know if it is weakness or wisdom to listen. I wish everyone would leave me alone to do my own thinking and my own deciding."

Madeline released his hands and put her arms up around his neck. She laid her cheek against his. "Oh, I am sorry, Dom," she said. "I am truly sorry I have made you feel inadequate. Your trouble is, not that you are immature, but that you are very sweet and sensitive. You hate to hurt anyone.

You want to please everyone and take the burden of the world upon your own shoulders. You are just like Edmund in that way. But it can't always be done, dear. Other people have to carry their own burdens for themselves. Sometimes you have to allow other people to suffer, Dom, even if they are people you love. Sometimes you can make the situation worse by trying to intervene."

"Or interfere," he said. "But if I have caused the suffering in the first place, Mad?"

"Look, Dom," she said, removing her cheek from his and looking earnestly into his eyes, "you compromised Alexandra, you offered for her, and she refused you. I imagine you probably apologized too. Your obligation ended there. You have to accept that. She refused you. What happened later between her and Edmund is between them. If there is a problem, it is his. And hers. Not yours, and not mine, even if we love both of them and want to see them happy. They are not our responsibility. They are adult, sensible people. They will work it out for themselves."

He drew a deep breath and blew it out from puffed cheeks. "Don Quixote, eh?" he said. "And I am not immature!"

"Don Quixote was a dear," she said. "Easily my favorite fictional character. Just as you are my favorite real character, Dom." She gave him a smacking kiss on the cheek.

"Well," he said, "we haven't exactly solved any of the world's problems, have we, Mad? Shall we go in search of luncheon? The bell must be about to ring any minute."

"An admirable idea," she said, getting to her feet and bending to fold her embroidery tidily. "When all else fails, eat. It sounds very sensible. And alarmingly fattening!"

• • •

ALEXANDRA HAD AGREED TO accompany her mother and Lady Amberley on an afternoon visit to Sir Peregrine and Lady Lampman. Sir Cedric had also declared his intention of making one of the party, and Lord Amberley had decided at luncheon that he could not possibly allow the older man to have three ladies all to himself for a whole afternoon.

The barouche was ordered around after all in preference to the carriage when the heavy clouds of the morning moved off and the sun decided to shine. It was blustery enough, it was true, to make Lady Beckworth look a little dubious, but it was a warm and healthful breeze, Lady Amberley declared firmly. Lord Amberley rode his horse.

Alexandra sat next to Sir Cedric, their backs to the horses. He smiled at her and patted her hand.

"Well, Miss Purnell," he said, "and were you pleased with Amberley's news at luncheon?"

"Yes, indeed," she said, forcing a smile to her lips. "It will be good to see Papa again."

"I am delighted for you, my dear," he said, "that he has changed his mind and decided to come for a couple of weeks. There is nothing like the presence of one's family to raise one's spirits, is there?"

"No," she said.

"I cannot say how gratified I am to know Beckworth is coming," Lady Beckworth said. "I have never been away from him before, you know, except at home when he has occasionally been called away on business. I find decisions too momentous to be made without the guidance of my husband."

Sir Cedric smiled at her. "It will be a happiness for everyone to have him here in time for Amberley's ball, ma'am," he said. "It is always a splendid event."

"It is one of the few occasions of the year when the state rooms are used," Lady Amberley said. "I am afraid we do indulge ourselves in lavish preparations and decorations. Of course"—she smiled warmly across at Alexandra—"a wedding is a perfect excuse for using them too. Perhaps we will not have to wait a full year this time before we dine again in the state dining room. But I am putting you to the blush, Alexandra. How unforgivable of me. Do look down, dear, and see the house and gardens from up here. I never tire of the view, I must confess."

Alexandra had been roundly scolded earlier that morning for allowing herself to be led off alone by Lord Amberley at the picnic when they might have joined the larger party who had gone down to the river. And they had been gone for longer than an hour, her mother had said, longer than the others. What would everyone think of her?

And now Papa had written to say that he was coming. And Mama was vastly relieved, as she had said a minute before. She had said the same thing to Alexandra before they left the house. Her father would control her behavior, Lady Beckworth had said. She would not dare do anything as improper as go off alone with her betrothed more than once or twice in a week once her father was there to keep an eye on her.

It was going to be difficult, Alexandra admitted to herself. It was all very well now to tell herself that the new Alexandra would stand up against him and assert herself. She was one-and-twenty, she could tell herself now, and officially betrothed. She did not have to allow her father or any man to dictate her every word and action. Unless she married another man, of course. Then she would become his property, his to command, his to punish if he so chose. But she did not have to allow that to become possible. The society in which she lived might impose all sorts of restrictions on the behavior of women, but it could not force any woman to marry against her will.

It was all very well to tell herself that she could now command her own destiny. But she knew that it would be harder to live up to her resolution once her father arrived. From the habit of a lifetime she had always obeyed his every command to the letter and without question—even to kneeling for long hours on the floor of her room, reading her Bible, when no one came to check up on her and it would have been easy to cheat and sit on a chair or lie on her bed. Even as recently as a few weeks before, she had submitted to those punishments. She had accepted Lord Amberley because her father had commanded her to do so and had promised that the beatings would resume if she did not.

She no longer had to submit to those beatings or to the hours, and sometimes days, of silent torture. Just that morning she had known an exhilaration at her own freedom, her own ability to free herself and live her own life. But the test would come when Papa arrived. Would she have the strength to do what she knew she had the right to do? It was impossible to tell. She could only hope that she would.

Her eyes rested on Lord Amberley, who was riding behind the barouche. The temptation, she knew, would be to turn to him if she found Papa difficult to deal with—*when* she found Papa difficult to deal with. He would help her, she knew instinctively. Kindly and courteous as he invariably was, she sensed a streak of iron in him. She had seen it once at Lady Sharp's soiree, when by sheer force of will, unaccompanied by any forceful words or actions, he had wrested respect for her out of the cream of the *ton*.

He would not allow Papa to bully her. He would protect her. He would, she was sure, even marry without further ado if she but hinted to him that she needed to be rescued from her father. It would be good to be rescued by the Earl of Amberley. Edmund. Good to relax, forget all her problems, and allow him to shoulder her burdens. Good to know that afterward she would not find a new bully to replace the old. Life could be good with him. He could be her friend as well as her protector. Her lover. The father of her children. Those children with whom he would climb up the most dangerous part of the cliff face. She would go with them.

It was only when Lord Amberley looked away from the valley and smiled warmly at her when he caught her eye that she realized the treacherous direction of her thoughts. She lifted her chin and gave him a half-smile in return.

It was not yet time for tea, Lady Lampman announced when they arrived at the neat stone house set among carefully tended gardens and orchards. Would they all care for a walk? She took Alexandra's arm resolutely as they left the house, and led the way along the hedge-lined laneway, in the opposite direction from that by which they had come in the barouche.

"I insist on plenty of exercise both morning and afternoon," she said, "even though Perry worries. He thinks it would be far better for me to sit at home with my feet on a stool. Can you imagine any life more dull, Miss Purnell?"

"No, indeed," Alexandra said fervently, thinking of all the years she had spent almost confined indoors. She was noticing for the first time—she could not understand how she had missed the clear evidence both at the Courtneys' dance and at church on Sunday—that Lady Lampman was with child.

"Perry is terrified, of course," Lady Lampman said with a quick and nervous smile at her companion. "Both for me and for..." She touched her abdomen and blushed. "I am thirty-seven years old, you know. No, you probably did not know, though I am sure you might have guessed. I think we both assumed I was too old."

"Are you pleased?" Alexandra was a little embarrassed, having been brought up to believe that talking about pregnancies was as unthinkable as talking about the marriage act.

She was favored with that nervous smile again. "Terrified," her companion said, "though Perry must never know. I pretend that it is a matter of no moment at all. But you cannot know what it means to me, Miss Purnell, to have the chance to present him with a child, just like any normal woman."

Alexandra gave her a look of surprise.

"Perry is only seven-and-twenty," Lady Lampman said. "He should be married to a sweet young thing who could fill a whole nursery for him, shouldn't he?"

Alexandra found the question quite impossible to answer. She did not even try.

"I am embarrassing you," Lady Lampman said. "Do you like it at Amberley? And are you planning to be wed soon? And are my questions impertinent? We will talk about the hedgerow if you wish."

Alexandra laughed. "I love Amberley," she said. "I am sure there can be no more beautiful place on earth. His lordship has shown me the place on the cliffs where he climbed as a boy with your husband. Sir Peregrine got stuck, it seems, and they were both caught. And thrashed."

Lady Lampman flashed her a broader smile. "Boys are horrors, are they not?" she said. "I wonder if our sons will ever try anything as foolish. Oh, Miss Purnell, I do so wish for a son. This will be my only chance, surely. Of course, first and foremost I wish for a live and healthy child. But a son! There could not be any greater happiness."

The woman looked stern and humorless. Alexandra had labeled her thus during their first meeting. And she had watched her husband all during the Courtney dance with eyes that Alexandra had labeled as jealous and possessive. How wrong first impressions can be, she thought as they walked on and climbed a low hill in order to circle around behind the house for their return.

Lady Lampman was a woman deeply in love. And perhaps painfully in love. She was ten years older than her husband—Alexandra did not know the story behind their union—and very insecure. She must wonder constantly whether he regretted their marriage, whether he looked with longing at younger women. And now she was bearing his child, terrified that she was too old to bring it alive and healthy into the world, painfully yearning to be able to present him with this one token of her love.

She wondered about Sir Peregrine and watched him curiously during tea, after they had returned to the house. He and Lord Amberley spent some time reminiscing about their boyhood years and laughing a great deal. Only once did she have any indication of his feelings for his wife. She was bending over the tea tray, pouring a second cup for Sir Cedric. Sir Peregrine's eyes were on her, on the slight swelling of her abdomen. His eyes followed her as she took the cup across the room though he continued with the story he was in the middle of telling. After his wife sat down, he got up and carried a footstool across to her. And he touched her shoulder lightly before returning to his own place.

They were small gestures and caused not the slightest pause in the conversation. But Alexandra smiled slightly to herself. It was a strange relationship—a ten-year gap in ages seemed enormous when the woman was the elder—but it was not without affection even on the husband's part.

She looked around the cozy parlor in which they sat. For the moment she was not directly involved in any of the three conversations in progress. But she felt an enormous and seductive contentment. She did love Amberley Court, as she had just admitted to Lady Lampman. And its surroundings. And she was beginning to love its people too—Lady Amberley, always so gracious and sensible; Sir Cedric, quiet, unassuming, part of the family though no blood relation; and Sir Peregrine and Lady Lampman, who were becoming for her no longer merely faces, but interesting and probably complex people.

How easy it would be to relax into the comfort of it all, to allow herself to become one of them. And how foolish not to, when the alternative was so unnecessary and so bleak. What a dreadful thing pride is, she thought as she met the blue and smiling eyes of her betrothed, watching her from across the room. She lowered her eyes to her teacup.

"Did you enjoy this afternoon?" he asked her later, when he took her for a stroll in the rose garden after their return. "Perry has always been one of my closest friends."

"Yes," she said. "I like them both."

"I think they are happy together," he said. "I am glad of it. I thought he was mad at the time, I must confess. Lady Lampman was living with her brother, our last rector, as his housekeeper. Perry was particularly friendly with him. He used to spend half his time at the rectory. And then she was left apparently quite destitute two years ago when the rector died suddenly."

"Poor lady," Alexandra said.

"The rest of us were busily thinking of a solution," Lord Amberley said. "Mama was even going to offer her the position of companion, though Mama would hate having such an employee. But Perry took the matter out of our hands by marrying her. I am afraid at the time I thought it a foolishly noble gesture and told him so. I had a rather painful jab on the nose for my pains." He laughed softly. "But I think he is fond of her. And she dotes on him."

"Yes," Alexandra said. "I hope she will be able to bear her child safely."

She was blushing furiously and biting her lip when Lord Amberley smiled down at her.

20

ALTHOUGH THE ANNUAL BALL AT AMBERLEY was to be held within a week, nevertheless it was decided that an informal garden party would be an appropriate welcoming gesture for the arrival of Lord Beckworth from London. The Carringtons, the Courtneys, and the Lampmans were to come, as well as the Misses Stanhope, the rector and his wife, and the two officers of the regiment. Tables were set up on the northern lawn, close to the trees and the river.

Lord Eden had spent an unhappy few days. His decision to buy a commission in the army and go to Spain if at all possible had been quite firmly made. It was true, he had decided, that sometimes one had to do what one wished to do, no matter how selfish one's behavior might seem to be. There were some things too important to be given up even for the sake of loved ones. For him, the active life of a soldier in the service of his country was essential. He felt that he could not be a whole person if he did not go. And if he were not a whole person, then he could never be a good son or brother—or husband.

He had not yet spoken to either his mother or his sister

about his decision to leave before the end of the summer. It was not cowardice or procrastination that held him back. It was just that he wished to tell them all of his plans, and he did not know himself what all his plans were. Was he going to marry Miss Purnell? Or at least, was he going to still try to persuade her to marry him?

He had been quite firm in his plans to do so. He had asked her, and he had even mentioned his intentions to Edmund. Neither had expressed marked opposition to the idea. But he could not shake from his mind what Madeline had said in the conservatory. She had echoed uncomfortably the very thoughts that had been in his own mind and that he had so ruthlessly quelled.

It was all very well to feel, as he had originally felt, that it was his responsibility to marry Miss Purnell, not Edmund's. It was fine at the start to fight against his brother's decision, to try to take an unwelcome betrothed off his hands. Even up to the moment when they had left London, the change would have been possible. Already there had been enough upheaval, enough scandal, surrounding both families, that one more odd incident would have made little difference.

But he had to admit that once they had all removed to Amberley, the situation had become remarkably formal and unchangeable. Miss Purnell had been introduced to everyone in the neighborhood as Edmund's betrothed. She had been entertained in the homes of many of their neighbors; she had attended church with Edmund; she had visited the Petersons and attended Joel's funeral with him; there was to be the ball within a week.

The thought now of his trying to take her away to marry her himself seemed almost incredibly naive. Certainly not noble. Madeline was right. He had already thought it himself. Edmund would find it difficult to hold his head up forever after. Miss Purnell would never be received again by respectable society. He would surely be banished from his childhood home.

And why was he trying to do such a thing? Because he loved Miss Purnell? He did not, though he did like her a great deal and respected her deeply. He wanted to marry her in order to save his brother from a life of misery. Would he not be plunging Edmund into a life of much deeper misery if he continued with his plans than if he allowed the marriage to take place? And he wanted to marry her so that he could take upon himself the duty of making her happy. Making her happy by changing her into a social pariah? It was a lunatic idea.

And yet, he thought every time the answer was obvious to him and he decided that he must drop his plans, if Edmund had a bad marriage, if Miss Purnell did, then he would never forgive himself for having been the cause of it all.

Life was just not easy, Lord Eden concluded. Adult life, that was. When one was a child, one frequently made wrong decisions and frequently got into trouble. But when one was a child, there was always someone there to pick one up and soothe one's hurt or else call one to task and mete out punishment. And always someone to explain exactly what it was one should have done. In childhood, it always seemed that there was an absolute answer to everything. If one did not have that answer oneself, an adult surely did. Mama did, or Sir Cedric, or Edmund.

But when one reached that longed-for goal of adulthood, where there was no longer anyone to lecture or scold or punish, one also became aware of the supreme joke of life—that there were no absolute answers after all, not, at least, to many of the thornier problems of life.

And then there was Susan! She was with Lieutenant Jennings during the first part of the garden party, until teatime, and he was content to leave it thus. He had avoided her company since his uncle's picnic. But when he turned away from the table, a loaded plate in his hand, he literally collided with her. A cucumber sandwich flew one way, a jam tart the other. Susan's hand flew to her mouth to stifle a shriek.

"Susan!" he said with a grin. "Do you see the effect you have on me? I cannot even keep a steady hand."

She blushed and lowered her lashes. "It was all my fault, my lord," she said. "I was not looking where I was going."

"How fortunate for me that you weren't," he said. "May I fill a plate for you?"

"Oh," she said breathlessly, "I am not hungry."

He did not think to ask what she was doing approaching the food table if she did not intend to eat. He put down his own plate gallantly and offered her his arm.

"By coincidence, neither am I," he said. "I was about to eat from force of habit only. Shall we walk down to the bridge?"

She peeped at him from beneath her lashes. "I am sure Mama would say that I may," she said. "The bridge can be seen from here."

"I think you must have worn green to torment me, Susan," he said as they began to walk, looking down at the pretty bonnet that was all he could see of her head for the moment. "It quite perfectly complements the auburn of your hair."

"I am sure I do not mean to torment you, my lord," she

said, looking up at him with her hazel eyes. "It would not be fitting, with you so far above me in rank."

"Ah," he said with a grin, "but beauty is the great leveler, Susan. If you were side by side with a duchess at the moment, no one would even notice the duchess standing there."

"Oh," she said, "you are funning me, my lord. Who would ever notice me if I were in such grand company?"

"I would, Susan, that is who," he said, patting her hand. "And every other man for a radius of five miles, I warrant you."

Her eyes brightened with tears and she lowered her lashes suddenly. "You are making fun of me, my lord," she said, her voice low.

"No. Susan!" His hand closed around hers as it rested on his arm. "Of course I am not. Do you not even realize how very lovely you are? And how utterly adorable?"

"I am nobody," she whispered.

"Susan!" he said, stopping and turning toward her. "Look at me. Please look at me."

She did so, her cheeks flaming, her eyes still bright with unshed tears. He looked hastily back the way they had come. They were hidden from the picnic site by a clump of bushes beside the river.

"Susan," he said gently, "you are someone, believe me. You are surely the prettiest and sweetest young lady of my acquaintance. In fact, I would go beyond saying you are someone. I would say you are everyone, Susan. To me you are everyone and everything. There. Does that reassure you?"

"Oh," she said, and two tears spilled over and began to trickle down her cheeks.

Lord Eden took her face in his hands and wiped the tears

away gently with his thumbs. And that little rosebud of a mouth, still formed into an "Oh," was not to be resisted. He lowered his own to it.

And then his hands came away from her face and gathered her slight, yielding body against his own. Her hands stole up to his shoulders. Her lips trembled beneath his and returned their pressure.

Lord Eden did not allow the embrace to be anything else but gentle. She felt very small and very fragile in his arms. She made him feel large and protective. He gave himself up to his love for her.

But only for as long as the kiss lasted. As soon as he lifted his head and found himself looking down into her large trusting eyes, he knew that he had just succeeded in complicating his life even further, just at a time when a contemplation of the tangles of his mind was already enough to give him a headache. He groaned.

"Oh, my sweet love," he said, "what a wretch I am! I have no right doing this, you know, no right giving in to my love for you. I have other obligations, Susan. I am not free. At least, at present I am not free."

Tears welled into her eyes again but did not spill over. "I cannot help loving you," she said. "It is not wrong to show you that I love you, is it? I cannot help myself. But I do not expect you to return my feelings. You are Lord Eden."

"Susan." He hugged her to him again and then held her at arm's length. "That has nothing to do with it. I wouldn't care if I were the King of England and you a milkmaid. I would still love you. But I have obligations. I am in a tangle."

"You love someone else," she said. "It is understandable that you do. You are so very handsome."

"No," he said. "At least... Susan, forgive me. I have acted

unpardonably this afternoon, setting my own needs and feelings before yours. Forgive me. Please forgive me."

"I forgive you," she said. "I love you, my lord."

Lord Eden closed his eyes briefly and released his hold of her arms. "I certainly do not deserve your love," he said. "I should take you back, Susan. Or would you prefer to walk on to the bridge? We are almost there."

"To the bridge, please," she said. "I would not wish Mama to see my tears. Are my eyes very red?" She raised perfect eyes and complexion to his gaze and looked anxiously into his eyes.

"You look quite beautiful," he said, raising one hand as if to touch her cheek, but lowering it again before he did so. He clasped his hands behind his back. "Let us stand on the bridge for a while, then. It was perfectly placed, was it not? The view is quite lovely in both directions."

"Yes," she said. "Did you know that the regiment may be going to Spain? That is what Lieutenant Jennings told Papa earlier."

"Yes," he said. "The whole neighborhood is agog with the news, though no one seems to know it if is quite certainly true."

"I think it is dreadful," she said, "to think of all those men going where there are guns and fighting. I do not know how they can even support the idea. I would die at the very thought."

"And yet that is the job of a soldier," he said, "to fight when it is necessary to do so."

"I would die," she said. "I would just die!"

MADELINE WAS SITTING ON the lawn with Captain Forbes, Sir Peregrine and Lady Lampman, Miss Letitia Stanhope, and her cousin Walter. She was gaily telling them stories about London and keeping them all laughing. She was trying desperately to fall in love with the captain.

He was very tall and very handsome, and looked perfectly magnificent in his regimentals. Only a few weeks before, she would have had to make no effort whatsoever to fall in love with him. In fact, she would have had to try very hard indeed not to do so. He would not, after all, be a desirable match for her. He was the younger son of a baronet, without property of his own and without fortune. He was, moreover, a soldier with the declared intention of making a lifetime career out of the army.

No, not a desirable match at all. It was not that she really needed to marry a fortune. Her dowry was extremely large. And she did not need to marry a prince or a duke. Her family was remarkably enlightened about the idea of marrying untitled people. But she really could not picture herself living the unsettled life of an officer's wife. Once she had almost done just that, of course, when she had tried to run away with Lieutenant Harris. But she had been barely eighteen at the time. Besides, she had admitted to herself afterward that she had probably left that letter almost deliberately where Edmund was bound to find it and put a stop to her plans. It had been easier to blame him for being a tyrant than to decide for herself that after all the elopement would just not do.

But this time it just could not be done. Although the captain showed her every deference and would need very little encouragement to be declaring himself, she just could not fall in love with him.

"Someone else tell a story," she said now, as the laughter died down following her latest anecdote. "Walter, you were in London for a few weeks. Something interesting must have happened to you."

"Well," he said, "there was the day I tried to get into White's with Hanbury. He said I could look older than I am if I pursed my lips and looked very stern."

"And it did not work, I take it," Sir Peregrine said with a grin.

"The years will pass quickly enough," Lady Lampman said, "and you will be able to join all the clubs you wish, Mr. Carrington."

It was an inspired moment to call Walter "Mr. Carrington," Madeline thought. He must appear little more than a babe to Lady Lampman. She flashed a curious look at the lady. She had always found her intriguing. So quiet and unassuming when she had been the rector's housekeeper that she had been scarcely noticeable. And then coming into a shocking prominence as the bride of Sir Peregrine.

Madeline had once fancied herself in love with him, and he had been in the habit of paying her lavish compliments and flirting outrageously with her. She realized now that his intentions had never been serious. But Lady Lampman! How could he have brought himself to such a thing as to marry her? She was so much older than he, and had no obvious attractions.

Madeline looked again, as she had looked many times, for signs of unhappiness or discontent in Sir Peregrine's face, and could find none. What an intriguing relationship theirs was! It was impossible to know if they were mildly contented or desperately unhappy. Impossible to know if Lady Lampman ruled him with a rod of iron, as she sometimes liked to fancy. The woman certainly watched him wherever he went when they were in company.

And she was with child. Madeline would have thought she was far too old.

"Yes, please, Perry," Lady Lampman said now, handing her husband her empty glass so that he might bring her more lemonade. And she followed him with her eyes as he crossed the lawn and stopped to talk briefly to the rector's wife. He was looking after his wife's needs—like an obedient puppy? Or like a devoted husband?

Madeline found her eyes straying up the river again, as they had against her will at least a dozen times in the past hour. But they were still not returning—Howard, Uncle William, Anna, and Mr. Purnell. They had gone to look at a good fishing spot, though what there was to see in a good fishing spot escaped Madeline's comprehension. She could have gone with them. Uncle William had asked her, and Howard had looked hopeful. Mr. Purnell had not looked at her at all. And of course she had not gone.

Did she love him? That was the word she had used to Dom a few days before. But was "love" a suitable word to describe her feelings for Mr. Purnell? Perhaps "obsession" was a better word. She certainly was obsessed. She avoided him at every moment of the day, and yet at every moment of the day she knew were he was and with whom. When he was within her sight, she tingled with awareness of him and studiously avoided looking at him. And found herself darting glances at him every few moments.

She was very much afraid of him. And she did not know why. There was his way of talking to her, of course. He had never made a secret of his dislike of her and had insulted her on more than one occasion. But then, that was not the sort of behavior that would make her cringe. If any man wished to talk to her in that way, well, she would give as good as she got, and better. She could even enjoy the banter. Not that she had had much practice at that sort of game, of course. In her experience men tended to be worshipful. And boring.

And there was the way he had treated her the last time they had been alone together. She had still not succeeded in shaking the memory of that kiss from her mind. And she was not sure that she had tried very hard. It had been a bruising and an insulting kiss, and she supposed quite sufficient to explain her fear of Mr. Purnell. But for all that, that was not the reason for her fear. Perhaps it was foolish of her to be so trusting, but she did not feel that she had been in danger of being ravished, or that she need fear such danger. She did not believe him quite that unprincipled.

No, she could not explain her fear. It was a fear of the unknown. And Mr. Purnell definitely represented the unknown. There was something about him, something locked up inside him, that frightened her. Not that she feared it would erupt in violence. She was not afraid of being physically harmed by Mr. Purnell.

What was she afraid of, then? Of falling in love with him so irrevocably that she would not be able to feel an interest in any other man ever again? Yes, she was afraid of that. Very afraid. She was two-and-twenty years old, and she wanted to be married. She wanted her life to settle down. She wanted to be in love, to marry, to have children.

And she was afraid of finding herself irreversibly in love and then discovering something dreadful about Mr. Purnell, something that should distance him totally from her regard. Not that it would matter anyway, of course. Not in her wildest imaginings could she ever picture Mr. Purnell loving her, wanting to spend his life or any part of it with her. And yet, in some small way he must share her obsession. She had never heard him treat any other lady as he treated her. He had apologized twice to her—once for what he had said, once for what he had done. And that kiss had been quite unpremeditated; she was sure of that.

"Oh, yes, thank you," she said, smiling up at Sir Peregrine, who had brought her a glass of lemonade too. "It is a warm afternoon. I should tell you about the time Lord Timmins brought me a glass of lemonade at Almack's and tripped just as he was holding it out to me, though no one could discover afterward what it was he had tripped over. The poor man. That was all of three years ago, and I have never seen him there since."

The others joined in her laughter. They were on their way back, she saw, Anna tripping along beside Mr. Purnell, her arm through his. He was looking down at her, an indulgent smile on his face. Madeline laughed at Sir Peregrine, who was declaring that he was terrified to hand his wife her lemonade lest he spill it all down the front of her dress.

ALEXANDRA HAD DREADED THE ARRIVAL of her father, and in the event had fallen into his arms and hugged him with a fervor that had surprised herself quite as much as it had him. She had never been separated from him for as long before, and seeing his familiar bulky figure step down from his carriage outside Lord Amberley's door had made her realize what she had not fully known until that moment: she loved him.

"Well, Alexandra," he had said, holding her at arm's length and glancing up the marble steps to where Lord Amberley and his mother waited, and to his wife at the bottom of the steps, "I see you have forgotten your manners, miss."

And yet, she had thought as he turned to greet Mama in

a far more restrained manner and to acknowledge his host and hostess, he had not been angry. His gruffness had hidden some pleasure. Or had she imagined that? Was it possible that Papa could be pleased at being hugged? She had never done such a thing before.

She had had very little private talk with him since. If Mama had recounted her misdeeds, he had not yet found the moment to take her to task about them. He had addressed one remark to her the night before after dinner.

"Well, Alexandra," he had said, "you will be pleased with the latest news from town, doubtless. The Duke of Peterleigh has just engaged himself to Lady Angela Page. She has made a fortunate catch, under the circumstances. She is seventeen years old."

What had she felt? Alexandra asked herself now. A sense of finality, as if a door had been finally closed in her face? Yes, she did feel that. Relief? Yes, definitely. It might so easily have been she. In fact, all her life she had expected that it would be she. And she knew now after a few weeks of rapid growing up that she would never have known a moment's happiness in her life if she had married his grace.

Indeed, she thought with some surprise, that ridiculous kidnapping that had been the origin of all her woes had probably been the single most fortunate thing that had ever happened to her. She was in a tangle, and there were worse days to come, but at least she had been made aware of herself as a distinct person, quite separate from her father or the Duke of Peterleigh or any other man. She had a great deal to thank Lord Eden for. She must tell him so when she had the chance, she thought with a smile.

"Alex," Lord Amberley said to her, taking her empty plate from her hand, "shall we stroll along beside the river with your mother and father? Perhaps we should cross the bridge first. I always prefer the walk at the other side."

She took her father's arm while Lord Amberley offered his to her mother.

"You have a very pleasant seat here, Amberley," Lord Beckworth said as they walked. "It is too bad that there has to be such a lot of wasted land."

"You refer to the valley?" Lord Amberley said.

"And to the land close to the sea," the other replied. "No good for anything but grazing sheep, I gather."

Lord Amberley smiled. "You are quite right," he said. "It is waste land, is it not? It is strange that the idea had not occurred to me until this very moment. And yet the valley and the cliffs are my favorite parts of my land, the parts that make it so very precious to me. Perhaps something is not valueless if it can warm one's heart."

"The hunting is good?" Lord Beckworth asked.

"Forbidden, I am afraid," Lord Amberley said, "though I do allow fishing. I have the notion, considered somewhat amusing by many who know me, if not downright lunatic, that wild animals have as much right to life as we do. Your next question is quite likely to be: do I eat meat? The answer is yes, unfortunately. I do not quite have the courage of my convictions, you see. If I lived quite alone, and prepared all my own food, perhaps I would abstain. But I always think how very inconvenient it would be to all concerned if I became so eccentric."

"Live without meat?" Lady Beckworth said. "It would not be possible, my lord, would it? You would not long survive, especially during the cold of the winter. It seems a strange notion to me."

"And quite unnecessary," Lord Beckworth said. "You have only to read your Bible, Amberley, to know that animals were created for man's food. It would be rebellion against God to refuse to accept his gift."

Lord Amberley smiled. "You are quite possibly right," he said, "though opinion on the matter does depend on which version of the Creation one reads."

"Hm," Lord Beckworth said. "I came down, Amberley, to settle the matter of your wedding. The end of summer, I thought, would be the perfect time. The end of August, perhaps, or the beginning of September. In St. George's. A large enough number will be in town or will return to town for the event if we send out the invitations without further delay."

Alexandra held her breath.

"Alex and I have not discussed the matter," Lord Amberley said. "We had certainly not thought of such an early wedding."

"The best possible thing," Lord Beckworth said. "Why wait?"

"Ours was a precipitate betrothal," Lord Amberley said. "We did not know each other at all, and have had only a few brief weeks to become acquainted. I do not wish to rush Alex into marriage."

"Alexandra will do as she is told," her father said. "This is entirely between you and me, Amberley. I should not have raised the matter until we were alone together, perhaps. But both Lady Beckworth and Alexandra need to know what we plan."

They had all stopped walking. Alexandra watched her betrothed with raised chin and compressed lips. He smiled at her.

"I would say rather that it is a matter between Alex and me," he said with quiet courtesy. "We will discuss the matter and let you know our decision while you are still here. I can understand your wish to know what our plans are. But I believe I can say with some certainty that we will not be marrying quite as soon as you suggest. And probably not in London."

"Not in London?" Lord Beckworth said, his brows drawing together. "You are to marry in the country, as if you are hiding your shame? Under the circumstances, Amberley, it is quite imperative that your wedding be a very public occasion."

"When I marry," Lord Amberley said, his voice no louder or less courteous than it had been at the start, "I will be marrying Alex, my lord, pledging myself to her for the rest of my life. Frankly, it will not concern me at that moment what the rest of the world thinks, or where the rest of the world is. Provided Alex is there, and the people we love most, I shall be entirely happy."

Papa was breathing rather heavily, Alexandra saw. Mama was looking frightened. Alexandra raised her chin another inch. And then the tension was broken by the sound of Uncle William's voice calling from across the river.

"No point in going any farther," he called to Lord Beckworth. "There are only more trees and more water up there." He laughed. "And the water is all coming this way."

"We have been showing Mr. Purnell one of the best fishing spots," Anna called gaily. She was clinging to his arm, looking very pleased with herself.

James Purnell looked assessingly at the group across the river and met his sister's eyes. They exchanged that smile of theirs that would have been almost undetectable to anyone else.

"I am quite fatigued," Lady Beckworth said petulantly as the other group continued on their way back to the house. "We must have walked for almost half a mile already."

Lord Beckworth took her arm.

"Alex," Lord Amberley said, "would you care to stroll a little farther before we turn back?"

She was aware of the look of surprise both her father and her mother gave her. She caught herself just in time before making the automatic reply.

"Yes, thank you," she said, and took his arm.

21

"YOU ARE UPSET," LORD AMBERLEY SAID, TOUCHing Alexandra's fingers lightly with his own. They had been walking in silence for a couple of minutes.

"Yes," she said.

"Because your father talked of our wedding?" he said. "He cannot force you into marrying me at the end of the summer, Alex, or at any other time. I will not allow it."

"I know," she said.

He looked down at her again after another minute of silence. Her expression had not relaxed at all or her chin dropped.

"What is it?" he said. "You had better tell me. I know you well enough to know when something is on your mind, but not well enough to read that mind."

"You will not allow it," she said, her voice tight with fury. "How grateful I must be."

"So," he said, "it is me you are angry with, not your father. You are angry because I spoke up to protect your interest. I cannot win at this game, can I, Alex?"

"How humiliating it is," she said, "to have two men arguing over me as if I were inanimate. Of course I am far less than inanimate. I am a woman, and as such cannot have a mind or a voice of my own. How very fortunate I am to have a champion."

He felt angry. He had never allowed himself to feel anger with her before. He had been too constantly aware of his obligation toward her, of his need to protect her, to make her happy if possible. But now he felt angry.

"And apparently no ears either," he said. Her head jerked around and she looked at him in surprise. His voice really had sounded far more irritated than he had intended. "Did you not listen to what was said, Alex?"

"Oh, yes," she said. "Very well. The question was, I believe, where and when we are to be wed. You were pleading my need to have longer in which to become acquainted with you. I do not want longer, my lord. I have had quite long enough, thank you. You are just my father in different clothing."

"Enough!" he said, his anger thoroughly aroused. "Your trouble, Alex, is that you have grown sorry for yourself in the past few weeks. Every man is your enemy. Someone who tries to give you orders is your enemy. Someone who tries to include you in decisions to be made about your own future is your enemy. What do you want? I give up."

"Someone who tries to include me in decisions!" she said. "Do you not see? I am included only because you choose to include me. What freedom does that give me? I am beholden to you for every favor. You should not be in a position to give me that choice. I should have the choice by right of my humanity."

"Nonsense!" he said. "You want the moon and the stars. You want what is beyond my power to give you, Alex. We live in a certain social system. And in that system, unfortunately for you, males are dominant. That is fact, my dear.

Neither of us is going to change that fact merely because we might wish to. If we wish to fight it, we can do so only within our individual lives. I feel no guilt for what I have said or done this afternoon. I was trying to protect your interests."

"Yes," she said bitterly. "Protect!"

"If you do not like it," he said, "you will have your chance next week to go and seek your fortune and your freedom as a governess or whatever else you choose. You may not like what you find, Alex. I think you are appallingly naive about the world in which we live. But at least you will have freely chosen your destiny."

"Yes," she said, "I will. And I will not come complaining to you if I do not like it. You may depend upon that."

"Frankly, Alex," he said, "once you are away from here, I will not spare a thought to caring how you like your life. I can scarce wait for the moment. Do you think my life has been pleasant for the past few weeks?"

He was appalled by his own words after they were spoken. They had been spoken in anger, an emotion that he rarely allowed in himself. They were vicious words that had been chosen to hurt. They had been chosen out of his own frustration and pain. They were unforgivable.

He looked down at her bent head. He could not see her face beneath the brim of her straw bonnet.

"Alex," he said softly, "I did not mean a word I said then. I was behaving like a petulant schoolboy, wanting to hurt you. Please forgive me if you can."

She looked up. Her dark eyes were suspiciously bright. They were also hostile. "No," she said, "don't ask forgiveness. You are too well-mannered by half. Your courtesy and your kindness are like a shield. I think I have just seen the real man behind that shield. And I respect you the more.

Why should you not wish to see the back of me? I have brought you nothing but trouble. And it is true that you have done a great deal for me. And I have been thoroughly ungrateful. I understand and appreciate, but I cannot accept what you have done for me and keep on doing. Of course you hate me. It would be strange if you did not."

"I don't hate you, Alex," he said. They had stopped walking. His hand was over hers.

"Well," she said, "once your ball is over, I will be leaving. We will both be glad. You will be able to get your life back to normal."

"Yes," he said.

"And this very naive young lady will find what the wide and wicked world is like," she said.

"Yes."

She smiled at him, a rather bleak effort, it was true. But he could not bring himself to return even as much.

"I wish we had met under different circumstances, Alex," he said. "I would like to have got to know you without all the bitterness you feel."

She shook her head. "There is no use in thinking thus," she said. "Without the scandal, you would have met me—if at all—as the Duchess of Peterleigh. And I think I would rather you did not have that pleasure. I have something to thank your brother for, you see."

"Are you going to marry Dom?" he asked quietly.

Her eyes widened. "Marry Lord Eden?" she said. "Of course not."

"He told me you had not said no," he said. "He had hopes that he would be able to persuade you."

"I was tempted," she said, "before I realized that I do not have to marry anyone. But not now. The answer will be no if he asks me again."

"But why were you tempted?" he asked. "If you felt marriage was necessary at the time, why be tempted when you were already safely betrothed to me?"

She shrugged.

"Do you have an aversion to me?" he asked. "But no, I do not believe it. When I have kissed you, you have responded to me."

She was examining the backs of her hands. "You have caused too much turmoil in my mind," she said. "Lord Eden has not. Lord Eden seems like a younger brother, though he is older than I."

He touched his fingers to her cheek. "I would like to have made love to you, Alex," he said. "I regret that I will never have the chance."

She looked up at him with wide eyes, her cheeks flaming.

He smiled. "You regret it too, do you not?"

She did not reply, though her eyes grew larger, if that were possible.

"Alex," he said with something like a groan, catching her by the shoulders and pulling her against him, "why is it that I could shake you and spurn you, that I cannot wait to see the end of you, and that I want to hold you and fold you into myself and love you and love you?"

She sagged against him and put her arms around his waist. But she said nothing, and she did not lift her head. He wrapped his arms around her and closed his eyes.

"Is there any hope?" he asked. "Is there any chance that you will change your mind and decide to stay with me? Is there any future for us, Alex?"

"No!" She raised her head and looked earnestly into his face. "No, Edmund. I would always be sorry if I stayed, always accuse myself of weakness. I would be restless and miserable, and I would make you miserable, as I have already done. Yes, I want you to make love to me. No! I want to make love to you. I want us to make love. I want you. I cannot deny that, and I would be foolish to try. You have held me, and you know that I have wanted you. But that is not enough. It is not enough to fall into each other's arms and assume that for the next fifty years or so we will live happily ever after. I am not sure I am capable of happiness. That I will have to discover. But I cannot be happy with you, Edmund. And I care for you too much to risk trying, for I would make you miserable. And you do not deserve misery."

He nodded his head and swallowed. "I don't know if you are the most courageous woman I have ever met or the most foolish," he said. "But I see that I have to let you go. There is to be no keeping you. I am sorry, Alex. I am truly sorry."

She raised herself on her toes and set her lips to his. He stood quite still. She removed her arms from around his waist and set her hands on either side of his face, her fingers pushing into his hair. She removed her mouth after a while, but she kept her hands where they were.

"I can tell you," she said. "I am a foolish woman. In years to come I will regret you, Edmund Raine. I know that as surely as I am standing here. I know just as surely that if I don't go, I will lose my self-respect. And I have been without that for so long—all my life, in fact—that I know life is not really worth living without it. I have to put it first. I have to, Edmund."

She kissed him once more and then released him. He let his arms drop to his sides.

"Papa will have a search party out if we are much

longer," she said. "As it is, I am in for a thundering scold. Take me back."

He smiled ruefully at her and gave her his arm.

MOST OF THE ATTENTION of the neighborhood was focused during the following week on the approaching ball. The annual event was always the highlight of the summer. On this occasion there was the added excitement of knowing that there were visitors at Amberley Court, most notably the young earl's new fiancée.

Alexandra had taken well in the neighborhood, far better than she had done in London. Most people admired her dark beauty, which had been largely lost on the *ton,* inundated as it was during the Season with young ladies of far more obvious and adorned prettiness. And her quiet dignity won the approval of those who knew they would look to her as the leading lady of that particular part of the county.

It had been observed that she was willing to be friendly, willing to listen, and willing to participate in any of the activities of village or countryside without in any way pushing herself forward or putting on airs because she was to be the Countess of Amberley. Even the poorer people of the village, most of whom worked for the earl, acknowledged her with a nod and a smile whenever they saw her. Her kindness to Mrs. Peterson and her sons and her appearance at Joel Peterson's funeral had not gone unnoticed.

Alexandra was not idle during the days leading up to the ball. She took tea most days with one of the neighbors, usually calling on them with Lady Amberley and sometimes with her mother and Madeline too. And she found herself having to fight against the warm feeling of belonging that was beginning to steal up on her. Mrs. Carrington, who insisted that she call her Aunt Viola, constantly protected her from Uncle William's teasing; Anna plied her with eager questions about London and the assemblies and balls; the Misses Stanhope displayed all their lacework and embroidery for her inspection; Mrs. Courtney showed her the large vegetable garden that she always planted and tended herself, although she now had a couple of servants who could do the work for her; the rector's wife told her about Lord Amberley's charitable works in the neighborhood, which were supposed to be a closely guarded secret; Lady Lampman showed her the large flower garden at the back of her house, which was the pride and joy of both her and her husband.

It was difficult to face the knowledge that she was an impostor. What would these people think of her when she left? That would not matter, of course. She would not know what they were thinking and saying, and consequently their opinion would not affect her. But what would they think of Lord Amberley? Would they feel sorry for him, or would they blame him?

It would be very unfair if they did the latter. Indeed, they must not blame him. She must be very sure that she was the one who broke the engagement, she decided. It was enough that she knew he was willing to do it, to prove to her that he was willing to allow her to take some of the burden of life upon her own shoulders. But she did not wish to humiliate him publicly. And it would be a dreadful humiliation for him to be known as a gentleman who had ended a formal betrothal.

Her relationship with her father was not as bad as she had expected it to be. It was true that he had taken her to task on a few issues, but he had not tried to dominate her every move. He had not tried to impose any punishments on her.

He did not like the Earl of Amberley. The man was a weakling, in his judgment.

"What in thunder does he mean by saying he has to talk the matter of the wedding over with you, Alexandra?" he asked the day after the garden party. "What does it have to do with you anyway?"

"It is my wedding you were discussing, Papa," she said. "Surely it is only natural that Lord Amberley and I should be the ones to make the decision."

"Nonsense!" he said. "Nothing would ever be decided if women had always to be consulted. You should feel thankful enough that you are to be respectably married, my girl. Let your menfolk take care of the practical matters."

"That is not the way it will be with me, Papa," she dared to say. She looked him carefully in the eye.

"Alexandra!" her mother said in a shocked whisper. "Remember to whom you are speaking."

But Papa did not explode as she had fully expected him to do. He looked at her long and hard, his eyes steely. "Who has been putting such nonsense into your head, Alexandra?" he said. "Amberley? He seems to have some strange notions. And that brother and sister of his seem a ramshackle pair. Well, you will be his problem soon. He will doubtless discover soon enough that you are a stubborn and a headstrong woman despite my training. He will have to learn how to handle you. You had better be careful, miss. Talk to him as you just did to me and he is likely to answer you with a heavy hand."

Alexandra did not reply, and the matter was not alluded to again. Her father's words to her tended to be confined to unimportant grumblings.

"You are foolish to have allowed Amberley to call you by your given name," he said once. "And 'Alex,' too. You should have more pride, girl. Is that the only liberty you have allowed him?"

It was a rhetorical question. He did not wait for an answer.

"The Courtneys are Amberley's tenants?" he said on the day she was to visit Mrs. Courtney with Lady Amberley. "And you are going to take tea with them, Alexandra? That is a foolish precedent to set, my girl, take my word for it. They will be expecting you to socialize with them forever after. It would be quite enough to stop your carriage as you drive past to inquire after their health."

Again he did not wait for an answer. Alexandra went on her way.

James stayed away from his father as much as possible, Alexandra was both relieved and disturbed to find. She so longed for a reconciliation between the two of them. She knew it was very improbable. Papa was not likely to admit that what he had done to James had been wrong, and James was unlikely to forgive him unless Papa did ask his pardon. But she always hoped. As things were, she was thankful that there was no open hostility between her father and her brother.

James spent much of his time alone or with one or more of the other men. He played endless games of billiards with Sir Cedric. If they were in company, he often allowed Anna Carrington to hang on his arm. Indeed, she seemed almost as taken with him as she was with Lord Eden. Surprisingly, James was willing to humor her. He seemed to understand the frustrations of being fifteen, so close to being grown-up and yet still a child.

It did Alexandra's heart good to see him listening

gravely to the girl's prattle, adjusting his stride to her tripping walk, and very often talking to her himself. James so rarely relaxed with anyone but her. But there was hope. She would never lose faith in her belief that there was hope for him.

And so the day of the ball arrived, and suddenly Amberley Court was a hive of industry, the state apartments being cleaned and prepared, masses of flowers being gathered and arranged under the supervision of Lady Amberley, and those guests who were from some distance away and had been invited to stay overnight beginning to arrive.

LORD EDEN STOOD JUST INSIDE the grand ballroom looking around him. The room was decked out this year all in pink and white carnations and roses and masses of ferns and other greenery, and smelled more like a garden than a room. The long mirrored wall doubled in number the flowers and the candle-laden chandeliers. The same mirrors multiplied the number of guests, so that the room looked crowded. As it was, it was surprising that an event in the country could draw so many guests. But the Amberley ball had always been a great attraction.

It had always been Lord Eden's favorite event of the year, even in those years when he had been too young to attend. He and Madeline had usually succeeded in stealing into the unused minstrel gallery to peer down at all the glittering gowns and waistcoats. He supposed now that his parents and, later, Edmund must have known very well that they were there. But it had added to the excitement to feel that what they were doing was strictly forbidden.

On this occasion he was not looking forward to the

evening with quite as much exuberance as usual. He felt rather as if he had the world on his back. He had talked to both his mother and Madeline that morning about his decision to leave in two days' time in order to buy his commission in the army.

Mama had not been bad. She had listened quietly to him, merely drawing herself up to her full height and clasping her hands before her while he talked.

"Yes, Dominic," she had said when he was finished, "I have known for a long time that this day was coming. But I have waited, dear, for you to come to me like this to tell me. Not ask me, but tell me. Now I know that your decision is definite, that you have finally grown up. And I see that I must let you go, though it breaks my heart to do so. You must do what you must, and I must suffer what I must. But I will always be proud of you, my son. And there is nothing you could ever do to forfeit my love for you. Remember that."

"I have tried, Mama," he had said, "to put it from my mind, knowing what you have suffered in the past. I have tried to be contented with my life as it is."

"Ah, no," she had said. "It is not in the nature of young people to be contented, Dominic, or to want what their parents want for them. I have had my chance, and now it is your turn. I married your papa. Your grandfather did not want me to do so. It was a brilliant match for me, of course, but I was only seventeen and he thought I should have a Season in London and meet some other young men before making a decision. But I have never been sorry that I defied him. I had twenty wonderful years with Papa. Twenty dreadfully short years. And I have you, dear, and Edmund, and Madeline. I have been well blessed. I can wish no better for you than that your decision will bring you as much happiness."

He had not seen his mother cry since that dreadful year following his father's death. He had held her that morning until she had herself under control again, and then kissed her and left her. He had not been able to think of anything more to say.

Madeline had been more of a problem. She had thrown every cushion she could lay her hands on at him—he had been thankful that they were not in the library—and refused to accept his decision.

"And what am I supposed to do when you are killed?" she had asked. And then she had added rather illogically, "But you will not care, will you?"

He had been unwise enough to grin and admit that, no, he probably would not care under those particular circumstances. He had been witness to a foot-stamping, screaming tantrum after that. But it had all turned out the same way as with Mama—she had ended up sobbing in his arms.

"I don't want you to go, Dom," she had said between hiccups and sobs. "I forbid you to go. I will never talk to you again if you go."

"I am going, Mad," he had said quietly, kissing the top of her head.

"I don't want you to go," she had wailed, so that he had been reminded of the times when they were children and she had been forbidden to join him on some escapade. "I'll die if you die, Dom."

"No you won't," he had said. "You will live on, Mad, so that you can tell your children and grandchildren about their brave Uncle Dominic."

"Their stupid, foolish, bullheaded, unfeeling Uncle Dominic, you mean," she had said petulantly.

"If you like." He had kissed the top of her head again.

"I hate you," she had said, pulling away from him. "I hate you, Dominic. Get out of here. I never want to see you again."

He had smiled ruefully and left her. And true to her word, she had not spoken to him all day. There had been a deal of sniffing and head-tossing when she was close to him, but not a word or a look. Sometimes it was not easy to be a twin, he thought.

He wished that was the sum of all his woes. If it were only a question of leaving Mama and Madeline, he would consider himself blessed indeed. But there was this stupid mess with Miss Purnell to be cleared up. And it was a mess indeed. He had asked her to marry him more than a week before, and he had had the feeling at the time that she might say yes. She must have expected him to bring the matter up again. He was honor-bound to ask her again, since she had not had a chance to give him an answer at that time.

And yet he had realized in the days since that it was not at all the thing to marry Miss Purnell. He would be hurting Edmund a great deal more if he did that than he had done originally by causing him to feel he must offer for Miss Purnell himself. But he had marched on with his scheme with great crusading zeal and his eyes firmly shut. Madeline had made an apt comparison by likening him to Don Quixote.

But he could not simply drop the matter quietly. He had already spoken to Miss Purnell and to Edmund. And what if she accepted him now after all? He would have to marry her, of course. What a coil! He must find time to talk to her tonight. He dared not postpone it until the next day, or he might lose his courage altogether. And how dreadful it would be to leave Amberley having begun something so important and not completed it.

And Susan! No, he would not think of Susan. He dared not. There were only so many burdens a man could bear without collapsing under the load. He must not think of Susan. He must not dance with her tonight. Or talk to her. Or look at her. She just looked so damned pretty in her pink gown that appeared as if it had been made especially to match the ballroom tonight. Pink should look dreadful with auburn hair. Well, on her it didn't. She looked deuced pretty.

The orchestra Edmund had hired at great expense were tuning up their instruments. Edmund was preparing to lead Miss Purnell into the opening set. Lord Eden looked about him for the eldest Miss Moffat, whom he had engaged for the first dance. He smiled as he caught her eye across the room. She was looking remarkably pretty too, and blushing most becomingly. He was going to concentrate on her prettiness for the next half-hour.

Susan was going to dance with Lieutenant Jennings, he could see.

LORD AMBERLEY LED ALEXANDRA onto the floor to begin the opening set. It should be a wonderfully happy occasion, he thought, gazing down at her. She looked breathtakingly beautiful, dressed as she was in a gown of pale lemon silk with a netted overdress. Nanny Rey must have had a battle royal with her over her hair, he guessed. She wore it in a topknot, with curls trailing along her neck and over her ears and temples.

Had she been this lovely in London? he wondered. Was it just that he saw her differently now, knowing something of the stubborn, courageous, independent, adorable, and thoroughly muddle-headed character behind the well-disciplined exterior? Was it that now he could see the beauty that had been there all the time? Or had she blossomed within the course of a few weeks? Had she really been the almost lifeless shell of a woman she had appeared when he first met her and was not a woman in full and beautiful bloom?

"You look very lovely, Alex," he said, holding one of her hands and waiting for the music to start.

"Thank you," she said. And then an almost impish look, which he knew he had never seen in London, flashed into her eyes. "And you look very handsome, Edmund."

He grinned. And the music began.

And so he began to enjoy his final evening as her betrothed. Tomorrow he must shock both their families and all their acquaintances and many with whom they were not even acquainted by announcing that he no longer had any intention of marrying her. Wherever would he find another Alexandra Purnell? It was perhaps as well that he had no intention of ever trying, or of finding any other woman, for that matter. He doubted anyway that any lady would be eager to accept his marriage proposal after tomorrow, for all his wealth and position. He was certainly about to forfeit his name of gentleman in perhaps the worst possible manner.

22

ALEXANDRA WAS GOING TO ENJOY THE BALL. She had decided that before it even started, and had even sat unprotesting while Nanny Rey dressed her hair in a style far more frivolous than any she had ever worn. She had chosen her dress with care for its lightness and daring lines. She had not worn it before. She might never again have the chance to attend such an event or to enjoy herself so much. She was going to make the most of her opportunity. There would be time enough tomorrow for the heartache and the regrets.

She was glad to see that Lord Amberley was in a mood to match her own. He was not looking unduly solemn or tragic or angry. He was smiling for his guests and smiling for her. And she was glad she was seeing his house at its very best. The state dining room had looked splendid indeed set for thirty guests, and the ballroom looked more breathtaking than any she had ever seen. She was glad it was all his. He would never be careless of such a possession.

"That should warm everyone up," he said to her with a smile as the vigorous country dance that opened the ball came to an end. "And here comes Dominic to claim your hand for the quadrille. I will wager you will not have a chance to sit down this evening, Alex."

She smiled at Lord Eden. How dear he too had become to her in the past couple of weeks. So handsome and boyishly charming, so very popular with the young girls of all classes. Susan Courtney sighed after him, and his cousin Anna and countless of the village maidens. She was going to miss him.

"Miss Purnell," he said, "you look quite dazzling. Edmund, Miss Moffat declares that she has no wish to go to St. James's or Almack's or any other fashionable assembly room. She declares that nothing could surpass this very ballroom."

Lord Amberley grinned. "I am surprised she even noticed her surroundings, Dom," he said. "She seemed to have eyes for no one but her partner."

Lord Eden flushed unexpectedly and reached for Alexandra's hand. "Shall we take our places, Miss Purnell?" he asked. "The members of the orchestra are very eager. They are almost ready to start again already."

She put her hand in his as Lord Amberley went off in search of his next partner.

"I must talk to you," Lord Eden said, looking at her with a mixture of eagerness and agitation. "I should have done so sooner and not left it for an occasion like this. May I talk to you later, Miss Purnell, or will you come walking with me now?"

"Perhaps we should talk now," she said, looking rather regretfully at the dancers taking their places around them.

He led her out through the French doors, which stretched the length of the ballroom opposite the mirrored wall. All had been left open against the warmth of the night. The terrace outside was almost deserted. It was too early for there to be many strollers seeking escape from the heat of the ballroom.

"I have procrastinated, ma'am," Lord Eden said, his voice now decidedly agitated. "I should have spoken with you privately days ago."

"Perhaps," she said calmly. "The last time we spoke, you asked me to marry you. I did not have a chance to give you my answer. We were interrupted by Anna. The answer was and is no, my lord, though I thank you most sincerely for your offer. You have a kind and generous heart."

He was silent for a while as they strolled and the music of the quadrille flowed round them. "I left it too late," he said. "I should have pressed my claim with more ardor while we were still in London. I have seen that since we have been here. I have seen that it is now impossible to change the situation without another huge scandal. Is that what has prompted your answer, Miss Purnell?"

"I have been touched by your loyalty to your brother and your concern for me," she said. "But I do not believe I would have accepted your offer, my lord, even if there had been no chance of further scandal."

"But in London," he said, "if I had known sooner what happened at Lady Sharp's and if I had returned to Curzon Street before Edmund, you would have accepted me, Miss Purnell? I cannot forgive myself for having been so tardy."

"No," she said, touching his hand lightly with hers for a moment. "Not even then. For you would have come and asked, you see, and my answer would have been the same as it was the first time."

"But is not that what Edmund did?" he asked.

"Not exactly," she said with a little smile. "By the time

your brother came to ask me for the second time, I really had little choice but to accept."

"We have made a mess of your life, Edmund and I between us, have we not?" he said, looking down at her with a frown.

"Not really," she said. "Had I not been mistaken for Madeline at the Easton ball, I would now be contemplating a betrothal to and matrimony with the Duke of Peterleigh. I think I have had a fortunate escape."

"I have to agree with you there," he said, looking somewhat cheered. "I would not like to think of you as that man's property, Miss Purnell. You have far too much character for that kind of life."

"Thank you," she said.

"And can you be happy with Edmund?" he asked somewhat wistfully. "You could not ask for a better man, you know. I do not know a better. I have always admired my brother's steadiness of character and his invariable kindness. He will certainly take care of you."

"Yes," Alexandra said, "he is good at taking care of people and shouldering their burdens."

"Isn't he, though?" Lord Eden said eagerly. "I am glad you have noticed that, Miss Purnell. I have always thought that perhaps one day someone would do the same for Edmund. Look after him, I mean, and help him with the problems of life. It is absurd to think of Edmund needing help, is it not? But sometimes I think perhaps he is more vulnerable than the rest of us put together. We have always come running to him. It is second nature to him now to rush in to help without a care for himself. And he has been doing it for ten years, Miss Purnell. He was only nineteen when Papa died. That seems very young to me now."

"Yes," Alexandra said, "it is."

"That is what I wanted to do for him now," he continued. "Relieve him of a burden, that is. I thought that if I could marry you..." He stopped both talking and walking. His eyes were closed in a grimace when Alexandra looked up at him. "Oh, ma'am, I am so sorry. I did not mean..."

She laughed. "I know what you meant," she said. "I know exactly what you meant, my lord. I am not offended."

"You are generous," he said. His face brightened suddenly, and it was the usual boyish, eager Lord Eden who looked down at her. "But I have just had a thought. Perhaps I have done that for him after all. Perhaps I have been responsible for giving him you. If you feel as I do, Miss Purnell, if you want to make Edmund's life less lonely, less burdensome, then you will be the best thing that has happened to him in ten years. And I will be responsible."

"Yes." Alexandra smiled up into his eager face. She felt as if she had a lump in her throat. She wanted to turn and run out into the darkness. "Yes, so you would."

"Do you care for Edmund?" he asked. "I have watched the two of you together, and sometimes I feel that you do care, both of you. But perhaps I am only seeing what I want to see. Do you care for him?"

"Yes," she said. "I care for him." She turned her face from him. "Very much," she added almost on a whisper.

He took her by the upper arms and squeezed them. "I am so glad," he said. "I am so happy, Miss Purnell. Did you know that I am leaving the day after tomorrow?"

"No," she said. "The army?"

He nodded, his face alight with eagerness. "I hope it will mean Spain," he said. "I hope I will be sent there as soon as possible. I want my chance for a jab at old Boney. I can scarcely wait."

"How does your family feel?" she asked.

He sobered slightly. "Edmund has been wonderful," he said. "He has urged me to do what I want to do. There have been tears from the women, of course, though Mama is just as insistent as Edmund that I must do with my life what I feel I must do. Madeline had the hysterics this morning when I told her, and has not talked to me since."

"Poor Madeline," she said. "She loves you very dearly, you know."

"I know," he said. "I have imagined how I would feel if I had to stand by and see her go voluntarily into great danger. I think I might have hysterics too."

"She will come to understand," she said. "She will do as you have done, you see. She will put herself in your place and know how important this is to you."

"Miss Purnell..." He looked earnestly down at her. "I must ask a favor of you. If anything happens to me, if I should be killed, will you look after Mad for me? It is a huge favor to ask, is it not, and I have thought of it now only on the spur of the moment. But you see, Mama and Edmund will have their own grief to contend with. But Madeline's will be different and many times worse. We are twins. Will you help her?"

Alexandra felt as if she were trapped at the bottom of a deep well. She was about to suffocate or drown. She smiled. "Madeline is a strong person," she said. "If such a thing were to happen, no one could help her, you know. Not your mother, not Edmund, and not I. But she would survive. You know that too. But why the talk of death? It is far more likely that you will come home the conquering hero."

He smiled. "I really do not feel the need for either death or heroism," he said. "Just to be able to be part of the army and part of the excitement and dirt and danger and exhaustion of a campaign. That is all I want, Miss Purnell: the chance to do my part. But the music is coming to an end. I must return you inside. I am glad we have had this talk."

She laughed. "And so you should be," she said. "You have been released from one problem anyway, sir."

He smiled ruefully. "You would not have been a problem, Miss Purnell," he said. "I would have been proud to fight for you."

MADELINE HAD BEEN SO furiously gay all evening that by midnight she was exhausted. She had laughed and chattered and flirted until she was convinced that the whole county must believe that Lady Madeline Raine was as empty-headed a young female as society could offer. She had refused a request to go outside walking with Captain Forbes, sensing that a proposal of marriage was imminent and terrified that in her present mood she might accept it. And her smile had not faltered since she had left her room before dinner.

She would not have believed how much effort and ingenuity it took to avoid two men. To avoid meeting their eyes, to avoid being close enough to them to hear what they were saying or to risk having to say something to them.

She would kill Dominic. She would save the French the trouble of blowing him off the face of the earth. She would do it for them. Why did he always have to be bursting with that crusading zeal? Why did he have to be a knight in shining armor? Why did he occasionally have to be Don Quixote? She did not want a brave, adventurous, chivalrous brother. She wouldn't care if he were the biggest coward in the kingdom, provided that she could know that he was safe. She just wanted Dominic.

And now he was going to go away and get himself killed.

And he did not care at all how she felt or what she would suffer. But she would not give him the satisfaction of pleading with him anymore, she had decided. She was not even going to speak to him again before he left.

Before he left! Panic grabbed at her when she remembered that he was going to go away in two days' time. She might never see him again. She would spend the following months and perhaps even years constantly waiting for news, constantly dreading that letter that would bring bad news. How did the army let one know of the death of a loved one in battle? She did not want to know. She shook her head and smiled more dazzlingly than she had intended at Howard Courtney.

She turned away and slipped out through the French doors. She had one dance free. The rector had engaged to dance with her, but he had been called away suddenly to a sick parishioner. It was no one belonging to the Amberley estate, she had been thankful to hear, or doubtless Edmund would have felt it imperative to go too. No one had yet noticed that she did not have a partner for the set then beginning. It was a delightful feeling to know that she had half an hour during which to be alone, during which to let her face relax and her pretense of enjoyment slip.

She would not wander on the terrace. Someone would notice her there. She slipped around to the front of the house and past the rose arbor. She would walk in the formal gardens for a while, where it was cool and quiet. No one else had wandered quite so far from the ballroom.

It was dreary not to be enjoying oneself at a ball, especially the Amberley ball. She could not remember such a thing happening before. But try as she would, she could not feel the gaiety she was acting. And she could not fall in love with Captain Forbes or any other of the young men who could have been hers at the lift of an eyebrow. How dull it was not to be in love, not to be involved in the intrigue of planning just how much she could allow herself to flirt and just when she must draw back and be the demure lady again.

She unconsciously followed the same path she had taken with James Purnell that first evening. How long ago that seemed! How she had changed since then. Then she had merely disliked him. She had not hated him. Or loved him. She trailed her hand in the basin of the fountain where he had done the same thing that evening. And she walked around the fountain. Just there he had stood when he had talked about his concern for Alexandra. Just there.

She must have looked at him for several seconds before she saw him. He was in the shadows, leaning back against the marble basin, his arms folded across his chest. It was only when he moved slightly that she realized that he was standing there.

"Oh," she said foolishly, "what are you doing out here?"

"Probably the same as you," he said. "Escaping. Although it looked to me as if you were having too merry a time to need escape. Did one of your partners abandon you?"

"The rector," she said. "He was called away."

"Poor Lady Madeline," he said. "A wallflower at her brother's own ball."

"Don't," she said.

He did not speak or move for a long time. She could not see his face to know what his expression was. It did not occur to her to turn and walk or run away.

"I could dance with you here if you wish," he said. "The music carries this far."

She shook her head.

They stood thus for a while longer until he finally uncrossed his ankles, pushed himself away from the basin, and came to stand in front of her. He slipped his right hand around her waist and extended his other hand for hers.

It was a waltz tune, faint in the distance, but quite loud enough to dance by. Madeline placed one hand on his shoulder and the other in his. She closed her eyes as they began to dance.

She would not have expected him to be a good dancer. The only time she had danced with him, at the Courtneys', she had not noticed. But here, where there were just the two of them and the darkness, she knew that he moved with the music, that he felt it with his body and could take her with him into its rhythm.

She did not know when her body first touched his or when both his arms moved around her waist and both of hers around his neck. She did not know when his cheek came to rest against the top of her head. They continued to move to the music and finally to sway to it. By that time she was in a world beyond reality.

When the music stopped, she lifted her face for his kiss. Not with the coyness and excited anticipation with which she had offered as much to other men. Not with fear of the man who had hurt and insulted her a week before. But without thought or clear intention. She offered herself to her lover.

She would not have known with her conscious mind that this was James Purnell, this man whose lips took hers with gentle tenderness. But with every other part of her being she knew her lover as she had always known he would be. She abandoned herself to him. She was his, and no other man would ever matter to her. *Could* ever matter to her.

He tasted her lips lightly, caressingly, opening his mouth

over hers, probing between her lips with his tongue, stroking the soft flesh behind with its tip. When she moaned, he removed his arms from her waist and took her head in his hands. He caressed her cheeks and her temples with gentle thumbs, his mouth moving over her face and back to hers, over her chin and along her throat.

His hands followed the line of her neck and her shoulders, touching her lightly, worshiping her flesh. And she gave herself to him, arching the lower half of her body against him, hunching her shoulders when he pulled her gown over her arms so that it would slip down more easily, moaning again when he took her breasts in his hands and sought out the nipples with his thumbs. She gasped and threw back her head when his mouth trailed kisses down her throat and took the place of his hands at her breasts. His hands moved lower, pushing downward on her hips, moving behind them to draw her closer.

"Madeline." His mouth was at her ear, over hers again. His hands were straining her to him. "Madeline."

She was aroused and languorous all at the same time. She did not know where they would make their bed. But it did not matter. She was his. She would let him decide. She would go where he wished to go, lie where he chose to lay her.

"My love," she said in wonder against his mouth, her hands twining themselves in his long dark hair. "Oh, James. My love."

When he held her head against his shoulder, she closed her eyes and abandoned herself to what he would do. She breathed in the smell of him, gloried in the roughness of his waistcoat against her naked breasts, felt her body humming with awareness and soon-to-be-satisfied desire.

But he held her quite still. She could both hear and feel

his heart thumping beneath her cheek. But she was aware with an extra sense that he was imposing control over himself. He was not going to take her. He was not going to dishonor her. She relaxed against him and closed her eyes. Perhaps she felt relief as well as regret, she thought. But whatever she felt, she knew that she was utterly, utterly happy.

She helped him when she felt his hands pulling at her dress. She covered herself before moving back a step and looking up at him. But she could not see his face. He was standing with his back to the fountain again.

"Go back to the ballroom, Madeline," he said, "while you are still reasonably safe."

She shook her head. "I am safe," she said. "I am where I want to be. And none of that was against my will."

"Then it should have been," he said. "I have warned you before to stay away from me for your own good."

She felt bewildered. His voice was flat, not the lover's voice that had spoken her name a mere few minutes before.

"I love you," she said.

He laughed low and harshly. "Love!" he said. "It is so easy to love, to make vows to last beyond the grave. So easy to forget again before the echo of the words has died away. I loved once and was destroyed by it. Never again!"

She swallowed painfully. "But you love me," she said. "I felt it. I did not imagine it."

"You confuse love and lust," he said. "For a few minutes I forgot that you are a little butterfly. I wanted you. Do you understand me? I wanted to mount your body and take my pleasure from you. There would have been nothing more. Nothing after. No love. Only satisfied lust."

"No." She shook her head. "Why do you hate yourself so much? Why will you not allow yourself to be touched? No, don't laugh. Don't say what I know you are about to say. I have touched you with my hands and my body. But I have never touched you. You have made yourself untouchable, James Purnell. But I have glimpsed you, for all that. I do not believe that you felt only lust a few minutes ago. I do not believe it."

"You are a dreamer," he said, "a romantic. You think it shameful that you have been panting to lie beneath me. You must dignify the bodily craving with the name of love."

"I love you," she said.

"Go away from me," he said. "Go away now."

Madeline looked at the still, dark figure in the shadows. Again, he might not have been there. There were miles and oceans between them. She turned and hurried away.

Purnell, his arms crossed over his chest, listened to her go, her slippers crunching lightly over the gravel walk. He let his head drop forward and closed his eyes.

LADY BECKWORTH CONGRATULATED LORD Amberley on the success of the ball. They were sitting with Lord Beckworth and Alexandra, Lady Amberley and Sir Cedric Harvey in the supper room after everyone else had returned to the ballroom.

"This ball always has been a gala occasion," Lady Amberley said. "And we have usually been fortunate with the weather, have we not, Edmund? It is such a disappointment when it is wet or cold and we have to keep the doors closed."

"We always welcome the excuse to open the state apartments to more than just visitors passing through," Lord Amberley said. "Such rooms were meant to be lived in, I think. They are not just museum pieces."

"This year I am hoping that the rooms will be used on more than this one occasion," Lady Amberley said, beaming at Alexandra.

Lord Beckworth did not miss her meaning. "And what have you decided, Amberley?" he said. "Is it to be St. George's in the early autumn? The invitations should go out soon."

"Oh," Lady Amberley said, looking at her son in surprise, "is the wedding to be in London? How foolish of me to have assumed that it would be here."

Lord Amberley looked at Alexandra and half-smiled. "Not St. George's, sir," he said. "Perhaps we can all gather again tomorrow and discuss the matter further. At present I am hosting a ball."

"There is not going to be a wedding," Alexandra said quietly. Lord Amberley reached for her hand, but she clasped both of hers very firmly in her lap. She raised her chin.

"What did you say, Alexandra?" Lord Beckworth's eyebrows had drawn together.

"There is not going to be a wedding," she said again more distinctly. "I have decided not to marry Lord Amberley."

"What in thunder are you talking about?" Lord Beckworth was on his feet. "Amberley, if you will excuse us, Alexandra and I will retire to her room for a while. The girl has clearly taken leave of her senses."

"No," Lord Amberley said. "What she says is quite true. And the decision has been mutually made. I have decided not to marry Alex either. It is an amicable agreement, you see."

"Edmund, my dear!" Lady Amberley too was on her feet. "Alexandra? What is this? You cannot be serious."

"But we are, Mama," Lord Amberley said. "We have

decided, I am afraid, that we would not suit and that we will each be far happier without the other."

"Alexandra!" Lady Amberley turned a face full of concern to her. "But I have grown to love you, my dear. I think of you already as my daughter. I am so very sorry."

"You cannot do this, Amberley," Lord Beckworth was saying. "Your word was given. This is insufferable."

"I am afraid it has been done," Lord Amberley said quietly. "The betrothal has been ended, sir."

"Alexandra," her mother said, "how could you do this to your papa, you ungrateful girl?"

Sir Cedric coughed. "Might I suggest that we follow Amberley's advice and gather downstairs tomorrow to discuss the matter?" he said. "My presence excepted, of course. This hardly seems the time or the place."

"You are quite right," Lord Amberley said, getting to his feet. "The music is beginning already, I hear. Alex, this is my dance, I believe?"

It seemed absurd, totally unreal, he thought a few minutes later, to be dancing with his betrothed—no, with his former betrothed—just a short while after such a scene, waltzing with her, smiling at his neighbors, smiling at her.

"I thought I was to be the one to break the engagement," he said.

"I changed my mind," she said. "There was no need for you to take any of the blame at all, you know."

"Your father would have eaten you for dessert if I had not," he said.

"That would have been my problem," she said.

"Ah, yes." He twirled her around one corner of the room. "I must never try to lighten your burdens, must I? Well, Alex, you are free now. No longer my responsibility. But I fear you are in for a thundering time of it. And don't tell me. I know. That is your problem, not mine."

He watched her as they danced—his beautiful dark-haired, dark-eyed Alex. No, not his any longer. But very beautiful and very desirable. He dared not let his thoughts slip past the moment, ahead into the next day and the next. And the next. It was hard to believe, looking at her now, so familiar, so beloved, that just a few weeks before he had not even known her.

He tried to remember her as she had looked to him that first time—disheveled, frightened, proud, defiant, voluptuously beautiful. Yes, it was clear to see now that she had been all of those things. And he remembered her as she had appeared on the second occasion, when he had made her his first offer. Or tried to remember. At the time he had thought her unlovely, unapproachable, cold.

Unlovely? He looked down at her shining dark hair and the teasing curls at her neck, at the dark lashes fanning her cheeks, the heightened color in those cheeks. He looked down at the creamy smooth skin of her shoulders and at the generous swelling of her breasts beneath the delicate fabric of her gown. Alex unlovely? She must be the most beautiful woman he had ever known.

And cold? He thought of her fierce independence and of the passion she had shown in his arms on more than one occasion. He thought of the music he had heard her create. Alex was probably capable of more feeling and more passion than even he could imagine.

She looked up at him. "What are you going to do?" she asked. "You will marry? You will have children?"

"I have been looking around the room wondering to whom I could pay my addresses before the end of the ball," he said.

"Oh!" she said, her eyes startled. "Oh, pray be serious."

He smiled. "No," he said. "I shall not marry, Alex. I don't think I could do so after knowing you."

She stared at him for several moments, her dark eyes wide and unfathomable. Then she looked sharply away.

"Excuse me," she said as soon as the music came to an end. "I must leave for a while."

He released his hold on her hand and watched her go, his smile firmly in place.

23

LORD EDEN WAS STANDING WITH HIS BACK TO one of the French windows, enjoying the coolness of the night air on his back and wondering if he should ask his Aunt Viola to dance the set that was forming or if that evening breeze was going to prove too tempting. He wished there were someone he could wander outside with, but he had to remember that this was Amberley and not London. It was not so easy here to indulge in a casual flirtation. Besides, he was not in the mood.

Suddenly a little pink whirlwind that was looking back over its shoulder collided with his chest and stepped with a light slippered foot on his toe.

"Oh!" Susan looked up at him, all blushes and confusion. "Oh, my lord, I do beg your pardon. I was not looking where I was going. I was going to slip outside for some fresh air."

"What?" he said, catching her by the arms to steady her. "Alone, Susan? You are not dancing?"

"I had promised to humor Colin and dance with him," she said. "But I told him I must go outside. It is so hot." Large hazel eyes gazed up into his.

Lord Eden felt every resolution slip from him. He could not let her go outside alone. True, this was the country and not town, but even so he had had painful proof within the past few weeks of what might happen to a young lady wandering alone outside a ballroom. Besides, she looked so deuced pretty.

"By strange coincidence I am partnerless for this set too," he said. "Perhaps you will save me from being a wallflower, Susan, and walk with me?"

"Oh." She giggled. "You a wallflower, my lord? How funny you are."

He was relieved to find that they were not the only couple on the terrace. Even so, their footsteps somehow took them to the far end of it, where the lights from the chandeliers did not reach. There they stopped and gazed out into the darkness.

"I think I have offended you," she said so quietly that he had to bend his head down to hear her.

"Offended me? You, Susan? Impossible," he said.

"You have not danced with me," she said. "I know I should not expect it because I am a mere nobody and you are Lord Eden. But I did think perhaps you would ask for one set."

He was quiet for a while. "It is not that I did not want to, Susan," he said. "Believe me, my dear, I have scarcely been aware of anyone all evening except you. I dared not dance with you or come near you, that is all."

"I have done something to offend you, then," she said, gazing up at him with troubled eyes.

"No." He smiled at her and resisted the urge to cup her face in his hands. "You have offended me only by being so very pretty and so very sweet, Susan. But I respect you too deeply, I love you too dearly to try to take advantage of you.

And I cannot offer you more than flirtation. Not now, anyway. Perhaps never."

Even in the half-light he could see her eyes brighten with tears. "I have never expected anything from you," she said. "I know I am unworthy."

"Susan!" he said. "Oh, don't say that. You are so very dear to me. I must take you back inside. I cannot trust myself to be with you any longer."

"I love you," she said, clasping her hands to her bosom. "Is that so very wrong? I would not demand anything. Only the chance to love you. Oh . . . No, I must not say more."

"I cannot offer you the life I would wish to offer you," he said. "Not at present anyway. It would be cruel to draw you into the life I am about to lead, Susan. I must not, dear. Come back with me now to the ballroom, or I will lose my resolution and hate myself for the rest of my life."

She put her hands to her mouth and looked at him with large tear-filled eyes.

Lord Eden raked one hand through his hair, leaving it looking considerably disheveled. "I am a monster," he said. "A monster. I have never wanted to make you cry, Susan. You were not made for tears. I cannot marry you, dear, and I will not offer you anything less."

One tear spilled over and trickled down her cheek. Suddenly Susan brushed past him and hurried in the direction of the ballroom.

Lord Eden did not turn to watch her go. He stood with teeth and fists clenched and eyes gazing fixedly up at the dark sky. Temptation had almost got the better of him. If she had stayed one second longer, he would have had her in his arms and then there would have been no letting her go until he had begged her to marry him.

The thought had been the first to leap to his mind when

Miss Purnell had refused him earlier. He was free, he had thought, free to marry Susan. But of course he was no more free than he had been before. He could never ask Susan to be an officer's wife, not during a time of war, anyway. She was so sweet and timid and fragile. It would be cruel to ask her to face the life of constant anxiety that must be the lot of every soldier's wife. And it would be self-indulgent in the extreme to ask her to wait for him, to wait until the war was over. It would be no less cruel to ask her to wait on the chance that he would still be alive and whole at the end of it all.

No, he had decided, he must leave her free to marry a man who could look after her and offer her the security she deserved. And she would have many an offer. Susan was not highly born, but she had the manners of a lady and the looks and character of an angel.

But the pain was somewhat hard to bear at the moment. He had found himself a few minutes before making the painful choice between Susan and the army. And he had chosen the army. He must live now by that decision. He must live with his misery and hope that the new life he faced would soon drown out all else but the adventure and excitement of military action.

If only he could have saved Susan from misery! If only he could convince himself that he had done nothing to encourage her. But he had flirted with her from the start and unconsciously done what he had always determined never to do. He had raised hopes where he could not fulfill them.

Lord Eden rested his arms on the stone balustrade that bordered the terrace and stared out into the night.

• • •

ALEXANDRA HAD BEEN IN the chapel for half an hour. She had taken a single candle with her and set it on the altar. And she had knelt at the back, looking up to the darkened windows, beyond which were the hills, as she had seen on two previous visits.

A God of love, he had said. Not a God of vengeance and restrictive commands, but a God of love. It had sounded wonderful. After a life in which she had been taught that she had to live up to the high expectations of a vengeful God, it had been a sweet, seductive idea that perhaps God was simply love.

But love is not a powerful enough force, she had discovered, to be God. Love is not enough. She loved the Earl of Amberley. Yes, she really did. She could not think of one way in which she did not love him. And she had reason to believe that perhaps he returned that love. And yet they had just publicly ended their betrothal. Tomorrow or the day after at the latest, she would be going away from him and would probably never see him again.

Love was not enough. Why not? she wondered. If God was love and God was everything, why was not love enough?

She had discovered that her self-respect was more important to her, her need to assert herself as a person. Lord Amberley was the kindest, most considerate man she could ever hope to find. He would be most women's dream of a husband, someone who would care for a wife and protect her for as long as they both lived.

But she had found his protectiveness suffocating. She would have had no sense of her own worth, of her own personhood, if she had allowed their marriage plans to proceed. She had to assert herself. She had to know that she could, if she must, exist without a man to dictate her every action or protect her from pain.

And so she had been forced to give up the one man who could have filled her life with joy and companionship. She had been forced to give up love in order that she might know herself as a person.

And now that it was done, did she feel more of a person? She had grown up for twenty-one years as the obedient daughter of a man who had given her not one moment of freedom, not one opportunity to think or do for herself. And she had been passed on to a man who would have protected her with his life for the rest of her days. In a strange way, opposites as they seemed to be, Papa and Lord Amberley were two sides of the same coin.

Yes, she felt more of a person now. She was in control of her own life. She was not happier. She was not at all happy, in fact. But then, she had not expected to be. Happiness was not the point at all. The point was that she was now a person as well as a woman. It was not a great victory. She could not now go out to conquer the world. She was, when all was said and done, still a woman living in a man's world. But she did not have to be a puppet, a simple possession.

Yes, she was unhappy. She could be with Edmund now, in the final hours of the ball, enjoying herself, looking at his handsome figure and knowing that he was hers, furthering her acquaintance with his relatives and friends. She could be looking forward to marriage with him, to a lifetime spent at Amberley. She could have been happy. She could have chosen love.

But she had not. And what about Edmund? Could she really accuse him of being similar to Papa in any way at all? When he had finally known what he was doing to her, he had not tried to justify his actions. He had understood and sympathized. He had made it easy for her to be free. He had even been prepared to take upon himself all the blame for the breakup of their engagement. He had not tried to hold her against her will. He had let her go.

Edmund lived by love. What greater sign of his love could he have given than his willingness to set her free? It sounded like a paradox. But Edmund had shown the ultimate unselfishness. He had ignored his own feelings entirely in a concern for her. He had even been willing to face about the worst scandal a gentleman could face. He was doing, in fact, what he had always done, according to his family: he was living for someone else.

He had never lived for himself, if other people were to be believed, and if the evidence of her own experience was typical. Always for others. One almost forgot that he too had needs. That he was a person. He had been left with the responsibility of being head of his family at the age of nineteen, and it seemed that he had taken that responsibility very seriously ever since.

How much freedom had Edmund ever known? In his own way, he had been as bound as she had ever been. Bound by his own concern for others and his desire to make life easier for them. He had added her to his list of responsibilities when his brother had spoiled her life. And he had protected his brother at the same time.

And what had been his reward? What had ever been his reward? Lord Eden was off to the wars to fulfill a life's dream. And she was on her way out of his life in search of a future of her own making. And Lord Amberley was left with his home and his estates and his dependents, his mother, his sister. His loneliness.

He *was* a lonely man. She had not realized it before. So many people depended upon him, and even loved him, that one tended to miss the obvious fact that he was lonely. He had no particularly close friend, no confidant, no lover.

She might have been all three.

And so which of them was in the more enviable situation now? He for whom love was all? Or she for whom self-respect was more important?

Who was the more selfish?

And therefore ultimately the more unhappy?

Alexandra, her elbows on the pew in front of her, her forehead resting on her clasped hands, could not answer her own questions. Or would not. She rose after a while and left the chapel, taking her candle with her. She must go back to the ballroom, she decided. She must see this night, at least, through to the end.

"Alex!" She turned as she passed through the great hall, having deposited her candle on a table. Her brother was hurrying down the stairs, no longer in his ball dress. He was wearing riding clothes.

"James?" she said.

He caught her by the hand and hurried her through the front doors, which stood open, and down the marble steps.

"I have been searching everywhere for you," he said. "I thought I was going to have to leave without speaking to you."

"To leave?" she asked, staring at him blankly. "Where are you going?"

"I am leaving," he said. "I can't stay any longer, Alex. Not even for another night. I have to go. It is not a dark night. I will be able to see where I am going."

"But it is past midnight," she said, "and in the middle of a ball. What has happened, James? Is it Papa? Has he said something?"

He shook his head and grasped both her hands in his. "I

cannot explain," he said. "Don't ask it of me, Alex. I have to go, that is all. I have left a letter for Mama and Papa. But I wanted to see you. You will be all right? You still feel as you have felt for the past week? You do not need me?"

She gazed at him in silence for a moment, biting her lip. "No," she said finally. "I want you to do what you must. But where will you go, James? This is so sudden, though I have known it is coming. I cannot think."

"Out of the country," he said. "I have to get right away. Canada, I think. There is room there, and opportunity. There is work there, and challenge, and it does not matter there who one is or what one possesses. I think Canada."

She clung to his hands and rested her forehead against his chest. "Go, then," she said. "Write to me."

"Yes," he said. "But I will not know where to write, Alex."

She frowned suddenly and looked up at him. "Write here," she said in some agitation. "Write here, James. I will let them know where I am going to be. Lady Amberley, maybe. Or Madeline."

They looked at each other with the desperation of an imminent parting.

"Live again, James," she pleaded. "Give life another chance. I love you."

"Yes," he said, taking her into his arms and hugging her so hard that she could not draw air into her lungs. "Yes. Alex."

And he was gone from her, striding in the direction of the stables without looking back. Alexandra stared wildly after him until he disappeared from sight. Then she hurried up the steps and into the house. She could not wait until he rode into sight again.

• • •

MANY OF THE GUESTS had left or were leaving when Alexandra returned to the ballroom. Lord Amberley stood just inside the doorway with Lord Eden, Madeline, and his mother, saying good night to an almost continuous stream of neighbors. She had no choice but to join them.

"A terrible ball, Edmund," his Uncle William was saying. "Terrible. Next year you will have to hire an orchestra that plays at half the speed. This one is like to kill us all from heart failure after torturing us with blisters. Terrible ball." He chuckled.

"Oh, William!" his wife said. "You know you have been saying all evening what a splendid time you have been having. Take no notice of him, Edmund. He is just a tease. Miss Purnell will be taking you seriously, William. She does not know you yet."

Lord Amberley smiled. "I did not notice you suffering, Uncle William," he said. "Every time I have spotted you this evening, you have been dancing."

"Merely practicing," his uncle said cheerfully. "Next year we will have to bring Anna. She almost drowned in her own tears this year because Viola said no—and I dare not defy Viola, you know. Next year, my boy, I will have to dance with Anna. And you had better reserve the opening set with her soon, Dominic, or she will break her heart."

Mr. and Mrs. Courtney were the next to leave. Their boys were close behind them, Susan hovering in the background, Lieutenant Jennings beside her.

"Well, your lordship," Mr. Courtney boomed, extending a large hand to his host, "a thoroughly grand evening, as always. My little one here will remember it for as long as she lives, I'll wager."

Lord Amberley smiled at Susan. "You have been a great

success, Susan," he said. "I am still chagrined over the fact that when I asked you, you had not one free set to offer me."

She blushed and hung her head.

"It is supposed to be a secret," Mr. Courtney whispered so loudly that no one in the group had any difficulty hearing. "I am not supposed to say anything until the lieutenant has had a chance to communicate the news to his family. But they will not mind present company knowing. Lieutenant Jennings here offered for Susan this afternoon, and Mrs. Courtney and I gave our blessing, and she has accepted him this evening." He beamed around at everyone who stood and listened to him.

"Papa!" Susan said in an agony of embarrassment, allowing the lieutenant to lift her hand and lay it on his sleeve.

"Well, then," Lord Amberley said, "my ball has been a memorable occasion indeed. My congratulations to you both."

Lieutenant Jennings bowed. Susan would not lift her head.

"My little girl the wife of an officer!" Mr. Courtney said. "Can you imagine it, my lord? My lady?"

"I am sure Susan will do very well," Lady Amberley said. "I believe she has a great deal more backbone than anyone gives her credit for. And is it true that the regiment may be going to Spain, Lieutenant?"

Madeline, who had not looked at or spoken to her brother all evening, moved quietly to his side and slid a hand through his arm. She laid a cheek lightly against his shoulder for a moment. He hugged her arm to his side, his own as taut as iron.

"We will be taking ourselves off to bed," Lord Beckworth said, approaching the door with his wife on his arm. He nodded stiffly and unsmilingly to his host. "We will talk to you in the morning, Amberley. And Alexandra." He gave her a direct and cold look. "Where is James?"

Alexandra hesitated. "He has left," she said. She looked up at Lord Amberley. "Did he tell you?"

"Yes," he said briefly. "I am glad he found you, Alex. He was looking for you."

"Left?" Lord Beckworth said. "What in thunder do you mean by that?"

"He has gone away, Papa," Alexandra said quietly. "I think permanently."

"In the middle of the night?" Lady Beckworth said. "And in the middle of a ball? What can have possessed him? There must be some mistake. Where is he going?"

"To Canada, he said." Alexandra looked around her. "He left you a letter. Perhaps I can accompany you upstairs, Mama."

She said a hurried good night to everyone else, linked her arm through her mother's, and left the ballroom.

Lord Eden's free hand had come across to grip his sister's. Looking down at their clasped hands, Madeline wondered idly whose knuckles were the whiter with tension, his or hers. She concentrated on their hands, giving them the whole of her attention. Only so could she save herself from falling down the long, dark tunnel that was waiting to receive her.

MORE THAN AN HOUR later Alexandra was standing at the window of her room, staring sightlessly out. She was brushing idly at her hair, though there was really no need to do so. Nanny Rey had already given it its obligatory two hundred strokes for the night. And her touch had been none too gentle either. She had been told about the broken engagement and their imminent departure from Amberley.

"You don't know your own mind," she had said, pulling out the last hairpin and spreading Alexandra's hair over her shoulders in preparation for brushing it. "All these years you have not been given a chance to live, and now, when you are being offered all that life has to give by way of happiness, you are not satisfied."

"I know I am being foolish," Alexandra had said meekly.

"Foolish?" The first vicious stroke of the brush had dragged Alexandra's whole head backward. "Lunatic, I would call it. Such a lovely lord that I can scarce believe he is real. And not good enough for you."

"Ah, I did not say that, Nanny," Alexandra had protested. "He is too good for me, perhaps. Goodness had nothing to do with it. I have to be free, that is all. For once in my life I have to be free."

"That is the silliest word I ever heard tell of," Nanny Rey had said, making no effort whatsoever to tease the brush through a tangled curl, but pulling at it unrelentingly. "I can see it being in the French language or the Italian language, but not in the English language. The English are supposed to be sensible people. Free! There is no such thing as freedom, I am here to tell you."

"If I were a man I could be free," Alexandra said. "Ouch, Nanny. Can you not be a little more gentle?"

"Do you want to go to bed with tangles?" Nanny Rey had asked severely. "Hold still now, lovey. Men are no more free than we are, I do assure you. We are all born to a certain way of life, and we have to make the best of it. The person does not live who can do just whatsoever he pleases. Oh, some of those Eastern princes, perhaps, with their harems and other heathen trappings, poor lost souls. But I'll wager even they have to do what is expected of them. What if one of them wants only one wife? Everyone will laugh at him and think he is less than a man. So he is forced to fill his harem with fifty wives."

"Ouch! Nanny!" Alexandra had complained.

"Hold still, lovey" had been the only sympathy she had received. "If you spend your life running around in search of freedom, you will be running to your dying day and still no nearer than when you started."

"Perhaps," Alexandra had said. She never had been able to argue with Nanny, whose homespun wisdom always sounded incontestable.

"If I were you, I would run to his lordship in the morning and beg his pardon," Nanny had said. "He will forgive you, lovey, and still marry you, I would wager. I have never known a kinder gentleman."

"Nor I," Alexandra had said. "But the deed is done anyway. I will want you to pack my bags tomorrow morning, Nanny, if you please."

And finally she had been left alone, unhappy, her victory feeling very hollow indeed. And James gone. Perhaps she would never see him again. Perhaps she would never even hear from him. There had been no time to think of a place where he could send a letter and she be sure to receive it. Lady Amberley or Madeline might be very reluctant to forward a letter to her under the circumstances. Lord Amberley would, her mind told her unbidden. But she shook off the thought.

And then she saw him. He was standing outside the house, his hands clasped behind him, his legs apart. He was looking up to the sky. She held her breath and watched him, the brush suspended in her hair. He stood there for a long time, not moving. The urge began to grow on her to go down to him, to stand beside him, to talk to him. She wanted to ask him what his thoughts were, what his feelings. Too late she had remembered that there were two people involved in any relationship. She had not been the only person involved in their betrothal. He had been too.

She would have to get dressed, she thought. She would not have to pause to do her hair. He would not mind if she merely tied it back at the nape of her neck. She removed the brush slowly from her hair and stared down at him, undecided.

But before she could put her half-formed plan into action, Lord Amberley moved. He strode away from the house in the direction of the stone bridge. He was no longer wearing his ball dress, she could see, but riding clothes. He did not go for a horse, though. He crossed the bridge, turned up the valley, and disappeared from view behind the trees.

Alexandra stood at her window for another half-hour, her forehead against the pane, waiting for him to return, knowing that he would not do so. She knew where he had gone. And as the minutes passed, she ached to follow him there. He wanted to be alone. That was why he had gone. She would be the last person he would want to see. She had told him once that it would be his private place. She would never go there again.

It was a losing battle. She lost it at the end of the half-hour, when she hurried across her bedchamber and into the dressing room, changed quickly into her green velvet riding skirt and green silk blouse, rejected the jacket, and reached for a woolen shawl. She did not possess a hair ribbon and could not at the moment think of anything else that would serve the same purpose of tying back her hair.

She tossed it back over her shoulders, drew the shawl around her, and let herself quietly out of her room.

A half-hour later she was not feeling at all sure that she had done the right thing to come. It was all wrong, of course, to pursue him here to his most private place, on the same night that she had told his mother and her own parents that they were no longer to be married. All wrong. Madness, in fact. But she held that awareness at bay. She did not have leisure to think about such matters. She needed all her wits to see where she was going.

Even though it was not a dark night, it was dark enough among the trees to make it very difficult to see the ground beneath her feet. If it had not been for the river flowing along beside her, she would have been hopelessly lost. And there was the constant worry that she would not know where to turn off in order to climb to the stone hut and that she really would be lost when she started to ascend.

She stood for a long time on the bank of the river at the spot she thought was the right one. She did not fancy at all the idea of climbing up among those dark trees. How could she tell who or what was up there?

She shrugged finally and turned resolutely upward. It was either that or return to Amberley again alone. And if she did get lost, it would not be forever. Dawn could not be too far in the future. Besides, all she had to do was go downward until she reached the valley floor and the river.

She thought she was not going to be able to find it. She must have wandered a little to her right in the ascent. But she did find it, more by luck than judgment, she thought. There it was, the small clearing among the trees, and the stone hut against the hill, its door standing open.

She stood for a long time, more reluctant than ever, now that she was there, to move forward and make her presence known. Why had she come anyway? What more was there to say? What comfort was she looking for? Or hoping to give?

She crossed slowly to the doorway and stood looking in. There was a candle burning on the table. He was lying on the straw bed, the blanket spread beneath him. He was wearing only his shirt and breeches. One leg was drawn up at the knee, his bare foot flat on the bed. One arm was across his eyes, the other reaching to the floor beside him.

She must have made some sound or created some shadow. He pulled his arm sharply away from his eyes suddenly and turned to look at her. There was a moment's pause, and then he was on his feet and coming toward her.

24

LORD AMBERLEY DID NOT KNOW QUITE HOW he had got through the ball. The necessity of circulating constantly among his guests, making conversation, dancing, making sure that everyone was enjoying himself, and of smiling, smiling, smiling, had been almost beyond his powers of endurance. Up until suppertime he had kept up his spirits tolerably well by blanking his mind to what he knew must come tomorrow. But even the night had been stolen from him. Lord Beckworth had asked an awkward question and Alex had answered it directly.

Somehow he had smoothed over the moment—with help from Sir Cedric, he seemed to remember. But there had been no more pretending after that. Dancing with Alex had been an agony. He had felt the need to smile even for her so that she would not suspect the full truth. And for the rest of the evening he had been left to worry about her, to wonder where she had gone, what she was doing. And the cold demeanor of Beckworth and the troubled, sympathetic glances of his mother had been equally disturbing.

He could not go to bed after the last guest had taken his leave or retired to his assigned room. He had sent the servants away, insisting that all the tasks of clearing away might be left for the morning. And he had gone to his own room, undressed, realized that he could not lie down, donned riding clothes, and gone back downstairs with the intention of saddling a horse and riding up onto the cliffs. Perhaps the sea air would drug his mind, tire him enough so that he could rest.

But he had changed his mind. Once outside, he had longed for peace and quiet, total solitude, so that he could get his mind in order for the coming day. It was not forgetfulness he needed at the moment, or sleep, but tranquillity of mind, the ability to deal with the difficult day ahead. He must appear calm. It must appear that what Alex wanted was what he wanted too.

And so, late as it was, he had gone striding off up the valley up to the hut, which had never failed him. He could not afford to spend more than a few hours there, but he would make them enough. He would be able to think better there, relax better there, than in his own room at home.

He had lit a candle, thrown off his coat, spread the blanket over the straw on the rough bed he had made several years before, and lain down. It was a warm night; he had left the door open. He stared up at the ceiling for a while, and then threw an arm over his weary eyes.

Alex. He had known her for only a few weeks. Before he had met her, he had thought himself quite self-sufficient. He really had not felt the need of anyone else to help him along with the business of living. It was true that he had contemplated marriage with Eunice, but more because he had felt that life would be pleasant and comfortable with her than because he had felt any real need of her.

Just a few weeks ago! Could he have changed so drastically in such a short time? Surely he was just as capable now of living alone, of relying on himself for all his needs? Surely another person could not so quickly and so easily have become indispensable to him?

The prospect of living out the rest of his life, all the years ahead, seemed so dreary without Alex. He had meant right from the start, of course, to love her. He had intended to marry her, and it had seemed to him that he must love his wife. But he had not known at that time what love was—not the total love of a man for a woman. He had felt affection before, and responsibility, and respect, and friendship, and sexual desire. He had felt them all. But never all together, centered in one person, with that indefinable something in addition to all the parts that made her like the half of his own soul.

He had not known that he would grow to love Alex like that for the simple reason that he had not known such a love existed. And how was he now to smile and let her go? And how was he to pick up the threads of his old life and carry on, seeing to Mama's comfort and Madeline's happiness, protecting them as best he could from the anxiety of knowing Dominic in the army and in battle, looking after the running of his estate, the welfare of those dependent upon him? He did not think he had the will to carry on.

Something was at the door. He pulled his arm from his eyes and turned quickly toward the opening, expecting to see a deer or some other wild animal. At first he could not see beyond the candlelight. And then he was on his feet and crossing the room to the door.

"Alex?" he said, looking out at her in some wonder.

"I promised I would never come here," she said.

He shook his head. "I told you that you did not need to make such a promise," he said.

There seemed to be nothing to say after that. They stared

at each other. She was wearing the blouse she had worn on that first occasion when he had brought her here. Her hair was loose and in riotous curls down her back. Her eyes were large and wary. She looked remarkably as she had the first time he saw her.

He reached out and touched his fingertips to her cheek. Then he ran the backs of his fingers along her jawline to her chin.

"Why did you come?" he asked.

He felt her swallow against his fingers. "I don't know," she said. And then she reached up and caught at his wrist. "Yes, I do know. I want to make love with you."

He closed his eyes briefly. "Alex," he said, "I cannot so dishonor you."

"I do not intend to marry," she said. "No one will ever know except you and me. It is what we both want, is it not?"

"In a marriage bed, dear," he said.

"No. Not there," she said. "There it would be my duty to submit to you. It would not be making love. I want to give myself to you freely. I am free now. I want to give."

"I may get you with child," he said.

She looked stricken for a moment, and then she shook her head.

He looked up to the sky behind her head. There were no stars, though it was not total blackness. When he looked back down at her, she was looking back, her dark eyes large and calm. She was waiting for what he would decide. She still held to his wrist.

He drew her inside the hut, leaving the door open behind her. He framed her face with gentle hands and threaded his fingers in her hair. He looked into her eyes and answered the question there with his own.

She reached up and began to unbutton her blouse. She

pulled it from the waistband of her skirt when she reached the lower buttons and shrugged it off her shoulders. She let it drop to the floor behind her. She reached behind her, worked at the buttons of her skirt, and let it also fall to the floor. She stood before him in a thin silk shift. His hands had remained in her hair, his fingers lightly massaging her head, his thumbs rubbing against her cheeks and temples. He watched her eyes as they roamed over his face and his shoulders and chest.

Then her hands were on his shoulders briefly and moved to undo the buttons of his shirt. Her fingers were trembling. He did not help her until she drew the garment free of his breeches and he lifted his arms so that she could pull it off over his head.

He could see through the thin shift that her breathing had quickened. She buried her face against his naked shoulder suddenly and set her hands at his waist.

"I am so very frightened," she said with a breathless laugh.

He hooked his thumbs beneath the straps of her shift, pulled it free of her shoulders, and slid it down her body. She straightened her arms downward without lifting her head. He undid the buttons of his breeches, slid them down over his hips, and kicked free of them, before putting his arms around her and drawing her against him. She gasped and lifted her head to look into his face.

"Shall I put out the candle?" he asked.

She shook her head. "No," she said. "I want to see you. I want you to see me."

He lowered his head and kissed her. And took instant fire. He had never held anyone quite so incredibly feminine, or anyone who put herself against him with quite such heated and naked abandon.

There was to be no gradual building of desire, no slow and erotic exploration, no careful preparation of an uninitiated virgin. Hands, lips, tongues, bodies touched ungently, urgently, with the mutual and desperate need for union and release. She clung to him, moved against him, moaned at his touch, at his kiss, which ravished her mouth.

He tumbled her to the bed, following her there in his urgency and drawn on top of her by the desperation of her arms. And without any further preparation, without any agonizing over how he might avoid giving her pain, he was between her thighs and stabbing deeply into her. She cried out and clung to him with both arms and legs when it seemed that he might draw back.

"No," she cried to him. "Come to me. Come to me. Oh, please, Edmund. Please."

And she pushed up against him, twisted against him while he drove into her all the unleashed power of his passion. They cried out together, clung tautly to each other, and descended together into the world beyond passion.

She was sobbing and trembling beneath him. Lord Amberley disengaged himself from her body and moved to her side. He gathered her into his arms, smoothing back her hair with one hand, feathering soft kisses over her face.

"I hurt you," he said. "I hurt you, Alex. I frightened you."

"No." She shook her head. She had stopped sobbing, though her body still shook against his. "No."

He watched her as her eyes fluttered closed and her body gradually grew still and relaxed. He listened to her breathing grow steady and slow. And he smiled in some wonder. He did not believe he had ever before put a woman to sleep.

She was beautiful. Quite incredibly beautiful. Her hair

was in wild disarray around her face and over her shoulders. Her cheeks were flushed, as far as he could see in the faint light of the candle, which was about to burn itself out. Her lips were parted in sleep. Her skin was petal smooth and creamy. Her breasts were firm and generous, her waist small, her hips provocative. Her legs—her long, shapely legs—he could feel against his own.

And she had given herself to him. Given with a passion he did not know women capable of. Given, merely because she was free to do so and wished to do so. And what of tomorrow? But he cut off the thought before it could even develop in his mind. Let tomorrow take care of itself. He would take the free gift of this very brief portion of the night.

He closed his eyes.

ALEXANDRA KNEW INSTANTLY WHERE she was when she woke up. She could feel her lover's arm warm beneath her head, his breath against her hair. She could feel the warmth of his body close to hers, the cool air from outside against her back. She opened her eyes and found that she could see part of his chest and one broad shoulder. But it was not candlelight by which she could see.

She turned her head and found that the world beyond the doorway was lightening. And she became aware of the early dawn chorus of birds in full progress.

"It is still very early," Lord Amberley said at her ear. "I have just been watching the sky lighten out there."

She turned back to look into his eyes. They were smiling back at her with that expression that had always had the power to make her catch her breath.

"Any regrets?" he asked softy.

She shook her head.

"I'm afraid I was very rough," he said. "Are you sore?"

Alexandra paused to consider. Yes, she was sore. She could feel where he had been. But it was a pleasant soreness, one which she would not have been without. She shook her head.

He continued to smile at her with his eyes. He reached up with his free hand and smoothed back the dark hair from her face.

"You have beautiful hair," he said. "You should not hide it so ruthlessly."

She reached an arm up over his broad shoulder, moved close against him, and kissed him. She felt him draw in a slow breath, and his arms closed around her.

They tasted each other's lips, nibbling, teasing with their teeth. She opened her mouth and relaxed as he slid the tip of his tongue up behind her teeth and along the roof of her mouth before circling her tongue and pushing slowly in and out of her mouth. She inhaled sharply.

And his hands roamed her body lightly, touching, exploring, rubbing, slowly but surely arousing. His mouth moved away from hers to trail kisses over her face, down over her chin and her throat to her breasts and back to her mouth again. She set her palms against his chest and spread her fingers wide. She could feel beneath the rough hair the muscles of his chest, his shoulders, his upper arms.

His hand went down between her legs, and his fingers searched and teased. She moaned, and her arms closed about his neck.

"Easy, love," he murmured against her ear. "Not so fast."

And he turned over onto his back and lifted her to lie on top of him. He took her legs between his own and held her head in his hands.

"I am going to show you how beautiful it can be," he said. "There is no hurry. We have hours yet before we will be missed. Slowly, love."

And he resumed the light exploration with his hands, the feathered kisses, the teasing, warm meeting of mouths. Alexandra became physical sensation only. And yet it was not entirely that. Not for one moment did she forget with whom she lay, who it was who was making such achingly wonderful love to her. And she knew that he was equally aware of her. His eyes were open as hers were. He murmured her name as she did his.

And finally he nudged his legs beneath hers, reached down to bring her knees up to hug his body, and lifted her slightly away from him. When his hands grasped her hips firmly and brought her back down to him, she found herself being deeply penetrated.

"Edmund," she whispered against his mouth, and pressed her knees to his sides.

"Easy, love," he said. "Slowly."

And he moved in her in a tantalizingly slow rhythm that had feeling gradually spiraling upward in her, through her womb into her breasts, into her throat. She lost touch with time and the world beyond her own body and that of the man who was creating such erotic feelings in her.

He took her by the shoulders eventually and lifted her upward so that she was kneeling over him, looking down into his eyes, her hair waving forward like a curtain on either side of her face.

"Ride me, Alex," he whispered, and she moved to find his rhythm until they were together and moving faster, her hands reaching down to his shoulders, his on her hips, their eyes looking deeply into each other's.

But she closed her eyes finally and bit down on her lower

lip. She was tight with desire, in an agony of raw wanting and wanting. And yet every muscle was clenched in protest, holding him away from the center of herself where no one but she had ever been before. And every inward thrust became a pain and an ecstasy, demanding the admittance that she dared not give and that she could not live without giving.

He moved unrelentingly on and she knelt astride his body, still now and taut, resisting the moment that she knew was inevitable, waiting in terror lest it happen, waiting in anguish lest it not happen.

Her body was opening to him, relaxing against him. And now that it had begun, now that there was no holding back the giving, she stopped fighting. She opened her eyes and looked down into his again and allowed each inward thrust of his body to push back the resistance of her muscles.

And then she knew herself fully opened, without defenses, and he paused on the brink of her.

"Alex," he whispered, "come down here to me." He reached up his arms and cupped her face in his hands as she came. He brought it close to his own and kissed her lips.

"Now," he said, and laid her head against his shoulder before reaching down to grasp her hips again and push himself firmly and very deeply into her once, twice, three times, until he was there, there with her, in her, part of her; and all feeling, all tension moved outward on soft waves of sensation until there was nothing left but herself and her lover, cradled in each other's arms, united at their core. Nothing else mattered or even existed. Just the two of them suspended in this moment of time. Life and death and heaven all combined in one timeless moment.

When she came to herself, her legs had somehow been

straightened to lie comfortably on either side of his. His arms were wrapped around her, and he was kissing her cheek and her temple—and her mouth when she turned her face toward his.

"Edmund," she murmured against his mouth. "You are beautiful. So beautiful."

"It was good for you," he said. "I am very happy that it was good for you, Alex. I have wanted to give you happiness."

She burrowed her head against his shoulder and reached up to touch his cheek with one hand. "That is all you ever want of life, is it not, Edmund?" she said. "To make other people happy. And what of yourself?"

He took her hand in his and kissed the palm, holding back her fingers with his thumb. "You cannot doubt that it was good for me too," he said. "You gave me everything, Alex. No one has ever done that for me before. Thank you."

He must have drifted off to sleep. Certainly he said no more, and his breathing was quiet and even. Alexandra did not. Utterly satiated and relaxed physically, still united with her lover, she began to return to her separate being mentally and emotionally. Her very separate being.

No one had ever given completely to Edmund before. He was respected, loved by so many people, and yet everyone was at the receiving end of his love. He gave so much that he gave also the impression that he did not need anything himself, that he was sufficient unto himself. She had given him her body, and he had thanked her as if it were the most precious gift of his life. And yet just a few hours before she had publicly withdrawn the gift of herself to him. She could have married him, spent her life giving her companionship, support, understanding, love, children. And she had chosen instead self-respect, freedom.

Selfishness!

And she would reap a just reward. She would spend her life reliving this hour, watching it fade in her memory and cloud her life. Everything in her future would be judged against this night of love and harmony and giving and receiving, and everything would be found wanting. All the happiness in her life was in the past already. In the past hour. All that was left of this night was the getting dressed when Edmund awoke and walking back to the house, perhaps together, perhaps separately.

She was justly served. She turned her head slightly and kissed the warm flesh of his shoulder where it met his neck. He did not stir.

LORD EDEN WAS UP very early the next morning. In truth, he had slept but little. A mood of restlessness drove him, the need to be gone on his way, without having the ritual of a final day to live through.

There was so much to be said to Edmund and Mama, and especially to Madeline. Too much to be said and too little time in which to say it. Oceans of time in which there was nothing to say. It was always like this at parting. He could remember it to a lesser degree every time he had left home for school or university. One felt the day before that one wanted to do and say so much, and yet one's actions felt paralyzed, one's tongue tied.

He wished he could snap his fingers and he would be on his way, all the farewells said. Once away, he could forget the sadness, the partings, though he would carry with him wherever he went his affection for those left behind. He would be able to concentrate on his future, on doing what he had always wanted to do.

And perhaps once away he would be able to blank his mind to a horribly bungled love affair. He had renounced Susan in his heart the night before and felt that heart breaking. The eternal noble gesture. Don Quixote. Susan must not be faced with the realities of war and mortality, so Susan must be given up. And Susan had promptly betrothed herself to an officer whose regiment might be off to Spain at any moment.

He might have had her after all. It seemed that she would not have said no. She had cried and told him she loved him, and then she had gone in and accepted another man's offer of marriage.

He had spent a couple of hours of sleeplessness in a fury against her. She had been playing with his emotions, dangling after the larger prize, he had thought at first. But his anger had faded. Susan, sweet little Susan, was incapable of such scheming duplicity. She really did love him and had hoped until that last moment that he would marry her. But Susan was a realist. She had always protested that she was not good enough for him. She had given in to reality and accepted a good man when he had offered.

And so, the morning after the ball, when he rose early and left his valet in his room packing the belongings that he would need to take with him, his feelings were battered and bruised, his need to be gone strong upon him, and an uncomfortable day of pain yawning ahead of him.

Edmund was not yet up, the butler informed him. It was unusual for Edmund to be in bed so late, but of course it had been a late night, and a demanding one on Edmund as host. Madeline, on the other hand, was up and out riding already. That was surprising, as Madeline was not an early riser at the best of times. But of course, she had her own reason to find sleep difficult.

"Where did she go?" he asked the butler.

"I am afraid I could not say, my lord," that individual said with a bow, and Lord Eden was left to stride out to the stables to see if anyone did know.

He found her less than an hour later galloping along the beach toward him as if she had all the hounds of hell at her heels. She slowed her horse when she saw him and came riding up to him, watching him warily.

"Are you talking to me today, Mad?" he asked, flashing her a grin.

"Yes," she said without any of the dash of spirit he expected.

"Are you still angry with me?" he asked.

She shook her head and turned her horse to walk along the beach in the direction of the black rock. Lord Eden brought his horse into step beside hers.

"I have always known that you would go," she said. "I just thought that perhaps if I ignored the fact, it would go away. Perhaps it would be easier to have a twin of the same gender, would it not, Dom? I feel so very close to you, and yet you are so very different from me that sometimes I cannot understand you at all. But one thing cannot be ignored, and must not be, since this may be the very last day I will spend with you. I love you more dearly than I could possibly say."

Lord Eden grinned across at her. "Perhaps I should get you to put this down in writing, Mad," he said. "It would be delicious ammunition to use against you in future arguments. 'Look,' I would be able to say when you are hurling cushions or books or hatchets at my head, while I wave a piece of paper in the air, 'you love me more than you could possibly say, Mad.'"

To his surprise, she raised eyes to his that were brimming

with tears. "Will there be future arguments?" she said, before breaking into loud and indelicate sobs.

"Mad!" he said. "Hey! For goodness' sake, stop this, will you? Anyone would swear that I was going to be led straight out to a firing squad or something as an initiation rite into the army. A surprising number of soldiers go home after war to tell the tale, you know, a large number of them with all four limbs too."

But her sobs only increased in volume as she flapped her hand around in search of a handkerchief and slapped at his as it reached across to take the reins of her horse.

"Hey, you goose," Lord Eden said, vaulting from the saddle of his horse and dragging his sister down from hers. He held her very tightly to him despite her effort to escape and her snorts and hiccups as she tried to control the humiliating tears. "I haven't seen you cry since Papa thrashed me when we were ten for pulling your hair and kicking you in the rear end, and then refused to do the same to you though you had contributed at least your equal share to the fight. Until yesterday, that is. And now again."

She snorted inelegantly. "I hate you," she said.

"No, you don't, love," he said cheerfully. "You love me more than you could possibly say. You see? I had no idea that I would have a chance to throw that back in your teeth quite so soon."

"Don't, Dom," she said, clinging to his arms suddenly and raising a red, tear-streaked face to his. "Don't act this way as if everything is normal and as if you are not going away forever tomorrow. Don't. I can't fight back today. It is not fair to fight with me when I am not in form."

He bent and kissed her forehead. "You are a goose," he said. "I have no intention of getting killed, I would have you know. I wouldn't give you the satisfaction of knowing yourself the oldest surviving twin. I intend to outlive you, little sister, by at least half an hour. First in and last out, so to speak. But not for fifty or sixty years at least yet, Mad. I'm not in any hurry. Are you?"

She clung to the lapels of his coat. "I wish I could go too," she said. "I wish women could go to war too, Dom."

He raised his eyes to the sky. "Heaven forbid!" he said. "I would spend more time fighting with you than with the French, Mad."

"Are you very unhappy about Susan?" she asked.

He looked into her eyes and then away over her head. "Yes," he said curtly. "Yes, I am. Just don't say anything more about her, Mad. All right?"

"All right," she said.

He looked down at her and took her hand in his as they strolled the remaining distance to the black rock.

"Something happened with Purnell last night?" he asked. "Do you want to talk about it? I won't pry if you would rather not."

He did not think she was going to answer. She took her hand from his as she sat down on the rock and spread her riding skirt carefully around her.

"I made a fool of myself," she said. "I offered myself to him, Dom. I mean really offered myself. I would have given everything."

Lord Eden sucked in his breath. "Mad, he didn't . . ." he said.

"No, he didn't," she said. "But I wanted him to and would have allowed him to. I thought everything was going to be all right between us. I thought he loved me. No! I *think* he *loves* me. But there is something. I don't know what. Something that makes him hate himself. And now I will never know. Canada! The other end of the world. He is going to Canada."

He reached out and touched her hand. "Winter will be here before you know it," he said. "You will be going to London with Mama, I expect, and soon you will be in love with someone else, Mad. Perhaps really in love this time. Happily-ever-after in love."

She smiled at him and squeezed his hand. "Yes, perhaps," she said. "Tall, I think. Blond. Broad-shouldered. White teeth. A deep musical voice."

"Forty thousand a year," Lord Eden said.

"Forty thousand a year," she agreed. "Let's see, what else?"

She jumped to her feet suddenly and made a dash for her horse, which was standing quietly with her brother's close by.

"Help me up, Dom," she said. "I'll race you back to the head of the valley. Help me up."

"I say," he said, rising to his feet in order to comply with her demand. "You aren't crying again, are you, Mad?"

"Of course I'm not crying, numbskull," she said, gaily, her face turned in to the horse's side. "How could I see to race you if I were crying? Help me up this instant!"

25

NANNY REY WAS BRUSHING ALEXANDRA'S hair and preparing to draw it back into its usual chignon. She teased the brush through the worst of the tangles and looked shrewdly over the tops of her spectacles at the mirrored image of her mistress. Alexandra was gazing off into the distance from slightly shadowed eyes. There was a flush of color high on her cheekbones.

"I took your green riding skirt downstairs to the kitchen to be washed and ironed," Nanny Rey said. "The hem was wet."

"Ah, yes," Alexandra said absently.

"And your shoes are drying before the kitchen fire. They werc soaked through."

"It was the dew," Alexandra said.

Mrs. Rey paused in her task and peered at the mirrored image, but Alexandra seemed oblivious of her presence.

"Not quite so severe, Nanny," she said when her hair was pulled back firmly from her face. "Could you get it to wave down over my ears, do you think? Would it look too frivolous?"

"Like this, lovey?" Mrs. Rey loosened her hold on the hair, which looped down over Alexandra's ears and immediately softened her features and showed off both the thickness and the shining waviness of her hair. "It would look very pretty, if you ask me, which you are doing."

"Yes, please." Alexandra smiled.

"We must not keep your Papa waiting, lovey," Nanny Rey said. "He said half an hour when I came up here, and there cannot be more than five minutes of that left."

"In his room, you said, Nanny?" Alexandra said. "I shall go now and be two minutes early. You have finished? Yes, I like it. Thank you." She stood up, turned around, and surprised her old nurse by bending and planting a kiss on her withered cheek.

"There," Nanny Rey said. "Get along with you now."

Alexandra did not look forward to the interview with her father, but she did not feel afraid, as she usually did. She took a deep breath before tapping at his door, and waited for his valet to open it to her.

"Good morning, Papa," she said, looking around the dressing room when she went in and seeing that they were alone. She folded her hands in front of her, drew back her shoulders, and lifted her chin.

"I don't know what is good about it, Alexandra," he said, turning at the opposite end of the room and glaring severely at her. "Your mother is unwell and confined to her bed until luncheon time at least, and our grand gentleman insists that an interview between himself and me is not satisfactory. It seems that you and your mother and his mother must be there too. So we must be kept waiting until this afternoon. A pretty situation this has turned out to be."

"But Lord Amberley is quite right, Papa," she said calmly. "What we have decided concerns both him and me, and it is right that we should communicate that decision to our parents and discuss the matter in a civilized manner."

"Silence, girl!" he roared. "When I want your opinion, I will ask for it. And you may be sure that you will have a long wait before that happens. Is a man not to be master of his own family any longer?"

Alexandra swallowed. "I will not be silent, Papa," she said evenly. "This is a matter that concerns me very directly. I will have a voice in what happens to me."

She wondered for a moment what he was about to do. He stood arrested, staring at her. She did not move or remove her eyes from his.

"What is this?" he said, his voice ominously quiet. "What ways have you picked up in this place of iniquity, Alexandra? Do you know that you are talking to your father, girl? And do you dare look me in the eye while you defy me? You had better go to your room and spend the hours until you are summoned downstairs on your knees begging for mercy. I shall make your excuses at luncheon."

"No," she said, "I will not do that, Papa. I will not be praying to that imaginary God of wrath and vengeance ever again. And I intend to ride out onto the cliffs this morning if our interview with his lordship has been delayed. I am a grown woman, Papa. I am one-and-twenty. And I have decided to take my life into my own hands. I do not know what I will do with it. I suppose I will have to take a position as a governess or something like that. I will decide that after I have left here."

"I will decide what is to happen to you after we have left here," Lord Beckworth blustered, striding across the room and glaring down at her. "I see that I will have to take responsibility for your immortal soul myself, Alexandra. You have let it slip to the devil."

"Papa," she said, letting her shoulders relax and her chin fall an inch, "must we be like this? Can we not just love?

When you arrived here a few days ago, I was so happy to see you. I realized how much I love you. You are my father, and I have spent my life with you. And you have cared for me. I know that you love me and James too. But you are so afraid to show it, so afraid of appearing weak and sinful. It is not sinful to love, Papa. God is love."

He gazed at her incredulously while she talked. One hand opened and closed at his side. "You are preaching to me?" he said.

She shook her head. "I just want to hug you, Papa," she said. "I just want to love you."

"I never heard such nonsense in my life," he said. "I would think you should love me too, Alexandra. Your soul would be in a sorry state if you did not. And I would think I love you too. Have I not devoted the past twenty-one years to bringing you to eternal salvation?"

"Papa," she said almost in a whisper, "I love you."

"Hm." The hand was opening and closing convulsively at his side. "I cannot think what can have come over you, Alexandra. You must be sickening for something. Go to your room, girl. I would advise you to lie down for an hour or two. I shall have to summon a physician when we return to town."

Alexandra closed the small distance between them and kissed him on the cheek before turning and whisking herself out of the room.

"What in thunder has come over the girl!" were the last words she heard before she closed the door behind her.

LORD AMBERLEY WAS IN his mother's sitting room. He was standing before her, both his hands in hers.

"Dear Edmund," she was saying. "I have been so happy

for you. I love Alexandra very dearly, and she has seemed so right for you. I thought that finally my son was to be rewarded for a lost youth and years of service to others. My firstborn son, Edmund. You are so very precious to me."

He was smiling. "You make it sound as if I have lived a life of misery and hardship, Mama," he said. "How very untrue. I have had you and Dominic and Madeline. I have had this home and wealth and comfort. Many people would give an arm and a leg for the privilege of enjoying such misery. Don't make a tragedy of what is happening now, dear. Alex and I are not right for each other. That is all. We will both be happier away from each other."

She looked searchingly into his smiling eyes. "Liar, Edmund," she said. "Oh, liar! Do you think I do not know you a great deal better than to believe that? You love her, do you not?"

"Yes, Mama," he said gently. "I love her. She is everything in life to me."

She looked stricken and squeezed his hands more tightly. "And there is no hope?" she asked. "None, Edmund?"

"No, Mama," he said. "I have given Alex her freedom because that is what she wants most and has been without all her life."

She nodded. "You have given," she said. "Yes, Edmund. And all is now said. I will not keep you. You must want to get away about your own business. Such meetings are a strain on you, are they not? I will see you at luncheon, dear."

She held up a cheek for his kiss and watched him leave the room. Sometimes he looked so much like his father that her heart ached with pain. But he was so much more vulnerable than his father, though not many people would suspect the fact. And she knew from long experience that the worse Edmund was hurting, the more firmly and gently he would smile.

How dreadful it was to be a mother, to have borne a child and suckled him at one's breast, to have watched him grow into manhood, and to know oneself powerless to shield him from harm and from suffering.

Lady Amberley sighed and turned back to her embroidery frame.

HE COULD NOT LEAVE her alone. He knew she had left the house. She had gone minutes before he had left the chapel, the butler told him. And when he stepped outside, he saw her ride alone up the hill to the west, on her way surely to the cliff top. It was where Alex would go this morning. And he had to follow her there. Perhaps she wanted to be alone. But there was so little time left. This might be his final chance to be alone with her. He had to go after her.

Lord Amberley rode up the hill slowly, battling with himself. Perhaps he should turn back and leave her to herself. There really was nothing more to be said, nothing more to be done. Better to remember those magical early hours of the morning and their silent, strangely peaceful walk back to the house together as his final encounter with her. Better not to spoil it now with the awkwardness of a lone meeting in the cold light of day, when as like as not they would not be able to find one thing to say to each other.

But he rode onward. He had to be alone with her one last time. Once more to see her, to look into her eyes, to touch her perhaps. He had not allowed his mind to dwell upon what had happened up in his hut early that morning. There was too much to be said and done that day, too much for which he must keep himself alert. He would open up the treasure of his memories when she was gone—tomorrow or the next day.

But he could not stop the memories and images as he rode on. Alex naked and unembarrassed and more beautiful than any woman he had seen or imagined. Alex hot and fierce with passion in his arms. Alex above him, moving to his rhythm, gazing down into his face with dark, luminous eyes and voluptuously waving hair. Alex with her soft, wet, womanly depths opening to him and giving all of herself so that they had met and united in an ecstasy of giving and receiving.

Alex!

He could see her as he rode across the plateau toward the cliffs. She stood looking out to sea, her hands at her sides. She was hatless. Her horse was grazing on the coarse grass a safe distance from the cliff.

She turned as he approached, and stood watching him. She did not come toward him or turn to move away. He left his horse beside hers and walked toward her. She did not smile or take her eyes from his face.

He smiled and stood beside her. He looked down at the sea below them. "It is almost calm today," he said.

"Yes," she said.

"Alex," he said, "you will not regret last night?"

"No."

"You will not forget?"

"No, never," she said. "How could I?"

"I am glad," he said.

There seemed to be nothing else to say. He stood beside her, his hands clasped behind his back, gazing down at the water, which he did not see.

"You will be leaving tomorrow?" he said.

"Yes."

"You will be happy, Alex?" he said. "You do not regret your decision?"

There was a pause. "No," she said.

He nodded and lifted his eyes to the distant horizon.

"What about you?" she asked suddenly, turning to look at him. "Tell me about you, Edmund. How do you feel about all this? How do you feel about last night? Will you be happy? Do you have any regrets?"

He turned his head to look back at her. His eyes were smiling. "I have grown fond of you, Alex," he said, "and I do not need to tell you how I felt about last night. I want you to be happy. If you are happy in what we have decided, then I am content. No regrets, dear."

She stared at him for a moment, her head shaking slowly from side to side. "No," she said. "That is not good enough, Edmund. I do not want to know how you think you should feel, or what you think you should do. You have given me so much, Edmund. You have always been so selfless. But you have never given me yourself. Your body, yes. But not you. I don't know you at all."

His smile spread downward to his mouth. "You are the important one here," he said. "I have had a happy life, Alex, and have been abundantly blessed. You have not. And if I can do one small thing to make you happy, then I will do it willingly. I have done it. I have set you free. It is what you wish, is it not?"

"Show me you are vulnerable," she said. "Show me one sign, Edmund. Are you hurt in any way? Even in the smallest way? Have I hurt you at all? Show me one chink in the armor. Show me that you are not all saint. Show me that you are a man who can feel and suffer. Please, Edmund. Tell me what I have done to you, what I am doing. If anything. Or tell me that you are happy to see me go."

For once his smile seemed frozen in place. And then it faded as she waited, her eyes holding his. "I love you," he said. "And I am raw with the pain of losing you. I have given all I can, Alex, because you are more important than anything else in my life. I will hurt and hurt when you leave, and I cannot see any end to the pain. Although my mind knows that I will live on and continue to function, and that I will laugh again and that a day will pass eventually in which I will not think of you, my heart cannot believe it today. There. Now, are you satisfied?"

There were tears in his eyes and he smiled at her again.

"Yes," she said. "Oh, yes."

She watched him swallow and bring himself under control, as the smile took firm control of his blue eyes again. "I thought it was freedom I wanted," she said, "until I had it and realized that that was not it at all. What I wanted, Edmund, what I have always wanted, is to be needed. I have always been cared for and trained and disciplined by Mama and Papa. I have been loved and protected by James. And I have been sheltered and treated with incredible kindness and courtesy by you and by your family. But I have never been needed. Feelings have always come to me from others. No one has ever seemed to need my feelings to flow back again. No one has ever really needed to be loved by me."

"I need you," he said. "My God, Alex, I need you."

"I know," she said. And suddenly she smiled dazzlingly at him. "Will you marry me, Edmund?"

He searched her eyes. "You know I will marry you anytime you say the word," he said.

"No." She shook her head. "Not good enough. I don't want you to marry me because I want you to. Not at all. I would rather be companion to a ninety-year-old crosspatch in the farthest corner of the Scottish Highlands. I really would. I want you to marry me because you want to. Or not marry me, as the case may be. But because of your feelings and your needs, Edmund."

"I don't want to continue living without you," he said. "I suppose I will if I must. I am not the suicidal type. But I don't want to, Alex. I want to take you up to my stone hut and keep you there all to myself for the rest of our lives. I want to love you and love you and forget that there is anyone else on this planet who might need me at some time in the future. I need you as I need this air we are breathing. Have I reassured you?"

"Yes," she said.

"Very well, then," he said. "Will you allow me to be the man here? I know that you do not think our society is very fair to women, but this is the society we live in, my dear. It is the only one we have, and if there is any marriage proposal to be made here, I am the one who is going to make it. Understood?"

"Yes, Edmund," she said.

"And you need not look so meek," he said. "You may fight me and fight me on this theme for the rest of our lives, but on this one occasion I insist on being the man. Will you marry me?"

"Yes, Edmund," she said.

His hands were cupping her face, his fingers threaded into the soft waves over her ears, his thumbs rubbing against her cheeks. He gazed into her eyes for several moments, his own serious and searching.

"Will you really?" he said. "It is not just because of the sad story I just told you?"

"Oh, yes," she said, "it is entirely because of that, Edmund. I would not marry you if my own need was the only inducement. I was never sure that that was not all until you said that you really wanted and needed me. I never knew that your wish to marry me was not just your excessive kindness and desire to protect what was weaker than yourself."

"Alex," he said. He was shaking his head. "Even after last night?"

"I asked you to do it," she said. "It could have just been that you wanted to make me happy."

"If you had had any experience in such matters," he said, "you could not possibly have just said that. I could not have done what I did to you, dear, and in just that way, if I was just intent on giving you a pleasant sensual experience. I was loving you, Alex, loving you with all of me. Yes, and asking and begging for all of you. You would have known that had it not been your first time. You would not have had to ask me this morning."

"Well," she said, placing a hand against his coat. "Well." She closed her eyes. "Oh, Edmund, I don't have to go away after all. I don't have to leave you. And I won't have to keep taking and taking from you. I will be able to give. You need me. You really need me! I think I need to shout or scream. I cannot grasp the truth of this yet. I don't have to go, Edmund?"

He was grinning at her when she opened her eyes. "I might ask you to move a hundred yards away if you really are going to scream," he said.

She giggled suddenly and threw her arms up around his neck. "Oh, Edmund," she said, "how I do love you. And you are quite right. Love is what is most important. But love that goes two ways. Love that gives and love that receives."

"You will have to teach me the latter," he said. "I am not used to being vulnerable, Alex. I will doubtless close up against you the very next time I feel hurt or suffering approaching and try to cope with it alone. You will have to teach me to let you in. It will not be easy, dear. I am afraid of disappointing you."

"No," she said. "Now that I know you need me, I am never going to forget it, and I am not going to let you forget it."

He bent his head and kissed her.

She clasped her arms more tightly about his neck when he lifted his head again. "Edmund," she said, "I have to get something off my conscience. It is wrong to keep a secret from one's betrothed, is it not? Especially a guilty one?"

He looked inquiringly and a little warily into her eyes. "What is it, love?" he asked.

"I lied," she said. "Last night I lied because I wanted you so badly. I really do not know when is the most likely time or the most unlikely to be got with child." She flushed quite hotly after the words were out of her mouth.

He laid his forehead against hers. "It seems I have no choice then, love," he said. "I will have to make an honest woman of you, won't I?"

"Yes, Edmund," she said.

"Soon," he said. "Very soon, Alex. And we will have to hope that you can lie as convincingly as you did last night if our first child is born a little less than nine months after the nuptials."

"Oh, Edmund," she said with perfect seriousness, gazing into his eyes, "I hope he is. Oh, I do hope he is. What a beautiful way for a child to begin."

He kissed her again. "All our children will begin as beautifully, Alex," he said. "I promise you." He grinned suddenly. "All one hundred and two of them. No, don't flinch, love. Remember there are twins on my side of the family."

"I want to go and tell Mama and Papa," she said. "Can we go and tell them, Edmund? Please?"

"About the one hundred and two children?" he asked with raised eyebrows, "or about the first of those, who may already be on the way?"

"Oh, do be serious now," she said. "About our marrying, Edmund. I want to tell them and your mother and Madeline and Lord Eden and Sir Cedric and Uncle William and Aunt Viola and every other person in the whole world. And James."

He drew her to him and rested a cheek against the top of her head. "He will be all right, Alex," he said. "I cannot pretend to know your brother or to understand him. There is much about him, I believe, that has not been told. But there is a strength in him, an instinct for survival, something. I don't know quite how to explain it, but I feel it. He will come back, dear, when he has found himself, and you will have a chance to give him your love as he has given you his."

She relaxed against him and allowed him to seek out her mouth with his. "Thank you," she said. "You know how very important he is to me, don't you?"

"Of course," he said. "Quite as dear as Dominic and Madeline are to me. And this is Dominic's last day at home, Alex. We must make the most of it."

"Yes," she said, smiling up into his eyes and moving back from him. She reached out a hand for his. "Take me home, Edmund."

He set his hand in hers and closed his fingers around it in a warm clasp. "There," he said. "You *are* home already, love. And so am I. Let's go back to Amberley."

About the Author

MARY BALOGH is the *New York Times* bestselling author of *Simply Unforgettable* and the acclaimed Slightly novels: *Slightly Married, Slightly Wicked, Slightly Scandalous, Slightly Tempted, Slightly Sinful,* and *Slightly Dangerous,* as well as the romances *No Man's Mistress, More Than a Mistress, A Summer to Remember,* and *One Night for Love.* A former teacher, she grew up in Wales and now lives in Canada.

Read on for a sneak peek

at the next breathtaking novel in

Mary Balogh's series featuring

the teachers at Miss Martin's School for Girls

Simply Magic

Coming in spring 2007

from Delacorte Press

THE *NEW YORK TIMES* BESTSELLING AUTHOR OF *SIMPLY LOVE*

MARY BALOGH

SIMPLY MAGIC

Simply Magic

On sale spring 2007

SUSANNA OSBOURNE HAD THOUGHT SHE WAS not going to be able to come to Barclay Court and had been disappointed even though she had tried to tell herself that it did not really matter.

She had remained at the school in Bath all summer with Claudia Martin to care for the charity pupils, who had nowhere else to go during the holiday. Anne Jewell, the other resident teacher, had gone to Wales for a month with her son, David, at the invitation of the Marquess of Hallmere, an old acquaintance of hers.

But while Anne was still away, Frances Marshall, Countess of Edgecombe, a former teacher at the school herself, had stopped off in Bath with the earl, her husband, on the way back to their home, Barclay Court in Somerset. They had been away for a few months in Austria and other European countries, where Frances had been engaged to sing. They had come to invite Claudia or Anne or Susanna to go home with them for two weeks. The three of them were still Frances's dearest female friends even though she had been married for two years.

Claudia had urged Susanna to go. She could manage the girls perfectly well alone, she had said, and there were always the non-resident teachers to appeal to if necessary. Besides, Anne would surely be back any day. But Susanna had a loyal heart. Claudia Martin had given her employment five years before when she had still been a charity pupil at the school herself, and she would not easily forget her gratitude or the obligation she felt to set duty before personal inclination.

She had told Frances without any hesitation at all that no, she would not go this time. And of course, Frances had not argued. She had understood. But then, just the day before Frances and the earl were to leave, Anne had come home and there had been no further necessity for Susanna to stay too.

And so here she was in Somerset during a particularly sunny and warm spell in late August. It was not the first time she had been here, but the wonder of such visits would never pall, she had been sure. Barclay Court was stately and spacious and lovely. Frances was as dear as ever, and the earl was exceedingly kind. The neighbors, she remembered, were amiable. She knew that Frances would go out of her way to entertain her royally. Not that any effort was necessary. Just the rare enjoyment of being on holiday was entertainment enough especially when the setting was so luxurious.

She and Frances were out for a visit to the Raycrofts, whom Susanna had particularly liked when she first met them. They had decided to walk rather than take a carriage since the weather was lovely and they had been traveling all of yesterday. When they were scarcely half a mile on their way, they had heard cheerful, laughing, youthful voices and had seen that the younger Raycrofts and Calverts were out walking too.

Susanna had felt her heart lift with gladness. Life had seemed very good indeed.

Until it no longer did.

Frances and Mr. Raycroft were talking about Vienna. Frances had been there very recently, and Mr. Raycroft's betrothed, Miss Hickmore, had just gone there with her parents to spend the autumn and winter months.

Mr. Raycroft, tall, loose-limbed, sandy-haired, his face good-humored more than it was handsome, had always been particularly amiable. Frances had once suggested, only half in jest, that Susanna set her cap at him. But he had shown no romantic partiality for her—and she had felt none for him. She felt no pang of regret to learn now of his betrothal, only a hope that Miss Hickmore was worthy of him.

He was gentleman enough to draw Susanna into the conversation, explaining that he was as ignorant as she of what such places as Vienna were really like, having never set foot outside the British Isles himself.

"It is undoubtedly a most lovely city," he said, smiling kindly at her, "though I am sure it cannot surpass London in beauty. Are you familiar with London, Miss Osbourne?"

She determinedly tried to concentrate upon the conversation rather than upon the other thoughts that whirled in jumbled disorder through her mind.

"Only very slightly," she said. "I spent a short time there as a girl but have not been since. I envy Frances's having seen Vienna and Paris and Rome."

"Lady Edgecombe," one of the young ladies called from behind them, "do you suppose there will be any waltzes at the assembly the week after next? I shall simply *die* if there is one and Mama forbids us to dance it as she surely will. Is it really quite shockingly *fast*?"

"I have no idea, Mary," Frances said while Susanna turned her head to see who had spoken. "I did not even know of the assembly, remember, until you mentioned it a few minutes ago. But I hope there will be a waltz. It is a lovely, romantic dance and really not shocking at all. At least, it has never seemed so to me."

And there he was in the middle of them, Susanna saw with a sinking heart, one lady on each arm as he had been when she first set eyes on him, the other two hovering about him as if he were the only man in the world of any significance—an opinion with which he undoubtedly concurred.

She was not inclined to think kindly of him though she would concede that he could not be blamed for his name.

Viscount Whitleaf.

She turned suddenly cold at the remembered name—as she had done a few minutes ago when Frances introduced her to him.

He was without any doubt the most handsome gentleman

she had ever set eyes upon—and she had thought so even before she was close enough to see that he had eyes of an extraordinary shade of violet. He looked as if his valet might well have poured him into his coat of dark blue superfine and his buff pantaloons. His Hessian boots looked supple and expensive, even with their shine marred by a light coating of dust from the lane, and his shirt was white and of the finest linen. His tall hat sat upon his dark hair at just the right angle to look slightly rakish but not askew. And he had the physique to display such clothes to full advantage. He was tall and slender, though his shoulders and chest were broad and his calves were shapely.

If there were any physical imperfection in his person, she certainly had not detected it.

The very sight of him amongst the Raycrofts and the Calverts had filled her with awed wonder.

Then Frances had mentioned his name.

And he had bowed with studied elegance—so out of place on a country lane—and smiled with practiced charm and paid her that lavish, ridiculous compliment while looking so deeply into her eyes that she would not have been surprised to discover that the hair on the back of her head was singed. He had white, straight, and even teeth to add to all his other perfections.

There had been delighted laughter from the other young ladies, but Susanna would not have known what to do or how to reply even if she had not still been stunned from hearing his name. Her mind had been paralyzed and it was only by sheer chance that her body had not followed suit.

Even if he could *not* help his name, Susanna thought now, remembering that it was not any *Viscount* Whitleaf against whom she held a grudge, nevertheless she already disliked him quite heartily. A gentleman ought to set about making a strange lady feel comfortable, not throw her into confusion. She did not know much about men, but she could recognize a vain and shallow one when she met him, one so wrapped up in the splendor of his own person that he expected every woman he encountered to fall prostrate at his feet.

Viscount Whitleaf was such a man. He lived up to his name.

She had accepted Mr. Raycroft's offered arm with gratitude. But with every step she had taken along the lane since, she had felt the presence of Viscount Whitleaf behind her like a hand all along her spine. She resented the feeling and despised herself for allowing it.

Of course the name *Osbourne* would probably mean nothing whatsoever to him. And he could not really be blamed for that either. He had been only a boy... But he *ought* to remember. It ought to be a name burned on his brain as his was on hers.

She wished fervently now that Anne had not returned to Bath when she had and that *she* had not come to Barclay Court with Frances and the earl. She wished herself back in the safety of the school—in the dreary, endless safety.

Though why *should* she? And why *should* she allow her holiday to be ruined by a shallow, conceited, careless man who clearly thought he only had to look at a woman with those fine violet eyes for her to fall head over ears in love with him?

Susanna turned to face the lane ahead again, unconsciously squaring her shoulders and lifting her chin as she did so, and asked Mr. Raycroft where he would go if he could choose anywhere in the world. Would he choose Greece, as she would?

"Greece would be well worth a visit, I believe, Miss Osbourne," he replied, "though I have been told that travel there is very uncomfortable indeed. I am a man who enjoys his creature comforts, you see."

"I do not blame you at all," Frances said. "And I can assure you that I have not yet seen a country to rival England in beauty. It feels very good to be home again."

They reached the village soon after that and stopped to speak with Mrs. Calvert, who came outside the house to greet them, though they declined her invitation to step inside. When they continued on their way without the Calvert sisters, Viscount Whitleaf walked ahead with Miss Raycroft on his arm, and the two of them chattered merrily all the way to

Hareford House, obviously very pleased with each other's company.

The two visitors drank tea with the Raycrofts and exchanged civilities for half an hour before Frances got to her feet and Susanna followed suit.

"I do not suppose," Frances said, "you would care to go walking again, Mr. Raycroft, after having been out once. Perhaps we may hope for you to call at Barclay Court tomorrow?"

"I seem to recall," Viscount Whitleaf said, "that your original invitation included me too, ma'am. And indeed I *would* care to go walking again today. I look forward to paying my respects to Edgecombe. Raycroft, are you coming too? Or am I to enjoy the pleasure of having two ladies to myself for the walk to Barclay Court?"

Susanna's eyes flew to Mr. Raycroft's face. She was vastly relieved when he expressed himself ready for further exercise.

Her relief was short-lived, however. She desperately hoped to maneuver matters so that she would walk with Frances or Mr. Raycroft, but as fate would have it, he was saying something to Frances as they descended the garden path and it was natural that he should offer her his arm after they had passed out through the gate. That left Susanna to walk behind with Viscount Whitleaf.

She could hardly have imagined a worse fate. She glanced up at him in a sort of sick dismay and clasped her hands firmly behind her back before he should feel obliged to offer his arm.

Whatever were they to talk about?

She was horrified to discover that she could *feel* him down her right side like a fever, even though there was a foot of air between their shoulders. Her stomach muscles were tied in knots—not to mention her tongue.

She despised the fact that she could feel none of the ease that Miss Raycroft and the Calvert sisters had felt with him earlier. He was only a man, after all—and a shallow man at that. He was not anyone she would wish to impress. All she need do was be polite.

Not a single polite topic presented itself to her searching brain.

She was twenty-three years old and as gauche as a girl just stepping out of the schoolroom for the first time. But then she never had stepped outside the schoolroom, had she?

She was twenty-three years old and had never had a beau.

She had never been kissed.

But such sadly pathetic thoughts did nothing to calm her agitation.

She might have spent the past eleven years in a convent, she thought ruefully, for all she knew about how to step into the world of men and feel at ease there.

BY THE TIME THEY WERE halfway to Barclay Court by Peter's estimation, he had spoken six words and Miss Osbourne had spoken one.

"What a lovely day it is!" he had said as a conversational overture at the outset, smiling genially down at her—or at the brim of her bonnet anyway, which was about on a level with his shoulder.

"Yes."

She walked very straight-backed. She held her hands firmly clasped behind her back, an unmistakable signal that she did not want him to offer his arm. He wondered if she simply had no conversation or if she was still bristling with indignation because he had compared her to a summer's day—though he was in good company there, was he not? Had not Shakespeare once done the same thing? He rather suspected that it was indignation that held her mute since she had been speaking in more than monosyllables with Mrs. Raycroft less than half an hour ago—though he would swear her eyes had never once strayed his way. He would have known if they had since his eyes had scarcely strayed anywhere else *but* at her.

He had been puzzling—he still was—over that strange thought he had had when his eyes first alit on her.

There she is.

There *who* was, for the love of God?

It was a novel experience to be in company with a lady who clearly did not want to be in company with him. Of course, he did not usually find himself in company with lady schoolteachers from Bath. They were, perhaps, a different breed from the women with whom he usually consorted. They were quite possibly made of sterner stuff.

"You were quite right," he said at last, merely to see how she would respond. "This summer day was not *really* made warmer and brighter by your presence in it. It was a foolish conceit."

She darted him a look, and in the moment before her bonnet brim hid her face from view again he was dazzled anew by the combination of bright auburn hair and sea green eyes—and by the healthy flush the fresh air had lent her creamy, flawless complexion.

"Yes," she agreed, doubling her contribution to their conversation since leaving Hareford House.

So she was not going to contradict him, was she? He could not resist continuing.

"It was my heart," he said, patting it with his right hand, "that was warmed and brightened."

This time she did not turn her face, but he amused himself with the fancy that the poke of her bonnet stiffened slightly.

"The heart," she said, "is merely an organ in the bosom."

Ah, a literalist. He smiled.

"With the function of a pump," he agreed. "But how unromantic a view of it. You would put generations of poets out of business with such a pronouncement, Miss Osbourne. Not to mention lovers."

"I am not a romantic," she said.

"Indeed?" he said. "How sad! There are no such things, then, you believe, as tender sensibilities? There is no part of one's anatomy or soul that can be warmed or brightened by the sight of beauty?"

He thought she was not going to answer. They came to the fork in the lane where they had met a couple of hours ago and followed Raycroft and Lady Edgecombe onto the branch that led to Barclay Court.

"You make a mockery of tender sensibilities," Miss

Osbourne said so softly that he bent his head toward her in case she had more to say.

She did not.

"Ah," he said, "you think me incapable of feeling the gentler emotions. Is that what you are saying?"

"I would not so presume," she said.

"But you would. You already have so presumed," he said. He was rather enjoying himself, he discovered, with this curiously serious, prim creature who looked so like an angel. "You told me I made a mockery of tender sensibilities."

"I beg your pardon," she said. "I ought not to have said such a thing."

"No, you ought not," he agreed. "You wounded me to the heart—to that chest organ, that mundane pump. How differently we view the world, Miss Osbourne. You listened to me pay you a lavish and foolish compliment and concluded that I know nothing about the finer human emotions. I on the other hand looked at you, serious and disapproving, and felt—ah, as if I had stepped into a moment that was simply magic."

"And now," she said, "you make a mockery of *me*."

She had a low, sweet voice even when she sounded indignant. She was small in stature and very slender, though she was curved in all the right places, by Jove. He wondered how well she controlled a class of girls, most of whom undoubtedly wished themselves anywhere else on earth but at school. Did they give her a rough time? Or was there steel in her character, as there appeared to be in her spine?

He would wager there was steel—and not a great deal of tenderness. Poor girls!

"I fear," he said, "that with a few foolish words I have forever condemned myself in your eyes, Miss Osbourne. Shall we change the subject? What have you been doing with your school holiday up until now?"

"It was not really a holiday," she said. "Almost half of the girls at the school are charity pupils. They remain there all year long and some of us stay too to care for them and to entertain them."

"Us?" he asked.

"There are three resident teachers," she told him. "There used to be four until Frances married the earl two years ago. Now there are Miss Martin, Miss Jewell, and I."

"And you all give up your holidays for the sake of *charity* girls?" he asked.

She turned to look at him again—a level, unsmiling look in which there might have been some reproof.

"I was one of them," she said, "from the age of twelve until Miss Martin made me a junior teacher when I was eighteen."

Ah.

Well.

Extraordinary.

He was walking and talking with an ex-charity schoolgirl turned teacher. It was no wonder they were having a difficult time of it communicating with each other. Two alien worlds had drifted onto the same country lane at the same moment, none too happily for either. Though that was not quite true—he was still enjoying himself.

"There is no question of *giving up* our holidays," she continued. "The school is our home and the girls our family. We welcome a break now and then, of course. Anne—Miss Jewell—has just returned from a month in Wales with her son, and now I am here for two weeks. Occasionally Claudia Martin will spend a few days away from the school too. But in the main I am happy—we are all happy—to be busy. A life of idleness would not suit me."

She was a prim miss right enough. She had nothing whatsoever to say about the weather, and had only brief reproaches to offer when he would have spoken of hearts and sensibilities. But she could wax eloquent about her school and the notion of teachers and charity pupils being a family.

Lord help him.

But she was more gloriously lovely than almost any other woman he had set eyes upon—and the word *almost* might even be withdrawn from that thought without any great exaggeration resulting. He had often thought fate was something of a joker, and now he was convinced of it. But the apparently huge contrast between her looks and her character and circumstances had him more fascinated than he could remember being with any other woman for a long time—perhaps ever.

"The implication being that idleness suits *me* very well indeed?" He laughed. "Miss Osbourne, you speak softly but with a barbed tongue. I daresay your pupils fear it."

She was not entirely wrong, though, was she? His life *was* idle—or had been for all of five years anyway. It was true that he intended to reform his ways and put idleness behind him in the very near future, but he had not really done so yet, had he? Thinking and planning were one thing; doing was another.

Yes, as he was now, today, Miss Osbourne was quite right about him. He had no defense to offer.

He wondered what it must be like to *have* to work for a living.

"I spoke of myself, sir—my lord," she said, "in answer to your question. I made no implication about you."

She had small, dainty feet, he could see—which was just as well considering her small stature. He had noticed during tea that her hands were small and delicate.

Miss Susanna Osbourne disapproved of him—probably disliked him too. In her world people worked. What had it been like, he wondered, to be a charity girl at the school where she now taught?

"Do you *like* teaching?" he asked.

"Very much," she said. "It is what I would choose to do with my life even if I had myriad choices."

"Indeed?" He wondered if she spoke the truth or only said what she had convinced herself was the truth. "You would choose teaching even above marriage and motherhood?"

There was a rather lengthy silence before she replied, and he regretted the question. It was unmannerly and might have touched her on the raw. But there was no recalling it.

"I suppose that even if I could imagine myriad choices," she said, "they would still have to be within the realm of the realistic."

Good lord!

"And marriage would not fit within such a realm?" he asked, surprised.

He did not realize until he found himself gazing at the tender flesh at the arch of her neck that she had dipped her head so far downward that she must have been able to see nothing more than her own feet. He *had* embarrassed her, dash it all. He was not usually so insensitive.

"No," she said. "It would not."

And of course he might have known it if he had stopped to consider. How often did one hear of a governess marrying? Yet a schoolteacher must have even fewer opportunities to meet eligible men. He wondered suddenly how the countess had met Edgecombe. He had not even known before today that she had been a schoolteacher at the time. There must be an interesting story behind that courtship.

In his world women had nothing to hope for or think about *but* marriage. His sisters had not considered their lives complete until they had all followed one another to the altar with eligible mates in order from the eldest to the youngest, at gratifyingly young ages—gratifying to them and even more so to his mother.

"Well," he said, "one never knows what the future holds, does one? But you must tell me some time what it is about teaching that you enjoy so much. Not today, though—I see we are approaching Barclay Court. We will talk more when we meet again during the next two weeks."

She stole a quick glance at him again and he laughed.

"I can see the wheels of your mind turning upon the hope that such a fate can be avoided," he said. "I assure you it can not. Neighbors in the country invariably live in one another's pockets. How else are they to avoid expiring of boredom? And I am to be at Hareford House for the next two weeks just as you are to be at Barclay Court. I am glad now that I decided not to return to my own home tomorrow as I had originally planned."

He spoke the truth and was surprised by it. Why on earth would he wish to extend an acquaintance with a woman from an alien world who disliked and disapproved of him? Just because she was dazzlingly beautiful? Or because he could not resist the unusual challenge of coaxing a smile and a kind word from her? Or because with her there might be a chance of actually conversing sensibly—about her life as a teacher? His conversation—and his life—had been far too trivial for far too long.

"I daresay," she said, "you will be busy with Miss Raycroft and the Misses Calvert."

"But of course." He chuckled. "They are delightful young ladies, and who can resist cultivating delight?"

"I do not believe," she said, "you expect me to answer that."

"Indeed not," he agreed. "It was a rhetorical question. But I will not be busy with them *all* the time, Miss Osbourne. Someone might misconstrue my interest in them if I were. Besides, with them I have felt no moment of magic."

He smiled down at her bonnet.

"I would ask you," she said as their feet crunched over the gravel of the terrace before the house, her voice as cold as the Arctic ice, "not to speak to me with such levity, my lord. I do not know how to respond. And moreover I do not *wish* to respond. I do not wish to have you single me out on any future occasion. I wish you would not."

Dash it all. Had he offended her more than he realized?

"Am I to look your way whenever we are in company together during the coming weeks, then, and pretend that I see only empty air?" he asked her. "I fear Edgecombe and his lady would consider me unpardonably ill-mannered. I shall bow to you each time instead and remark upon the fineness or inclemency of the weather—without drawing any comparisons with your person. Shall I? Will you tolerate that much attention from me?"

She hesitated.

"Yes," she said, ending their conversation as monosyllabically as she had begun it.

Edgecombe must have observed their approach and was coming out through the front doors and down the horseshoe steps to greet them, a smile of welcome on his face.

"You *did* persuade him to come, then, Frances," he said,

setting one hand at the small of the countess's back and smiling briefly and warmly down at her. "Raycroft—good to see you again. And Whitleaf is staying with you? This *is* a pleasure. Do come inside. Did you enjoy the walk, Susanna? And did you find Mrs. and Miss Raycroft at home?"

He smiled kindly at the schoolteacher and offered her his arm, which she took without hesitation.

"We met Miss Raycroft at the fork in the road," she said. "She was out walking with her brother and the Calvert sisters. We walked back to the village together and then on to Hareford House, where we took tea with Mrs. Raycroft. It was indeed a pleasant outing. There can be nowhere lovelier than the Somerset countryside."

Her voice was light and happy. Peter smiled ruefully to himself as he followed them up the steps and into the house, the countess between him and Raycroft.

By the time he stepped over the threshold, Miss Osbourne was already moving off in the direction of the staircase without a backward glance.

"You will wish to entertain Mr. Raycroft and Lord Whitleaf in the library, Lucius," the countess said. "We will not disturb you."

"Thank you," he said, setting a hand at her back again. "The vicar called. I daresay by now you know all about the village assembly the week after next?"

"Of course," she said.

"I said we would attend," he told her, "on condition that there be at least one waltz. The vicar has promised to see to it."

He grinned at her and she smiled back, her face alight with amusement, before turning to follow Miss Osbourne up the stairs.

"Right." Edgecombe turned his attention back to his visitors, rubbing his hands together as he did so. "Shall we step into the library? We will have some refreshments, and you can both tell me everything I missed in London during the Season. I *have* heard that you are finally betrothed to Miss Hickmore, Raycroft. My felicitations. A fine choice, if you were to ask me."